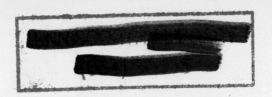

The Music in
my Head

Mark Hudson

F/459378

JONATHAN CAPE
LONDON

Published by Jonathan Cape 1998

2 4 6 8 10 9 7 5 3 1

First published in Great Britain in 1998 by
Jonathan Cape
Random House, 20 Vauxhall Bridge Road,
London SW1V 2SA

Random House Australia (Pty) Limited
20 Alfred Street, Milsons Point, Sydney,
New South Wales 2061, Australia

Random House New Zealand Limited
18 Poland Road, Glenfield,
Auckland 10, New Zealand

Random House South Africa (Pty) Limited
Endulini, 5A Jubilee Road, Parktown 2193, South Africa

Random House UK Limited Reg. No. 954009

A CIP catalogue record for this book
is available from the British Library

ISBN 0 224 04383 8

Typeset by Deltatype Limited, Birkenhead, Merseyside

Printed and bound in Great Britain by
Mackays of Chatham PLC

For my parents

This is a novel. All characters are fictitious. Although mention is made of Wolof language and culture, the social and political situations described are totally imaginary. Only the music is real.

One

Can you fax music? I've no idea. But I've got paper massing in ever higher drifts as the printers in my offices grind out further missives from every corner of the known universe. And I'm quite sure *some* of it must be music. I've got jiffy bags stuffed with CDs piling up, waiting to be opened in mailrooms, hallways, cubby holes and PO boxes. I've got crates, packages and holdalls full of records and cassettes, wrapped in leaves, straw, fur, fish-skin and God knows what else, sent from everywhere from Manhattan to Manchuria to Madagascar, dumped in darkened rooms, waiting till I find the time to unpack them and add them to the collection that must rank as one of the world's great cultural archives.

All around I've got impulse purchases, gifts, promotional freebies from everywhere from the heart of the metropolitan Coca-Cola complex to places so obscure, so unlikely, you wouldn't even think they had record companies. I've got plastic bags containing one title it took me months to track down, next to the stock of entire record companies, the recorded output of entire countries, picked up with the stroke of a pen.

And still it keeps on coming. Wherever I go I've got musicians, producers and promoters camping out in my hotel foyers. Hands thrust more cassettes, more CDs, more records through my taxi windows. And it's not just that they think I may be able to help them move their careers forward. They know I not only already have the rest of their oeuvre, I know it better then they do

1

themselves. I can hear things in their music even they're not aware of. I've got records so obscure even the people who made them don't know they exist, records so rare and so valuable it makes me feel slightly queasy thinking about them.

And always I want more. As soon as I get a moment to myself, I'm off in search of the junkshop, the market stall, the booth at the back of the bazaar that's got that *particular* title the acquisition of which fulfils one tiny, infinitesimal aspect of my life's dream.

Ten years, man. Ten years. And sometimes even I feel tired. Ten years. You can't blame yourself, you can't blame the world, you can't blame anybody if the sight of those far-flung corners, viewed casually from twenty-five thousand feet – like the view of Marrakesh, surrounded by the crumpled cardboard curtain of the Atlas, I have at this moment – does not invoke the exploratory buzz of a decade ago, if the mere sight of my fellow passengers, seen momentarily between the headrests garbed in the fantastic costumes of our destination, does not evoke the same giddy excitement it did then. Things move on. You move on. Or you should do. So you shouldn't blame yourself if, when you move about as much as I do, if you shade the globe with the cross-hatching of your flightpaths to the extent that I do, if you find yourself becoming just a little bit blasé – if you experience, in those rare moments when you actually have time to think, a certain feeling of jadedness.

But then, as the blue darkness begins to settle over the wastes of bare Mauretanian rock, dense and liquid, swelling beneath a thin scattering of cloud, like the bass throbbing elastic under the timbales and clanking piano of the music pumping through your headphones, you begin to recall, not so much with your mind as your fingertips, your solar plexus, your very viscera, something of the purpose, the deep-seated motivation, the underlying historical logic of your journey.

Tito and Celia. El Rey del Timbal. La Madre Rumba. El Pareja Real de la Salsa. The shiny urgency of those cross-rhythms, the awesome, magisterial power of that dark and unmistakable larynx calling out its rambunctious exhortations from the street

2

corners and teeming tenements of Brooklyn, from the rooftops and fire-escapes of the Lower East Side, across the glittering Manhattan nightscape, over the great, grey void of the Atlantic to the ancient gods of Africa.

> Elube Chango!
> Elube Oshun!
> Elube Ogun!
> Elube, lube yumbbala!
> Elube Chango, *señores!*

That's right, man. You're on your way to Africa! What else are you supposed to listen to?

The world turns. And as it does, the processes of flux and upheaval, with their attendant cultural cross-currents, grow faster by the day. Transfers of musical influence and style, carried on the tides of movement and conquest over hundreds of years, can be buzzed down the information superhighway in a matter of moments. And we're not talking about tasteful producer-led fusions cobbled together in San Francisco, Munich or Wiltshire. I'm talking about the real thing. Stuff that's coming through raw and unmediated, with the scent of the musicians' sweat still on it. Music that's stubborn, cantankerous, downright bloody-minded in its refusal to be accommodated by the norms of the Western market. There's so much flooding through all the time. And it's not all good. Most of it's fucking appalling. That's why you need someone out there to sift through it all, someone like me, constantly cruising the intercultural flightpaths as I pursue my interests in music publishing, promotion and management – and of course, my small but highly influential record label – who can sort through the kitsch and the schmaltz, separate the bogus modernisation from the even more bogus authenticity to find those moments, mere minutes, which when we hear them we say, *That is it!*

In Delhi, I'm in the courtyards of the great mosques with the

3

sufis, seers and poets. In Casablanca, I'm on the massive sprawling housing estates where extended families are trying to live the life of the desert in two-room apartments: a world of backstreet bars acrid with cheap perfume and even cheaper synthesisers. I'm at the mixing desk in tiny smoke-filled studios, turning it up for leather-jacketed juvenile delinquents who sing with the voices of fifty-year-old women, but bellowed out with a fifteen-year-old's compelling randy urgency, piling on Berber rhythms, House beats, fairground wurlitzers, sampled police whistles – mixing it up, churning it up, making it bump and bounce till it's so funky you can hardly stand it.

In Marrakesh, I'm in the Place Djmaa-el-fnaa, with the gnawa men – the black trance dancers, keepers of the ancient pulse, the subsonic sway of Black Africa. People who think nothing of going to 'the other side' and back several times in the course of a day.

My time in Spain is always one long juerga. Gypsies come from the four corners of Andalusia to chill with me. In Sevilla at feria time, I'm welcomed in any casseta I care to enter, honoured and feted, and plied with drink and the most incredible tapas till dawn, as black-eyed conchitas twist and twirl, kicking the massive flounces of their dresses into kaleidoscopic vortexes before my manzanilla-besmeared eyes, their elegant arms raised, writhing snakelike as the snapping rhythms of their castanuelas bounce against the dry and world-weary thrumming of the guitar . . . But, of course, I like to be where the real musicians are. Those whose voices testify to the most unspeakable levels of dissipation and abuse, to the closest identification with the age-old agonies of their race. They tell me where they'll be performing, and I join them in the most exclusive and impenetrable of the cassetas.

As preparations begin for the departure to El Rocio, the hermandads vie for the honour of having me march with them. Out there in the sun-bleached pathways of the mirasmas, we stop continually for impromptu sevillanas and fandangos, ice-cold manzanilla cutting to the quick of our sun-dazed sensibilities, jarring and jolting us into rhythm to the stabbing dry-gut staccato of the never-silent guitars.

4

In Baranquilla, I'm down there in the thick of the carnival crowds, carried for days and nights on the tide of ecstatic bikini-clad dancers, constantly checking and making notes on the different bands, till the time comes when, like as not, I'm called from the crowd and carried bodily to the judges' platform to decide the destiny of the congo de oro.

In Bahia, I'm with the trance dancers in the houses of the orishas – the ancient gods of Africa – whose rituals were kept alive through the secret religions of the slaves. I'm with the afoshes – the great percussion schools of the Brazilian slums. Casual labourers at the docks by day, street-cleaners – the anonymous shadow people of some of the most horrendous places on earth. People who have nothing to live for but music. People who yet, in the world of the orishas, form a kind of aristocracy – the Lords of Rhythm. Those are the kind of people I like to be with. And if there's a price to be paid for spending time with people who through force of economic and social circum-stance have no option but to be on nodding terms with unnamable evil, that comes with the territory.

But mostly, I like to be in Africa. Because it is to Africa that anyone with any feeling for Black Music – and most of us did start with Black Music, didn't we? – must finally go, to make obeisance, to prostrate themselves on the hard, red earth and make an offering at the shrine of the Black Soul.

Oh, yes. The moment you set foot on African soil, you realise what it's all been about: that Robert Johnson, Aretha and even the Supremes are in fact African music.

And that's where I'm going now, to N'Galam, the tropics' most stylishly dodgy musical capital, the city with the hardest hustlers, the most voracious taxi-drivers and the most arrogantly beautiful women on earth – a place which, while regarding itself as the Athens of Africa, was recently described by the *Economist* as 'one of the least secure places in the world' – to see the mainman, the man with the most spine-tinglingly beautiful voice, the man now universally regarded as Africa's Greatest Musician. And who was it first called him that? That's right. Me.

The doorbell just went. A nineteen-sixties doorbell. The sort that goes *bling*. Two mellow and bell-like mid tones, eliding together, what they call in drumming a 'flam'. You know, *bling*. The sort of bell that immediately says suburbia: a frosted-glass panelled door with wrought-iron behind it. Bland in a way which when you examine it, is very slightly sinister. And there it is again.

I don't think I'm going to answer it. No. That would be stupid. And it's not that I'm worried – not any more than any moderately prudent citizen of this country has a right to be. It's just that I can't think who would have a good reason to be out there. I mean a positive reason. I mean who might be out there that I might actually want to see. And the list of people that I might actually want to see, is very very short.

Bling. I can feel it in my chest. My arms. In the side of my head. Why the side? Why not the middle? My breath is short. And I'm walking doubled up. Why? It's virtually pitch dark in here. I've just realised that since the first *bling* I've walked backwards and forwards across this room in every possible direction. I'm like a headless chicken. And now it's going *bling-bling-bling-bling-bling* like they've got their hand jammed on it, which they obviously have. I'm halfway upstairs, thin light streaming from the curtained window on the upper landing, and I'm through the door into the spare room over the front door, the one filled with what She calls 'your crap', dazzled from the sudden brilliance from the uncurtained window, so I can hardly see. My eyes are gluey as I clamber doubled-up towards the hard silver brightness, between the piles of boxes and crates – boxes and crates full of records, full of CDs and cassettes, and all the attendant paper-work, all the press releases and programmes, all the stuff that may be crap, but which when collated over decades, hoarded for several more, suddenly constitutes a valuable archive... My cheek's resting on the cold of the window sill. If they were to stand back on the driveway, and look carefully along the bottom of this window, they might be able to spy the top right-hand side of my unkempt and greasy barnet, unseen, except by my immediate family, for several weeks ... But no, they're just round the side of the house among the bins. I can hear the grinding of

6

the heavily-laden iron on tar. The bin men? Why would they be ringing the bell? The rubber lid flumphs back onto the bin. Checking out if I've been here! Two guys in dark-blue crombies. Bad sign! Short, thinning hair. Bad sign! Hard, hard faces. Very bad sign! Wiping their hands fastidiously after touching the bins and chucking the tissues down in my driveway. Bastards!

Now they're in the grass, poking in the undergrowth the chairman of the residents' association's complained to Her about. Residents' association? You don't come to a place like this to be bothered by residents' associations. But I didn't say that. I didn't say anything. That's what made Her start crying . . . Now what are they doing? One of them's pulled a bit of sodden, water-logged cardboard box out of the nettles. He curses, seeing it's not remotely relevant, and he's got his hands wet and his shoes and his trousers and the bottom of his precious crombie. It's a cold day to be getting wet. I can see their breath in the air . . .

Yes, he's annoyed, and he's banging on the door. Hammering on it, hard. Shit! I'm crouching down now against the freezing radiator. If they come in . . .

Then I hear the car engine growling into life and they're gone. I'm getting back down. Into the frowzy warmth. I'm going to put something on. Oh, yeah. I'm going to put on 'Nonguini'. I deserve 'Nonguini' after that.

'Nonguini . . . Nonguini . . . Mbaye Bouna Njai, nonguini.'

'Going up and down, going up and down. Mbaye Bouna Njai is going up and down.'

The warmth enfolds me. Breathing on me. Holding me. 'Nonguini.' Even in the darkness I find it with ease. I press power, and the amp and tuner cast their faint spectral glimmer. The graphic equaliser sparkles into life. Yes, they seem to say, you *shall* have music.

The abrupt bounce of the intro booms out. 'Ndeysan!' growls Pape Seck. 'Aha!' And we're into the main groove. 'Nonguini, Nonguini . . . Nongui-nonguini!' The latiny bass line, like the lyric, is propelled relentlessly up and down by the bulbous pummel-ling talking drum and the robust slapping of the congas. 'Nongui, nongui . . . Nongui, nongui . . .' You could dance to the singing alone on this. The tama, the talking drum, comes burbling and throbbing out of the mix, bobbing on the rhythm as it bubbles and rolls, ushering in a lonesome, soulful trumpet, spraying its tender rasping notes all over the front and back of the song. 'Nongui, nongui . . .' And you can't help smiling, you can't help shaking and nodding in time. Oh, yes. I wouldn't go anywhere without this. I had to leave a load of stuff with that bastard Paul. He's probably sold it all by now. But I'm not bothered. That was all the freebies, the mainstream stuff. Africa as put out by the Western majors. Stuff the likes of Ahmadou Toure and Michael Heaven have put their spoke into. The sort of stuff you could just go out and *buy*. Oh, yes. I mean, I did actually buy this. And I'm not telling you where. But believe me, *buying it* was the least part of it. I often play people things and they say, 'Hey! This is really good! Where can I get a copy?' And I just laugh. I say, 'You can't. There's absolutely no way you could get a copy of this. If you actually went to N'Galam you couldn't get a copy of this. Sajar Jopp hasn't got a copy of this. Pape Seck hasn't got a copy of this. Matter of fact, last time I went to N'Galam, Sajar Jopp asked me if he could have this copy, and I said, no.'

I click on the Anglepoise and look at the cover – stare at it, analyse it for what must be the millionth time. Sajar, his long torso improbably clothed in a tight-fitting white-collared City shirt, stares coolly back at the camera, his long-lashed slightly bloodshot eyes having that satiated steamed-over look that might make you think he was stoned – wrongly, since Sajar has never indulged – but in fact just mean that he's a cool guy, a dude from the mean streets of N'Galam. And while his friend beside him, the animateur and dancer Alhaji Samb, holding up a pair of enormous maracas, beams back at the viewer in a friendly way, Sajar has that slightly aloof, slightly arrogant look he always has had, that look which as far as I know he was born with that says, 'I don't have to try, I'm already *it*.' Yes, that was the way Sajar looked before he decided to move outside the culture into which he was born, the world of the Medina, the old native quarter of N'Galam, that dodgy, cantankerous environment whose mores, whose dangers and pitfalls he understood intuitively, before he

8

realised he had to kowtow to and charm the hacks and time-servers of the multinational Coca-Cola complex, before he was corrupted . . . The way he looked when I first knew him.

Yes, I'm on my way to talk through projects with Sajar, to chill, chew the fat and generally keep myself in the frame, while keeping an eye out for stuff that can be licensed and lucratively fed through to the majors, and of course for acts for my own label. And the plane is in that moment of suspension, of yawning ineluctable imminence before it begins its slow descent into the blue darkness. And I'm starting to feel very slightly sick. Not just because of the mediocre plastic meal I've just eaten. But because there are in relation to Africa certain phenomena, certain . . . incidents, which while far from representing the totality of the continent, far from representing even one per cent of its everyday reality, should, I've come to think, be borne in mind, purely as a matter of prudence when visiting the place. The only trouble is, that once admitted to the back of the mind, they have a way of sneaking their way to the front at the most inopportune moments. And, to be honest, it's getting worse. Every time I make this journey the more the dark visitants seem to swarm in around me, like the large brown mosquitoes massing over the swamps round N'Galam airport. Talking of which, I mustn't forget to take my anti-malarials.

'Er . . . madame. Je veux . . . er take . . .' I make a gesture indicating swallowing, '. . . une medicine.'

'Vous voulez prendre un medicament? You need some wat-teur?'

'Yeah.'

'I'm coming.'

I read the warning on the container: 'May cause dizziness or loss of balance. If affected, do not attempt to drive or operate heavy machinery.' Fucking great. What if you're planning to spend years in the tropics? Fortunately, I can't drive and I can't see myself encountering too many pieces of major plant over the coming weeks.

'Here you are, sir.'

9

'Cheers.' I gulp it down, holding her deep walnut gaze, the contours of her fetchingly chunky shoulders. She's got a pleasingly maternal presence – somewhat younger than me, but still maternal. That's nice.

'Not long now, sir, and you will be enjoying your holiday.'

Something in the look I give her – something I'm totally unaware of – makes her flinch in apology.

'I'm sorry, sir. I realise, of course, you are going to work.'

Work? Work! Shit! What am I radiating here? Sniffiness, English stiffness or sheer terror? Christ! I thought I'd arranged everything before I came, phoning Sajar, making sure his brother Abdou knew to meet me at the airport. Oh, yes. You've got to be met. Flying into N'Galam at two in the morning and not being met? Cannot be done. Yes, you, O tyro-backpacker on no matter how stringent a budget – don't even think of trying it!

But what if he's got the date or the time wrong? What if – more likely – he's totally forgotten about it? What if he's placidly drinking tea, watching Schwarzenegger videos, or fucking his brains out with some floozy, leaving me at the mercy of all the rangy, smooth-talking, cold-eyed hustlers, all the touts, conmen, drug dealers, muggers and madmen that throng the concourses of N'Galam airport, of all the cackling, bloodshot, fake taxi-drivers, armed robbers, sorcerers' apprentices, changeling children and wolfish insistent bastards who mill in the darkness outside – not to mention the impostor baggage-handlers, bent policemen, kleptomaniac customs officials, black-market money-changers, corrupt immigration officials who pollute the airport's inner workings – all waiting to confiscate my possessions, steal my documents, strip me, prostrate me, dismember me for amulets – or at the very least, put me in the wrong taxi?

Everyone else sits, staring ahead. The citizens of Tekrur mellow, in serene expectation, returning, after how many months, how many years, to the country of their ancestors. The Indians and Lebanese, with their characteristic look of supercilious resilience, the knowledge that in whatever country, under whatever circumstances, they will tough it out. The other

10

Europeans, mentally preparing themselves for the great confrontation. The couple on the other side of the aisle, with their two young kids and the deep, permanent brownness and slightly dazed equanimity of people who have come to terms with the tropics. Aid workers perhaps in some remote outpost, people who have broken through the skin of Africa as represented by airports, hotels and rapacious, thieving cities like N'Galam, and gone deep into its other reality. People with a slightly complacent look that suggests they know they are about to be *met*.

I've got to fill in one of those cards about where you're from, how long you're staying and where. A pilot, an African, has the only pen, and there's a queue. You never think of these things. I grab the pen ahead of an Indian and a Frenchman who looks too mild for his own good, and fill the card in, glancing up at the immigration official, a big bloke in a safari suit, cool and anonymous behind tonton macoute shades.

'Excusez moi, monsieur. You have not filled in the section where it says where you will stay.'

'I haven't?'

'You have not.'

'I'll be ... with friends.'

'The name and address of your friends?'

'Er ...' I don't want to seem too bigheaded. Don't want a shake down and a body search just for seeming cocky. 'Jopp,' I mumble.

'Pardonnez moi?'

'Jopp! Sajar Jopp!'

'You're staying with Sajar Jopp?'

'Yeah.'

'You know Sajar Jopp?'

'Yeah.'

'Welcome to Tekrur, my friend.'

There's a crowd forming round the beaten-in, antique conveyor belt. Passengers, porters in robes or shabby fatigues with big laminated name-tags, guys with placards looking around for this person or that delegation. Abdou is nowhere to be seen, and there are no signs for Litchfield.

11

Everyone's black. The big, shining porters overshadowing the whites, who already seem pale, ghostlike, almost invisible. Everyone's speaking in the deep elastic vowels and hard contemptuous consonants of the Wolof language. Exchanging formal courtesies, making what are no doubt fairly mundane enquiries, with exaggerated rhetorical force. The occasional chuckle breaking through the all-pervasive musk-like cool. Because you've got to be cool here. You've got to be cool at all costs. Not just because there's an edge to this place that's getting sharper by the day. Not just because you could be robbed, sold into slavery, have your throat cut before you've even noticed what's going on. But because that's the prevailing ethos of the place. That's what it's all about. And when I say cool, I don't mean a spaced-out, mellow cool. I mean a sharp, hard-eyed cool. It's tough. That's inescapable. But it's not aggressive. Just cool.

And that's your insurance policy. Not just that if you're cool and you respect their cool they'll respect yours. But that all these . . . unmentionable things I was alluding to earlier, that you read about happening in other parts of Africa, won't happen to you here. Because they're not cool. And that's how they see them-selves here – though they'd never admit it – as the most civilised Africans, the coolest Africans. And you of course know the coolest of them all: Sajar Jopp.

So everyone's standing there in various postures of slightly absent-minded cool, waiting for the conveyor belt to judder into action. Not wanting to give anyone another excuse for a body search, I've got my money-belt and all my documents leaning against my leg in a Tesco's carrier bag. Trying to appear nonchalant, I don't clutch it earnestly to me, but have the other leg poised to grip it. I avoid eye contact.

Eventually the conveyor grumbles and lurches into life, and after an age the first bag appears. I seize mine and head rapidly through customs. Indians, Lebanese and Tekrurians are having to open huge crates, bundles and packages. There's a lot of negotiating to be done tonight, and no one's interested in my meagre holdall. I'm free. Ahead, a small doorway leads directly into Africa.

There's a great crowd of figures draining the light of the sodium-lit concourse, filling the air with the minty tang of their body odour. Immediately in front of me, a grinning gnome-like figure holds a sheet of A4 paper above his head, with the word 'LITCH' printed large upon it. Thank Christ for that. A taller figure stands stone-faced beside him. The gnome seizes my bag and follows Stone Face into the crowd. Soft voices paw the air all around me.

'Which hotel?'

'You want taxi?'

'English? Americain?'

Stone Face suddenly stops and points at the piece of paper. 'C'est vous?'

I try to catch my breath in the thick air. 'Oui.'

They're suspicious. *They're* suspicious? Gnome's brilliantly coloured bowling shirt is filthy, while Stone Face has none of the suavity, the easygoing urbanity I expect of Sajar's people. And they've got my bag!

Outside, we're into total darkness. They scuttle on, me having to virtually run to keep up. I realise they've seen Abdou's sign and have cut in a confederate in the airport administration to make a replica. Abdou's back in there pathetically holding up an identical sign, and I'm about to be hit over the head.

A light goes on in a car, and I make out the outline of a dark BMW. I'm momentarily reassured. Thieves don't drive BMWs. Not these kind of thieves in a place like this. The back seat is heaped with dirty laundry. My bag is thrown on top of it, and I make to clamber after it. But Gnome gestures me to the front.

'Any ten franc?' he asks.

'What?'

'Ten franc piece. Francs français.'

I do have one, and I find myself giving it to him.

'Any more?'

'No.'

This is all wrong. Sajar's people don't beg off visitors. But then he's gone, and I realise he's got nothing to do with Sajar – just another small-time airport hustler slightly known to the driver.

13

We're moving smoothly, but very fast, out of the airport complex, and I'm really getting worried. Not only can this guy not speak English, he can hardly speak French. I mean I can hardly speak French, but this guy can *really* hardly speak French. And his speech is none too clear. If it's possible to slur in your throat, he's doing it. I look at him. The hard features, absorbed in the too-fast driving, baseball cap pushed back on his head. The guy's a thug. Sajar wouldn't employ someone like this. The car's been stolen. I'm going to be taken to some lonely piece of waste ground and my throat's going to be cut.

'Where's Sajar?'

'Erh?'

'Sajar! Où est-il?'

'Sajar . . . Il est . . .' The words get lost in his growling gargle. Something about Sajar having to see friends.

Cheers, Sajar. There he is, chatting suavely with friends or relaxing in front of the telly, leaving me to be shaken down by all the thugs of N'Galam. And anyway, the guy's bluffing. Sajar? He doesn't know what the fuck I'm talking about.

We're powering down a dusty dual carriageway at about ninety miles an hour, and I'm about to open the door, when he says, 'You know Michael?'

Michael? Michael Heaven. An English rock musician who likes to hang out with Sajar. I breathe more easily. We're getting into qualifying information.

'Yeah, I know Michael.'

He looks into the rearview mirror. 'You know Sairz?'

'Who?'

'Sairz! Il est touzur avec Michael.'

'Serge?'

'Ouah!' He chuckles at the hilarious wickedness of Serge – whoever the fuck he is. He carries on talking in his gargling pidgin-French. I keep saying oui, but he can tell I can't understand, and he doesn't like it. Thinks I'm looking down on him.

'Look, man,' I say at length. 'I can't speak French.'

'Erh?'

14

'I said I can't speak French.'

'You are French!'

'No.'

He hits the wheel and lets out a throaty guffaw. 'You're not French?'

'No.'

He throws up his hands – disconcerting given the speed at which we're travelling. But I don't care. Things are getting more into the groove they ought to be in. 'Tu es *bandit!*' he says with approval.

Suddenly I realise there's music playing – there probably has been all the time. Wiry acoustic guitar, syncopated with the bumping rhythms of a bulbous balafong. A deep-voiced man is half-singing, half-talking, his voice swaying to fit in all the full, round vowels, while a couple of girls give nasal sing-song support. A sharp-voiced drum comes snapping into the mix, counterpointing the vocal line. Yes, man. We are in Africa. Fucking brilliant! But what is it?

'Serahule music . . . You know Tekrur Orientale? Mali?'

He begins rummaging in the glove compartment for the cassette case, peering into the dimness, as a dark shape comes looming in front of the car.

'Look . . . !'

He swerves to miss a woman, her head piled high with a great bundle of clothes, calabashes, basins and God knows what else. I turn to see her continuing her progress, untroubled, across the carriageway. The driver hits the wheel, and gives another roaring satanic cackle.

Two

I'm in Africa. I must be, because everyone's walking round with
I ♥ Africa carrier bags. Or rather the few people I can see, as I
peer round the heavy curtains at the corner of my hotel room,
look as though they must be: moving across the patch of glittering
sand far below, between the backs of the worn and dustily
anonymous modern buildings, in their white starched robes –
their carrier bags swinging gently beside them – with that stately
majestic slowness. Overhead the heat swells into the iron sky,
carrying the eagles and vultures high above the vast rotunda of
the Banque des Etats de l'Afrique Ouest – the buttresses
projecting between the perpendicular rows of windows of
Africa's own cathedral of Mammon, decorated with narrow semi-
abstract reliefs no doubt illustrating something like African
Achievement. Oh, yes, it's all going on out there. But I'm not
happy. Because while African civilisation is going on down there:
a bunch of guys sitting in the doorway beyond, reduced to dark
outlines by the pitiless brilliance, just sitting there with that
ineffable African patience, not waiting, just there ... Yes, while
that's going on down there, I'm up here, skulking in the thickly
curtained dimness of a plastic and Formica chain-hotel room.
And I can't at the moment see any way I'm going to get beyond
that.

Normally when I'm here, I stay in Sajar's old compound, down in

16

the Medina, close to the Corniche Ouest – where he grew up, and where his father went on living till he bought him that new house. So when the driver brought me here last night, I was surprised. But I couldn't, on barely a moment's reflection, say that I minded. Firstly, they had this all arranged, and secondly, while anywhere else in the world this would be just a mediocre hotel for commercial travellers, here in Africa it's major luxury. And it's expensive. But if it costs slightly over half the average annual income of a Tekrurian peasant, as I happened to notice as I was checking in, it's no skin off my nose. Because if you're in the media, you don't pay. There's always someone to whom it's useful to have you somewhere or give you something. Obviously I don't pay for records, CDs or any of that. Nor do I pay for books, tickets to concerts, films, theatres, or even, should I choose to go, opera and ballet. It may seem incredible to you. It seemed incredible to me when I first realised it. I mean, in this instance, I did actually pay for my plane ticket. But that's unusual. In general, if you're in the media, you don't pay for anything.

And of course when you're in Africa with Sajar Jopp, things operate in a different groove. You don't bother with things like customs and immigration controls. When you're with Sajar at an African airport, you get waved through a side door. And here in Sajar's own city, they couldn't wish for better PR than to have someone like me, Sajar's guest, staying here. Sajar'll sing a song for the manager and that'll be that.

And let's face it, there are times when, tired after a long flight and faced with things like air-conditioning, ensuite bathroom, swimming-pool and excellent laundry service, you think, Why not?

The moment I step out of the lift, my head starts spinning. Either that, or it's the foyer – milling with people who were up before me, gleaming between the golden spotlights and the reflected glow of the brilliance outside, African pop bubbling gently in the background – that's going round and round. The restaurant is deserted. I woke early, but now suddenly, it's late. I approach a big-hipped woman in glasses.

17

'Est-ce que le petit déjeuner est er . . .'

She mutters something.

'Pardon?'

'Room service!'

Back in my room, I'm frantically dialling. I'd better eat something. I'm not at all hungry. In fact I feel slightly sick. But I'd better eat something. Then I'll feel better. Then I'll phone Sajar.

I've no sooner parked my grateful thighs on the toilet than there's a rap at the door. The waiter, a slight figure in a maroon high-collared jacket, stands there with the tray, his mournful features suffused with a mixture of reproach and disdain. I dare say he looks even more disdainful and reproachful as he returns tipless along the corridor.

I don't want the coffee or the croissant, but I force them down. Now I feel really sick.

There's the briefest and most fugitive of grunts on the other end of the line. It could be 'Oui.' It could be the second half of 'Allo.' It could just be a grunt.

'Is Sajar there?'

There's another grunt signifying non-comprehension.

'Est-ce que Sajar est là?'

'Il n'est pas là.'

'Er . . .' God, this is hard work. 'Où est-il?'

There's one of those bouts of nasal gargling of which the French language seems largely to consist, tinged with a guttural African gruffness.

'Donc,' I conclude. 'Il n'est pas là.'

'C'est ça.'

'Merci.'

There's another grunt and the phone goes dead.

Fucking bastard.

I've stayed in this hotel before. I've no idea when or why, but I must have done, because there's something altogether too familiar about the dull steel interior of the lift, with its framed adverts for breakfast and day-trips to bird sanctuaries, about the white polystyrene tiles of the humming corridors, about those

18

photographic blow-ups of traditional Tekrurian glass paintings, with their bright graphic images of musicians, holy men and cow-eyed coiffured women, at the end of each corridor opposite the lift, about the view onto the serenely glowing Atlantic from the window beside it. Yes, I've definitely been here before. And last time, I had a sea view – the Island of Slaves virtually underneath my window, dissolving into the gluey grey ocean haze – not looking down between anonymous dust-worn official buildings onto a scruffy bit of street. And I'm right by the lift – pinging, sighing and wheezing all hours of the day and night. Christ, I may not be paying, but I didn't come all this way to overlook their fucking dustbins.

Once again I'm back in the foyer, and the place is packed. There's some kind of conference on and it must be their coffee break, because the place is milling with elegant, sleekly fitting suits, magnificently starched robes, major leather attaché cases and ostentatiously large name-tags. Oh yes, they know how to wear suits here, and they certainly know how to wear robes. This is Africa as the Anglo-Saxon mind can't conceive of it. Africa as suave, Africa as urbane, Africa as stylish – where everyone's a docteur, everyone's a maître. They may be up to their necks in it, but at least it's *their* corruption, if you know what I mean.

I recognise people from the plane, specially here for the Congrès des Avocats. And everyone's a cool guy. Everyone's pressing flesh, squeezing elbows, gripping shoulders, networking in that effortless, masterful way that's the very stuff of culture here – smiling as one must, magnificently with frequent lubricious chuckles of acknowledgement. Oh, yes. Everyone's cool. And standing in the middle of the room looking straight at me, and smiling magnificently, is the coolest, most sleekly suited, the most foxily elegant and suavely moustached of them all. Prosper Mbodj, Sajar's lawyer. I make my way over to him, my hand extended, my smile – I like to think – equally magnificent. At the last moment his eyes lock onto mine with a faint flicker of alarm. He wasn't looking at me at all, he just happened to be staring into space smiling magnificently.

'Mbodj!' I take his hand.

19

The computer of his mind whirs into action.

'Nigel!'

'Litch.'

'Litch! Yes! How are you?'

'Sorted.'

'All right! Here on business?'

'I've come to see Sajar.' Come on, man. Why else would I be here?

'Of course. You are the guy who is always with Sajar.'

'Yeah.'

'Okay . . . It's some time since we've seen you.' For a split second I can see his computer flickering overtime. 'And how long will you stay?'

'Er, two we . . . A month . . .'

'We must meet. Talk, eat, chew the fat. Have a few beers.'

He turns, sees someone else, and leaves me hanging in mid-foyer, as his voice goes up a couple of registers into a spluttering high-fiving greeting. You just can't get the same effect in English.

Back at the counter. At each of my tentative 'Excusez mois', the woman – hair braided tightly back from sculpted brow, air of serene inner emptiness which must on no account be disturbed – turns to some other customer who has just arrived at the counter. If I wasn't feeling so bad, I might start running through all the various reasons why these people always have to be like this. Instead, I try a different tack.

'Oy, missiz!'

She flashes me a different look – hard, hostile, but very slightly worried.

'Est-ce que c'est possible à avoir une chambre avec un vista de la mer?'

Moving some imaginary object disdainfully round the back of her teeth, she glances down at the register. 'Come back at twelve o' clock.'

I'm lying on my bed. The lift is pinging and groaning two feet from my mind, and the room is going round. I hardly slept last night. Too wound up from the flight, and the mad ride from the

20

airport. From the thought that I was in Africa, and when I woke up I'd be *in it*.

But I'm not *in it*. I'm in this hotel. I could stand on the polished compacted marble floor of the air-conditioned foyer, look out through the glass doors, down the bleak driveway, past the security checkpoint, at the shimmering whiteness of Africa, at the taxi-drivers standing chatting before they retreat from the heat of the day, and beyond them, the sellers of crap wooden sculptures sprawled under the shade trees. Africa is fifty yards away, but I'm too ill to go down into it. I'm missing it.

Normally when I arrive in N'Galam, I head straight for the Marché Hakim Nder, that great hive of traditional African commerce at the crossroads where the road through the Plateau, the airy official district – the European City – begins its descent towards the teeming, chaotic sprawl of the quartiers populaires. The great entrance, where between the tightly packed arcades of stalls, you can see the mustard-coloured ramparts of the main building, a mad colonial fantasy of a Soudanese mosque, swarming with beggars, hustlers and pickpockets, porters twisting their barrows through the throng, women with their basins and calabashes of fruit, spices, sauce and God knows what else, squeezed squatting into every crack and crevice, boys holding out slabs of meat – one on each palm. And up in the great halls, the butchers themselves whistling and shouting, rolling their blood-shot eyes as they hack into the carcasses, holding up great handfuls of flesh to passers-by; the stick-chewing marchandes hissing over the banks of gleaming vegetables, the sacks of spices of every colour of the earth. And down in the dingy bowels of the building, the fruits of the sea: the great mounds of squid and octopus, fish the length of a man slithering over the swimming counters. The whole place delirious with the reek of rotting fish, urine, split innards, rank flesh, pepper and the yellow overmastering stench of dried fish. And, beyond the market itself, the labyrinth of the cloth vendors, where after a few moments you lose any sense of where you are in relation to the street outside: the berobed merchants sprawled on their bales and bolts, beneath the glistening lengths of silk and indigo, watching you slow-eyed

21

and half-amused, remote in their *Arabian Nights* world that moves to its own ineluctable rhythms, to the whirring and thrumming of the sewing machines in the cavernous, unseen sweatshops all around us, to the whizzing needles of the cobblers and embroiderers of the robes of the faithful, to the counting of banknotes greasy, black and clothlike with use. Oh, yes. The Marché Hakim Nder is a place with its own codes, its unseen traps and pitfalls; a place to be entered with caution, where the unwary could easily trip, be fleeced, bartered, sold into slavery, disappear without trace before they've even noticed what's happening.

But I've been all over it. There isn't an inch, nook or crevice of that place I haven't explored and made my own. And mostly, I go there for the music. Not stuff by the country's most well-known artists – the kind of thing you can buy at the HMV shop in London. I'm talking about the stuff that never gets to the West, by people you've never heard of – culture music, heavy culture music. And as you approach the Marché Hakim Nder, it's as though you're hitting a wall of music: squealing rock guitars, mellifluous, cascading African guitars, tinny horns, hard, cracking drum rhythms, buzzing and blaring from a thousand speakers, cohering along the packed avenues of stalls into a seething, bubbling river of sound. Mountains of cassettes are crammed into tiny booths, piled beside stalls selling aluminium pots, enamelware, plastic sandals and Vick's Colic Rub. Rock, jazz, reggae, blues, French M.O.R. and probably even classical if you wanted it. And, of course, African music. Every kind of African music you could possibly imagine. Silkily sinuous Zairean soukous, brittle, plangent Kenyan guitars, the lugubrious drone of the great Egyptian orchestras; the flutings of pygmies, the humming of bushmen; tumbling balafongs, tinkling thumb pianos, pumping mbiras, cascading koras; the grinding of ritis, the booming of budongos; the buzzing of hard gut harps . . . Oh, yes. Any record or cassette you could possibly want – I swear that it's in there. At some stall in the deepest, darkest recesses of the market, they'll have it. I couldn't swear by the condition, but it'll be there somewhere.

Some nights I dream I'm walking in the Marché Hakim Nder,

sating myself, gorging myself on the most recherché, the most obscure, the most unknown music. In alleyways and stalls that are strangely deserted, I find cassettes I've been searching for for years, cassettes by familiar artists that I didn't know existed, cassettes which, from the picture on the cover, the track listing and the personnel, I realise with a quivering excitement, I've been waiting for, I've been dreaming of. Sounds that fulfil my deepest musical fantasies. The music only I know about.

As I move from stall to stall, sampling and buying at my leisure, a crowd gathers round me: apaches, hucksters, panhandlers, moneychangers, madmen – the wolves of the gutter – gather round to see what I'm going to buy next, to see if I'm going to pick out the particular things that have been turning them on, the things no mere tourist would think of asking for, the deeply cultural, the recondite, the things they think of as most exclusively *theirs*. I pick out a cassette with a man and a young boy on the cover, incongruously dressed in velvet jackets and bow ties. A man steps from the crowd, forefinger raised, eyes virtually popping from his head with enthusiasm as he extols the virtues of the cassette. The crowd all grunt in urgent agreement. They're all raising their hands, disclaiming. They're poor men, but they've got nothing to gain from this. They want nothing from me. But they know I love music. I pause for a moment. I hold the cassette between forefinger and thumb, a frown of theatrical doubt on my brow, then my expression clears and I hand it to the stallholder. There's a great roar of delight as I put my hand in my pocket. Everyone's grabbing me by the shoulders and slapping each other's hands. 'Bon choix, gorgi! Bon choix!' Good choice, old man! The news is caught on the gusts of the market's gossip, hooted and hissed by the stick-chewing women, barked by the butchers, cackling with approbation as they hack ever harder into their sides of meat, thrusting their hands into great mounds of liver. Till, within seconds, it's all over the market.

I never thought much about cassettes before I went to Africa. Compared to vinyl they lacked atmosphere – and of course the visual potential of the cover. People who actually chose cassettes over vinyl for reasons of economy and convenience always seemed fatally lacking in style, even sexually inadequate. Cassettes were of use only for the car or the Walkman. But in Africa, this most despised of formats came into its own. In Africa, I came face to face with the majesty of the cassette. In Africa, the microgrooves of the vinyl record were worn within days by the sandpaper of the wind, by the paws of the uncontainable children fumbling through Daddy's records when he's out, shredding the covers as they go. So, while in the fifties and sixties the buzzing, the crackling, the wind-worn scurfing of much-handled vinyl – sounds as much a part of the music as the bands fighting through from underneath – were the characteristic sound of the African bar, by the seventies the cassette, the cheapest, simplest means of reproduction, was the means by which the vast majority of the people, not only in Africa, but the entire world, received their music. And as I came to realise that in Africa, the record scarcely existed, so the cassettes with their neat little covers came to have the cute and addictive desirability that chocolate bars had for me as a kid.

Somewhere out there is Sajar Jopp. He could be touring in the U.S. or Japan with his band the Super Lumière d'Afrique, rubbing shoulders with film stars, supermodels and heads of state. He could be giving his views on the responsibilities of the African artist at a Pan-African cultural festival in Ouagadougou or Dar-es-Salaam. Or he could be filming the video for his latest single on a rubbish dump in Kensal Rise. Since Sajar first played in England – can it be ten years, *ten years* ago? – you find him in the most surprising places. He's toured the world with some of the world's biggest, most influential and richest stars. He's been a UNESCO ambassador for the Year of the Child. And at these stadium-filling mega-jamborees for worthy causes – relayed by satellite to every corner of the known universe – Sajar's always there – appearing to rapturous applause even from people who don't know who he is. In all that time, he's kept his position as the African star most likely to carry the music over to a mainstream Western audience.

24

He never has of course, but he's somehow managed to hold the imagination of the Western media. Just when you thought no one could possibly need to hear any more about Sajar Jopp, there's another TV documentary, another spread in the weekend funnies. His almond eyes, dazzling smile and rangy clean-limbed physique haven't done him any harm with lady researchers and film directors wanting expenses-paid trips to the tropics' most dodgily attractive style capital. But more than that, more than his cool charm, more than the ineffable beauty of his voice, he's got mystique. Somehow, no matter how far you go with Sajar, you never quite get to the bottom of him.

And through all of this, his position in his own society has become more and more important, till the poet of urbanisation, the bumptious street urchin made good, is now without doubt the most famous person in the country, bigger than the President, bigger than the marabouts, the Great Holy Men, leaders of the all-powerful religious brotherhoods.

Oh, yes. Sajar is out there. And he's not far away. I say that, not just because I obviously checked before I came out here, but because I can feel his presence out there, brooding over the battered, sun-tormented rooftops of the city.

Another approach, another language.

''lo.' It's that grunt again – for the nth time.

'Salaam aleikum.'

'Aleikum salaam,' comes the gruff and suspicious response.

'Sama wai nangadef?' You can't be flat or hesitant in this language, you've got to punch in there with a raffish, exultant swagger.

There's a slight pause at the other end. Got the bastard off guard! He wasn't expecting that. 'Man gi fi rek,' he concedes reluctantly, as though he were choking blood to do it.

'Ana sa wa kir?'

'Nyung far,' he grunts. Now he's really pissed off.

'Dafa bah loll,' I pronounce, concluding the formal greetings which in Africa always precede even the most mundane of enquiries. 'That's very good.' And well put. Most people now say

25

'terop' for 'very', a corruption of the French 'trop'. Far better to say 'loll'. That's pure Wolof – *deep* Wolof. He grunts in response.

'Ana Sajar?' (I think you probably need subtitles here: 'Where is Sajar?')

'Sajar nekou fi.' ('Sajar is not here.')

'Fan?' ('Where?')

He comes back with a long sentence. A very long sentence. Unnecessarily long, in my view.

I pause.

'Sajar is not here.'

'You speak English?'

'Yes.'

'Why didn't you say so in the first place?'

'You kept phoning up, asking for Sajar in French. And I kept telling you he is not here.'

'Where is he?'

'He is not here yet. When he arrives I will tell him you have phoned.'

'Who are you?' I ask in a loaded tone, implying that when Sajar arrives he is going to be in deep shit.

'Sanyang,' he says with a solidity and a matter-of-factness that suggest that his position in Sajar's operation is unlikely to be shaken by the complaints of an unknown foreigner. 'Who are you?'

'I,' I breathe, enjoying the moment, 'am Litch.'

'Ah.'

'You've heard of me?'

'No. But when Sajar arrives, I will tell him you have called.'

Yes, it's all going on out there now, only half a mile or so away. I could just jump in a taxi and go there. But apart from the fact that I'm too ill to think of going anywhere, at the back of my mind there's the memory of the feeling I had last night as we drove through the city in Sajar's BMW. Along the dusty half-formed boulevards, the ramshackle buildings set back on the earth verges, the smell of drains, dried fish and an indeterminate human tang that penetrated the closed windows, the air-conditioning, as though we were going ever deeper into the fetid interstices of a great body. The buildings becoming bigger, the deep darkness away from the feeble street-lighting milling with figures, rickety stalls along the roadside, as though the markets of the night were in full swing. Robed figures, turbanned women, full-hipped girls, rangy loose-limbed young men ambling or just standing, half in, half out of the road, their features caught indifferent in the headlights. Silhouettes moving in the turquoise-painted dimness of tiny shops. Africa. I could have described it all down to the last detail. But there's no substitute for the actual sensation of the myriad, teeming enormity closing around your flabby, hapless whiteness – no substitute for actually *being there!* In all my scheming, my planning, my endless promoting, I always forget one thing. That Africa is Africa. And as we ascended towards the Plateau, past the shuttered booths of the Marché Hakim Nder, the great heaps of rubbish, the sweepers moving oblivious before the oncoming traffic, the ragged night people lolling expressionless along the roadside, a skinny kid, his spindly limbs protruding from a dusty hooded sweatshirt standing uncaring in our pathway – the driver, equally uncaring, hardly bothering to miss him – I had a feeling I had never had before, that if I had been put out onto the street there, if I had been put out even up on the Plateau itself, even in the daytime, I would not survive. I would not make it.

I keep seeing this kid. Is it . . . ? I can't see the face, but she's got the same hair – fair, wavy – like her mother's hair, like Her hair, only longer. And I'm trying to see, is that her? It could be. 'Cept she's got this coat on. One of those coats with a velvet collar, tweed. Like Prince Charles and Princess Anne used to wear when they were about six. And you can't tell what colour they were, 'cause the photographs were all black and white. And I'm thinking, Why would she be wearing that? She hasn't got a coat like that. But nobody's got a coat like that now. So that proves nothing.

27

Three

I feel terrible, man. I feel really bad. And every time I pass those photographic blow-ups of glass paintings by the lifts, as I'm coming and going to and from the foyer, I feel worse. I don't know why. You get an image in your mind when you feel nauseous, and it keeps flashing in front of your mind, reproaching and mocking you. And this one, this cartoon row of figures marching to fight the colonialists, seems to be saying, Why have you come here? – Why have you come here? – Why have you come here?

Just at this moment however, even more than whether I give a fuck if I see or speak to Sajar, I'm thinking about how I started shaking as I ate that cheese sandwich in the hotel restaurant. I'm still shaking. And I feel faint. And I'm thinking about how the nurse, as she was pumping me with yellow fever vaccine yesterday morning (it can't only have been yesterday morning!) said my biggest danger was getting bitten by mosquitoes, and how if I experienced flu symptoms I should consult a doctor immediately.

Now I'm back in the foyer, clutching the counter for support. One of the receptionists (they seem to change every hour) narrows his eyes at me.

'Est-ce que il y a un ... directoire téléphonique?'

He narrows his eyes still further in pained incomprehension.

'Telephone book!'

28

Pouting with distaste, he heaves a large volume from behind the counter, and slamming it down in front of me, turns immediately to the next customer.

I rifle manically through the pages of Jopps, Faals and Njais. What the fuck is this? When in doubt phone the British Embassy.

I'm back in my room, and the phone's ringing.

'British Embassy.'

'Could I speak to the Ambassador's wife?'

'The Ambassador's wife? One moment please.'

'Hello?' The voice is smooth and low, with an appropriate mixture of languidity and caution.

'Oh, yeah er ... Sorry to bother you. My name's Andrew Litchfield. I'm in N'Galam researching an article on intercultural finance structures ...'

'Gosh ...'

'That's right. Anyway, I arrived last night and I feel *really bad*. I'm wondering if you could recommend a doctor.'

'Well er ... How exactly do you feel?'

'Flu symptoms.'

'Oh, Lord. Yes. Well, one can't be too careful. I er ... yes. There's a Dr Khalidy who the embassy use. He's Franco-Lebanese and he's er ... awfully nice. Where are you exactly?'

'The Belotel.'

'The Belotel ... Oh, Lord, yes. What time is it ... ? Well, I mean, I would offer to drive you myself, but I've got an appointment at four. Er ... I mean, I'd just jump in a cab if I were you, and see Dr Khalidy. I mean er ... phone first.'

I'm almost in tears with gratitude. The English are a remarkable race.

Dr Khalidy isn't back till three. On the dot I phone. He doesn't speak English, but he has a way of dragging out the word, 'Oueeee ...' that suggests he would react with the same wry, impeturbable assurance no matter what disaster arose. But don't be too complacent, I tell myself. It's you who's ill, not him. This is N'Galam. And life is cheap.

I'm walking down the hotel drive. As though floating. As

though in a dream. I'm walking towards the line. Towards the light of Africa. The guys on the front desk watch in mild astonishment. The security guards sheltering in their pillbox at the front gate, off-duty hotel staff sitting smoking in the shade beside them, all stare. Who is this guy? What is he doing? Why didn't he order a taxi up at the hotel doors like everyone else? Because, ill or not, I'm not going to be ripped off. The price will be a quarter at the bottom of the drive of what it would be at the top.

Those taxi-drivers who are not asleep in their vehicles stand watching me in the blazing sunlight ahead. And then I'm in Africa, in the crumbling sandy street, with the sunlight hitting me. The first taxi-driver looks doubtful at the question of this drained, pale, lank-haired apparition from the hotel.

'Rue Joseph Gomis?'

The question spreads among the drivers starting to wake up. Rue Joseph Gomis? That's one of the troubles of orientation in N'Galam. They keep renaming the streets.

They consult a gaunt, grey-bearded man, somnolent in his voiture, who seems to have a position of respect among them – le gazeteer ambulant. Yes, he knows it. Used to be Rue de Rennes. I'm waved in and the vehicle clatters and clanks into motion.

Where do I want in Rue Joseph Gomis?

Fifty-four.

The doctor's?

Oui.

This guy knows it all. He wears a woolly hat and a tattered robe, habitual garb of the older faithful of N'Galam. On the dashboard is a strip of that embossed lettering you peel off in strips: 'Sop Mam Cheickh Falilou Jarra'. Sort of I ♥ My Holy Man. In this place they're relying totally on the baraka – the spiritual power – of their marabouts, their Holy Men, to get them to the place they're really concerned about. Paradise. In this world, the White Man has been given everything and the Black Man nothing. But in the Next World, if God's commands are obeyed, the position will be reversed. You get people coming up to you, a portrait of their marabout round their neck, and just shoving their hands in your pockets. And to them it's cool, because it's *for their marabout* . . . But this guy's not like that. He's more into somnolent fatalism. He's just somebody's grandad.

I'm looking intently ahead along the dusty back street, the brilliant light through the shade trees reflecting the white dust onto the grimy colonial buildings, as though we're just below the surface of the still afternoon world. On each street corner, and at each building entrance, men sit in ones and twos and small groups, elbows resting on knees as though asleep. Others are sprawled fast asleep on mats or bits of cardboard on the sidewalk. Guys just stand leaning against cars, staring into space. This is the world of the African street: people moving, not discrete, closed off from each other, but just standing there, or sitting or lying, totally chilled out, as though the street is one big living-room. But I'm not fully taking this in, any more than I'm noticing the fact that the windscreen is shattered into a great spider's web, that the passenger door doesn't close properly, that there are wires hanging out everywhere, that the foam is bursting out of the seats, or that everything is covered in that grey encrustation of dust and indescribable other matter that *is* Africa, or indeed than I'm paying attention to the driver's amiable but meaningless small talk, which I can't understand. No, I'm thinking that in my haste I've neglected to bring the package containing sterilised needles and other medicinal essentials of tropical travel, and far from getting the driver to turn back so I can get them, I'm passively allowing myself to be taken on towards the circumstances that will bring about my death.

I'm on a bridge. The footbridge over the dual carriageway between the Leisure Centre and the railway station. It's about five or six o'clock – dark, freezing – and I'm walking against the tide of people flooding over the bridge into the station to get home. And I keep glimpsing this figure, through all these other milling figures, holding onto the railing of the bridge, her head not even reaching the top, peering down onto the river of headlights pouring up from the roundabout by the Confederation Life building. And I'm just glimpsing in the frosty glare of the lights, the flurry of shadows, this fair hair and that coat with the velvet

31

collar. I can't see the face. But I'm thinking, That *is her*. But what's she doing there? On her own? I'm trying to get to her, pushing through all these people. They've got no substance. They're just ... blurs. But I'm hardly moving. It's like I'm wading knee-deep in glue. I still haven't seen her face. And just as she's turning, the shadows close in around her.

Dr Khalidy's surgery is located through a darkened doorway, up a dark staircase and through another open door: a large, bare, gloomy room – clean, but the walls having their own grey accretion of desolation, as though somehow encrusted with the collective sadness of all the colonialists, the expats and émigrés, the solitary misplaced traders, stuck here over decades in the endless burning brilliance. Light comes from a high window. Very little equipment, and what there is apparently not added to since the 1950s. In this Graham Greene film set I'm going to be pumped full of HIV, Hepatitis B, bubonic plague and a myriad hideous tropical ailments with a rusting antique syringe used on all the whores and pederasts of N'Galam. I could, at the moment of inoculation, simply tell him to wait while I rush back to the hotel for my syringes. But in my current state I know I will lack the willpower for even so mundane an act of self-preservation.

Dr Khalidy, a stocky middle-aged man in steel-rimmed glasses, turns to greet me.

'Bonjour Monsieur Litchfield. Asseyez voooous.'

What seems to be the trouble? Say, Aah! Poke, poke, poke. Let's take your blood pressure. Lie down. Breathe in... Christ, German, though it's a hideous fucking language, is just English that happens to be in a different language. But French is a whole different way of thinking, a whole different civilisation, a whole different mind-set. Docteur Khalidy however, seems to think I speak it pretty well.

He's absolutely sure I haven't got malaria. Even if I'd been bitten by a thousand mosquitoes at the airport, I couldn't possibly have malaria. He's convinced it's the anti-malarials I've taken. Anofilene. He's constantly having people coming in here –

32

'surtout les Anglo-Saxons' – who've taken Anofilene, and don't know what's going on.

'*Oui?*' I already feel a hundred times better.

'Oueee . . . Don't take any more. Rest. Drink a lot. Peepee a lot. Get it out of your system, and I will give you another formula. No more meetings today. Rest! Regardez la mer!'

'D'accord!' Christ, the guy's talking horse sense!

'That will be ten thousand francs.'

Thirteen-odd quid. Not bad. And I didn't even see a syringe. I peel up my shirt and fumble in my money belt, giving Dr Khalidy an embarrassed grin.

'Non, non. C'est bon. C'est sûr. C'est beaucoup plus sûr.'

I step out into the street, taking care not to look at the group of raggedly berobed guys I'd seen sitting just down the street, with their marabout badges – not that they represented any threat to me, staring into space, absorbed in their own seraphic stupor – one incongruously in a Russian fur hat, earflaps askew. But you find yourself exercising a prudent sixth sense: don't stare, know what you're doing, glide coolly over the world. That's what you've got to do if you know what you're doing.

And I can hear the rumble and clatter of drumming. Not the earthy reassuring throbbing you probably imagine. These are the Wolof rhythms of N'Galam, hard, urban – in-your-face. A jaunty thrusting back beat, hard, staccato rolls bumping off apparently at random, booming and echoing metallic against the buildings.

> Oom-RAKADAK-um
> Oom-RAKADAK-um
> Oom-RAKADAK-um
> braba-bam-bam!

The sound gets suddenly louder and two girls come sauntering round the corner, all big pout and shades – a huge boom-box thudding and rattling on a shoulder – electrically coloured cycling shorts skin-tight over their robust haunches. The rhythm shifts, and they go striding off up the street, their big hips moving

33

unconsciously in time. A woman calls me to buy oranges. I wave my thanks and flag down a taxi, all in one deftly elegant gesture. Inside there's more music. Different music, but the rhythm dovetailing with the one outside. Here it's all one rhythmic flow, and you've got to get synchronised with it. That's the secret!

It's ndagga. N'Galam music. The same bumping rattle I heard just now, balanced by plangent guitar, coolly blaring horns and Sidi Taal's husky just-got-out-of-bed vocals. Sidi Taal, the spaced-out street guru of N'Galam, the man who talks to the students, the unemployed, the rastamen, ghaddafists, radicals and discontented. Oh, yes. Me and Sidi go back a long way. You probably thought Sajar Jopp was all Tekrur had to offer, but the place is erupting and exploding with music of every description.

Outside, the crumbling streets are waking up to Sidi's cooled-out proclamations. This is how I remember it. A European city falling to bits under the sun. And it looks more desiccated and dishevelled, its buildings grimier and more run-down than ever. But with what style, eh? Everyone out there's *big* – not physically big, but making a big impression – sauntering, proud, through the late-afternoon air, the smell of drains and petrol. Everyone's exerting their cool. And that's the way you've got to be. If you exert your cool, you'll be all right.

The car's in as bad a condition as the one earlier, though in different ways, and there's the name of a different marabout on the dashboard. I didn't discuss the price before getting in, as you're supposed to, but it'll be all right. The driver, tall, blacker than his black robe, is gauntly intent on his driving. He's another talibe. God will reward him for his honesty. But also, while you've got to faire attention at all times, you've got to have some trust. And achieving the right balance between caution and conciliation is something you only achieve over a long period. But believe me, it's crucial. Because how people treat you depends, to a large extent, on *you*.

Back at the hotel, in that eternal waiting-room, that VIP lounge of the soul, suspended over the sea on the edge of Africa, I get my room changed to one on the tenth floor, last but one on the right-hand corridor. I sink down on the bed. Silence, save for the hum of other people's air-conditioners, and far below, the sound of the waves on the rocks, and beyond that the faint laughter of the taxi-drivers, waiting outside the restaurant on the other side of the corniche at the back of the hotel. I lie there. There's a time to chill. A time to regard la mer. A time to regard le télé. This is it.

I was on a beach. I was washed up – almost literally. I mean, I had plenty of money. I'd been through successful treatments for alcohol and cocaine addiction. My marriage was holding together, just. But I felt empty and defeated. One day, on a whim, I took a package tour to Badiya, a tiny former-British colony in West Africa, dwarfed by the French-speaking territory of Tekrur, that was then opening up as a winter sunshine destination. Not that I knew it at the time. I just opened the brochure at random, hardly even aware of what I was doing.

I didn't go to the pool. I didn't go to the nightclubs. I didn't go on any day excursions. I just sat under a palm tree staring into space, hardly even aware of where I was. From being a mod and a teenage vandal in New Malden, I took acid a week before my O-levels and spent my seventeenth birthday bombed out of my mind in a hotel in Katmandu. By the mid-seventies I was leading a life of relative sedateness promoting pub rock gigs, but supporting a major cocaine habit, as well as a wife and a serious house in Ladbroke Grove. Punk was the period when I really cleaned up, when many of the people I'd nurtured through gigs in lavatories made it big-time. I went on through New Romanti-cism, Electropop and all the other shit. By that time I was part of the machine: sucking it all in and spewing it out. But I didn't particularly give a fuck. Then one day, it all just fell apart . . .

So there I was, sitting on that beach, staring out at the Atlantic breakers, at almost the most far-western point of the African continent, under the grey rustling leaves of the palms, but not seeing any of it. I wasn't a wreck. I'd been a wreck. Now I was the dried-out shell of a wreck. Or that's how I felt. Like the blurred after-image of a human being . . . I tell a lie. I'm letting subjective

35

memory get the better of me here. I didn't feel anything. I was completely numb.

Then one day I heard music. I heard a voice speaking to me inside my head. A voice, tender, intimate, crooning, stroking a song into insistent animation. Against a lilting, Cuban-sounding backing of liquid guitar and slapping congas, the singer teased out an exquisitely haunting melody, with that kind of non-European quality of yearning . . . What was it? Arabic? Andalusian? Something vaguely Islamic. And while the singer himself sounded almost heartbreakingly young, there was behind his voice a sense of knowledge, ageless, mysterious, *other*. And I can remember being extremely conscious of the singer's gums, of the flesh of the inside of his mouth. It is such qualities, I know from long experience, that make a voice *inimitable*.

The rhythm tautened, became faster. The singer took up a fervent rhythmic refrain as the number came to a crashing conclusion. The song had had something of the enchanted quality of music heard in the last exquisite moments of sleep, whose essence permeates deliciously the first blurred hour of waking before it disappears forever. This music however was perfectly real, as I realised when I came to, feeling a faint breeze on my face, and hearing, for the first time, the rustle of the palm leaves high above me. Some yards away, a figure sat on the trunk of a felled palm listening to a transistor radio. I could hear the announcer talking in a stilted English. I got to my feet and staggered towards the man. I had to find out the name of the singer. 'Cause I know from bitter experience that if you don't ask immediately, you never, ever find out. He turned in alarm at my approach, a burly middle aged man in a kind of gown. 'That music,' I said. 'What was it?'

He seemed taken aback by the abruptness of my approach. But I kept repeating the question, rephrasing it with what I felt to be appropriate gestures. At last he understood, and beamed with pleasure. At first I couldn't hear what he was saying, unaccustomed as I was in those days to hearing foreign names.

'Sajar Jopp?' I said after several attempts.

'Sajar Jopp. That music, Sajar Jopp.'

36

'Is it a group or a singer?'

'Sajar Jopp is in N'Galam.' And he burst into a big African laugh.

'But who is he?'

'Sajar Jopp?' A knowing gleam came into his eye, and lifting a forefinger he launched into a monologue on the subject of Sajar Jopp, in some African language I realise in retrospect was probably Wolof, though at the time I'd never heard of any African language, apart from maybe Zulu. He carried on chuckling to himself as I staggered off along the beach.

That night I sat in the hotel restaurant, alone among the package tourists. For the first time I realised that I actually was *somewhere*. The waiters in their red pyjama uniforms, so courteous and patient with Leighton Buzzard Man on holiday, had their own life, their own reality away from here. It occurred to me that any one of them could probably have told me everything I wanted to know about Sajar Jopp. But I didn't ask them. I didn't want to know quite yet. Experience had taught me that the best musicians have really very little to offer, and I wanted to spin this fragile spell out as long as possible.

The next day, I took a taxi to the local market. It was nearly midday as I stepped into the screaming brilliance of the sun's glare, and already the place was virtually deserted. Three girls came running towards me with these huge basins of lettuce. 'Salaad! Salaad!' they kept shouting. No, no. No salad, I said, and kept on walking. The place seemed to me an amazingly sad dump: a shambles of rusting, beaten-in corrugated iron, the traders mostly asleep among their bales of cloth and rotten fruit. The smell of drains, rank meat and a harsh yellow reek I later came to know as dried fish. Big women in incredibly coloured turbans watching me with this amazing clear-eyed impassivity. And already I could feel this other immensity opening up beyond this, that I was putting a toe into another reality, another civilisation, another way of being: Africa.

No one bothered me. They could tell I wasn't into anything they had to offer. And there, at the back of the market, I found this stall, like an open-fronted shack, stacked to the ceiling with hi-fi gear, where two guys in shades were calmly pirating cassettes. And in a way, I knew where I was, because although they were Africans, and they were grumpy bastards, they were after all 'Music People'. And I soon realised they knew more English than they were letting on. Sajar Jopp, I kept saying. The owner, the wiry one in the cut-off Levi jacket, slipped a cassette into one of the decks and turned up the volume. The rattle of drums came spitting from the speakers. There were a couple of seconds of the voice I'd heard the day before, howling through the tinny distortion. Then he ripped it out of the deck, snapped it back in the case and handed it to me. I bought four more, hoping the song I had heard on the beach would be among them. This wasn't the place for prolonged listening. The cassettes, marked only – and shamelessly – with the owner's stamp, were of horrendous quality, but there was no point importing original copies, as no one could afford to buy them. If I wanted to buy an original copy, I would have to go to N'Galam, the owner scowled.

And if I went to N'Galam, would I find Sajar Jopp there? He shrugged. Possibly.

But who was Sajar Jopp?

He snorted. Then he sniggered and broke into a wry chuckle. He turned to his colleague who laughed too. 'Hurh! Sajar Jopp!'

Why were they laughing?

The owner looked at me, then turned away. 'No,' he said, as though I could never possibly understand.

I was on a bus. How I got on it – how I knew which one and where it was going – I'll never know, but there I was in a wreck of a bus grinding over the shimmering asphalt in the heat of the day, the hard earth scrub of the African bush rolling away in every direction. Every so often we'd pass villages of mud huts – groups of ragged and naked children watching us pass, old men, their features reduced to black outlines beneath conical straw hats, sitting, apparently asleep. Mud huts. *Mud huts!* I had to keep pinching myself. But this was no dream, man. I was *in it!*

There are certain things which, while you haven't actually

planned them, fall in with the general pattern of your life, which even if you didn't expect them, seem somehow no more than your due. But this wasn't like that. This was something totally *extra* – that I'd never thought about, that it had never even occurred to me would happen. A few days ago I was absorbed in the pains, the speechless agony of my life. And now, while the other mugs were sitting by the pool or off on silly little day trips to baboon sanctuaries, I'd scarpered across the border into a country I'd never even heard of, on a *bus* – with the real people. The real people, muffled in their shawls and turbans, sprawled out in their ragged European trousers, seemed to be nearly all asleep. But I was wide awake. And the fact that I hadn't planned this, the fact that it had never even occurred to me, was all part of the pleasure – as though I'd stolen the experience, filched it. No, it was a gift. On my way to what I already realised was one of the great cities of Africa, the metropolitan magnet of the savannah, towards Sajar Jopp and the music in my head.

As we hit the hazy glittering immensity of the Atlantic, the bus started to fill up, mostly with big women in brilliantly coloured robes dragging great bags and bundles, and we entered the string of battered corrugated-iron towns that continues almost unbroken along the coast, and right into the centre of N'Galam. At each stop the crowds of women and children besieging the bus, holding up their handfuls of fruit, plastic bagfuls of water and biscuits, grew larger and more desperate, many fighting their way onto the bus, the groups of youths hanging out on the crumbling corners, more numerous and more hard-eyed. Blind people and cripples tried to push their way through the throng, singing out in hard nasal voices, reaching up at the bus windows for charity. One old man stayed on the bus, facing the passengers as he sang, tin outstretched, tearing phrases apparently impulsively from the air, his dark voice harshly and tarrily nasal – admonishing as much as imploring – and I thought, there's everything in there: Howling Wolf's blues, the rawest, hardest flamenco, the towering mystery of the call of the muezzin . . . And I felt a shiver down my spine as I realised that *that* was what I was heading towards. And I clasped my bag closer, because I spoke virtually no French, and I had no entrée in this city, other than the name Sajar Jopp. And what would he be like? A pretty puppet in gold robes, his strings pulled by corrupt and conniving relatives, or a glittery megalomaniac in dated seventies threads, like Sly Stone as a witch doctor? I would find out all too soon. And I had a slight feeling of queasiness, of the slightly nauseous excitement I used to feel on meeting brilliant musicians – before I became completely blasé.

We were on a freeway, huge billboards for airlines and cigarettes obscuring the sprawl of rusting, dustworn shacks. There was an underpass, then a dry and deserted railway track running beneath the road, and it was as though we were in a provincial town in some indeterminately dry and drab corner of Europe. The people crossing the streets in their long gowns and turbans looked as though they were in fancy dress. Then the bus had stopped, and everyone was shoving their way off. The evening sun fell on the scene outside in great bars of gold, but the air was black with spilt engine oil, singed tyres and the crowds of people fighting their way in and out of battered vans, old buses, taxis and pick-ups, among the milling touts, crippled and blind beggars, hawkers of water, cloth, cassettes and Vick's Colic Rub. Before I had time even to think what I should be doing, I heard a hissing and a man in a filthy white cap and his boss-eyed sidekick were beckoning me into the crowd. I was about to follow them when a hard voice cut into the back of my neck.

'No, my friend!'

I turned to see a tout, tall, eagle-eyed in a pith helmet pointing at me. 'For where?'

'Sajar Jopp.'

His eyes narrowed.

'I want to see Sajar Jopp!' I blurted almost querulously.

'You want Sajar Jopp . . . lui-même?'

'Er . . . oui.'

Having been about to follow two seedy malingerers to God knew what indignities, I had now submitted my destiny totally to this man, who had forced himself on me through sheer power of will. He led me a couple of yards to a large and battered saloon car, and immediately began hauling the passengers out. 'No, no . . .' I said. And the passengers protested equally vehemently, a large woman in red robes making a particular meal of it. The tout paid no attention, but opened one of the passenger doors, threw my bag in and gestured me to follow.

'I . . .' I faltered before obeying.

'You can pay the driver,' he snapped, as I fumbled for my wallet. 'But, if you wish, you can also give me something.'

I took out an English five-pound note, which he took, snapping out the creases in a single expert gesture. He banged on the roof, and the vehicle heaved away, honking into the throng, the disappointed passengers hammering on the roof. We passed into a dim alley, along the narrow sides of which women squatted behind bowls of fruit and God knows whatever else they were selling. I was shaking inside. Now what was going to happen?

But up on the main boulevards, white-gloved policemen waved the traffic past patisseries that might have been transplanted from the Champs Elysées in every detail including, I surmised, the prices. Well-scrubbed children of various races made their way home from the exclusive schools, nannies pushed prams past gleaming pharmacies and cream-coloured official buildings. There were a lot of whites about. French, I assumed. All looking very big and pink and confident in their smart tropical gear. And there were a lot of people who could have been Arabs. Lebanese? But mostly they were black. Black and handsome. And self-possessed and coolly purposeful even when they did not appear to be doing anything. So this is Africa, I thought. Not lions and tigers and safari parks, but this dusty, dishevelled version of Europe populated by these black, black, self-assured people.

We passed into the back streets. More and more people outside. Hanging out of shop doorways. Old men in incredible robes sitting in dining-chairs on the pavements. The rattling of crafts-men's hammers – silversmiths. People hammering on car parts behind stockades of corrugated iron. Children sanding car doors on the pavements by hand. Oil, ashes and behind a wickerwork screen, a pile of charcoal fifteen feet high. Huge mechanics, like

41

oily titans, on their way home. Huge piles of cooking-pots stacked along the pavements; lines of bedsteads; suitcases beaten out of old tins. The workshops were shacks, their roofs held down with lumps of rock. Between them were heaps of board and old corrugate. Houses! With washing drying outside. It might have been depressing if the people emerging had not looked so singularly undowntrodden.

We passed briefly onto the sea front, and then back into a long avenue of small boxlike concrete houses laid out on a grid, with alleys running off to right and left, and lines of brilliantly coloured washing hanging everywhere. Kids played football in the street, and along the shattered pavements, women and girls queued at standpipes. It seemed a workaday, proletarian kind of an area, the African equivalent of a council estate. At the corner of two such thoroughfares, the car slowed. A group of young men sat looking dazed and weary, like labourers benumbed by a hard day's work in the sun. The driver gestured me to get out. As I crossed the street the men watched without curiosity, though I couldn't imagine that too many whites could have come that way. I approached the nearest of them, a lean youth with slanting eyes, his torso, naked to the waist, covered in dust. 'Excuse me,' I said. 'Where can I find Sajar Jopp?'

'I'm Sajar Jopp,' said the youth. 'Can I help you?'

That's how, without meaning to, without even knowing what I was doing, I became 'the man who got there first'. And I thought Sajar was just a regular guy. I didn't realise how unusual it was even then, to find Sajar sitting out in the street – that in the eyes of everyone around him, he'd already achieved a position of almost mythical greatness.

Four

The gardeners, or whatever they are, are all massive cheerful
blokes in dark blue overalls and they move in great gangs,
dividing into groups of two or three, before regrouping, like some
protean collective organism that cannot be completely broken
down. They're heaving huge potted plants back and forth over
the poolside terrace, bits of the stage they're busy erecting over
the pool itself and trestle tables that the waiters are laying in the
shade opposite the restaurant – presumably for the avocats'
lunch. Beplaited girls in quasi-traditional uniforms move with a
superb and ineffable slowness between the restaurant and the
tables, while the dapper waiters in their maroon pyjama uniforms
lollop backwards and forwards fetching cutlery, unfolding table-
cloths, ordering each other sternly but good-naturedly about.
Nobody's hurrying, but at the same time nobody's dawdling.
This is Africa. The sun is out, but not yet too hot. The birds are
twittering in the palms and bougainvillea. Everything will find its
own pace – its own rhythm.

I'm sitting by the pool under one of those thatched umbrella
things – 'cause while I don't feel too bad, the doctor told me not to
overdo it, and we don't want the world to start revolving again,
do we? So I just chill, enjoying the neo-colonial pantomime of the
hotel, savouring its mindless but deep-seated hierarchical order,
which, you feel, would just keep going on endlessly, regardless of

whether anyone was actually staying here or not. And that is very, very African . . .

I divide my time between lengthy sessions in my room with CNN, the poolside and the foyer, where there's une promotion marocaine on, the back of the place half-blocked with stalls trying to unload the usual ornamental crap, the hangers of djellabahs, gilt-embroidered and sequinned kaftans filling half the walls, and the slumped, jaded forms of the stallholders and their stupefied Tekrurian assistants most of the furniture. I squeeze onto the end of one of the sofas and sit there for hours speechless among them and the other denizens of the foyer. Beside me's the bloke who's supposed to be photographing the delegates of the congrès d'avocats, but has camped out here permanently in the hope of bedding one or several of the stallholders' assistants. There are the members of the 'orchestra' specially flown in from Marrakesh to play in the restaurant over the course of the promotion, playing cards in the corner while the porters, two powerfully built men in dun-coloured safari suits – the one hunched and loping, eyes downcast, the other majestically upright, a serene smirk on his eagle's features, who misses nothing – patrol the compact-marble expanses. And there are even some hotel patrons: that Ethiopian, delegate at a conference on environmental issues, who speaks no French, and spends a lot of time sitting staring eagerly at nothing; the two non-Tekrurian Africans in glasses, who are perpetually in hushed conference and always order the cheapest thing on the restaurant menu, who I take to be Mozambican film-makers travelling the world on UNESCO money in search of finance for Marxist epics that will never be made. There are a few Europeans, hard-faced businessmen, who pause in the foyer only long enough for their limo to pull up on the other side of the glass doors, and a few uncertain tourists, their knees white beneath their too-new shorts. But mostly, there are those people of indeterminate race, who seem perpetually suspended on the trailways of international trade and intrigue, unnoticed surfers of the medium waves of international commerce, who are merchants before they are members of any religion or ethnic group, who trade not because they have an inordinate love of money, but

44

because they have no home but business. What are they? Parsees? Sindis? Mozarbites? Smyrna Greeks? Bokhara Jews? Packing their civilisation in a briefcase, mistrusted wherever they go, secure only in the knowledge that everything – particularly in a place like this – is going to be negotiable. And of course, me. An anonymous white man in specially designed 'savannah' trousers that not only drip-dry in five minutes, rolling up to the size of a fountain pen, but are considered stylish items of apparel by London clubbers who have no intention of straying near the burning immensities of the earth.

And I feel I could go on with this sedentary existence practically forever: approaching that African condition of not watching, not waiting, not expecting, not anticipating – just being.

'Monsieur, telephone.'

As I follow the waiter inside, I feel a sense of things at last falling into place. The foyer has its usual hum of comings and goings, but I'm not aware of it, I'm about to speak to Sajar. I can feel the glow, the big smile on my face.

'Yea . . .'

The syllable is big with a ripe, exultant chuckle. I'm halfway through it, when I hear heavy breath at the other end. This isn't Sajar. Who the fuck is it?

'Litch?'

The voice is thick and husky, and so clear and so loud I feel whoever it is must be actually in the building, actually in the foyer. I freeze to the roots. I can feel them watching me: not only whoever's speaking, but the guy behind the desk and the hall porter, 'cause let's face it, they could all be in on it.

'I want to see you!'

Be careful, man. If you get roped into the wrong scam here, you could end up in the *wrong* prison. And don't think that because you're in a French-owned chain hotel, that there's any security here. Not at all.

'Who is this?'

'Daouda,' says the voice, thick and complacent as though providing me with detailed information rather than just the equivalent of Dave.

45

'Daouda who?'

'Daouda Mboob.'

'I don't know you.'

'No, I know .. I need to talk to you.'

'About what?'

'Music!'

Christ, man. Another musician trying his luck. I relax.

'That's great, man. But I'm like mega-busy. I've got meetings all day, and I'm checking out bands at night. So . . .'

His voice becomes more agitated and forceful. 'Mane, amna fi cassette bou nekh-a-nekh-a-nekh! And I know you're definitely the best person to hear it.'

'Yeah, okay. If you send it to Sajar Jopp's office, he'll pass it on to me. All right?'

Fucking hell, man. I'm just sitting there minding my own business, and this guy has to phone up, bringing the teeming unruly airs of the quartiers populaires, the scent of *reality* in here.

I'd better make a phone call.

'. . . lo?'

Christ! Him again.

''Ello! Est-ce que Salimata est là?'

'Un instant.'

At last. Somebody is there. Salimata. Sajar's younger sister. His favourite. The one who spent two years in England at his expense doing a computer course so the third wave could hit Tekrur. And we all helped. The number of wet afternoons I spent watching bad Richard Gere films in otherwise empty cinemas is nobody's business. Still, there were compensating factors. Salimata. Cool, cool eyes. Full Egyptian mouth, set in one of those shapely, pendulous jawlines . . .

'Hello?'

'Yeah, Salimata! Litch!'

'Hello, Litch.'

'How's it going?'

'Fine.'

Gordon Bennett! Let's get some fucking enthusiasm going here! Anyone would think the woman didn't even *know* me.

'So, er ... how is everything?'

'Fine.'

'Is er ... Sajar there?'

'He's not here.'

'Well.' Come on, man. Show some muscle! 'Where *is* he?'

There's a slight pause as she takes in the implications of my tone. 'What exactly is it that you want?'

What exactly is it that I want? I can't believe I'm hearing this. *What exactly is it that I want?* She's putting that question to me? To *me*? I mean, who is *she*? A jumped-up secretary, who happens to be Sajar's sister! Some *silly little girl!* Trying to tell me *I* need a reason to speak to Sajar Jopp!

'I want to talk to him,' I say, trying to inject some real annoyance into my voice, but I still sound desperately limp. '. . . about business.'

'Phone back in . . .' I can hear her pouting as she decides how many hours I should be kept hanging around. 'Phone back tomorrow.'

You assume everywhere is approaching the safe, anodyne blandness of a Midwestern retail park, don't you? Well, I do. I assume everywhere's losing it, succumbing to the dead, homogenising hand of consumer capitalism. But they're not. They'd like to be! But the overwhelming economic facts mean that they just can't make it. And when you get out into the desiccated, black-patina'd wreck of a city, and find that all the old codes, the old routes, the teeming, intractable, irremediable *stuff* is still going on, you have that same intoxicating, but terrifying rush you always did get on realising that not only is *Africa still Africa* – but in its sheer tenacity in remaining so, in retaining the essence of what it has always been, Africa is more Africa than ever.

Yes, Africa is still Africa, because it can't afford to be anything else. And I'm out here in it. And that rush seems more intoxicating, more terrifying and delirium-inducing, because of the feeling, the knowledge that I really shouldn't be here. I should be sitting quietly by the pool. I mean, I knew the sun was going to be hot, but I didn't realise it was going to be hitting me with quite such vehemence, blasting up off the glittering white dust with such fierceness you wouldn't think you were wearing shades. And the people don't care. Because lolling and loping and lolloping along the crumbling sidewalks, leaning and sprawling against their stalls, sucking on their chewing-sticks with their characteristic abstracted indifference, they're black. Oh, yes. They've got the protective purple blackness, and that indifference, which far more than hostility is the feeling coming at you along these edgy streets. Oh, yes. Just because they think they'd like to get into a bit of consumer capitalism and you come from near the heartland of that, doesn't mean they give a fuck about *you*. And that indifference is all part of the intoxication and the intensity of the hit you're getting from the sheer scale of it all, a hit the force of which makes you realise how long it must be – much longer than you thought – since you last came here.

Out of the brilliance comes the brooding immemorial grimness of the dockyard walls, and along the crumbling pavements beneath, the sore-like growths of ragged and not-so-ragged stalls, these encrustations of tenuous African commerce, that could, like the red termite tracks, like the webs of spiders, like all the other unnamable accumulations of matter that announce the African process of decay, be swept away with the movement of a hand, only to immediately begin to gather again.

I'm feeling all this rather than looking at it. Because if you look, if you pause to ponder, you get the guys walking in step, the 'Yes, my friend! From England?' And before you know where you are they've got the gold out, and as we all know, if you get offered gold in Africa, it means you're about to be mugged. I've already had a couple of guys sidling up, murmuring, but the moment I got a few yards beyond their stall they gave up.

'Yes, my friend!'

Shit.

The voice is coming not from beside me, but from the ground behind. I've turned before I've thought what I'm doing, and there's this guy, his pin-like legs twisted useless beneath him on a trolley like a tea-tray on tiny wheels, propelling himself quickly along with his hands, and he's beaming most amiably. 'How are you?'

From the other direction a thick-set middle-aged woman with no legs is heaving herself over the rubble towards me with her muscular arms. I'm quivering inside. I've got to get moving. I'd like to help these people, but I can't be getting money out here. Those of the stallholders, strollers and liggers who can be bothered to look, titter with bemusement and disgust as the sweating, desperate toubab, the rich bastard, picks up his pace. There's a young woman cross-eyed with a narrow pinhead and a dazed smile, walking on the spikes of her elbows and knees, her bony calves twisted upwards behind her. 'Monsieur!' And they don't seem abject, they don't seem pathetic, these people. I mean, they *are* abject, they *are* pathetic. But they don't see it like that. They know exactly what they're doing. It's me, my body swarming with panic and shame, who's losing it. In a hideous rushing instant, I recall delightedly hyping this place from the comfort of some record exec's office, larding on the atmosphere, telling him that the beggars here – even the most horribly deformed – had the same pride, the same assertive chutzpah as everyone else, and I remember thinking, even as I was saying it, that this was the most criminally dishonest bullshit. *But it was true, wasn't it!* It's just one of those things which, if you're not actually *there*, you cannot get yourself to believe.

As I reach the corner, a figure crawls crab-like from the shadows. I glance down at this bearded tough-looking guy. 'Please, my friend!' he says in English in a voice of hard authority. 'I am *asking* for your help!'

I put my hand into my pocket.

Up on the Plateau, the official quarter of embassies and government buildings, the shade trees have grown huge and massively gnarled, their great trunks half-filling the pavement, splitting and upturning the blackened paving-stones. A group of young girls, one French, one Lebanese, one Tekrurian, come tumbling along the pavement towards me giggling and chewing their haversack

49

straps. Three twelve-year-olds on their way home from their privileged private school, at large on these edgy pavements – not bothered by anyone or anything, a picture of robust multiracial good health. While I, my dizziness partly quelled by a Coke in a fly-blown Lebanese patisserie, am still queasy and more than a little shaky.

On the other side of the street is a long art-deco apartment block. I imagine it just built: brilliant white, streamlined, exhilaratingly modern – *the* new place to live in N'Galam. In those days, you'd see fewer blacks in this part of town than you would in say, Marseilles. Even a few years after independence, this was still basically a French city. The streets were still swept every day for the nannies pushing the gleaming prams of the toubabs; the memsahibs, or whatever the French call them, stepping cheerfully out on their shopping expeditions. Now, crouching behind its screen of overgrown shade trees, this block looks grey, tired and exhausted – succumbing, like everything else, to the blackening patina and crumbling neglect.

Over a dustblown shopfront, I pick out in relief – in letters that would mark themselves out immediately anywhere in the world as 'French' – the words 'Café-Restaurant – la Maquisette.' I remember the place well. Formica-topped tables, big photographic blow-ups of engravings of the Isle des Esclaves, café crême and excellent croissants served by hunched and ancient waiters, while boy hawkers stood waving their wares at the windows and newspaper-sellers slunk in to serve the sleek-suited and starch-robed customers, and a pink and very tough-looking Frenchman watched hard-eyed from the till. Now it's boarded up, screened with wicker, the narrow entrance filled with rags, rubbish and other detritus of human occupation. I'm in some rundown indeterminately aged main street of the European mind, blackened by handling, worn by African dust, faded through the filter of overgrown shade trees by the African sun. On the other side of the street, between an incongruously well-kept pharmacy and a Lebanese alimentation, the turbanned elders sit outside a mosque, saying their beads, a couple of leprous beggars seated along the wall beside them, stumps prominently displayed. The odd turbanned woman squats along the kerbside behind a pile of oranges. Otherwise, the place is practically deserted.

Past the open-fronted shops of the Lebanese cloth vendors I reach the great crossroads where the Avenue Wagane Diouf descends towards the quartiers populaires. And there on the far corner, sticking up against the shuddering metal sky, are the battered ochre ramparts of the Marché Hakim Nder. *The Marché Hakim Nder!* Stations of my mind! How much time have I spent thinking about, dreaming about – never mind actually being *in* – the Marché Hakim Nder. It never was much of an architectural masterpiece, but now standing stark against the empty afternoon sky, surrounded by its mess of ramshackle stalls, a hand-painted hoarding for Jumbo Cube masking much of its upper portion, it looks pathetically ramshackle and decrepit. Is that it? The great library, the great repository of the soul of Africa's music? Music ... I've been here how many days, and I've hardly heard any music, let alone bought any. I've hardly thought about music. The normally crowded and extremely dodgy entrance is deserted except for a few porters and beggars slumped in the afternoon heat. Even at this time of day there'll be a few stalls open. I could just slip over there and cop a handful of cassettes. Something to listen to and pore over back at the hotel. But I'd be no more than half-way over the street than the touts and hustlers would be waking, emerging from the woodwork, materialising from the pavement and on me like a pack of dogs. Already I can sense dark figures making their way towards me on this side of the street, feel hard eyes upon me from among the few people seated on the bent and twisted crash railing. Time to get out of here. There's a taxi ...

The sun has retreated into the pall of grey dust over the city, but it's still unnervingly bright as the taxi lurches onto a traffic roundabout crumbling into heaps of sand and rubble. 'This is the Medina,' says the driver. There's a petrol station with a bunch of beggars hanging listlessly about. There's the famous patisserie where Sajar always goes for croissants and hot milk at dawn, after he's played at his club. A block along is the even more famous

Savannah Nightclub – the birthplace of Tekrurian music, home of the legendary Star Band of N'Galam, where Sajar got his first gig singing Cuban rumba at the age of fifteen, where the use of Wolof language and rhythm in the pop context really got going. Yes, this is the Medina, the old 'native quarter' of N'Galam, the original quartier populaire, where Sajar Jopp was born and grew up. Reading those articles on Sajar, mostly written by people who haven't been within a thousand miles of here, and listening to all the media yuppies who came foraging here – 'of course *I* stayed in the Med*i*na' – you'd think it was this great fount of irrepressible street energy, one of les endroits le plus funky du monde. I mean, look at it, man. What a dump! The Savannah Nightclub is just another crumbling nondescript building, the famous patisserie is just a ... patisserie, and the whole atmosphere in the grey deserted mid-afternoon is seedily torpid beyond belief.

'N'Galam's Medina, a lovely area of sandy tree-lined streets, where one can easily shop for souvenirs and fruit.' Who the fuck wrote that? Yeah, that's right. It was me. 'Cause when you're trying to mould and manipulate thought, particularly in relation to something most people are going to be as inherently indifferent to as African music, you've got to cover every angle. Half the time you're giving the journalists so much information you're practically writing the articles for them. And as you'll know if you've ever done any journalism, it's not difficult. In fact, it's criminally easy.

'So where do you want to go?'

Yeah, good question.

'Do you know Nyanya Guisse's place?'

Nyanya Guisse is the percussionist, the dancer, rapper and rabble-rouser of Sajar's band. While Fafa Mbaye, a simple homely dude, looks after the tama, the talking drum, its gurgling, undulating roll the animating principle of Tekrurian music, Nyanya's the master of the djembe, the bougarabou, the rock-hard, long-sticked sabar – whose dry, cracking rhythms keep up this constant probing punctuation beneath the seething river of music. But it's his voice that's the most remarkable thing about him, cavernously resonant, using parts of his vocal apparatus other people don't even have – you can hear his anecdotes and cajoling catchphrases coming from several blocks away, trailing the chuckles and gasps of his admirers, acolytes and hangers-on. And on stage, bellowing an audience into a slavering frenzy with his furious bumping alliteration, his visceral free-jazz gobbledygook, his ancestral exhortations ghosting Sajar's golden shriek, he's the one who, no matter how much time Sajar spends amid the bland temptations of the West, keeps the danger, the street edge, in the music. And he's the one whose roguish charms the researchers and lady directors all fall for ('Oh, he's lovely!'), whose blokish highfiving backchat wins over the suits and bigwigs ('Yeah! There is my *man!'*). But when you're here for any length of time, when you're actually *in* Sajar's operation, you realise that here's someone whose ego – *monstrous* as a matter of course – must be assuaged at all points, someone who, if you haven't got him on your side, you can forget it.

The taxi stops along a track between breeze-block compound walls. I pay the driver and head into a yard where a group of women are laughing as they fan a charcoal brazier. They stop in mid-motion.

'Salaam aleikum.'

'Aleikum salaam.'

'Nangendef?'

Murmured responses.

Oh, yes. You can't just walk in and blurt out your enquiry. You've got to greet, break the ice, schmooze, even if only at the most pefunctory level.

The women stand, frozen, expressionless.

'Ana Nyanya Guisse?'

One of them points through a door.

I'm in a courtyard with low corrugated-iron eaves. Voices come from an open door on the far side. I head over there.

'Salaam aleikum.'

Grunted cursory, 'Aleikum salaam.'

A bunch of dudes lounge on a double bed in the turquoise-painted room. The conversation has stopped. Some look at me, expressionless. Others stare at the floor.

'Ana Nyanya Guisse?'

One of the guys grunts something to the effect that Nyanya is here or is coming. Another gets up from a wooden armchair and gestures me to sit down. I sink gratefully down. 'Cause it's hot. It's really hot. These guys are young, the usual collection of fashion rastas in expensive glasses and assorted baseball-cap wearers – probably some of Nyanya's brothers, all drummers, and their mates. In the past I'd have got some chat going about the percussion scene in N'Galam, but I'm too tired, too fucked. I'll have to do it another time. Inhibited by my presence, their conversation never really recovers. One by one they saunter out, and before I know where I am I'm sitting there on my own. Great, man. So much for African hospitality.

I'm starting to doze off when I hear Nyanya's resonantly purple tones out in the courtyard. What's he saying? What does it matter? The guy could make the phonebook sound like a masterpiece of lascivious portent. A spluttering laugh breaks through the mass of writhing labial consonants. Someone else is chuckling. Yes, the guy's in anecdote mode. When isn't he?

Nyanya ambles slowly through the door like he's just got out of bed – which he probably has – blocking out half the light in the room, slightly taller than I remember him, resplendent in a shiny lilac-and-turquoise tracksuit, peering down at me, slightly cross-eyed, with that unmistakable gap-toothed smile.

'Yeah, man! Ça va?'

'Bien, bien. Nangadef?'

'Jamm' rek. How is England?'

'Fine.'

'Everything fine?'

'Yeah. How . . . ?'

Someone's calling him from outside. He turns his head, still holding my hand, and shouts back. Then he slips his hand from mine and goes back out into the yard.

'Sajar Jopp is a philosopher!' this guy is saying. 'He is saying things that are relevant to every African person. He is advising us to do good, to work very hard for Africa. That is why we all like him so much. And he has a lot of . . . African philosophy, *deep stuff*, in his paroles. But you know that! I think you know that!'

He looks at me knowingly, according me moral parity, sitting on his bed in a voluminous mustard-coloured robe, Cindy Crawford's oiled thighs and Samantha Fox's bloated breasts glowing out of the big posters above him. He rolls himself tiny spliffs the size of matchsticks.

'I don't live here, you know. I live in Paris. Does that surprise you?'

Not really, no.

'Oui! I can't live here, there is nothing here – économiquement. So I go to Paris – chercher l'argent! Je suis tunneleur. I dig tunnels – for the métro. It's hard, yeah! Very hard! Paris is not a friendly place. But if I feel sad or lonely, I just listen to Sajar's music and I feel much, much calmer.'

Who is he? I've no idea. But that doesn't matter. He just turned up at Nyanya's and said why didn't I come round the corner to his place for 'thé chinois'. So we've just sat here, as the colour comes back into the world – the commuters flooding back into the Medina, the taxis, minibuses and pickups jamming the round-abouts and thoroughfares, the scraps of markets along the crumbling verges humming and buzzing again – as guys bring us glasses of sweet green tea.

And while the guy's such a nice guy – just like hundreds, thousands of other well-meaning ordinary people who've given me their views on any number of subjects over the years – I'm finding his folk homilies far from reassuring. 'Cause I'm not thinking that I no longer have the time and the patience for the endless sitting around, the hours of Chinese-tea philosophy, the pointless meaningless bonhomie that *is* Africa. I'm not thinking that I no longer find it picturesque and meaningful, that I no longer feel privileged to be with the *real people*, that I've long since done all that and can't understand why I'm back here again still doing it. I'm not even thinking that Nyanya's family didn't even accord me the basic rudiments of African courtesy, that Nyanya

55

himself behaved as though he didn't even know who I was. I'm thinking that after all I've done for Sajar Jopp, without payment, because I love Africa, because I feel I owe Africa one, for what I can only describe as 'political reasons' – because I feel it's important for Africa to have someone out there having his CDs flogged cheap with ten pints of milk, someone universally regarded as its 'greatest musician', despite the fact that Africa is so far from being a heterodox cultural reality, the term is almost meaningless – in spite of all that, I've been here however many days, and Sajar hasn't even acknowledged my presence in any way. I mean, who the fuck does Sajar Jopp think he is?

'I like people like you,' says my host, now quite stoned. 'You don't just hide in your hotel. You come out and spend time with the people. You get close to them. That's good.'

'Yeah,' I say, not really listening.

I'm in the kitchen, washing up. There's a lot. There always is. 'Cause I leave it till there's virtually nothing left to use before I do it. It pisses Her off, but I don't mean to do it. It just seems to get to that point amazingly quickly, considering how much stuff we've got. And I'm getting to the point washing these endless glasses, where I'm just standing there, my hands in the washing-up gloves just resting in the grey lukewarm water . . . Then I look up, and there's a stepladder standing in the middle of the terrace, and the kid's standing on top of it. And I'm wondering what that's doing there and what she's doing on it, and I can see that it's already moving. And she's looking straight at me, smiling as the stepladder sways from side to side, like she's dancing in mid-air. I'm pulling at the yellow gloves as I run to the back door. But it's locked.

The muzak in this place is starting to get on my nerves. You can hear it very faintly the moment you get out of your room. Then in the lift it's clearly audible. In the foyer it's always bubbling away under the clamour of new arrivals, the dazed, bored conversations of the stallholders and their even more bored Tekrurian assistants, and of course in the restaurant, as I try to complete my nauseous breakfasts. Even as the Moroccan orchestra go through their crashing droning paces, there's the mildly frightening thought that that muzak is still actually going on underneath it all. Yes, you say, but this is African music. What are you complaining about? You came here for this.

Yeah, man. But this is the *wrong* African music. And they only seem to have three cassettes, the same few tracks of which keep coming round and round with speaker-booting regularity. Not that it is completely bad music. That's perhaps the worst thing about it. And it's music that I already know all too well.

But it's not Tekrurian music. Oh, no. They wouldn't do that. That would be too close to home. Bringing the sound of the blaring quartiers populaires into the hotel foyer. No, no. You pay to come to a place like this as a refuge from all of that. No, this is music that is not only not from here, it has also gone through several processes of displacement from the actuality of Africa. But it is still not totally unconnected from the story I'm in the process of unfolding to you.

There was a time, a few years back, and I'm sure you remember it, when it seemed as though not only the music of Africa, but sounds from all kinds of improbable places – everything from Bulgarian women's choirs to Colombian salsa to sufi singing from Pakistan – anywhere it seemed that wasn't in the Anglo-American mainstream was going to take a major share of the Western record market. Suddenly, music that some of us had been fighting for for God knows how long was this month's thing. TV companies were wildly commissioning documentaries on everything from Antillean zouk to Mongolian throat-singing. Newspapers, with financial assistance from the multinational majors, were flying planeloads of journalists halfway round the world to interview the rai rebels of Algiers, the sufis of Lahore and the ancient praise-singers of West Africa. And particularly the praise-singers. Oh, yes. Suddenly the West woke up to the glory and majesty of the griot tradition. Suddenly the keepers of Africa's ancient lore were big business. Anyone who could find their way round a kora was television. Anyone who looked good in robes was sex. And anyone who could actually explain what a griot was was a media pundit. It was called, this sudden heady craze – World Music. *World Music!* You remember it, don't you? You probably bought a couple of the CDs. You probably went to the odd gig.

Right, you say, and you were involved?

Involved? Listen, I didn't see any of the documentaries. I didn't read the articles. I was too busy out there manipulating and masterminding it all. For three years my phone didn't stop ringing. You want an African star on your record label, but you don't know where to start looking? Ask Litch. You think you ought to have something musically 'Worldish' for your late-night TV programme, but you've no idea what? Ask Litch. I'm the man who made the connections, who put it all together. I must have been asked in as consultant on a hundred TV documentaries, put my spoke into a thousand newspaper and magazine articles, setting them right on a million points of detail as everyone from the *Wall Street Journal* to the *Radio Times* got crushed to death trying to clamber aboard the Great World Wagon. And it was all down to one man.

Who? you ask. You?

No, not me.

Sajar Jopp?

No, not Sajar Jopp. Cherry Jatta Samba.

Who he?

An albino of a certain age, short, his features set in a mask of gnarled melancholy, Cherry Jatta Samba was about the most unlikely person ever to become an international recording star.

Cherry was a Maninka from the Mande, from a tiny village in a remote hinterland near the source not only of several of Africa's mightiest rivers, but of much that is most significant in African civilisation. Where we're sitting now, at the gateway to Africa, on the coast, the people have lived for centuries in a state of brash, cynical collusion with the slave traders and colonists. But travel seven-odd hundred miles east of here, take an unspeakably insanitary train packed with commerçants, thieves, migrant workers and a few hundred of those stoic-faced people who,

58

clutching their bales and baskets and live animals, are forever hanging around the bus depots and taxi stops, undertaking the most horrendously arduous journeys for God knows what reason... Take that train, as I have many times, into the unchanging immensity of the savannah – unchanging except that it grows imperceptibly ever drier and barer and hotter. You'll arrive in Nyaani, capital of the Mande. And that, my man, is an *African* city, a one-storey sprawl of pitted earth boulevards under a tower of heat so massive, so palpable, it seems to cast a suffocating shadow over the earth. And when you get out into the villages of the brittle glittering bush, you'll find yourself in a world where the rhythms of an ancient way of life still hold sway, where despite the strict observance of Islam, Africa's traditional beliefs are most deeply and profoundly felt. A place where everything moves slowly, where everything is old, where even the children seem weighed down by a body of ancient and arcane knowledge, where people live their lives stoned on the heat and the heavy presence of tradition. This was once the heartland of Africa's greatest medieval empire – Mande, Manding, Mali, whatever you want to call it. The source of the feudal system that still holds sway to some extent over the whole of the savannah. The source of the griot tradition itself.

Cherry was from a family of impoverished peasants who traced their ancestry back to Sunjatta – the Lion of Mande – the founder of the Mali Empire. In this world of piffling village prestige, the birth of an albino was seen as a disgrace and a portent of ill-fortune. Disowned by his parents, tormented mercilessly by other children, forced to sit in the dust outside the schoolroom, listening to the lessons through the open window, he was sent to tend the swine, and there, bellowing into the bush, he discovered his voice. Swooping with an awesome power through the cadences of the griots, it radiated an indefinable and inimitable quality of intelligence. According to the old feudal hierarchy, however, he was precluded from making use of this gift, for he was – horrendous irony – a noble. Prevented from fulfilling his ambition to become a teacher by poor eyesight, and sustained only by his Islamic faith, he ran away to the capital,

59

Nyaani, where he slept at night in the market place with all the other rogues and runaways. Yes, those were the only kind of people who would accept him, the outsiders: beggars, prostitutes, criminals, dissidents and ... musicians. After many adventures he joined the so-called Rail Band, formed to play in the buffet at Nyaani station, who were at that time the country's leading combo. Here we have the classic pattern: amplified dance music discovered through imitation of the Cuban orchestras, then the gradual rediscovery of traditional rhythms and melodies. Not here the frenetic urban rhythms of N'Galam with their complex time-changes, but cheap guitars and Hammond organs spacing out through the rippling open-ended textures of the kora, ngoni and balafong. The great praise epics of the savannahs – of the kings and heroes of the old empires – declaimed in nightclubs to the sound of clanking melancholy guitars and counterpointing submarine bass, echoed by horn refrains every bit as portentous and ancient-sounding as the epics themselves.

Cherry, the man with a voice in a million, the Domingo of African song, now a national hero, formed the band Les Visiteurs du Soir with Guinean guitar genius Soriba Sissokho. They decamped to Abidjan, the torrid and heartless cocoa megalopolis on the Gulf of Guinea, West Africa's economic miracle, to which – before prices crashed – millions of economic migrants were drawn. There they became Les Visiteurs Internationeaux and recorded their masterpiece, the seminal *Horomo*. Thrill to the awe-inspiring praise-singing of the title track with its pychedelic organ, its tragic horn refrains and impromptu trumpet rendering of 'Summertime'. Sizzle to the incendiary guitar work-out 'N'toman' – a bubbling balafong and a brace of silver trumpets carrying Sissokho's molten guitar to the flooding ecstasy of the conclusion. Yes! It *is* a masterpiece. An African *Sergeant Pepper*. The *Pet Sounds* of the savannahs. The *Trout Mask Replica* of the Mande world. Go on, buy yourself a copy. If it doesn't take you to the higher ground, I'll refund your money – personally.

What a time that was! A time of incredible excitement and optimism. The continent on a cusp of inspiration between the complex order and antique grace of the Cuban orchestral style (and as you know, I love that music), and the amazing, apparently inexhaustible riches of Africa's traditional musics, all waiting to be discovered. From Zaire, where the soukous of people like Franco and Tabou Ley Rochereau still had those deep rich harmonies complementing the touchingly earnest lead vocals, to Tekrur, where Sajar and Lumière d'Afrique were going through their most inventive period, the music of those times had a kind of innocence, a mellow dignity and nobility. While much has been produced since that could claim to be, on some levels, more authentically African, I doubt if the music of those times has been surpassed in terms of sheer beauty and inspiration.

But things in Africa were becoming worse by the day. You had powercuts restricting your performance and rehearsal time, small-time promoters keeping you in hock for the price of a set of guitar strings, lavatorial studios, tyrants and military dictators locking you up or forcing you to sing their praises.

Soon everyone was decamping to New York, Brussels, Amsterdam, London and Paris – particularly Paris, the meeting-place of the Francophone world. Quaint local styles like Zairean soukous, Camerounian Makossa and particularly Antillean zouk, were given a sleek digital respray to create monstrous supra-national genres that found favour wherever African people had batteries for their radio cassette players. Later, you'd get these fucking naive English journalists going over there to write articles on the 'World Music Capital'. And you'd get the French going on about how it was all part of how they were plus ouvert aux autres cultures. What bollocks! The music was created in crummy little studios by musicians living on these grim housing estates in the northern suburbs, pressed as quickly and cheaply as possible, and whooshed off to Africa and the Antilles before it had time to be impinged upon by French values, or indeed even heard by the French. So it had fuck-all to do with the French. Okay?

Meanwhile, back in Africa, the old Cuban-modelled, often state-sponsored orchestras, who had made the great breakthroughs in African music, were going out of business. You'd arrive in some of these countries, and there wasn't a single musician left. They were all in Paris, living in council flats in St-

Denis and Montreuil, or fifteen to a room in the Goutte d'Or, spending their days scheming in grim little cafés. That's where you'd see Cherry and his mates – just more Africans in cheap clothes, sitting out the time before deportation. At that point, no one could see any commercial mileage in the griot tradition. It was too tied to specific languages and cultural traditions for the Paris scene with its emphasis on polyglot danceability. But I could see the whole 'World' thing coming and I told various relatively enlightened people in the Western majors that they should sign Cherry, but they still looked on African music as just tropical goodtime, and to them he was just too weird. It was an attitude they were to bitterly regret.

So, I could see that one day someone was going to make a vast amount of money out of Cherry. I could have done it myself. I probably should have. But at that time, I was too busy *living it*, too busy *out there*, to be bogged down with all of that. And I didn't need the money. At that time the ackers were flooding in. I was just doing what I loved doing, and people were falling over themselves to pay me for it.

Eventually, Cherry signed to Ahmadou Toure, Africa's self-styled 'greatest producer'. Son of an influential marabout, encyclopaedic on Cuban music, and indeed on virtually everything else, he's incredibly charming and extremely dangerous. Oh, yes. The day Toure buys a baseball bat is the day I get out of African music. American-educated, but Paris-based, moving between secret addresses, doing his business from his car, he specialises in taking musicians raw from Africa, giving them an acceptable international gloss while retaining the music's authentic spirit, and if at all possible licensing them to the majors for vast sums. His conveyor-belt was well oiled. At one point he seemed about to sew up the whole of West Africa and a fair amount of Central Africa too. Through a web of sub-producers he recorded traditional musicians in tiny primitive studios in Africa, buying the material outright, and flooding the markets and roadside booths from Kinshasa to Nouakchott with the results. Artists with potential were given a more considered treatment in the medium-tech environment of JBZ Studios in Abidjan, while the real work took place in Paris, where he had teams of musicians, arrangers and producers from all parts of the Francophone world working twenty-four hours a day. All Toure did was to wander into the studio occasionally and say, 'too African', 'too modern'. If he determined the balance of influences was all right, he'd leave them to it. The homogenised blandness of these products was generally overriden by their brash, shiny energy.

Cherry's record, *Bakumba*, was largely the work of two French arrangers. A Mande-style girlie chorus with just the right amount of authentic sing-song nasality, traces of the old Visiteurs' Mandingo guitar, synthesised kora, digitally funky Afro-Paris rhythms, everything shiny and super-sharp, a few 'African' sound effects – the buzz of insects, howling hyenas – the sort of thing no African musician in Africa would have thought of putting into their music – and BIG synthesisers, huge and magisterial chords, evoking the sheer scale and majesty of Africa as seen on wildlife documentaries, out of which Cherry's voice, 'the raw cry of Africa, full of pain and mystical anguish', came at you in widescreen dimensions. As cinema-style hokum it worked remarkably well, and it did contain moments of genuine beauty. Oh yes, that voice, caressing the unguent syllables of the Maninka language, was inimitable, and you can't deny they set it off a treat.

It had nothing to do with the Afro-Antillean dance floor. God knows who they thought it was *for*. But it found its rightful market with remarkable ease: the CD players of enlightened yuppies who had had their horizons broadened on backpacking holidays and wanted to relive the experience between trips to the local Homebase. And it sold. Not like Michael Jackson or Pink Floyd. But in terms of Africa, where everything was pirated, it was unprecedented. There *were* those who said that this wasn't actually African music. But Cherry was well pleased. He even bought himself a face-lift.

Suddenly every Western major needed an African star on its roster. Cherry signed to Virgin, for ten times what they'd have paid if they'd done it when I told them to, Sajar to Motivate. And *Bakumba*'s balance of Western production values and African authenticity became the grail, the benchmark by which all their efforts were to be judged. Sajar in particular became obsessed with it for a while. The music itself was not seen as problematic, either by artists or companies. It was just *there* – a raw and unquenchable resource. If it was placed in the right production context it would sell. But repeating, let alone surpassing or finding a commercially viable variant on the magic formula of *Bakumba*, proved surprisingly difficult. Sajar never managed it, and Cherry certainly didn't. He was termed 'extremely difficult' and 'a manic-depressive control freak' by the big boys at Virgin, and after two unsatisfactory albums he disappeared from view. Sajar got himself into all kinds of tangles I'll tell you about later, and the Western majors withdrew from the tricky, complex and commercially unrewarding waters of African music. The yuppies moved on, putting their four or five World Music purchases to the back of their CD collections, and African music was once more the province of the diehards and the nutters – two categories in which I am proud to include myself.

And so, this is the kind of music that constantly infiltrates one's mind in the hotel foyer: not *Bakumba* but a lame soundalike or one of Cherry's duff follow-ups. Did I say that though it was all recorded in Paris that there was nothing remotely French about this music? Well, I'm not sure that's quite true. As I go up to reception for the hundredth time, to see if there are any messages for me, and for the *n*th time hear the chorus of Cherry's 'Non pas bouger', I reflect that the music does have a kind of tweeness about it, a measure of that inescapable petit-bourgeois blandness that the French take with them wherever they go – the quality that makes France inherently antithetical to the whole concept of rock'n'roll.

God, you do go on, I hear you complain. It's a pleasant enough sound!

It may be. But I know too much about it. That's the problem. I know too much.

Five

I still don't feel at all well.

What's the matter with you? you ask. What are your symptoms.

Unwellness. I'm just not up to it. Okay? I think I'm going to sit by the pool.

It's hazy out here. It's warm, but it's not immensely hot. A group of young, casually well-dressed Tekrurians are sitting and standing around the next table, their conversation in Wolof, their throaty chuckling booming and crackling all too noisily around me. There's one guy with a particularly throaty and fruity voice, a real Wolof voice – and it's starting to get on my nerves in a big way. He seems to be telling some kind of joke, to which his companions respond, spluttering helplessly through their teeth, racked by shoulder-shaking guffaws at his lubricious elastic vowels and ostentatiously explosive consonants. God, they know how to talk here – and they love their language, launching into it with an athletic self-congratulatory verve, brandishing it like a lascivious weapon – the language that says they've made it to the big city, that they belong here. But why do they have to do it near me? There's eight tables round this pool. Why do they have to have their joke-telling competition, their recollection of sexual exploits or whatever it is, right behind my head?

And who are they? And why are they here anyway? Are they

friends of the staff? Friends of the management? Some of us are actually paying to be here.

The Moroccans have gone. When I came down yesterday morning, the stalls, the orchestra, the terminally languid stallholders and their stupefied Tekrurian assistants and the photographer from the Congrès des Avocats had all disappeared without trace, as though they'd never been there. When I arrived, I resented their presence, jamming the place up with their rubbishy souvenirs, monopolising the sofas. But they did at least give the place a sense of life. Now it seems even more sterile and cynically plastic. It seems like a completely different hotel, one which, although it professes to be completely full, has very few guests – or few that one actually sees. And now there are fewer guests about, the waiters who padded so soundlessly and slinkily about in their maroon uniforms, are brusquer, more arrogant, more inclined to have their differences in front of me, to bark orders to other parts of the hotel from directly behind my head, to fill the poolside with their friends and relations, to noise their language, the argot of taxi-drivers, pickpockets and muggers, about the place as though the guests were utterly peripheral to the purpose of the place. Or more to the point, as though I do not have the rights of a full guest, or am not even there at all.

Yes, people pay handsomely to stay in places like this, to keep Africa at bay – so that one can meet its unmanageable teeming chaos, its endemic horror and corruption on more equal terms. And now here is the continent as represented by its raffish, ithyphallic dialects thrusting its way arrogantly to the poolside of this French-owned hotel.

The sun's out and I'm going to go and lie down under the umbrellas on the other side of the pool. There's signs in the lift telling one not to take the room towels to the piscine. Large towels are provided down there. Nice.

Behind the thatched poolside bar is a pile of thick blue towels, and nearby a heap of mattresses for reclining. I help myself to a towel and drag one of the mattresses off under the umbrellas. Normally space is at a premium here, but today it's deserted. I lie

66

down gratefully, face against the blue towel on the blue canvas of the mattress. I'm exhausted. I don't feel like I've slept since I got here. I could just fall asleep. But just as I'm starting to doze off, I feel a tickling on my calf. I slap out instinctively. But then there's another. Flies. Shit. Now I've got to go back up to the tenth floor for my insect repellent. I stagger groggily back into the hotel, into the lift, and up to my room, catching sight of my reflection. I look fucking awful: paler than when I got here, with a hunted look in the eye. And while I've got to be losing weight, bits I've never seen before seem to be appearing on my face. Don't look, man. Do *not* look!

I lard myself in repellent. But the flies seem impervious to its noxious reek. Talking of reeks, what's that fucking smell? It's not me is it? It's like rotting fish. I raise my head, and peer through the wire mesh with its thin and unconvincing overhang of bougainvillea. Through my shades, I can see the silhouettes of the people walking on the corniche below, and raising my shades I perceive on the slope immediately beneath the fence a great mound of fish and animal bones, mango stones, maize cobs, dead cats and other unspeakable detritus through which the rats, vultures and human scavengers of N'Galam have been rummaging – bringing with them the flies who've aleady feasted royally at every open sewer and latrine in the city. And why is it only me who notices? The svelte, sleekly tanned Frenchwomen sunning themselves here yesterday afternoon didn't appear to be plagued by squadrons of disease-ridden flies, didn't appear to notice they virtually had their heads in a festering garbage tip, didn't realise this place isn't a hotel at all, but the desiccated shell of a European business, run for their own benefit by the cynically conniving staff, who would, given the chance, bleed the place dry in a week. It's a good thing I haven't brought anything of remote value, they'll already have been through my bags several times a day. And don't try putting them in the hotel safe! That's the *worst* thing you can do.

There's a sudden bump against my mattress, and I look up blinking to see a dark, burly shape standing over me – the shaven-headed pool attendant. He just kicked my mattress! And with me lying on it!

I should be on my feet, finger raised, he lumbering unsteadily backward toward the pool. 'Listen motherfucker, you do *not* kick my mattress!' At which point he would hopefully step backwards into the pool to the derision of all. But I haven't got the energy for that. I just lie there, squinting up at him in the brilliance, as he blurts some question at me in his clipped Wolof-French. What's he on about?

'Vous êtes en quel chambre? Le numéro?'

Now he's accusing me of being an illegal interloper by the pool, a non-resident, a false-toubab – a tramp. I've only been sitting here every day for a week. I can feel the dudes on the other side of the pool go silent as they watch this degrading exhibition. Yes, this time it's a white man who's getting it! I'm too fucked even to speak, and after rummaging under the towel, just hold up my key tag. He looks at it suspiciously, then turns and lumbers slowly back to his seat.

I glance up and as I thought, the guys over the pool are looking at me. I lie down. I'm virtually in tears. I shouldn't be here. And I'm not going to be here. I'm getting the fuck out!

Somewhere out there is Sajar Jopp. And somewhere out there, in a living-room perhaps, the shabby curtains closed against the heat of the day, on a dusty housing estate on the outskirts of N'Galam, not far from the lighthouse at the very westernmost point of the African continent, a telephone is ringing. It goes on ringing in that low, slow way that telephones do everywhere but in Britain, with these low dull beeps and gaps so long you keep thinking you've been cut off. I decided to go through the matted, multi-annexed and becarded volume of my filofax with a fine-tooth comb. I found this number scrawled minutely down the side of Sajar's entry, and as soon as I read it back to myself, I knew exactly what it was. There's a click and someone's answered. The voice is dry and weary, heavy with decades of effort, as though the person's been buried by exhaustion; and at the same time there's a degree of caution – caution and a kind of curtness.

'Allo?'

'Sajar?'

'Oui.' A spark, a very, very faint spark of enthusiasm comes into Sajar's voice. 'Hey . . . !' The yo-my-man-gimme-five tone of Sajar the international traveller and intimate of the rockocracy rears its head – rather unconvincingly – but at least he knows who it is. 'Litch.'

'Yeah. How's it going?'

'Fine.' The tone of gruff indifference returns though always with Sajar, however gruff, there's that hint of gold shining through – the gold of the world's most miraculous voice. 'How is England?'

'England? England's cool.'

'Oh.'

'Listen, man, I've been here nearly a week.'

'I know.'

'I've been ill.' I load the sentence with reproach.

'I know, I know.'

Got him on the defensive now. So why didn't you come and see me you bastard? I don't say it, but my silence implies it.

'We have er . . .' It always sounds strange when Sajar speaks English. Sweet, but not quite natural. '. . . lost a cousin.'

'A cousin?'

'Yes . . . He died.'

'Sorry, man.'

'It's okay. And I've been er . . . en train d'enregistrer un album.'

'An album?' You mean all the time I've been sitting here, he's been recording an album? Why didn't he get me down there? Once again he can sense my tone.

'Non. It was not my music. It was some . . . traditional music. Old music.'

'I like old music!' He knows fucking well I like the old music the best.

Sajar laughs. A dry and practised snigger. 'Litch!'

'Yeah!'

'I have to go.'

69

Go? What does he mean go? We've just started talking. 'Look, man. Can we meet?'

A pause. 'Oui.'

'Quand? Aujourd'hui?'

'Demain.'

'Chez toi?'

'Non. Au studio.'

I'm in the foyer. I've got my Ray-Ban Wayfarers on. And I'm getting my knickers in a twist. Remind me to get some lighter shades. If I look through the glass doors, the blazing heat at the bottom of the drive is just the right level of modulated sepia. Everything else is in total fucking darkness. I take them off. Christ, that's better. I've got the myriad pockets of my Striders packed with cameras, tape recorders, notebooks – and of course all my crucial documents. In my Tesco's carrier bag I've got spare cassettes, films. You need all that. You never know what *crucial* event you'll encounter, and I'm a congenital archivist. I have that element in my personality – I can't help it.

It's five o'clock, but outside it's still bright, still hot, though there's a bit more shouting and wandering about at the taxi rank. Sajar's moved his studio so many times. But his latest one is, I've learnt, quite walkable.

I turn to the desk clerk, a sharp-faced, young-looking bloke who's been watching me. 'Ma ne, ana studio bi Sajar Jopp?'

'Le studio d'enregistrement de Sajar Jopp?'

'Oui.'

He seems neither surprised nor impressed by the question, as though every bugger who came here hung out with Sajar Jopp, and launches into detailed directions, from which I learn that basically it's 'ici'.

'C'est ici?'

'Oui.' He waves vaguely at the glass doors. 'Justement.' And he goes back to work. Donning my shades, I head out through the glass doors, down the drive, into the afternoon's residual brilliance and into Africa.

There's the usual murmured offers of the taxi-drivers, then this

70

tall guy in a robe, dreadlocks poking from under a black beret, is immediately on my case with a fake papyrus scroll.

'Yes, my friend. Where from? England? Come and see my things. Many beautiful objects. Ancient Egypt, Africa. Everything.'

I curl my lip in a sneer, grateful for the darkness of my Ray-Bans. 'Next time,' I grunt.

'Okay, my friend.'

Ahead, below the anonymous, indeterminately modern buildings of the commercial quarter, the crumbling pavements peter out into heaps of sand and breezeblock. You can't tell whether everything's half-finished or half-started – burgeoning or decaying. That's Africa.

The street is virtually deserted – thank God – just the odd person sitting about, apparently half-asleep in a doorway. And even then, they wouldn't be fussed by me. Not everyone here is solely bent on robbing and hassling me. It's good to remember that. I pass the end of the main street that runs along to the Place de la République, where there are a lot more people hanging about. But even so, nobody's going to do anything to me. I'm on my way to Sajar Jopp.

But where the hell is he? I stop and ask two policemen guarding an official building. They look at each other quizzically.

'Sajar Jopp?' asks one.

'Oui. Son studio.'

'Studio?' asks the other.

They don't know what I'm talking about. They can't speak French. In fact they're not policemen at all. They're private security guards outside somebody's office – country bumpkins in uniform, fingering their side-handled truncheons and wishing they were sub-machine guns.

I cut back up onto the main road, asking at a big gloomy old hotel, going farther along by the big cinema showing Indian films, then I'm back on the narrow street – more of an anonymous, sand-dusted lane – that leads to the hotel. I'm virtually there when I ask a couple of guys sitting on a doorstep. It's back the way I've just come – two blocks. And there, sure enough, is a

71

doorway in a narrow frontage, totally anonymous except for a small plaque saying, 'Studio Njambour. Props: S. Jopp, A. Jopp, P. Mbodj.' So this is the great studio we've all heard so much about. The great 'African Cause' on which Sajar has expended so much effort. The security grille is pulled two-thirds of the way back and one of the double doors is ajar.

I knock tentatively. 'Venez,' comes a harsh voice from within.

As my eyes get used to the darkness, I can see that the minuscule lobby is packed with people. Squeezed into the sofa on the left, sprawled against the walls, while others squat around their ankles – their eyes large and lemur-like against the darkness, suffused with that African impassivity, that stillness that is not waiting, not anticipation, not indolence, not even patience – is just being there.

I give out some of the greetings necessary on entering a room, then squeeze myself up against a bit of wall. A slight young man gets up from the sofa and gestures me to his place. I sink back gratefully.

'Jerejef,' I gasp. It's really hot in this place, and stuffy. I can hardly breathe.

The lad murmurs in surprise, 'Deganga Olof?'

'Deydet,' I wave my hand deprecatingly. 'Touti rek.'

There are muted chuckles of approval before silence returns. Everyone just sits and stands and squats, staring into space. Did I say they weren't waiting? Of course they're waiting. They're not going to sit for hours in a dark airless cubbyhole for no reason. They're not totally stupid. They're all waiting for the person everyone in this goddamn country is waiting for: Sajar Jopp.

Everywhere you go with Sajar, there's a queue forming in the corridor, there's a little crowd of supplicants, petitioners, syco-phants, beggars and creeps loitering at the door. And that's not to mention all the members of his band, other artists he's working with, all the various managers, technicians, functionaries, roadies and courtiers, all the siblings, cousins and childhood friends he's put in positions of power around him, all of whom have legitimate questions and demands. It's like going around with an eighteenth-century monarch. Sajar the embodied state, with all his myriad minions swarming around him, watching his minutest biological functions, waiting with the most mundane enquiries, because in the country of Sajar, every detail has to come back to the great head, the intuitive, improvisatory intelligence at the centre of the monstrous corpus he's created from nothing. Incredibly inefficient, but without that, every franc would have been 'eaten', all their gear and resources would have simply disappeared. As it is, millions evaporated, people buggered about pursuing their private internal wars at his expense, blew up the lighting rig and mixing desk several times over. But all these incompetents and minor malefactors were kept on the payroll, because they were the people he'd got there with, part of the social structure of his world, people to whom he was bound by subtle but profound ties of obligation – people whose presence was essential to the health and well-being of the organism as a whole. And each of these people had dozens of dependants, people who were themselves Sajar's relatives and family friends, figures from his childhood – from the old world of the Medina, from which he drew so much of his strength and inspiration.

The thin, sad-looking youth who gave me his seat, who appears to be in charge of the studio, looks at me. 'Sajar dit qu'il vient a quel heure?'

'Je croix que cinq.'

'Dix-sept heures?'

'Oui.'

Those with watches glance at them. Five minutes to go. Oh yes, despite the silence, the apparent impassivity of everybody there, the sense of tension and anticipation is so thick you could cut it with a knife. Everyone – that older bloke in robes, the young dudes, one in shades, a crown of dreadlocks sticking in all directions, the other in beret and motorcycle boots, who must be a rap group, and the others, all men, who could be there for any reason, just more Tekrurian men, apparently no different from all the thousands and thousands of others, standing and sitting and wandering about in the streets outside – all are waiting for Sajar.

At five o'clock precisely, and Sajar is always on time, a dark shape slides across the bright chink of doorway. There's the low squeak of brakes. A car door clicks. The studio door opens, and Sajar's lean silhouette is framed by blazing light. 'Ça va?' he grunts to the world in general.

As he entered, everyone leant almost imperceptibly forward. And now he's coming round greeting everyone, shaking hands with a brisk and blokish informality. 'Ça va? Nangadef? Bien. Yeah.' Dressed in shirt and jeans, he looks no different from anyone else there. But always there's this practised, almost military, edge of authority, that both puts you at ease and keeps you at a distance. And no matter how much he's laying on the charm, if you stare into his eyes, there's always this look of wariness, of watchfulness.

'Hey!' he says – his standard greeting for whites – then he goes straight into the studio, gesturing to the man in robes to follow him, and shuts the door.

The mood relaxes. People get up and wander out into the street. Some of the people who were apparently just chilling disappear altogether. There's some banter, some laughter, some slapping of hands. A bit more like normal African life in fact. I get talking with the guy in the beret and motorcycle boots. Yes, he is a rapper. And am I producer? Yeah, I produce. And do I compose film music? Can't quite see why the one should presuppose the other, but I guess that's what the last white man he met sitting here was doing. I mean, don't think I'm the only white person who goes to see Sajar. I was the first. But now it's a continual fucking procession: producers, film music composers, film makers, journalists, all the flotsam and jetsam of the international culture circuit. And particularly Afro-American arts groupies who've got a vague idea they'd like to do something to unite Tekrurian and American Blacks – the kind of thing Sajar's very susceptible to. And how's he supposed to know who's kosher? Film music? Yeah, I do a bit of film music. I mean, I don't actually compose music, I'm more of a consultant. I advise people on what music they should put in their films. His eyes widen. Can he give me a copy of his latest cassette? For sure ... But I'm only half-listening. My eyes keep glancing back to the door behind which Sajar is holding his audiences. There he is, just a few yards

74

away . . . And anyway, I've heard plenty of Tekrurian rap, and none of it's that amazing. The grooves don't have the killer instinct and the 'homeboy' choruses lack conviction . . . Maybe I'd like to come to one of their gigs? No problem. When? Okay, if he tells Sajar when the next one is, he can tell me. He's over the moon. Well, at least I've made somebody happy.

By the time Sajar comes out of the studio, the light outside has softened. It's that precious mellow time in Africa, just before nightfall. Everyone else has gone except for the sad-faced young caretaker, who I gather lives on the premises, in that tiny room about six foot by four, just off the tiny, perpetually crowded lobby. Oh, yes. This is Africa, man. Sajar, relaxed, but still remote in whatever preoccupations were aroused by his meetings, comes and sits down on the sofa next to me. He doesn't look at me. He doesn't speak to me. He just sits there, staring out at the sandy street. A street trader lollops past, pausing to hold up a pair of plastic sandals. 'Bah'na,' says Sajar. 'It's good.' The standard way to fob off the thousands of vendors who throng the streets of N'Galam, but he says it pleasantly enough. Oh, yes. He's generally pleasant. Particularly with ordinary people, people who've got nothing to do with his work. He's nice to old ladies. I've always admired that about him. I'm a lot like that myself.

I steal a glance at him. Last time I saw him, in London, nearly a year ago, he looked drawn and haggard, abstracted. Worn down by his business affairs, by all the mad, time-wasting schemes I'm always warning him not to get involved in. By the contrasting expectations of his millions of fans here, his expanding coterie of admirers in the West, his record company . . . It goes on. Sajar, as always, knackering himself with everything but the music.

But today he looks remarkably fresh and rested. Maybe now he's handed over business matters to his siblings he's got more time for himself. I had heard he'd filled out a bit. And I saw pictures of him where he looked almost chubby. But now he looks hardly different from when I first met him. Slightly suaver, more mature. And there's no doubt he's a handsome geezer.

He might almost be unaware of my presence. But I'm not bothered by that. He can sit like this indefinitely, with people he

75

knows and trusts – just staring into space, enjoying the tranquil-lity. It's a sign that you've been accepted. But always there's that slight sense of mystery. Here one is, in intimate proximity to the man to whom millions are looking for inspiration, who all around him would dream of being, accepted into his inner circle. But always one is wondering exactly what is going on inside that handsome head. It's that sense of mystery that keeps one coming back. And one does keep coming back, doesn't one?

Then Sajar breathes out, shifts slightly on the sofa and looks me full in the face for the first time. 'So,' he says. 'Where's my money?'

Six

I feel like I'm under water. Money ... Money ... The word sounds muffled, pumping softly through my temples. Then suddenly I'm shooting up into brilliance, water, hard diamonds showering everywhere, and sound, the great shout of the upper world ... *Money?*

'What money?'

'La tournée des Etats-Unis de quatre-vingts-sept. Les advances de Shanachie et Rough Trade.'

Money from his American tour in 1987. Advances from two small independent record labels to whom he'd licensed old material. I remember the deals very well, though apart from facilitating the initial talks, I had little enough to do with any of it. But the American tour ... Was I even on it?

'Yes, you were. You know you were.'

Yeah, okay. Now I come to think of it, that was the one where I nearly came to blows with Michael Heaven. But come on. Let's be clear about this. Why would I have the money?

'Why would I have the money?'

'We er ... We gave you the money to keep for us.' He looks at me calmly, but gravely, his almond eyes filled with a sad but magnanimous honesty. 'You know that.' And he looks past me out into the street. Behind him in the dimness, the sad lemur eyes of the caretaker look in the same direction – how much of this he

77

can understand I've no idea, and at this point in time I don't particularly give a fuck.

Now I come to think about it, they did used to pay their cheques into one of my bank accounts – before they had one of their own – then they'd take the cash away in a suitcase. And I didn't ask any more, because I didn't want to be implicated when they got done for currency smuggling or whatever else they were up to. So basically, I was just cashing cheques for them. I thought at the time it was a ridiculous way of doing it. But I was involved. I was part of the whole enterprise. I had to help in any way I could.

And I mean, let's be realistic. I mean, no disrespect to the Tekrurians, but do they strike you as the sort of people to just leave several grand lying around in someone else's bank account, if you know what I mean? And who was it? Mbaye Njai, who used to collect the money?

'No, no . . .' says Sajar, meaning that his former manager, as a Tekrurian citizen, would never do something so heinous as misappropriating his money, despite the fact that he himself had sacked the guy for that very thing.

'C'était une époque confusée,' says Sajar.

It certainly was. There were all kinds of flakey people wandering about claiming to be Sajar's manager in le monde ailleurs – and he agreed to all of them out of politeness. But not me. I've never claimed to be anything to Sajar other than a friend. And this is what I get for it.

'How much?'

'Twenty-five thousand.'

'CFA?'

'Livres.'

Twenty-five large? *Twenty-five thousand English pounds?*

Sajar's on his feet trying to calm me. What the fuck's going on round here? Where did he hear this from?

'Someone,' he says, a trifle sheepishly.

'Who?'

'Someone I normally believe.'

A very African reply. Someone in whom he's placed his trust

has told him this, therefore he has to believe it. What about the trust he's placed in me? What about the trust *I've* placed in *him*? I get to my feet.

Sajar looks at his watch. 'I have to go.' He turns in the doorway. 'It's not a problem. But we have to have the money.'

It's the next day. But I haven't been anywhere, and I haven't slept. I'm still here. In the foyer.

It's nearly one, and I'm waiting for Abdou, Sajar's brother, to come and pick me up and take me to Sajar's club, the Jambar, where he's playing tonight.

It's late. The man who's been buffing the marble floor is putting his machine away. The amateurish-looking prostitutes who normally sit on the sofa against the wall leading out onto the terrace have either found gigs for the night or simply given up and gone home. The place is deserted except for the night clerks on the front desk, and amazingly bleak in its gleaming nocturnal brightness. There's just this Arabic-looking bloke on the next sofa, unshaven, with a nervous tic, a habit of trying to suck his upper lip into his nose at moments of particular concentration. And he's sucking on his biro, sighing and wheezing and fretting over some kind of language primer. I've noticed it's from Arabic to some European tongue, but which one and why he's doing it in the foyer of this hotel at one in the morning, I can't even be bothered to wonder.

I feel fucked. You know how tired you get, when you feel that if you don't actually go to bed *now*, you won't be able to stand it? That's how I felt about ten hours ago. I'm forcing myself to keep going. And the night's hardly started. Because in Africa, in fact in just about everywhere south of Bognor, everything that's meaningful musically takes place at night. In fact it doesn't even start till quite a long time after everything that's meaningful musically north of Bognor has long since finished. And it goes on till just before dawn, what the Spanish call the 'madrugada' – the time of happenings. Because there are certain kinds of music that only acquire their full meaning, that only sound the way they really should, deep in the bosom of the night. So if you want to work your way into the sinew and the texture, if you want the full revelation of the Berbers, Kabyles, Arabs, Greeks, Turks, Gitanos, Spaniards, Cubans, Brazilians and all the others whose music is worth a light, you've got to adjust. You've got to siesta. Siesta? I can hardly sleep at night, let alone the bloody afternoon. Abdou probably got up at a magnificent two in the afternoon, and is just getting into his stride. While I've been up since eight, *yesterday*, I had my dinner at eight, *yesterday* evening, which now seems about two weeks ago, and I'm so tired my exhaustion has achieved an independent identity of its own, and is following me round shadowlike. So I've got these two people to think of, me and my exhaustion, which is very inconvenient since I'm so tired I can hardly look after myself. Basically I'm falling apart.

Through the glass doors I can just make out the shadows of the taxi-drivers peering in to see if I'm likely to want a cab. Oh, yes. Down there at the bottom of the drive, in Africa, things are just getting started. But here in the foyer, it's the dead of the numb and neutral night. We're on two different time zones here.

The money, man. I can't stop thinking about the money. I've spent so much time thinking about the money, I've half convinced myself I have had it. I mean, I can't be expected to know exactly what's gone in and out of all my many accounts over a ten-year period. That's why you employ an accountant. Or that's why you *should* employ an accountant.

But I haven't had it. I just know I haven't. But even if I had I wouldn't give it to them. I wouldn't give it to them, 'cause I couldn't. I mean, you just don't have a spare twenty-five k lying about, do you? And I'm trying to imagine what would happen, and how nasty it could get. Being roughed up on a piece of waste ground near the airport. Languishing in some hideously insanitary cell. Wouldn't happen, man. Or it might. But something far worse could happen. I could lose Sajar's good will. And with it the access, the uniquely privileged *in* I have to Tekrurian life and culture. Because while Sajar Jopp isn't the be-all and end-all . . . Okay, Sajar Jopp is the be-all and end-all. He's become the be-all and end-all. I've *made* him the be-all and end-all. That's the fucking problem.

'Escuse me?'

'Yeah, what?'

'Speak English?'

'I am English.'

'Thank you. This, I think it's mistake?'

The Arab-looking guy's showing me his primer. There seems to be a misprint in his conjugations, declensions or whatever they are. Something like 'I are going'.

'Yeah. It's a mistake, man. Must be a misprint.'

'I think so.' His hawkish Maghrebian features crease towards the bridge of his nose. Well spotted, geezer. 'I learning English.'

'Nice one.'

Yeah, the idea that I might not be able to come here. Or that I might have to enter the country furtively and deal only with Sajar's enemies. I mean, I love dealing with Sajar's enemies, but I don't want to deal *only* with them. No, no. That's inconceivable. That can't be allowed to happen.

'English very good.'

'That's right.'

I wish this guy would shut up. I'm trying to worry about the money.

'I am er ... Algérien.' He smiles, raising his eyebrows.

'Great ...'

Here's Abdou. Same rangy prat. Half-arrogant, half-apologetic as ever. I wave to the Algerian, and I'm off. Instantly I'm in Sajar's world, and it's the same as always.

'Litch! How are you?'

'Fine.'

'You're feeling better?'

'For sure.'

We go out and climb into his Renault. His girlfriend, one of Sajar's backing singers, is slumped morosely in the back. We exchange curt greetings.

'I meant to come and see you,' says Abdou, putting the car in gear, 'but things have been ... difficult.'

Difficult? Things have been fucking difficult. But what does *he* mean? How much does he know? How much does anyone know?

Has Sajar told his entire staff? No. As few people as possible will know. That's Sajar's way. But don't think Sajar went back through the accounts himself. There are no accounts for that period anyway. That's the whole point. Someone's told him this. Someone with a vested interest.

'For sure,' I say, totally neutral.

We roll on through the dark and largely deserted streets of the lower commercial quarter – just the odd muffled figure strolling slowly along, or a group of guys playing cards in a doorway. Abdou and his girlfriend were obviously in the middle of an argument when they arrived, which they now continue. I pay no attention, looking out instead on the sombre empty boulevards. Then as we hit the avenue to the quartiers populaires, we're suddenly into the crowded, fetid, sodium-tinged African night: the night stalls, the poky shack shops, the pedestrians spilling heedless from the crumbling pavements, the guy in a wheelchair spinning himself around the taxis jamming around the road into the Medina. Abdou curses as we miss the guy by about half an inch. Once again I'm back in it. But this time it's different. I'm merely glancing at it from a lordly indifferent distance. I'm on my way to Sajar Jopp's club, in Sajar's brother's car. And this, I now realise, is how I've become increasingly used to viewing Africa, from inside the manicured, pristine bubble of Sajar Jopp's operation.

The club is set back from a busy highway on a broad verge of dust. Abdou parks the car in a side alley, and we push our way through the crowd milling outside – trying to force their way in and out of the too-small entrance, or just standing and watching, hoping. Abdou shouts to the guy on the door and the crowd parts for us. Inside, it's brilliantly lit, laminated collages on the white walls, with constructions of old shoes and tin cans placed carelessly about. What the fuck's this?

'It's a gallery,' says Abdou with an embarrassed shrug. 'Sajar says we have to invest in the economy of art.'

Does he, indeed? Yeah, I bet he does. Now who's he been talking to?

That's right, an African night club. You were probably

imagining some crumbling fly-blown shebeen, stinking of urine, with piss-artists accosting you about neo-colonialism and Rasta-fari, a heavy ganja haze and knife fights galore. You didn't expect an avant-garde art gallery in the foyer, did you? Mais, ça c'est l'Afrique de nos jours. L'Afrique de Sajar. Capisce?

All around people are holding vehement conversations, slapping hands, exploding into spluttered laughter. There's that heightened, slightly unhinged feeling of African celebration. Celebrating what? La musica. Because from inside the club itself are pumping, at considerable volume, the rippling, liquid rhythms of the Super Lumière d'Afrique – the ascending silvery chord progression of the song 'Sakhodougou', with the braying tones of second vocalist Leyti Mbaye, Sajar's cousin.

'Where's Sajar?' I shout to Abdou.

'He's here. But . . .' He holds up his hands placatingly. 'I think it's better if you see him later.'

'For sure.'

As we're about to go into the club, a huge bloke comes bursting heedlessly through the door, laughing demonically, and knocking me flying. Everyone seems big here. Not because they're all particularly big, or because I'm particularly small – because I'm not. But because I'm white. That's one of the things I always forget – that I'm white.

What did this place used to be like? A bit of a dump, wasn't it? Not romantically seedy like you're thinking, but African in the sense that it was a bit ramshackle, everything a bit cracked, mottled and marked. Now it's been renovated in a manner designed to ruthlessly expunge any trace of the African or the exotic. It's all clean lines, the curving staircase up to the balcony, the white jackets of the waiters – glowing under the ultraviolet light – giving an art-deco, ocean-liner feel, and a mirrored ball over the dancefloor. The whole feel is nineteen-thirties out of nineteen-seventies. Abdou leads me up onto the balcony and sits me down in a prime position with a bottle of Coke. I need it. It's fiendishly hot. I'm so knackered I'm on total remote control. I don't think anything would have any effect on me now. I've been led through the teeming, dust-laden African night, through an avant-garde art gallery full of neo-dadaist crap, into a nightclub modelled on a disco in somewhere like Kingston-on-Thames circa 1974 – where up in the darkness of the totally unlit stage, probably the best band in the world are going through their paces.

Oh, yes. With a burbling roll on Fafa Mbaye's talking drum, they're into a new number, and I'm immediately absorbed into the glistening, shimmering wall of funk – not with my mind, because let's face it, I've only heard this song about two thousand million times before, but with my knees, my neck, the very marrow of my being. This is the melancholy cadences of the khalam re-heard through the transmogrifying prisms of jazz funk, jazz fusion, a bit of slippery, crotch-grabbing James Brown soul, and a hundred other influences you can't quite identify and can't be bothered to try, because when you're *here*, when you're *in it*, you just accept it as what's happening. And when like these guys you've been playing together every day, sometimes twice a day, for fifteen years, and you can come at the material with a pure jazz freedom that is beyond telepathy, and you're playing at your home club, where you've got the freedom to space out long, long into the night . . . Well, it doesn't get any better than that. Believe me, because I do know.

Where's Sajar? I haven't got the energy to look at my watch, but it must be well, well after two, and he'd normally be on by now.

This place has definitely moved upmarket. It's mostly younger civil-servant types and kids in very clean jeans and trainers, whose parents must have money or they couldn't afford to get in here. And there are a fair number of whites. A couple of parties of businessmen and their Tekrurian hosts – all in *suits* for Christ's sake, a few aid workers on leave and some backpacker types. What are *they* doing here? Don't they know they've got to go sightseeing in the morning?

About two feet from me, there's this svelte and amazingly cool dudette, who judging from that tawny, aquiline profile has got to be Fulani, with relaxed hair and a raw silk suit, who's living the music totally, arching her back, swivelling her hips, doing these shapely, elegant arm movements they do in the traditional dances, raising one arm and thrusting her hips, forward with a slinky nonchalance that should be illegal. Yes, man! And they call this a Muslim country! She keeps running her finger down the front of her skirt, as they do at these all-night drum and dance sessions, shimmying their long dresses up and down their thighs as they roll their big arses. But you're not supposed to do it in an already absurdly short skirt. And it's all totally cool, totally knowing – and at the same time she's oblivious, miles away in her own private world of rhythm, her every movement mastered by the pumping, poking rhythms from the stage.

The guy next to me, a stocky bloke in robes, sees me clocking her and pokes me in the shoulder, tittering through his teeth. He leans over and speaks in my ear.

'Eh?'

'Litch!'

'Yeah. Who are you?'

'Sanyang.'

'Who?'

'Sajar's office. You are always phoning.' It's *him*, the grumpy grunting bastard.

I lean forward. 'Tu es bandit!' I say.

'Thank you,' he says, and we grip hands warmly.

Someone out there wants to spoil all this for me – wants to blow my connection with it. And they could be here. They could be in this room now. Because in Africa, it's incredibly easy to blow it with people without even realising you're doing it. Oh, yes. Don't think all this exultant highfiving bonhomie means it's all relaxed and easy-going. Are you kidding? You've got to be so careful. I look down over the milling dancers. There could be someone down there now, someone I don't even remember meeting, who's been waiting years to avenge some imagined, or not so imagined, slight.

I feel this gravelly breathing in my ear.

What's that?

'*Michael*,' says Sanyang. 'How is *Michael*?'

'Who?'

'Your friend, Michael . . .'

'Michael Heaven?'

'Yes.'

Michael Heaven! Why didn't I think of that before?

'Excuse me, man.'

I push my way down the staircase. Beside the club entrance is a door marked 'Privée.' I open it into a deserted corridor. On the left is a door. I barge straight in. Abdou's sitting on a table in a white-tiled changing room, the backing singer in his arms. They look up, startled and embarrassed.

'Where's Sajar?'

'Sajar? Oh, er . . . Sajar can't make it tonight.'

They're out there again. The crombie men. The short, thinning-hair merchants. I've got my back to the wall beside the inner front door – 'cause there's like a tiny glassed-in porch – just out of sight, and I'm not breathing. They've done the hand-on-the-bell bit, and it's gone quiet. I'm standing here on this bank, this great reef of unopened mail that's built up behind the front door. Stuff to me She's said She's no way going to deal with. Stuff, I surmise, relating to the studio bills, the pressing deal and all the other stuff. Stuff that I'm definitely *going* to deal with. And stuff that's got nothing to do with any of that, but I can't bring myself to open or even pick up. 'Cause it's just too risky.

They're talking. *There's someone else out there.* And I'm straining every nerve-ending over the grinding of passing cars and all the miscellaneous gruntings and roarings of the universe you never notice till such moments, to hear who it is.

'Is your daddy in?'

No . . . *No!* What's she doing there. She should be at school. *She cannot be there.*

I can't hear what she says.

'Is your mummy around?'

I can't hear, man. I can't fucking hear what she's saying.

'Why don't you come with us?'

I'm hanging there against the darkened wall, digging my fingers into my face.

No.

Oh, yes. In those days, Sajar didn't have any idea. In those days, if *you'd* gone up to Sajar and said, 'I really love your music, man. I want to represent you,' he'd just have shrugged and said, 'Okay.' He had no way of judging, see. In the mythological world of his childhood, the world in which most adult Tekrurians still live, all whites were uniformly rich and powerful. He didn't realise there were gradations. He didn't realise the vast majority of whites are fucking creeps and losers – though he soon learnt. And going back even further, to the time when he met me, I was the first white man he'd really got to know. And although it was all to do with music – and he knew I had a really deep and intuitive understanding of his music – there was the exhilarating novelty of having a white man as a friend. That's why he gave me total access to every aspect of his affairs. Because although in a way they didn't like the whites, resented them as slave-traders, colonialists and exploiters, and although they're all intensely and pathologically suspicious of each other, they had a curious and paradoxical expectation that the white man would behave honourably. It's a good thing I turned out to be such a nice guy.

Black music. That's what you want, isn't it? *Black music.* You're at a party somewhere in Middle England. The guests are lolloping around, as they do, to this really tepid *white* dance music. Then suddenly, another sound cuts in: harder, more twitchily edgy, and there's a *black* voice: thick, dark, huskily authoritative. And the people, even in a place like that, can dig it. Their movements become lither, more sexy, more . . . *black.* Don't get me wrong, I'm not talking about race here. I'm talking about cultural values. I mean, I'm white myself; it's nothing to be ashamed of.

You see I never was interested in the Beatles. Or the Rolling Stones. Or Manfred Mann. The Moody Blues. Pink Floyd. The Cream. Led Zeppelin, the Blue Oyster Cult, Peters and Lee or Captain Beefheart. I mean, let's be fair, looking back on it, some of that music is actually quite amusing. But at the time I didn't listen to it, because I was deeply, deeply into the seam they themselves had stolen it all from: the raw spirituality, the harsh eroticism, the dark electric pain, the sheer abrasive catharsis of the blues. Music that wasn't trying to be something. Music that *was* something.

So, I hear you say, if you're so into the authentic reality of *black* music, how come you spent so long working with *white* musicians? Well, I mean, firstly, I didn't have much choice. You can't just buy a one-way ticket from New Malden to Muscle Shoals and expect to be given a gig – not unless you've got even more chutzpah than I have. But I can honestly say that all the musicians I worked with – well, most of them – had a degree of genuine blues-feeling. They all worshipped at the shrine of the Black Soul. That's the way it's been with many of our century's finest spirits. Stravinsky, Picasso, and no doubt Einstein too. They all dug black music.

And as I've said, the moment I arrived in Africa, the moment I felt the heat of the hard red earth beneath my feet, I made certain profound and essential realisations about the nature of that music. University professors have spent their lives trying to establish connections between the music of the griots and the deep rural blues, between the techniques of the khalam, the five-string lute of the Wolof griots, and the banjo-picking of the sharecroppers. But to me it was absolutely self-evident. Blind Lemon Jefferson was a griot! To me, Sajar Jopp is just a soul singer. Why not?

That's why I was so pissed off when he got involved with that phoney Michael Heaven.

That's right. Michael Heaven.

I mean, no disrespect, right. But even *you* know who Michael Heaven is. More than that, you've got a pretty clear idea of what he and his entire project are all about. Because if you've been alive in Britain over the last twenty years in any state other than comatose it's been fucking unavoidable. Right? And what you know about him, over and above the fact that he's the thinking woman's bit of crumpet, the Nice Man of Rock who effortlessly bridges AOR, World Music and the avant garde, that he gets up on stage at stadia throughout the world without apparently making a prat of himself – despite the fact that he's my age, at least – that he represents the politically correct face of multimillionairedom – because he does such a lot of good things with it! – over and above all that, you know he used to front a progressive rock band called Opus in star-spangled loon pants. But unlike most of the rest of the class of '72, he hasn't been relegated to a hilariously bathetic footnote in the annals of rock fatuity. He used the fame and the wealth – particularly the wealth – to launch himself to his current position as contender for the *Sunday Times* Guide to One Hundred Makers of the Post-Modern World, or whatever it is.

But if the very mention of Heaven's origins in star-spangled loondom provokes in you a hoot of harsh and derisive laughter, a splutter of righteous indignation that this apparently diffident, but in fact monstrously be-egoed public schoolboy from Maidenhead with his baggage of unlistenable concept albums has the temerity to stray near the portals of the Shrine of the Black Soul, you do not tell him that. *You do not tell him!* Because while he is, as I say, apparently modest, even shy, it's typical of the kind of guy he is that he will, while making amused and deprecating comments on the absurd pretensions of those times, not only maintain that he and his cohorts were in fact actually subverting those pretensions through their whimsical English irony, but that they did actually make some very good music. And it's equally typical of him, and of most 'great artists', that he makes frequent reference to his life and works in a way that assumes a biographer's level of intimacy and fascination with the said oeuvre on the part of the listener. And if you allow him to realise – as I did one afternoon at a dance in Sajar's old familial compound, he and I in the seats of honour under the mango tree, the drums thrashing with amazing ferocity, unbelievable robes flying everywhere, eyes rolling, teeth flashing, buttocks and thighs thrusting every which way in the unbelievable heat – that you'd far rather be taking all that in than hearing about his latest project with Brian Eno, you can tell from the intensity and bitterness of the silence that follows that he does *not* like it. So I was careful what I said to him after that. Because I didn't want my name to be added to the as yet unpublished, as yet unknown list of people whose lives have been destroyed by Michael

Heaven. Oh, yes. While it may be axiomatic that Michael is *a nice man*, you will by now have realised that behind that diffident, long-lashed exterior, there lurks just another grotesque and inflated rock'n'roll spider.

Seven

In June 1984, Sajar did his first British gig in a converted cinema near Victoria Station. There'd been an attempt at the very beginning of the decade by Island Records and Virgin to promote Sunny Ade and Ebenezer Obey, rival stars of Nigerian juju music, as the next big thing – the people who were going to do for African music in the eighties what Bob Marley did for reggae in the seventies. I remember it well. The summer of '82. And I love that music: an endless, open-ended flow of mellifluous multi-layered guitars and bubbling talking drums, sweet 'n' soulful, with Hawaiian steel guitar cutting a bizarre swathe through it all. It was marketed as summer goodtime music, the ideal soundtrack for barbecues and open-topped motoring. Then summer came to an end, and everyone forgot it instantly. Sunny and Ebenezer couldn't get arrested. They went back to Nigeria and dug themselves deeper into their own indigenous furrow. Which, as far as I'm concerned was the best thing they possibly could have done.

Then a couple of years later, someone else decided to have a crack at the African chestnut, and a season of concerts by Africa's most significant stars was put on in this old cinema. Tabou Ley Rochereau, Franco and T.P.O.K. Jazz, Ambassadeurs, Manu Dibango. The list was a roll call of the greats – like an African Woodstock on a weekly basis. Zairean soukous had replaced juju as the great hope for African music. Down there in the mad military kleptocracy in the torrid belly of Africa, things were so bad that the only option – for those who could afford it – was to drink, dance and try to forget. The beautiful, soulful old Congolese rumba music had been extended into endless boisterously jovial guitar workouts that were popular the length and breadth of the continent. But onto an optimistic new Afrocompilation, Island had put one track by the already defunct Lumière d'Afrique: Sajar and Papa Gorgi Ngom declaiming through a lilting Afro-Cuban lullaby: Papa Gorgi's dark invocatory tones mingling hauntingly with Sajar's youthful screech. They sounded about as welcome amid all that glossy tumbling soukous hedonism as a couple of penniless seers turning up at a tacky nouveau-riche party. But those who value their opinions on such things: the journalists, deejays and A + R men, the self-appointed hipocracy who were scrambling onto the Afro-bandwagon, gleaned something new from it. African music was not just tropical good-time, it could be *meaningful*.

The musicians all stayed at 'Clarissa's', a dingy boarding house in Kensal Rise hung with grisly images of the sacred heart, run by a massive Sierra Leonean woman. The place bubbled the whole season, the musicians' bookings overlapping with each other, some enjoying themselves so much they refused to go home, drinking and grooving and exchanging ideas long into every night, sleeping in the cupboards, on the stairs and the kitchen table. It was an unofficial summit, a Platonic Symposium of African music. And I was omnipresent. Camping out under the kitchen table, partaking in the debates and dialogues, the dawn jam sessions, the massive afternoon breakfasts of pepper soup and refried Djolof rice.

Sajar's band were the last to perform in the season. By that time most of the other Africans had gone home. But everyone who mattered in the little world of people who might be able to do African music some good was there. They're a funny bunch. They've managed to establish themselves as someone in the little world of London, and they can't conceive that there might be anything more important than that. They love African music, they may love Latin music, and of course, reggae, hip-hop . . . America

92

they can relate to because of telly. Jamaica they can conceive of because there are Jamaicans in their road. But they never think about Africa. Not about the reality of Africa. It's just a great big incomprehensible otherness, and the few Africans they've met through the business are just these rather jovial, graceful people. Like Jamaicans only more different. But they don't really think about them. If people can dig the music in Camden Town, that's the be-all and end-all as far as they're concerned. I used to be like that myself, until . . . Until I went on a secret sub-holiday in Africa. And I was broadened. He just turned round and said, 'I'm Sajar Jopp.' And the next day was the first day of the rest of my life.

A year later, almost to the day, we were backstage at this cinema, which I'd last visited to see *The Aristocats* on a tab of Blue Cheer. It was an oddly cold evening in June, and Sajar's band were standing around shivering in these patchwork clothes, which made them look like a bunch of dervishes. They looked black away from Africa. They looked so black it was almost shocking – the whites of their eyes, diffident in this alien white country where they didn't speak French, standing out in the backstage gloom. They had that soft, slightly vulnerable look, that blooming look of wholeness, of spacious slowness, that marks out Africans, African Africans, in London. They made the people scurrying around them – the roadies, the electricians, stage staff, security – look grey, withered, almost skeletal in comparison.

Sajar was nervous as hell, but trying to hide it, telling the others, who sat or stood staring into space, that it was just another gig. I went and whispered in his ear. 'Don't worry, man. They're gonna love it!' He turned, gave me a grin of childish enthusiasm, then clasped me tightly to him in the darkness.

I was down on the floor when they came on stage. I didn't want to miss that. There were a fair number of people, but I don't know how the promoters recouped their expenses, for, as I say, few were from the class of people who actually pay for their tickets. They stood around, morosely indifferent through the disco, their characteristic look of 'so impress me' touched with an edge of faint involuntary expectation, as though even they could tell they were about to see something rather special. Christ, they looked exotic as they came on stage – so black, and swathed in all manner of scarves and their patchwork motley, and clutching their electric guitars. The two guitarists struck up a jangling ascending riff, a sound of stars and space and fervent mystical expectation. The horns gave out a blaring rejoinder, and the whole band came in. The audience were immediately enthralled. What the hell was this? Then Sajar began to sing. All eyes were on his mouth, as he went higher and higher, his mouth getting wider, his eyes and the rest of his face disappearing till there was just this yawning gap of teeth and tongue and epiglottis, and he took them to the sunburst heights of his ecstatic wail.

It was much later, when up on stage they were performing the songs of the Gor Yallah, the guardians of Kagor, the holy city of the great marabout Mam Jarra, everyone beating drums and calling the names of the great ones, that I noticed a figure standing near me, his even features stone-like and intent, silhouetted beneath the darkness of the balcony, not dancing or hooting with approbation as most of the rest of the audience now were, but absorbed in concentration. I knew that chiselled, rather morose profile. But from where?

Gestu de Dakar. Now they were a good band. They were a fucking good band. They only made one album, as far as I know, and 'Djirim' was the opener and the stand-out track. This wah-wah guitar, squeaky, slightly out of tune, grabs a phrase. The rest of the band kick back. Another phrase. They kick back again. Then they go into this round-the-houses preamble of the sort that was obligatory on African songs about ten years ago. Then they hit the main riff, this delicious descending wah-wah run, with bass and timbales pumping behind and a slightly blaring soprano sax floating in behind the melody line. Then the singer comes in, all earnest and well-manneredly soulful, like a lovelorn student teacher, his every phrase repeated by a real nasal earthy griot voice, like the beggar moaning on the corner, and the blaring, wailing sax. After a couple of verses we go into a squeakily staccato guitar solo – wah-wah still on – that explores the melody with an exquisitely elegant symmetry, constantly mirroring back on itself with echoes of melodies you aren't sure you even heard, and it's all taken in one great gulp like a sung sentence, riven with endless sub-clauses that somehow never loses its thread ... It's Proustian, man. Or is it Joycean? No, it's Proustian. It continues over a kick round the timbales, then the sax comes soaring in over the top with an exquisitely minor-key solo. Then the lead vocal comes back in, duelling with these swiping wah-wah guitar chords. The other voice comes in and they take it to a rousingly crashing finale. The song's all about polygamy, about how if your mother dies, you'll be left in the care of the co-wife – the stranger who is eating everything your mother strove for. Not so culturally specific as it might first appear, eh? And I think anyone could relate to the exquisite yearning melancholy of the singing, the lyrical Proustian – yes, Proustian – soloing, the sheer sense of spontaneity, redolent of another time and another place.

I sometimes try to imagine the day they recorded that song. I can see the streets of white dust deserted in the heat of mid-afternoon. Only a pariah dog licking its sores near the entrance to a run-down colonial building, and through the courtyard, I can hear the bass and timbales pumping from the primitive studio, and the soaring of the sax. A simpler place and time? Has there ever been such a thing? The music doesn't quite sound like anything you've ever heard before. But how sure of themselves they sound, those musicians, how rooted. Not straining after the attention of fickle Westerners. And their sheer improvisatory élan. I mean, they knew what they were doing by any standards. But who were they playing for? Who was listening? Who appreciated the brilliance of their playing? Did it go unheard? Not at all. I can see the dancers now in tumbledown provincial nightclubs, in village discos under the stars, fenced off with palm leaves, twisting and jumping through every familiar note of that guitar solo, 'demonstrating' as they call it, with expressive postures and grimaces, through 'their' solo. Oh yes, they were appreciated all right. But what happened to them? Did they go on to become mainstays of more famous groups? Did they open a petrol station

95

on the proceeds and forget all about music? Or did they just die, in that sudden, inexplicable tropical way? And where had they thought it was getting them, making that record? To stardom in the greater world? A steadier string of gigs? Or readies up front? Or were they just there for the pleasure of playing music? Who were these people? I did not know their names, had no idea what they even looked like. I had acquired the cassette almost by accident, had never heard anyone else even say the group's name. The cassette was a copy. Where were the originals? Where were the master tapes? Were they stolen, destroyed – or maybe like so much of Africa's music, like indeed so much of Africa itself, they had simply disappeared, disintegrated, worn away into the glistening dust of the continent. I sometimes wonder if I'm the only person who knows about this music. In fact, I sometimes wonder if I've imagined it.

'Saraba' by Abdoulaye Diabate and the Sanou Diouf Orchestra, that's another piece of unknown music. Now, when I think about it, the eponymous Sanou Diouf, is, I'm absolutely sure, the guy playing sax on Gestu de Dakar's record. But as for Abdoulaye Diabate – never been heard of before or since. There is a well-known Abdoulaye Diabate in Mali, but this is a completely different person. It starts in tourist-hotel mode, like the token ballad from your poolside entertainment, plangent soprano sax over rather plodding rhythm section. Then the vocal comes in, and it's somehow so exquisite, so excruciatingly poignant in its yearning intensity you can hardly stand it – like the ancient griots of Mali heard through the transmogrifying prism of Luther Vandross. Who is this Abdoulaye Diabate, you wonder. Where is he? Sign him up! Let's all get rich! But you know it won't happen. It's just going to be one of those things that's let go. Then the sax comes back in, flooding the track with its luminous colours, and then, just when you think your cup is running over, the kora, the twenty-one-string Mandinka harp, starts to pick its way up out of the mix, the myriad notes tinkling and tumbling like raindrops dancing in a beam of golden sunlight as they give a bouncing syncopated reinforcement to the melodic line. If, when I'm dying, they play that music, I think I might quite enjoy it. But then, when you're dying, you probably aren't even able to enjoy music. That's probably the awful tragic pity of it.

Afterwards, backstage, the musicians, still hyper-charged by the energy of the performance, were rushing around in a state of slightly unhinged glee, like footballers after a goal's been scored. When you've been around musicians as long as I have, you know when to stand well back. People began to filter in. Record company people, journalists, stylemongers, prominent Tekrurian people from London. Everyone embracing, shaking hands, smiling with delight and congratulation. Sajar, in the middle of everything, smiling easily, princelike, graciously accepting it all with the expertly feigned surprise of the true royal – the person who knows they are the real thing and nothing else will do. 'You enjoyed it . . . ? Oh!' Shaking hands with everyone, smiling for everyone, disarming everyone. Wooing everyone without having to *do* anything. 'Sajar's a*may*zing!' they would say for years after. I just laughed. They didn't realise there was an entire country of people like that.

Then I noticed the figure in the dark suit, hanging hesitantly on the edge of the group. Smaller then you'd expect. The suit expensively rumpled. The treble-figure haircut subtly, but attractively, greying. The pasty features with their characteristic sculpted intentness. At the same moment everyone else seemed to notice. Was it, could it be, *him*? Sajar turned, and the crowd spontaneously parted between them. The white man, with his well-cultivated air of diffidence, smarting beneath the burden of his own greatness. The African having no idea who this person was, but sensing immediately that here was someone of status, of rank. And the two embraced warmly, to the gasped approbation of everyone there. How a*may*zing! How *African*! And the two men spoke to each other as though no one else was there. Heaven spoke of his longstanding love of African music, of its purity, its elemental spiritual energy. Of how he bought his first African record at the age of ten. Of how this was 'l'expérience la plus profonde, la plus captivante' he had yet had of the music. Sajar said he was very happy to see him there, and that if he wanted to know more of African music he should come to Tekrur and stay with him in his house. Everyone listened, enchanted. They knew they were privileged to be observing this encounter between two of the most extraordinary musical spirits of our time.

Michael Heaven did go to Tekrur. He didn't stay in Sajar's house. He stayed in the most expensive hotel in N'Galam. But they were together a lot. Heaven took his tape recorder to do some field recordings, and he had a great time. He had a fucking brilliant time! How do I know? I was with him the whole time. I'm the one who told him which musicians to record. I introduced him to the most dangerously hard-edged drummers. I used up my contacts among the deepest, the most heavy-duty, the most *in there* griots of Tekrur. I told him how to behave, how to comport himself in that society. I kept him company. Because, if the truth be known, the Great World Man was more than a little intimidated by the gangs of howling kids who followed him everywhere, the larger-than-life women accosting him with brazen familiarity, the hustlers shoving their hands in his pockets at every opportunity. Let's face it, the guy was scared shitless.

You've probably got the impression I don't like Michael, that I resent him, even that I'm the tiniest bit jealous of him. Far from it. He did absorb his Tekrurian field recordings into a limp 'experimental' album, without troubling to thank me in the credits. But I don't hold grudges about things like that. He's a rock star and a multi-multi-multi-millionaire. But so what? As I've said, I don't give a shit about white music anyway. No, when I actually got to know him, I didn't think he was such a bad bloke. But, like a lot of white people when they come into contact with Africa, he felt he had to 'do something about it' – he had to put his spoke in. He got Sajar set up with the Motivate Corporation, and when the time came for Sajar to do his Great World Music Album, the one that was going to be his big chance to break through to the mainstream record buyer, Heaven found him a producer. Then, thinking he was doing Sajar a great favour, he put himself all over it. They got very excited. You kept hearing about how this record was going to take African music to another

98

level, that it brought Africa, the Caribbean and the West together in a way that had never been heard before, that it was going to fundamentally change a lot of people's ideas about what music could be. Of course, it bombed. Whether or not Heaven found out that I'd been advising Sajar the whole time not to use that producer and that he should have been approaching the whole project in a completely different way, I don't know. But the next time I met him out here, he was really jumpy. He left the country without even saying goodbye to me, and I haven't spoken to him since.

Beneath, beside and below the plateau of Tesco's car park is this massive traffic roundabout – and it *is* massive, it must be one of the biggest traffic roundabouts in the world – under which the ill-lit sluices of the pedestrian underpasses feed into a central open area where the footpaths and cycle routes converge round a single colossally tall streetlight. And as you enter this area, from the direction of our house, you can see high above the lip of the roundabout and its unseen traffic, the red and blue lights of Tesco's. And you think, I'm there. But you're not. Though it's only a few yards above you, the pedestrian footpaths take you ever further in the opposite direction, till you're on the other side of the adjacent dual carriageway. Then you take a footbridge that delivers you into the back section of the supermarket car park. The local advertising rags that come through our door are full of stories of pensioners being mugged on this bridge, of women being robbed in Tesco's car park in broad daylight, of car-jackings from outside the station opposite. But though I'm the last person not to turn a drama into a crisis, and I'm no stranger to *the edge*, I don't feel it here. All I can feel is this kind of numbness. The dark, windswept figures scurrying past me on the footbridge, the occasional – very occasional – person I meet in the underpasses, don't have the reality to me to pose any kind of threat. They're just shadows. Up there on the footbridge, the drizzling night mingling with the ever-present orange glare of the streetlamps, hanging in hazy curtains from the eternity of the night above. And always as I head out into the drizzle – because in this place it's always drizzling – it's night. The day with its changes of light and atmosphere, reminding me of the passage of time, of the forces pressing in on me . . . No, I can't be doing with that. But the night, the orange drizzling night, like the even glow of the supermarket, is neutral, doesn't demand anything. That's why I like the nullitude of winter: the short days, when often the grey pall never manages to lift. But now, whatever month it is, the days are getting longer . . . I'm having to go out later and later. And there's the nasty thought that soon I'll have to go out when it's light to catch Tesco's at all.

'Do you know Sajar Jopp's house?' I ask the driver.

Thinking I'm just making whimsical conversation, he grunts something to the effect of not having time to talk about things like that. He's off his manor here, and he's still smarting from the cool authority with which I put him right on the price.

We've passed the beachside fish market of Soumbedioune, with its grotty ribbon development of villages artisanales – drums and wooden antelopes piled up for sale at the roadside – and we're slowly ascending past turnoffs into dusty nondescript housing developments, towards the lighthouse of the Pointe des Alcaldes. Sajar lived out this way last time I was here, but precisely where, and whether or not I'm going to the same house, I've no idea.

Opposite the slope of the lighthouse is a long white wall, relatively new, but already crumbling, one entrance in which leads through into a private estate of modest-sized dwellings crouching behind more dust-eroded white walls. None of the houses are numbered and the driver's getting into a bit of a flap. We stop to ask a woman, ambling slowly along in the shade.

'C'est la maison de Sajar Jopp,' I hiss to the driver.

His heart is momentarily in his mouth. He's supposed to drop me at the *actual* house of Sajar Jopp? He's awestruck.

Sajar's house is just back the way we've come: no different from any of the others. I'd heard some rumour about him having built a large and luxurious mansion. This isn't it.

A group of kids are standing outside the gate.

C'est la maison de Sajar Jopp?

Oui . . . oui . . . oui . . .

Through a barred metal gate I can see into a bleak little yard with one tree in a corner. Incredible Sajar's still living in a place like this. I ring the bell and a dog starts barking. A harsh voice silences it, and a thick-set man comes out into the yard and peers suspiciously out. He sees the white man.

'Litch?'

'Oui.'

He unlocks the gate.

'Tell Sajar there are some people here who would like to talk to him,' says one of the kids.

'Sure,' I say.

The butler leads me into the dark bare hallway, not dirty but with that used patina that white walls quickly acquire in the tropics. The house is quiet, muffled, as though everyone is still asleep. He takes me to the living-room and slightly opens one of the curtains. Through the louvred window, I can see that there are heavy bars. The window is large by African standards, where even in modern houses, the windows tend to be narrow and slit-like, and in general they keep the curtains closed. The room itself is scruffy: the ceiling peeling, the walls marked with kids' scrawling, the curtains grubby and hanging any old how, foam stuffing bursting out of the mediocre G-plan-style suite. A modern African painting of no great distinction hangs skew-whiff on one wall, and opposite a hideous kitsch still-life of apples in a bowl. It's quite a lot scruffier than many moderately prosperous Tekrurian houses I've been in, except that there is *a lot* of electronic hardware: a massive telly, several pairs of black speakers piled ziggurat-like with loads of amplifiers, video players, faxes and answering machines littered about the place. Piles of video tapes, but no records, CDs or cassettes. Typical.

And it's good to see Sajar hasn't gone the way of neo-classical atriums, marble floors and gold bathtaps. He's still basically of the people. He never has been into *things*. He's into doing, not having. He's got his own sense of style, but he's never been into the Armani suits, the perfumes and accessories, the high life in Paris, New York and Rome. He only eats Tekrurian food and

McDonalds. He's only interested in football, music and women. He's just a working-class bloke. Like me.

But I've got things to say here. And how am I going to put it to him that his great friend Michael Heaven, to whom he still feels he owes so much, has been dragging Sajar's financial situation into his personal vendettas and manipulative head games? That Michael and his whole way of doing things are a liability? That his album would not only have been *better*, but probably far more commercial, if I'd done it?

And am I going to say any of that to him? You must be joking. Any reference to Heaven has got to be handled very, very delicately.

There's a shuffling out in the passage, then a tall figure, a cloth draped over its head, enters the room and sinks down into one of the sofas. She pulls aside the cloth and fastens it loosely into a turban. Then she turns to me. It's Sajar's mother, looking a bit older, a bit graver. And she's quite a woman. Intelligent, feisty, ambitious. I always felt she had a lot to do with Sajar's success: always pushing, always adoring, always inspiring, and enjoying his wealth and success. But I also felt she never got over the fact that Sajar got married – that all the material fruits were being directed towards another woman.

We exchange formal greetings.

'You know me,' I say.

She looks again, and a smile spreads over her face.

'Michael!'

'No, not Michael. Litch.'

'Yes, Litch.'

Sajar's wife comes in. She's small and rather mousey-looking, but there's toughness there, a strong will. That, I've been told, was the attraction. She put him in his place, and wasn't the least bit interested in his music. But you could have knocked me down with a feather when he got married. He'd had children with various women, but I always thought he was basically gay.

She comes over and shakes hands with me in the upfront way of modern Tekrurian women.

'How are you?'

102

'Fine.'

'How is England?'

'Fine . . . Mingi doh?'

'Wow. Bah'na.'

'We've met,' I say. 'In England.'

'Oh, yes,' she says, nodding, clearly not remembering at all. Don't these people have *any* memory for faces? She seems remote and preoccupied and goes and sits by the mother. Soon a strained, hectoring tone comes into their conversation, which I imagine must be fairly continual. God, it must be awful. The interminable territorial bickering of Sajar's women! Then Sajar himself appears, looking rumpled and saturnine. The two women get up and leave. Sajar sees me.

'Litch!'

'Yeah, man. How are you?'

'Tired.'

Still groggy with sleep, Sajar wanders over, and sinks down into the sofa adjacent to mine.

'We were up till five again. Playing at the club.'

'It's too much, man.'

'Yeah.'

He leans forward, and helps himself to water from a plastic bottle. He drinks long then gasps and sinks back. Then, without looking at me, and as though not addressing me personally, but some generalised listener, he asks, 'How do you see Tekrur now?'

How do I see Tekrur now? What a question! I shrug. 'The same.'

'No. It's not the same. Tekrur is now a very difficult place. There are many problems. Many problems.'

The voice is Sajar's – there's that unmistakable touch of gold coming through the thick sleepy gruffness. But the tone I don't recognise. Sajar's conversation tends to be fairly functional. By his standards, this is a soliloquy. And he's staring into space, not really talking to me at all. I must keep him going. It could be interesting.

'What . . . sort of problems?'

'Poverty. Corruption. Le moins d'éducation . . . Violence.'

103

'Violence?'

'Oui! I can't walk in the street now. It's impossible.' He laughs mirthlessly. 'I can't do it.'

God, I've never heard him talking like this before. I mean, he's always gone on about Africa's problems, about how everyone must do what they can to build the New African Society. But that was just spiel, another angle for self-promotion. Sajar's always been so blithe. I've never known him really let anything get to him. But now he sounds almost despairing.

'So,' I say, half joking, 'What are you going to do about it?'

He gives me a dark look. But again, it's as though it's not really me he's seeing. 'Nothing,' he says. 'I can't do anything.'

A woman comes in with a large covered basin which she sets down on the coffee-table. Lunch is served. I'd better speak while he's in this bizarrely talkative frame of mind. I may not get another chance. I can already hear other voices out in the hallway. Soon the room will be full of people.

'Listen, man, about this mon –'

But Sajar raises his hand commandingly. 'No. Not now.'

The room is full of hoarse ribald laughter and robust good-natured greetings.

'Mister Toubab! Back again?'

'Can't keep away.'

'That's right! Found anything good?'

'I'm on it.'

He chuckles and slaps my hand. This is Mbaye Fall, Sajar's old bass player, now a freelance producer. He and I go back a *long* way. 'So, the great explorer of World Music is among us again. Maybe I'm going to point you towards some new Tekrurian artists.'

'Produced by you?'

'Of course. But this is heavy music,' he warns, finger raised. 'Typical, *typical* Tekrurian music! Can you handle it?'

'Try me!'

He turns and talks to someone else in robust and elastic Wolof. Meanwhile, Sajar has asked Abdou to get something from the other room. Now he thrusts a sheaf of papers into my hand. 'What is this?'

It's a pile of press releases, faxes, letters, prospective programmes and other bumph announcing the launch of something called 'Sahelfest 2000' – a kind of stadium mega-gig designed to 'raise the consciousness of African Youth' on stuff like deforestation and conservation. Sort of an eco-BandAid – 'cept it's actually taking place *in* Africa, and it's more Black Music orientated. And the impression they're giving is that anyone who's ever been anyone in African, Jamaican, Black American or British music is going to be descending on this place. And there'll be poetry and exhibitions – the whole thing broadcast live round the world by satellite. Sounds fantastic, you say. That's right. Every few years they have one of these jamborees with monumental profile-raising agendas on Human Rights, Understanding African Culture, Refugees or whatever. The artists get good publicity, middle-men make millions and within a fortnight no one can quite remember what it was all about – even if you don't learn later that thousands of people's lives were ruined through the 'aid' created. Still, they're normally quite good fun while they're on, with plenty of opportunities for stirring, schmoozing, networking, ligging and 'doing oneself some good'. And this one not only looks a lot cooler and more African-orientated than most, it seems comparatively well-organised. They're about to wrap up sponsorship deals with at least four multinational companies. I mean, I can already tell you exactly what it'll be like. Sajar'll do a song and the dudes on the corner will all nod their heads wisely about how we must respect Uncle Elephant and Father Lion. But will one single glass of tea be prevented from being brewed on charcoal burnt from Tekrur's few remaining hectares of virgin forest? Je croix pas.

The latest communiqué is a letter from London from someone called Gabriella Malinowski, telling Sajar how crucial his involvement is, and saying how honoured they'd be if he agreed to be on the consultative panel.

At my elbow, Sajar is getting ever so slightly agitated.

'I can't do it.' He looks at me, wide-eyed and earnest. 'I always do these things, but I can't do any more.'

That's right, UNESCO, Amnesty International, Oxfam and hundreds of other charities, NGOs, conferences, benefits and festivals – Sajar, ever obliging, ever on the lookout for an opportunity to promote Africa, its music, its culture, and of course himself, has always said yes to everything. But it can't go on. He needs to draw the line. He needs time and some space, for himself and for his music.

'What shall I do?' he asks, looking almost hunted. 'They are coming here next week to discuss it.'

I ponder for a moment. 'Tell them you'll help in any way you can, but you can't actually *do* anything.'

'Yeah,' says Sajar. 'That's good.'

The lid is removed, and everyone positions themselves round the coffee-table. Salimata, Sajar's soignée, but too cool sister has joined us. She gives me a sheepish half-smile and raises her eyebrows. 'Litch,' she breathes.

'My woman,' I grunt.

Then we all dig our spoons into the mound of rice smothered in gristly meat and groundnut sauce, which we shower with Maggi sauce – that essential mainstay of African cuisine – and all kinds of fearsome red relishes. This is simple, earthy peasant food. Once again, I'm back in the bosom of Sajar's operation, in the close, intimate family environment to which only those closest to him are admittted. Yes, here I am sitting next to Africa's greatest musician in this hot stuffy room, which you could describe as the very heart of the world's music. Sajar, the mood of uncertainty and despair to which I was privy a few moments ago now utterly dispelled, as though it never happened – something in fact, only I know about – is telling some anecdote in robust and guttural Wolof through mouthfuls of food, to which the others all respond with sniggers and throaty chuckles.

'Litch!' he says. 'Can you understand what I'm saying?'

'No,' I say.

At which the others all laugh in affectionate approval.

On the way back into town, the car is stopped three times at police checkpoints. They peer into the car, but they're not interested in me. This is Tekrur, the coolest country in Africa. They don't bother whites here. And anyway, I'm too preoccupied to bother with that. I'm thinking about Sahelfest 2000. And I'm just a little miffed that I wasn't already aware of it. I don't like the idea that there's anything going on that's even vaguely connected with African music, particularly when it's originating in the London area, that I'm not party to. And I like to be in on it from the earliest possible stage, because that's when you can really exert some influence. And, I'm not boasting, but I am usually the first person they come to anyway. So I'm a little concerned that they managed to get this project so far down the line without me having heard a single word about it. If I didn't know better, I might start wondering if I was slipping, that my communications channels were getting clogged. And I still haven't worked out if this is an environmental event masquerading as a cultural event or vice versa, and I suspect the latter, because the tone of the blurb was less wellingtons and well-digging – still less crystals up the Niger – and more kind of abstract, theoretical and left-wing. And whether that's going to be a Great Enabling Factor or a pain in the arse we'll find out as things pan out. Because although one can scoff at this kind of worthy well-meaning event, one can't ignore them. If one's an expert – as I undoubtedly am – one's got to be seen to be an expert. And they can provide rich opportunities for the exploitation of my innumerable contacts, my myriad archives, libraries and research repositories, and all the performers, projects, albums and audio-visual material in which I have points, percentages, royalties and residuals. And when one considers there's not just the official programme, but all the TV, radio and satellite spin-offs, all the thousands of inches of newspaper and magazine print that need to be pushed in the direction I deem appropriate, that means there's a lot of work to be done. I can see I'm going to have to hire an assistant. I'm running through a list of potential candidates when the car pulls up at the Belotel. I squeeze the driver's cheek, and charge into the foyer. A diminutive man in a blue suit, who I've learnt is the assistant manager, comes darting forward, paper in hand.

'Monsieur Litchfield . . . ?'

I put up my hand. 'Jerejef. Mangi nyow, wai!' I stride into the lift as the doors are closing. It pings its way too slowly to the top, then I'm along the corridor in a couple of bounds, wrench the door open and get straight on the blower. It may be 7 p.m. G.M.T., but at the Sahelfest 2000 office in Islington, they'll still be hard at it.

'Hello?' The voice is tense and suspicious. Can this be the right number?

'Is that Sahelfest 2000?'

'Yes, it is.'

'Right. Gabriella Malinowski please.'

'This is Gabriella Malinowski.'

Without even having thought about it, I'd figured Gabriella as junker lesbian Eurotrash, Swiss-educated, motivated to Save the Tribespeople via childhood sojourns in Kenya with big-game-hunting aristo father, getting to grips with Sahelian drought through champagne receptions at the Musée de l'Homme. Not an uptight hostile Englishwoman.

'Okay . . .'

'Who is this?'

'My name's Simon Henchard. I'm a freelance journalist and I'm phoning to find out more about Sahelfest 2000.'

'You've read the programme, presumably.'

'Yeah, but I'm interested to know who'll be appearing at the concert.'

'Who are you, exactly?'

Grief, man. We're getting specific! 'I'm a freelance journalist working mainly for the *Guardian*.'

There's a pause. The *Guardian* is clearly *not enough*.

'I also write for . . . *Vanity Fair, Elle, GQ,* the *Daily Express, NME, Loaded . . . Esquire*.' How much more does she want? 'And I do a weekly column that's syndicated to the *New York Times, Le Monde, Frankfurter Allgemeine* . . . The usual stuff!'

Her voice has by now thawed very slightly. 'I had to check,

because we've had a lot of journalists phoning who aren't the sort of people we want to deal with.' I can't believe I'm hearing this. Doesn't this woman realise that the essence of PR is that you've got to be prepared to lick the arse of anyone who shows the slightest possibility of generating even one sentence of copy in any organ no matter how ignominious?

'Of course,' I say.

'Now the thing about Sahelfest 2000 that makes it different to similar events in the past, which you of course know about . . .'

'Of course.'

'. . . is that the impetus is coming not from Western NGOs, charities and governments, but from within Africa itself. This is going to be Africa for Africa. Africa standing up for itself and defining its own debates and agendas!'

I like listening to this woman. There's something in her cold and slightly barmy arrogance I find quite stirring. And she's confiding in me. She's telling me everything. I mean, I could be anyone. I could be making it all up. And I like the sound of her voice. Its very froideur hints at the fire beneath.

'We want to break down this Western division between science and culture, between art and technology. Just as we want Africa to propose the solutions to its own developmental problems, we want the artistes involved in this festival to be involved in setting the parameters for debate around the context of their work.'

I see her as a brilliant academic, breaking out into the field of practical action. Shielded from the world by the long years of toil on her ground-breaking post-structuralist thesis, she's now launched into the wicked realities of media manipulation and international fund-raising. London based, but Swiss-educated by millionaire industrialist father, she combines international breadth with Anglophone user-friendliness.

Hold on, she's talking to me.

'So what sort of journalist are you?'

'How d'you mean?'

'Well, some journalists seem to be able to decide to write an article, do it and it will be published. While others seem to have to

109

dither around asking dozens of different people, and it never comes to anything. Which are you?'

I've got a warm glow in my chest. My voice is thick with the constrictions of desire. 'Oh, the first sort.'

'That's wonderful!' Now she sounds like she's going to propose to me. 'Perhaps we should have lunch and discuss the possibilities.'

'We definitely should.'

'We want this thing to be different from all similar events. Which means that Michael Heaven isn't going to be involved.'

I chuckle – a laugh hoarse with immemorial knowing.

'SENSOR (a hippy front organisation for Heaven) aren't going to be involved.'

This is too beautiful!

'And Andrew "Litch" Litchfield, or whatever he calls himself, definitely isn't going to be involved.' *What?* 'The last thing African musicians need is fat middle-aged white men telling them what their music ought to be about.'

Fucking anorexic yuppie academics. Fucking privately educated, stuck-up, sharp-elbowed, careerist sound-bite merchants. Sitting there in her ch-chi little office, lecturing *me* about African culture. *'Africa for Africa!'* I should have said, 'If it's Africa for Africa, why the fuck are you involved?' Or maybe, more coolly, 'Oh, you're African are you?' These people are all the same. Jetting the world on Rockefeller Foundation grants, pronouncing to each other about African culture at a continual round of conferences, seminars and symposia, writing unreadable articles in user-hostile post-structuralist magazines read by six people. And they've even been to Africa. Oh, yes. They're in Ouagadougou for the film festival, Jo'burg for the biennale, Dakar for the symposium on Negritude and Neo-Platonism. They've even attended a ceremony for the propitiation of the water spirits in Oshogbo with Ulli Beier, Suzanne Wenger and Twins Seven-Seven. But have they actually put one foot in the dark, irremediable and excruciating reality of Africa? Have they gone into it and lived it? Have they made the sacrifices, have they acquired the sense of personal abnegation necessary to share the joys and sorrows, the ecstasies and unfathomable agonies of the African people? Have they fuck. For them Africa's just a peg to hang their careers on, an annexe of fucking academe, a happy hunting ground for their neo-colonial researchings, a backdrop for the charade of the theoretical bickerings through which they hustle each other on and off the ladder of academic esteem. Africa the abject continent lying there gleaming silver in the evening light waiting to be fucked and looted by these people, the same as she's been fucked and looted by everyone else. And how does she know whether I'm fat or not? Fat! Believe it or not, I've never actually been called fat before. Perusing myself in the mirror, I concede I'm no waif. In fact, with my lank colourless hair, my pale haunted eyes, the feral channels – revealed for the first time by the pitiless light over the bathroom sink – carving down towards the slack and sullen mouth, lines of sweat dripping down my mottled chest onto the grey and greasy folds of my gut, I have to admit that it presents a fairly unpleasant spectacle. And yes, there's some more superfluous padding round my arse and thighs. But I'm not queuing up to jump on your media-friendly bandwagon of prepacked culture with its callow manicured narcissism, Ms Malinowski. Because as you didn't realise as you spoke to me on the phone, I'm already *out there*. Yes, I reflect with a smirk that puts a slightly frightening light into my blue-grey eyes, everything you see here is a result of what I've lived. I see myself, the only portrait in a book of harrowing photographs by Don McCullin: 'The man who's *seen it.*' Fat!

I lie down. The air-conditioning's off. I let the evening warmth lay itself on my fatness. Yeah! So what? I can hear the laughter of the taxi-drivers far, far below, carried on the Atlantic breezes. That harsh visceral chuckling, that speaks of both the callousness and the raffish freewheeling joys of the African city. Yes, my friend. *That* is African culture, the African culture of which Mlle Malinowski and her ilk know nothing. Gabriella Malinowski. Sitting there in her office in Islington getting Africa all organised. You can't feel angry with someone like that. I feel almost *sorry* for her. Gabriella! And the thing was, I actually liked her! I still do. That's always been one of my problems. I actually *like* women.

Eight

I'm in the Marché Hakim Nder. Or rather, I'm on the edge of it, in that whirring, jangling lane that runs parallel with the Rue Maurice Njai, lined with stalls selling watches, Walkmans, batteries and . . . cassettes. But I'm not happy. There are too many eyes on me, the hard eyes of the stallholders perusing me from their dark booths, their touts cruising the pathways, the slip-streams of the shoppers and pedestrians, eyeing me up and down, assessing the wealth betokened by the bulges in my trousers, checking out my camera, counting the money in the hidden pockets of my Striders. Oh, yes. I've already been picked over, there's nothing left to be revealed, and now, their eyes darting piranha-like, I can feel them all around, walking in step, ready to move in for the kill. And the tragically ironic thing is, I *do* want to buy. I want to buy, but I don't want to be hustled.

It's about six, approaching the most exhilarating time of day, when everyone is on the street, and even down here in the teeming ratruns of the Marché Hakim Nder you can feel the reflected glow of the blessed evening light bouncing off the tall buildings into the boiling air, and the tumultuous clamour below – the people packing up great bundles and bales, heaving huge sacks on and off the barrows that twist their way through the throng, the impassive, stick-chewing market women, their heads piled with towering contructions of bowls and basins, swaying deftly though the mayhem, and the overwhelming impersonal

113

force of the people pressing out from the pavements, spilling from the sidestreets, pouring across the Avenue Wagane Diouf towards the open-fronted shops of the cloth-vendors on the Rue de Chon. Like all covered markets, this place was created to get the hawkers off the streets. But now the Marché Hakim Nder is spreading like some monstrous growth, erupting over the city, absorbing, subsuming everything around it into its relentless teeming energy. Each time I come here, it seems to have expanded another three blocks. Ten times as many bana-bana men – marchands ambulants – seem to be heading out each morning from their wholesalers deep within the market. And I'm thinking that in the past – not *ten years ago* – I wandered all over this market, thought nothing of straying off into the dark labyrinth beyond the cramped booths, whereas now I'm scared half-shitless straying even into its built-up edges.

In England, I expect to be subjected to robbery with violence once every ten, maybe fifteen years. *Here*, it doesn't matter how long my stay, if it's only three days, something always happens, even if I'm not actually mugged, even if it's just a mood, a feeling, the sense that something's about to happen – to jolt you out of your complacency, to remind you that you're white, that you don't belong here, you're a target.

Of course, if you're here for any length of time, you develop a looser, slacker rhythm whereby if something does happen, you take it in your stride. But I can't do that any more. I can no longer say, 'Yeah, man, cool!' or 'Yes, I do like black people, but I can't talk now, right?' and pass blithely on. Now all I can feel is the sweat-stained shirt revealing the overloaded contours of the money-belt round my querulous girth, the pathetic gaucheness conferred by my quivering pallidity – my *whiteness*. Now all I can do is ask not *if* something's going to happen, but when . . . *When?*

Ahead is a cassette stall. I can't see anything else. I'm focusing totally on this one stall with this bunch of guys sprawled round the car in front of it, chatting, chilling, pressing flesh. Guys who look a bit more urbane and well-heeled – not much, but a bit – than the rest of the anonymous throng, whose expansive gestures and relatively clean leisurewear speak of a certain maturity and respectability. I think I'm just going to slope up unnoticed, briefly peruse and maybe even buy some cassettes, and then get the fuck back to the hotel.

They continue their elastic chuckling, utterly oblivious, as I squeeze in behind them. And my brain goes into salivating overdrive, like a kid gone ape in a sweetshop, as I scan the images of the griots on the myriad dinky cassette covers – the fantastically turbanned women in their cloth-of-gold, their glacé silk, their necks, wrists and ears heavy with chunky or, their broad cheeks larded with lightener, their kohled eyes staring back with deceptive placidity, rolling towards heaven, gazing into the middle distance with a calm that belies the rawness and potency of the sounds within. Yes, these women have been busy. Time was when only the likes of Sajar got to make a cassette, and you only heard the griots at private ceremonies or occasionally on the radio. But now they're all at it – from the most revered matriarchs to the funkiest slinkiest dudettes, they're all teaming up with whizzkid garage producers, Wolof rappers, moonlighting members of Sajar's band, Lebanese cowboy guitarists, accompanied by everything from a single lute to a baroque mayhem of swirling synthesisers, flailing drums and slippery, insistent guitars with the magisterial, imprecatory tones of the women themselves towering above it all. And the men, urbane in fake Armani suits or magnificently starched robes, and all those old guys in dark glasses, the masters of language, people regarded as the very soul of the culture – they've all got cassettes out too. Not only must cassette production have quadrupled since I was last here, but the griots are more active and *out there* than they've ever been.

I'm suddenly aware that it's gone quiet behind me.

'Yes, my friend!'

It's happening, man. This is it.

'M'sieur . . .'

I turn. This blunt-faced guy's right behind me, fixing me with dull expressionless eyes. I can't feel anything. My soul's gone into spasm.

'Litch?'

'Ye . . .'

115

'You don't know me?'

'No.'

'Daouda . . .'

What?

'Daouda Mboob. I phoned you at your hotel. About my cassette.'

I'm exhaling. The blood's rushing back into my face. I'm almost in tears. I seize his hand. 'Nice, man! Nice!'

'How are you?' he's asking.

'Fine. Fine. Alhamdoulilahi! Jerejef sunu borom guiss na la!' I've developed a sudden inexplicable fluency in the Wolof language.

'Mister Litch!' he chuckles.

The others look on in various states of pity, derision and aloofness. I'd better greet them all formally, because you only get one bite at the cherry here, and if you alienate people by failing to schmooze them enough on first meeting, that's it.

'Tu me connais pas?' asks the broad, cool-faced guy in the shell suit.

Those luminous, snake-like eyes, that demeanour of impressive musk-like cool, that husky just-got-out-of-bed growl. You know what it's like when you're talking to someone and they get bigger and bigger . . . Shit, man! It's Sidi Taal! The gorgui, the guv'nor, the laid-back mainman of Tekrurian music, the voice of the streets – second only to Sajar in the pantheon. What's the matter with me, man?

'You just slip into the country without contacting anyone, eh?'

'No, man. It's been difficult.'

He shrugs. 'It's difficult if you want it to be difficult.'

'We must meet very soon.'

'It's up to you.'

With him is producer and entrepreneur Saliou Faye, Ahmadou Toure's sidekick, the guy who controls most of the musical connections between here and Paris. That shy-looking man is Babacar Mbaye, a geography teacher who manages a couple of leading griots in his spare time. And those moody-looking dudes in baseball caps, leaning against the car, are Militant Black

116

Rearmament, Tekrur's leading rap duo. Soon we're all embracing, punching shoulders, squeezing forearms and highfiving like there's no tomorrow. Behind the counter is Aliou Ndoye, Tekrur's principal cassette distributor. I'd imagined a fat bloke in a suit with a warehouse and a forklift truck. In fact he looks about fourteen, with a shy smile and just this telephone-box-sized booth, a telephone and a calculator. But it's like this whole scenario – finding the crème de la crème of Tekrurian music chilling against a parked car in the Marché Hakim Nder. It's the sort of thing you'd dream of happening if you came here, but you'd assume never would, like meeting Mick Jagger, Phil Spector and Harvey Goldsmith sharing a Woodbine outside Top Man. But here you are. We are here. And it's happening. That's what Africa's like. That's why I love it.

When I first came here, ten years ago, the main, virtually the only TV advert was this manicured black family in a gleaming white kitchen, tucking into food made with Maggi Cube. It could have been anywhere in the francophone world – the Antilles, Abidjan, even France itself. When I returned five years later, the same family were in the same kitchen, but wearing robes, and the voice-over was in Wolof. And there was another advert. A group of berobed elders at some traditional ceremony, say a baptism, squatting round a bowl of food, calling to one of their fellows to join them. He wanders off, uninterested, till someone calls, 'Wait . . . !'

He stops in his tracks.

'It's made with . . . Maggi Cube!'

He turns to the camera in big and beaming close-up, eyes lighting up behind his shades, and rushes to his place at the bowlside.

And there's another one, for Jumbo Cube, Maggi's locally manufactured competitor, shot in a cardboard studio on video, where this massive blindfolded woman is being fed spoonfuls of fish and rice made with Jumbo Cube or a leading competitor. On tasting the Jumbo version, she goes into flesh-shaking ecstasy. 'Wow, wow! Li nekh'na loll! Jarow lak!' Lots of hooting and hollering in the background, and the berobed presenter wags his finger at the camera, spluttering with eye-popping rhetorical force something to the effect of, 'That's why ninety-nine per cent of Tekrurian housewives prefer Jumbo Cube!'

But you don't want to hear about that. You've heard the griots on Radio 3. You went to their concert at the Queen Elizabeth Hall. And you don't want to see them in TV adverts for Jumbo Cube. You don't want to know about the Africa of railway lines, underpasses, TV adverts and kitsch music. If you were here, you'd be itching to get out of this cynical, cruel, chaotic city and into the 'real Africa' the Sunday supplements have sold you. An Africa of masked dancers, honeycomb villages and majestic gliding rivers. And if you want that, you probably will find it. But will it *mean* anything? Because in Africa, reality lies in what is behind outward appearance. More than that, the thrust of its civilisation resides in its people to the extent that in Africa, the social, the communal, interacting dimension is *everything*. So what's the point of travelling thousands of miles to places that may look picturesque, but where because you know nobody, the underlying reality is going to elude you totally, when the elemental mystery you crave may be revealed to you right here, in the middle of all this hideous chaos and degradation?

You're as bad as Michael Heaven. He was obsessed with visiting the Dogon, a tribe in Mali, whose extraordinary cosmology and ritual life, carried on in honeycomb villages under this incredible lunar-like escarpment, have made them the country's number one tourist attraction. Pretty spectacular, but it's all been ruined by the snapping shutters and fatuous expectations of 'overlanders' and yuppie backpackers. But Heaven was determined to do some recording in one of these villages, and even do the video for his latest single there. So we took him to this village twenty miles outside N'Galam, where bare-breasted women were pounding millet outside thatched huts under monumental baobabs that glittered silver in the midday heat, and the elders sat gaunt and inscrutable in the kind of straw hats seen on ancient Greek vases – though there was a certain absence of escarpments.

I said, 'Is this all right?'

118

He said, 'Are these people Dogon?'

I said, 'No, the Dogon live a thousand miles to the east. But Mike, in Africa reality lies not in . . .' And I gave him the whole spiel, with a force and an eloquence that really should have been recorded.

He still wanted to go and see the Dogon. And I think he did in the end, though he ended up filming his video in a quarry near Newbury.

I'm sitting in a chi-chi Lebanese café just off the Avenue Wagane Diouf. It's virtually empty, and unlike the Belotel, with its drive, fences and security gates, there's the smoked glass of the bar window, then the crumbling, desiccated reality of the beggars and the marchands ambulants begins immediately. There's a brief pause in the bland international pop that plays continually, and I'm aware of this other voice, calling slowly and clearly from the street, and getting nearer all the time. A man's voice, deep and full, rising in nasal intensity in a tone stern, austere, admonitory, singing out – what is it, the suras? – the verses of the Koran. Then this figure appears, moving slowly and steadily past the window, a gaunt old man in a black robe with a stick. Yes, a blind beggar. And what a voice! As he moves slowly past, his voice rings out with that hard invocatory ring, which like his measured tread is all part of the fatalism, the stoic endurance of the Muslim world with its ever-present sense of the harshness and inevitability of divine justice – a world view so at odds with the callow hedonism of this bar it's nerve-janglingly hilarious. I slip out into the foyer, onto the front step, just as the old man is getting there, and slip a coin into his hand. 'Thank you,' he says, and proceeds on up the street. The moment his voice fades, the music resumes. Christ, it's so bland, I can hardly even describe it. It manages to include a bit of France, a bit of America, a bit of the Antilles, without representing any of them.

But that old guy's voice! I still get the same frisson whenever I hear a voice like that. One day, I'm going to do an album consisting entirely of blind beggars of N'Galam, recorded with such frightening aural veracity, they're actually *in* your living-room! And unlike someone like Michael Heaven, I'm not going to cushion the blow, tarting it up with 'ambient' soundscapes and all that balls, I'm just going to leave it there, in all its hard, imprecatory majesty – a stark and spine-chilling reproach to your entire world view.

Papa Gorgi Ngom had a voice very like that. Papa Gorgi – Sajar's old co-singer and rival in the original Lumière d'Afrique. He's only in his early forties, he's younger than me, but he still sounds like that. He sounded like that when he was twenty. He probably came out of th e womb singing with that hard and nasal, that unyielding seerlike edge.

And I haven't seen him for years. In fact meeting up with him was definitely on my list of things to do this trip. But so far I've done nothing about it. That's the trouble. You make plans, lists and agendas from the cloistered calm of your British operation, and when you get here, things go off on their own tangents – it's not so much a question of hitting the hard realities of here, as the fact that here has different rhythms and different imperatives which carry you off in other directions. I mean, if one is to take an informed historical overview of Tekrurian music, one has to say that Papa Gorgi Ngom is a figure of incalculable importance. But here now, there's so much going on, people haven't got time to look back. Papa Gorgi is an almost totally forgotten figure – someone who used to be in a band that happened to have Sajar Jopp in it twenty years ago. The fact that these guys were the first authentic Tekrurian pop stars is by the by. That'll have to wait for the historical reassessment, and *that* is a long way off. But one mustn't be complacent. It doesn't matter that I've been throwing Papa Gorgi's name into conversations with the deejays, executives and journalists who think they know something about World Music to looks of total bemusement and mystification, it doesn't matter that I'm one of the tiny handful of people in the West who have the slightest idea of what Tekrurian music is about – one day, totally out of the blue, some chi-chi little record label's going to dig up some acoustic album Papa Gorgi did on the side donkeys' years ago – so quietly even I wasn't aware of it – and it'll be hailed as a lost masterpiece by a neglected genius, and I won't make a penny from it. That's the trouble with being permanently in the vanguard, you end up unwittingly earning fortunes for the suits, the users and the free-lunch merchants. But not any more. This time, it's my turn.

The trouble with Papa Gorgi is that he always was a difficult bastard. If Sajar Jopp is the Paul McCartney of Tekrurian music, Papa Gorgi is the John Lennon. He's a genius, but he's got this tormented, self-destructive, cantankerous side to his personality. It was his jealousy of Sajar that broke up the original Lumière d'Afrique. And while Sajar had Super Lumière up and running almost immediately, Papa Gorgi and guitarist Salifou Nyang floundered about for years, drinking and grumbling and wondering what to do next. Then Mor Jeng, a car dealer and import/export millionaire said that if they could get a band together, he would provide the equipment. One night, they invited me to a rehearsal in Jeng's garage. Abdoulai Jallo, the sound engineer, a shy, nervous bloke, but the nearest thing this country's ever produced to a technical genius, had a four-track plugged into the mixing desk.

You couldn't by conventional standards have chosen a worse place to record, a great booming hangar full of scrap metal – and they were putting reverb on everything. Nyang, a Hendrix freak, was playing howling fuzz-box guitar. Talking drums were being put through echo chambers. The works! I'm thinking, Yeah, great idea, man, but it's going to be totally fucking inaudible.

Just before dawn, Jallo had finished tinkering with the one song, and we all got round to listen. The sound was like a great black hole, out of which the splintering shards of Salifou Nyang's guitar ushered in an itchy, scratching rhythm that went undulating endlessly up and down, while Papa Gorgi came down like the wolf on the fold – letting rip with a fierce, apocalyptic grandeur, colliding immediately with the talking drum, which came booming and reverberating right into the middle of your brain, knocking you totally off balance, while the tumbas and timbales went on rattling away, like a relentless hammering on hub-caps and dustbin-lids – and miles above it all, a single sax, mildly distorted by reverb, floated like a fading star.

121

Exciting? It was fucking terrifying, man! It made Iggy Pop sound like Derek Nimmo. It went on for about seven minutes, by which time we were all totally shattered. The musicians looked at each other uncertainly. They were just hearing it in terms of their own performances. They weren't capable of evaluating it as an overall sound experience – except Jallo, of course. He looked at me with an embarrassed half smile, then turned back to his four-track with a shy tilt of the head that said, 'I'm just going to tinker with this, grease it up with a bit of smarm and schmaltz, make it sound a bit more like Earth, Wind and Fire.'

My voice rang out, hard and magisterial, 'Don't even *think* of touching that!'

They all looked at each other, shrugged, and the tape was given to a boy who ran with it like the wind to the national radio station, where the announcer was just finishing reading the eight o'clock news. '. . . in the east of the country, where the Minister of Agriculture will be visiting a rice irrigation programme later this afternoon. And the weather outlook for Tekrur today is hot . . . and dry! Now here's a new group who I'm sure we'll be hearing a lot more about – Orchestre Fin de Siècle . . .' He'd named the group without even consulting them. And there was the squeal-ing, peremptory guitar, the humping rattling rhythm, the boom-ing declamatory vocal, and the unbelievable psychedelic talking drum reverberating through parts of your brain you didn't even know existed. The switchboard jammed. Crowds formed outside the radio building. All with the same question on their lips, 'What the hell is that?' When it was over, the breathless deejay played it again, and again. In fact, he played it non-stop all day long. The city went mad. The song resounded over every compound fence, from every market stall and taxi. Everyone was working and moving and thinking in time to it. That night, the club was packed to see the group playing live. Another song was recorded, and the next day two more. The master was flown to Paris for immediate duplication, and the next day five thousand copies of Orchestre Fin de Siècle were sold in the Marché Hakim Nder. The population was jubilant. Sajar Jopp was finished. He could never cap this. Papa Gorgi and the lads were the toast of Tekrur. Women thronged to them wherever they went.

When Sajar found out I'd been involved, he went bananas. He didn't speak to me for a year. But of course, when everything settled down – which it inevitably did – everything went back to normal. Sajar responded with 'Njouga', one of his most famous songs, and he was back on top again. Fin de Siècle made two more cassettes, more or less the same as the first, and gradually people lost interest. You see, Papa Gorgi and his mates weren't bothered about the future. They weren't, like Sajar, always thinking about the next step. As long as they left the club with a good-looking woman, a bottle of beer and a loaded spliff, they were happy. So they gradually disappeared from view. I have heard odd things about Papa Gorgi over the years – bad things – that he's suffered from severe depression, that he was seriously injured in a motor-cycle accident, that he's an alcoholic, that his last band went bust because he drank the profits. And of course, the usual stuff about how Sajar destroyed him through supernatural means. But he's a talented bloke, and these things always come round in circles. So I think it's high time I masterminded the Papa Gorgi revival, before someone else does.

Nine

I'm bored. I'm *really* bored. I'd forgotten how boring Africa can be. And it's the afternoons that are the worst. This great stillness and brightness with nothing going on. It's a long time since lunch – fish and rice – which we ate sweating in Doudou's room. Now we've gone dehors to try to keep cool, laying the mats out on the sand under the tree on the street corner for a game of cards. Did I want to play? No, thanks. I've never got the hang of these African card games, though they all seem immensely uninteresting. Anyway, I didn't come here to play knockout whist or whatever it is. But now they've got their afternoon-long tournament under way, I realise that's all there is. There's a ledge cut in the tree trunk, which I'm sitting on, leaning back against the sloping trunk. And I'm stuck here, the young people with their card game at my feet, the little girls sprawled in a languid stupor chatting and plaiting each others' hair, and all around, the empty white shambles of the street. Crumbling graffiti-spattered walls, a gang of kids running barefoot over the white-hot asphalt showing through the sand. Overhead, a chaos of telegraph poles and wires. At the other side of the road junction, on the ground floor of a three-storey residential building, a shop. A parked car. The occasional taxi grinding slowly and unhurriedly past. We're in Mbar, one of the more central quartiers populaires. There it is, on the left of the main road to the airport – just past the Medina – on the other side of the stinking canal. A drab, workaday kind of a place, nothing much to come here to see, but not so terrible – just ordinary people, the vast majority of them unemployed, getting on with their lives with remarkable placidity. People wander slowly past, elders in robes, young dudes in vests, shorts, shell suits, jeans, young women in everything from fluorescent cycling shorts to traditional patterned prints, grunting greetings, or pausing for an exchange of chuckling banter. Yes. Apart from the urban detail, we could be in a village in the middle of nowhere. This is Africa, man. The afternoon card game under the tree on the corner, the girls plaiting and inspecting each other for lice, remote in their slow and spacious languor, their murmured conversations, their hermetic female preoccupations – before the evening round of domestic tasks begins. The only difference is that in the villages of the bush, they'd be carrying great iron tubs of water on their heads – here they've got taps. Well, some of them have. Yes, this is Africa. You're sitting in the unchanging pattern of the essential Africa, and you're bored out of your mind. The young people, the affable, easy-going young men, the stick-chewing young women in traditional dress, apparently bovine, but with that African resilience very much there beneath the surface, they've all greeted me, they've all done some banter with me, tested my Wolof – bad, but that's cool. And now they're happy to leave me be. I can spend as much time with them as I want. I can eat their food, find a space on one of their beds, and that's cool. This is the Africa Africans miss when they're away. The Africa of chilling, the Africa of being with people, of just *being*. And this is the Africa the Plateau and all its works – plastic overpriced hotels like the Belotel, with their guards, security fences and electrified bougainvillea hedges – exist to keep at bay. The unmanageable, unhygienic, disease-ridden, uneducated, unpredictable Africa from which all the hustlers, hawkers and touts came swarming each morning. And that's what gives the would-be manicured European world, the 'controlled environment' of the Plateau, its sense of tension – the idea that it will be invaded by the denizens of the barbaric underworlds of the quartiers populaires, the eagle-eyed thieves, muggers and murderers that stalk its streets. But once you're actually out here, it's surprisingly placid with none of the semiological complexities, the edginess, the terrifying cultural and economic dislocations, none of the posturing, preposterous francophone bullshit you find at the harsh interface of the European and African worlds. Here there's none of that constant need to ask yourself what the fuck continent, what the fuck world, you're in. This is Africa. Everyone's speaking Wolof, everyone's a Muslim and, it goes without saying, everyone's poor. If you live in a place like this, it's part of your essential world-view that you're poor. But no one's going to bother you here. The people who're going to give you a hard time are back up on the Plateau, loitering in the streets round your hotel. They'd never think of looking for you here. Even the taxi-drivers are more human here. And it's a little bit boring. Check. It's incredibly boring. I could get someone to take me to the little market a few streets away, to get some cassettes. But when I got there, I'd find he'd been leaving them out in the sun, or he'd been slipping them out of their cellophane covers to make his own pirate copies, thereby subjecting them to all the lacerating dust, static and electromagnetic malevolence of his gear. And you'd have to say you'd leave it for this time, while the guy who brought you there has already told him you're going to buy *massive* quantities. So the owner gets the hump and your guy feels ashamed and annoyed with you, and they both feel you're somehow belittling not only the production standards of their country's cassette-duplicating industry, but the cultural achievements of their entire race. So it's better not to risk it. It's definitely better not to risk it.

So here I sit, almost a prisoner, as the slow hours drift through the white heat of the afternoon, and the card players work through all the endless permutations of their tournament. Everybody's happy. It's only you, the white man – you have to destroy time's ineffable equilibrium by wanting to actually *do* something. But you can't help it. That's the way you are. Not like that woman over there, the one leaning forward as a younger girl with a baby on her back picks through her thick Nubian tresses for nits – the one with the exquisite pouting profile. There is something about the hauntingly perfect ovalness of her face, the steady implacable

126

coolness of her gaze, the no doubt exquisitely aromatic silkiness of her inner vestiges, that proclaims an ease, a languorous sultry self-sufficiency. Immersed in the stupefying hypnotic fatalism of the African woman's world, she doesn't have to keep reminding herself how big her record collection is in order to justify her existence. She's beautiful, and from where I'm sitting, that's enough.

I should try to be more like her: leaning back on the tree trunk, my hands resting easily on my parted thighs, seated in immemorial potency. Requiring nothing, yielding nothing, radiating a still and ruthless composure – a basalt monument to my own cool . . .

The woman gets up, and I realise she's about twelve.

Yeah, yeah. All right. I couldn't tell from that angle. And anyway, the women here develop at a different rate. That's right, you say. They develop more *slowly*! So don't try that, you sad onanist!

But in Africa, it's all around you. The rhythms of the women's world of domestic labour and childbirth – that endless inescapable cycle of pregnancy, birth, confinement, breast-feeding. And although as a man, you're more distanced from it, in a ritual sense, than you would be in Europe, in fact it's all going on continually, right under your nose. It's like a kind of buzz, a perfume of which you're continually half-aware, comfortingly subsuming some essential part of you into the seraphic fug of the women's world.

But I can't quite work out how this particular compound operates. Because normally the eldest male member is the compound head. But here it's the oldest woman, who Doudou calls his grandmother – he is in fact only a friend of the family who rents a room, though because he's the most educated person – he's an accountant – he's taken on the status of an elder and adviser. Otherwise the place seems to consist entirely of divorced women and their progeny. 'Cause there's part of at least one other family living in the rooms on the other side of the yard – and that's where the funky women, the real foxes are at. I keep getting glimpses of long, caramel thighs, of coolly disapproving eyes regarding me from around long braids, as they go about their pounding and water-fetching half-naked. Christ, man, it doesn't bear thinking about.

Yes. He's at it again! *Litchfield!* You're here to work, not daydream about African jailbait. Work? Whatever happened to that? I haven't had even one conference, let alone got anything actually organised since I've been here – unless you count bumping into Sidi Taal in the street. And I don't. All that's happened is that Africa's Greatest Musician has accused me of robbing him. And I can't quite get my head round the reality of even that. But of course even now, I am working. I'm working, because I'm in it. I'm *in it* – and I'm bored out of my mind.

Much later, far, far into the whiteness of the afternoon, I become aware of a rhythm, resonating blunt into the empty air. The kids along the street rapping on old plastic canisters – a stick in one hand, the other left bare, like the real drummers here. Oh, yes, after years of exposure to this kind of thing, you can identify the sound: the hard sting of stick on empty plastic. At first just an aimless endless thrashing, echoing and resounding against the crumbling walls and corrugated iron roofs. But then there's a particular rhythm they keep coming back to, that their hard sticks find in unison: that ends with two raps apart, then two close together: brap ... brap ... bra-brap!

Yes, that's familiar. And it's hardly surprising. If you hang around places like this long enough it gets in your blood and bones, without you even being aware of it. And they're playing it at a slower than usual tempo, thwacking out the insistent coda with an earnest deliberate relish ...

Thwack ... thwack ... thwa-thwack!
Tumbi dudlu ba-ba ... baba dubidum
... *urgh ... urgh ... ur-urgh!*

Oh, yes. There's no doubting what *that* rhythm's all about! Because it's not just the sounds themselves, it's the spaces around them. If I was to hit that coda out for you now, it would just be four slaps of a stick. But put it in context, and you've got that swinging volley of rhythm ... Hurum bi dubbadoo rapbap ... dubidum ...

Then there's a pause with maybe one deep *dum* you can hardly hear, making your bangles roll and your hips gyrate, before the sticks poke in together ...

Crack! Crack! ... Crack-Crack!

But as I say, man. You've gotta hear it in situ. You've gotta *be there*. And as I sit here on this endless supine African afternoon, it's the only hint of the other side of the African coin: the wild side.

Doudou, the acountant, sticks his head up between games. Lord, he'd almost forgotten I was here! It's a holiday, I say, isn't that the time for les manifestations? Les manifestations, les évènements traditionels, généralement avec danse de tam-tams. Oui, quelque chose assez amusant et un peu fou pour les femmes et les enfants. Yes, yes. Doudou nods. He's a reasonable, thoughtful, civilised sort of a bloke, happy to be a Frenchman if that's what I want him to be. In general, yes. But at the moment, it's not common. It's rare. He shrugs. It's the economic conditions. And of course, les temps modernes. There isn't the interest.

One of the women asks what I said. He explains and she protests vigorously in Wolof, pointing to a small poster on the other side of the street beside the shop. Doudou apologises with mildly bemused surprise. There will in fact be a manifestation today, of the simba – 'le faux lion'. Yeah, yeah. I've heard of this, but I've never actually seen it. A masquerade based on a ceremony where a man is possessed by the spirit of a lion, the totem of the clan of Njai, of Njaajan Njai, mythic ancestor of the Wolof people, founder of the Djolof empire. Sajar himself used it as part of his stage act for a time, particularly for a song about the Lions – the Tekrurian national football team.

It starts at five. One hour's time. I'm not interested, assumes Doudou. I'm interested. Vraiment? He thought I was only interested in modern music, Sajar Jopp-type music, not mad antics for women and kids. He asks the women where it's

129

happening. C'est un peut loin, he says hopefully. That's no problem. He shrugs. Okay, then. No peace for the wicked, he's thinking.

C'est un peu sauvage, n'est ce pas?

Le simba? He's back in the card game now. Pas vraiment.

Pas dangereux?

Pas du tout! C'est seulement pour l'amusement! If they catch you without a ticket, they make you dance. C'est pas grave.

I don't know whether to be relieved or disappointed. Don't know whether I would have liked something dangerous or not.

The afternoon wears endlessly on. Then all of a sudden, the colour is rushing visibly back into the world, the slanting bars of golden light cut down over the iron rooftops, and it's evening. The interminable card game is over and everyone is on their feet. D'accord? says Doudou, probably unaware of how reproachful his look is.

The place turns out not to be very far at all. Round a couple of corners of the sandy street, greeting everyone as we pass, along a stretch of wide road lined with raggedy stalls, the sun low and red behind us, casting our shadows long over the sand and asphalt ahead, and we can already hear the nasally exultant singing of the griots, horrifyingly distorted through loudspeakers, booming out over the rooftops, as though some slightly deranged religious ceremony were taking place.

Shit! A shiver passes up my spine. And at the same time a wave of exhaustion and slight nausea. Can I do this? Am I well enough to be doing this? Shouldn't I be back at the Belotel, lying on my bed with the air-conditioning on? And under the singing is the mid-paced cracking of the drums, just starting to get into their stride, and holding back as the excitement builds to the appropriate pitch. Yes, man! You're in it. The drums! And the thing that's always disconcerting when you first hear real drums in Africa is how loud they are: their volume all part of the wood and the skin and the earth and the very heat itself. Somehow you just don't get that same sound outside Africa. No, it's not going to be dangerous. But these things have a habit of getting a bit over-excited. There's going to be a lot of pushing and jostling, a lot of charging about. I'm already shaking. I don't want to be here. I want to go home. We turn a corner, and the drumming and the mad-sounding singing is suddenly much louder. The broad street ahead is blocked by a great crowd of people, all with their backs to us, with a few kids and young guys lingering along the street, looking watchfully back towards the crowd. Suddenly, without warning, half the crowd starts stampeding towards us in this sudden desperate shuffling of feet. You can feel the energy of terror. Then, as suddenly, they stop and fall back towards the dancing circle.

I eye Doudou with alarm.

'No, no. You will be fine.' I can tell he's now glad he came, caught up in the adrenalin, the electric tension crackling through the dusty evening air. 'As long as you have a ticket . . .'

A ticket! I haven't got a ticket! Gimme a ticket!

He laughs. 'Okay. Okay.' Then he calls to a young man and buys us all tickets.

I secrete mine deep in one of the hidden pockets of my Striders. If I lose my ticket I'm doomed.

We reach the edge of the crowd, the usual bickering, chattering, giggling young women and girls – though they're paying more than usual attention to what's going on in the centre. All around the middle of the central square of the quartier are seated hundreds of kids, legs outstretched. Behind them, more kids, and behind them the young women and matrons in brilliant turbans and boubous, and behind them are crowded hundreds and hundreds more onlookers and, pushing and thrusting among their legs, all the young men and kids who deliberately haven't bought tickets. Immediately in front of us are the drummers, a ragged bunch of guys, among whom the tempo is rapidly building. It's loud, man, and it makes you shake inside. Over on the other side, two griots, a man and a woman in robes, are bellowing into microphones, a harsh incantatory singing, horrendously distorted so that not one syllable is audible, but adding greatly to the sense of derangement and panic. Patrolling the edges of the circle are two tall women in grotesquely bright

131

dresses and cheap wigs of bobbed straight hair. But it's the way they walk that gives them away. That's right, they're men! Men dressed as women, their faces thickly painted with the features of lions. In the centre of the circle is a mound of sand with three large plastic basins of liquid, and beside that, something or someone draped in the tricolour of the Tekrurian flag. A guy comes over, raises the edge of the flag, and appears to speak to whatever or whoever is underneath it. The figure moves and there's a roar of trepidation from the crowd. All around people are shoving, jostling and arguing, kids without tickets are pushing between our legs. The demented wailing of the griots goes on unabated, of which I can catch only the word 'Njai' – the gainde, the simba, the lion! It's chilling, man! And where *is* the lion?

All the time, the drum rhythms are pumping, and at each mini-crescendo, the men-women, prancing and cavorting in the middle of the circle, rolling their eyes and smiling with sinister glee, perform a vigorous stamping dance, at the final beat of which they raise their skirts, thrusting their belegginged loins at the crowd.

Suddenly there's a wave of panic. Women are screaming and hollering, the kids between our legs are desperately trying to shove their way back out of the crowd. Half the crowd is now running desperately back down the road along which we came. Then they suddenly stop, turn, and we see a bizarre figure, a brown blur, seemingly half-human, half-animal, dragging a whimpering child through the crowd. The child, a boy, blubbering, insensible with terror, is hauled into the centre of the circle and thrown down by the basins of water, where the gainde, a thickly made-up figure in a crown and cloak of fur, his massively muscular body bristling with hundreds of amulets and gris-gris, stands over him, his bulging loins alarmingly close to the child's miserable face. The audience howl with a mixture of derision and sympathy, the drummers hammer and flail, the men-women leap and cavort, as the lion's arms swing wildly above the gibbering child, finally bringing a blow down hard in the centre of his back, rubbing sand in his hair and sending him howling back into the crowd.

That's a bit much! Doudou smiles at me weakly, and I can tell he thinks so too. And he said all they did was make you dance! The gainde turns and looks hungrily into the crowd, as whatever it is under the flag moves again, to squeals and roars from the crowd. I'm not feeling at all well. I can feel the drums pumping in my head, and the tension is becoming unbearable. Because I know that when they see me, they're going to get me in that circle whether I've got a ticket or not. They're going to throw me down in the sand and humiliate me, to the mixed horror and delight of everybody there. Why? Because I'm white. And because I'm there. I'm almost in tears with the injustice of it. And I'm not well.

I can just see two of the drummers over the wildly heaving shoulders of the crowd. One, a little bloke in a bandanna, has got his drum balanced on a chair beside him, and he's just thrashing out this steady metallic rhythm:

Burrak-a-tak!
Burrak-a-tak!

His mate, seated beside him, has got the deep-pitched lead drum, the mbungbung, clenched between his knees as he pummels out these punching, furious cross-rhythms – beats heard deep under the main drag of the rhythm, in your solar plexus and deep underneath your brain – flailing demonically at the hard dry skin, his face a contorted mask of effort. I don't know what they put in my lunch, but it wants to come out – urgently! But I can't leave. All these people have come here for my benefit. And if the lion sees me trying to slope off alone, that'll be it.

My entire body's becoming a critical mass of pressure. And if I don't drink something soon, my head feels as though it's going to explode. You idiot! You haven't drunk since lunchtime. This is Africa! The tropics! You've allowed yourself to get dehydrated, and you've been dragged to this mad African mayhem, where you're going to collapse fatally, your bowels exploding over the

133

crowd as you go. It's getting darker by the moment, the ashy, dusty air thickening all around, as fights start to break out among the boys and youths on the edge of the crowd. The rhythmic mayhem that's turned me into a jangling wreck is spreading its emotional chaos. Suddenly I feel a jab in my ribs. I turn and look straight into the face of the lion. Another lion! Where's he popped up from? Shit! He wants my ticket! I'm searching furiously through the pockets of my Striders, and I can't find it. The lion, short and horrifyingly muscular, his oiled torso so laden with leather gris-gris it's almost invisible, his midriff festooned with whip-like leather belts sewn with bits of the Koran, mirrors to ward off the evil eye, bits of horn, necklaces of cowries, his eyes bulging and gleaming through his thick make-up, is pulling on my arm. Come on, into the circle! Everyone else is remonstrating with him, 'Please, leave him! He's a foreigner, he doesn't know the rules, he's too old for this and he's not well!' But the lion's going to have me. I'm going to be dragged in there, where I'll shit myself in front of everybody. And I'm still desperately fumbling with the zip of my second secret pocket. *Where the fuck is it?* Gottit! Right at the bottom. A tiny, flimsy bit of paper, already crushed into a ball. I unravel it, shaking, and having inspected it, the lion heads off up the street, creating a stampede of panic as he goes. My heart's pounding, my head's creaking, and what about my bowels? My legs feel weak. I look at Doudou. Let's go, man! But he's already absorbed in something else. The louts, dudes and assorted riff-raff of N'Galam scattered by the lion are already pressing in around us. The crowd heaves as two guys go for each other, a guy in a red bandanna aiming kung-fu kicks at another's head. We move away. But I don't like it. All these people have got knives. Haven't they? Meanwhile, back in the circle, the flag's been removed, revealing the most major of the lions. He's built like a brick shit-house, and there is something unnervingly animal about his eyes, gleaming feral through the black bandit mask of make-up. He moves slowly and theatrically, his eyes suddenly twitching back and forth over the audience, while the griots go into overdrive. All I can pick out is 'Njai'. Njai Jatta Njai. Dom ou Gainde Njai. Njai, the lion, Njai! Njai, son of the Lion!

134

Sahare wale! The drums have hit a steady tumbling beat. But instead of being able to sway in time, we're being shoved back and forth as more fights break out around us. I'm looking at the lions, but all I can think of is the story of that American girl who went to do good in the townships of South Africa. That blue-eyed, corn-fed golden girl, who everybody loved, who was dragged from her car and stuck full of holes by a bunch of knife-wielding 'comrades'. What had she done? What had she *done*? She'd done nothing other than go there to help out – succeeding, earning herself a position of trust and affection among the women with whom she worked. But she was *white*, wasn't she? 'We don't want you,' they said to her black friends as they dragged her from the car, laughing as their eager blades went to work. Yes, she was white. I'm white. I'm the only white person here. That's why I'm going to get it. Yes, you say, but that was in South Africa. This is Tekrur. There's absolutely no comparison. Why have you got to bring in South Africa and Liberia? *Liberia?* Who mentioned Liberia? Do *not* mention Liberia!

In the circle, the lions – and there are five of them – are doing a frenzied, stamping dance. Yes, it's all cohering. It's getting there. And I recognise the rhythm. It's *that* rhythm – and it's fast.

Nga-dugudu-dungung . . . Rabadan . . .

And the drummers thrash down hard:

Ba – ba – ba-bah!

Once established, there's no stopping them. The lions are in the crowd, the stampede, and at each coda the audience goes wild:

Tass . . . Tass . . . Tass-tass!

The lead drummer's got a long, sharp-voiced drum round his waist, and he's out there in the middle of the circle adding furious, shattering syncopations, while this old woman's dancing with her legs wide apart, and at every coda she thrusts her loins forward:

Urgh! .... Urgh! ... Ur-urgh!

I can't stand it! I love it, but I can't stand it! I've got to get out of here before I shit myself, and before the white blubber of my flesh gives me away to the knives of N'Galam. Really! I've got to go! Then suddenly, everyone's looking at me. What's going on? The shorter of the men-women, the one with the cheeky impish grin, is beckoning me into the circle. Everyone's tittering with glee. The crowd parts. No! No! Everyone's gesturing me smiling into the circle. No, I can't. I look at Doudou. He's smiling and pointing into the circle. I tell him to come with me, and he follows as I'm led to the Simba – the greatest of the lions – the Domou Gainde, the son of a lion himself. There's a sharp intake of breath from the crowd, a great boggling of eyeballs. 'You must dance!' hisses Doudou. There's a great roar from the crowd as I start to swing my limbs in time. Yes, the white man is doing it! But the lion gestures me sternly to stop. I must dance as *he* tells me. He leans forward, making sweeping movements with his arms, which I try to copy, then these weird mystical hand movements – and I'm shaking so much I can hardly do 'em. But I've acquitted myself, and he waves me sternly from his sight. But the man-woman gestures me back, and he, the lion and I line up, as a well-dressed Tekrurian steps from the crowd and snaps our picture. 'Thank you, my friend,' he says, slapping me on the shoulder. 'Another one for the archive!'

The crowd is in uproar, everyone grabbing me, slapping my back and roaring with delight as I step from the circle. I'm trembling so much I can hardly walk. All I've got to do is get back to the house before I crap myself.

'Why don't you come with us?'
I'm standing there behind the door. I hear the car door shutting. *Get out there, man.*
I'm through the front door. Then the porch door. The rush of

cold air. And there's the bloke from next-door, locking his car door. He turns and sees me.

'Any chance of you trimming this hedge back?'

I just stand there on the driveway in my dressing-gown, looking at him. Then I turn and head back into the house to put something on. Something sweet and soulful. Something to block it all out.

It's one o'clock in the morning by the time I stagger up the drive of the Belotel, encrusted from head to foot in sweat, filth and every form of unnamable pollution – my own and other people's.

'Hey! Copain!'

The voice is right beside me, barking virtually in my fucking ear. Shit. *Now what?*

'Tu viens de quoi? Erh? Chercher *jigennes*?' and there's a raw and jagged guffaw, like a Southend bootboy with a major throat infection. I know that laugh.

An arm grabs me round the neck, and there's a demonic snigger in my ear.

'Tu es bad boy, erh?'

That's right. Sajar's driver.

Thanks for scaring the shit out of me, man.

'T'aimes la musique tekrurienne?' he asks as we go careering over the crossroads by the Marché Hakim Nder.

'Je l'adore.'

'Tu l'adores!' he hits the wheel with enthusiasm, tittering through his teeth. 'Tu es vagabond!'

We come to another junction – a sea of broken glass glowing spectrally in the feeble streetlight. He ploughs straight into it.

'What's happened?'

'Avec quoi?'

'The er . . . verre, sur la rue.'

'C'est les er . . . les chauffeurs fous. Erh?' He rolls his eyes, twisting his finger against his temple. '*Fous?*'

I turn and see the back of a guy in a wheelchair, leisurely wheeling himself down the centre of our lane. I can practically

137

count the lines on his neck as we bear down on him at a speed that's going to wipe him from the face of the earth and not do us any good either.

'*Regard!*'

He flicks the wheel and we go spinning into deep space. 'Tu vois, erh?' he says turning to me with a triumphant leer. '*Fou!*'

'Er ... where are we going?'

'*Going?*'

'Er ... où on va?'

'C'est Sajar. He wants to see you.'

Christ, man. Sajar and his money. I can't bear it. I should have been in bed hours ago.

On the highway past the Medina, we pull off, swaying and bumping over the broad dust verge, scattering beggars, promenading youth and women – still trying to offload their three oranges – and plunge into a black gap between the buildings. This isn't where Sajar lives.

'Na-a-awnh!' He scoffs at the absurdity of the suggestion. 'C'est la maison de Nyanya Guisse!'

Nyanya Guisse! What the hell are we doing here?

The car stops. The driver shouts at the kids who are already gathering round 'Sajar Jopp's car'. Then he gestures me through the ill-lit gateway.

Ahead is a dim doorway. Inside, two guys in baseball caps are standing under a lightbulb so dim it would be probably be lighter if they turned it off. I proffer greetings, taking their hands for the cursory shake as is obligatory here. They respond, totally non-committal.

'Where's Sajar?'

They look blank.

'Where's Nyanya?'

One of them flicks his hand at the doorway ahead. The courtyard is in darkness, and on the far side, a doorway with music and light and laughter coming from it.

Nyanya Guisse in gold-embroidered tarboush and blue damask gown is sprawled on the bed, holding court to various louts, dudes and members of Sajar's band, all ranged and sprawled and spreadeagled over the rest of the bed, the furniture, the walls and each other. Nyanya holds up a hand graciously.

'Yeah, man. Nice to see you. Have a seat, wai!'

Total remote control. Does he remember me even from the other day?

The others take my hand half-heartedly. I nod to lead guitarist Mamadou Faye, rhythm guitarist Tapha Jain and bass player Doudou Ndow. They nod back with a kind of absent courtesy, as though they can't understand why I'm paying particular attention to them.

We're already back into the lubricious anecdote, being retailed in a succession of elastic expostulations each more eye-poppingly forceful than the last, with guffaws, interlocutions from the others, over which Nyanya exerts a kind of editorial control – his tone of droll and immemorial knowing eliciting grunts and nods of assent and amusement. The story, if it had any point, comes to an end and someone else takes over.

I'm sat behind the only pillar in the room – a pillar, what do they need a pillar for? – totally blocked out. Ignored. Nobody's casting so much as a glance in my direction. Don't they have even the slightest curiosity as to what the fuck I'm doing here? If I didn't know Africa, I'd be really hurt. If I didn't know Africa I'd have tears in my eyes, man. But this *is* Africa. You can just come and join them. But it's up to you to fit in, to earn your place. Oh, yes, it's always up to you. Particularly if you're white, you've got to prove *your* good intentions to *them*. You've got to make all the running. And of course, if you're white, your novelty value, your instant celebrity potential, may give you advantages in some quarters. But not here. *Among these guys?* Are you kidding? These guys have seen it all ten times over, and they weren't interested in the first place. These guys are ten times better travelled than you or I will ever be. So don't come in here all white and wide-eyed and expect to be patted on the head: these guys are as blasé as it gets. And of course, they're musicians. And believe me, because I do know, there is no more callous, mean-spirited and begrudging group of people than musicians. It doesn't matter that you take them from gigs in toilets to Madison Square Garden, breaking up

139

your marriage, losing your house and bankrupting yourself in the process, they will always regard you as an outsider and an exploiter. You go to the ends of the earth for them because you believe in their talent, because you believe in *them*, and they'll drop you without a second thought. The idea that they had any obligation towards you would never enter their head in a million years. And this is true regardless of culture, from Javanese gamelans to the Royal Philharmonic: basically they're all just bastards. Believe me, there's no pain like the pain you feel the first time you've been *fucked* by musicians.

Take that guy there sniggering away at the current anecdote, which I can't believe can be that funny, Tapha Jain, Sajar's rhythm guitarist, one of the older, and actually one of the more mature and responsible members of the group, drawing on a Benson with that gaunt urbanity and neat moustache that say, 'Yes, I'm urban.' Oh, yes. I've been all over this country with that guy, sharing not only the japes and jests, but the same bed, the same bowl of food, falling asleep on each other's shoulders during endless hours in airless tour buses. Oh, yes, you can't hide on an African tour – you're literally *one*. But now he's totally ignoring me. He's behaving as though he doesn't even know me. As though he's got no idea who I am. Maybe he doesn't recognise me. Maybe he's forgotten. Maybe . . . Maybe he genuinely has no idea who I am!

I go into a kind of stupor. You cannot sit for hours listening to energetic conversations not one word of which you can understand, in hot rooms in the middle of the night, particularly when you're not feeling that great, without going into a kind of stupor. I look at my watch. Oh, yes. Time. I'd forgotten that existed. That European thing of instinctively knowing what time it is? Of looking at your watch and it always being within ten minutes of what you thought it would be? Forget that. That doesn't work here. I feel like I'm looking down at my watch through a great chasm.

It's half past three!

I lean over to the guy nearest me. He turns, his eyes narrowing in annoyance – like, how dare I interrupt this incredibly good anecdote! Then his eyes widen in alarm. *Sajar?* I'm looking for Sajar, *here*?

Tapha Jain leans across. What's the matter?

'You want to see Sajar?' he asks in English. 'Sajar is not here.'

'The driver brought me here to see him.'

He looks back at me, genuinely concerned – and mystified. He turns to Nyanya Guisse. The room falls silent. Sajar? everyone's wondering.

'Yeah,' says Nyanya Guisse. 'Sajar was going to come here, but he decided not to.'

Tapha Jain shrugs. 'It's too late, now. Maybe if you telephone him tomorrow.'

'You know me, man,' I say.

His eyes narrow.

'Dans les Etats-Unis?'

'Oui. Et ici. Beaucoup, beaucoup de fois. Une grande tournée!'

'C'est sûr!' he nods, wrinkling his nose and showing his gums. 'Nice time, eh?'

'I remember you, man,' bellows bassplayer Doudou Ndow from his position prostrate beneath the bed-head.

'How could we forget?' asks Nyanya Guisse, hurt that I could think of it. Everyone else nods in agreement.

I get to my feet and they all shout to me to sit down. 'Stay and chat with us.' I say I've got to work in the morning. Okay, they say, work is important. Nyanya sends his nephew to help me find a cab. I'm asleep on my feet. Did they remember me? Did they fuck.

Ten

Who does Sajar Jopp think he is? Someone comes two thousand miles to see you. Someone who's put themselves out for you and your family on many, many occasions. *Put themselves out?* Someone who's got their muscle behind you, who's talked about you, written about you, hyped you relentlessly, made connections, opened doors for you, ensured the red carpet's laid out for you at every possible juncture, for the sole reason that they believe in you and your work, that they actually love what you do, comes all the way to your country for the sole purpose of seeing you, and you ignore them totally. Would you do that? No, you wouldn't. So who is Sajar Jopp anyway?

Sajar Jopp is a fucking chancer, who's somehow managed to convince the entire media of the Western world – and let's face it, that's the media that counts – that he's the only Tekrurian musician of any consequence, that all the stylistic breakthroughs and developments that have taken place here over the last twenty years, which in reality have had the input of hundreds of people, were created totally by him – off the top of his head, as it were. Having ingratiated himself with some of the world's richest, most powerful and influential rock stars, he assumed a totally spurious mantle of 'Africa's greatest musician' – a distinction which, since Africa is not a single heterogeneous cultural entity, cannot be evaluated, other than by the number of column inches generated in the Western media, and thus immediately became a de facto actuality. So having achieved this position of international greatness, he returned to his own country, to consolidate a dominance that had itself been achieved largely by destroying other people's careers. And who's allowed him to get away with it? Me, that's who!

Wait a minute, you're saying. What about Michael Heaven? Surely the person who really got Sajar exposure in the West, the person who took him on all those mega-tours, who escorted him personally onto the stage at all those immense good-cause jamborees – like the AIDS gig – that were broadcast live to every corner of the known universe, was Michael Heaven? No. *No.* Because I doubt very much if it hadn't been for all my diamond-honed hustling, my hypercharged mythmaking, my relentless going on, that Michael Heaven would have been that interested. I mean, the guy's no fool. He makes out he's been into African music since he was six, but the fact is, he could see it coming, he could feel the buzz. And the buzz was created by me. But all those prestige events are in a way irrelevant, less important than getting through to the people who write the blurb for the *Radio Times* ('a profile of Africa's greatest musician') and the cheap-CDs-with-four-pints offers ('superb new album by Africa's greatest musician'), because those are the things people absorb without realising it, and the people who write them are amazingly open to modest coercion, and if you can get things said enough times in those kind of places, it becomes *reality*, man.

So, although just about everybody in the West has now heard of Sajar Jopp, could they actually name a single one of his songs, could they hum one of his tunes, could they even identify his voice – inimitable though it undoubtedly is? Of course not. Have all these albums he's recorded for the Western majors with the input of his rockstar friends actually made a dent in the market, let alone the collective consciousness? Have they fuck. Because they are, in fact, extremely dull. His live shows are full of colour and spectacle, and a controlled African 'wildness' he thinks the West wants, but is he actually personally that charismatic? Questionable. Sajar in interviews is incredibly boring, because he always says what he thinks people want to hear. Sajar himself is incredibly boring. He's never read a book in his life, except for a hagiographic biography of himself. He's not interested in anything other than furthering his own career.

So why, you ask, have you bothered? I've bothered because I love Africa. I care about Africa. And when you let Africa get into you. When you've really *seen it*. When you've allowed Africa to become an abiding, a dominating feature in your life, you realise how amazingly little regard or feeling for Africa most people have. Even very well educated people know *amazingly* little about Africa, and it doesn't even occur to them that they ought to know about it. Africa is just this chaotic, dangerous, amorphous mass of backwardness, a repository for Western pity and disgust, a destination for the odd safari holiday. The idea that Africa might have a 'greatest musician', and that they ought to know about him, is not something that even occurs to them. So I decided it would be good for them, and good for Africa, if they did know, and if, despite all the horrors, Africa had someone out there selling his CDs with four pints of milk. That's why I did it.

And of course, I did it because Sajar's a genius. Oh, yes. He's a genius all right. But although he craves international fame and acceptance more than anything else, it's the very things that make him a genius – the things I personally would want to listen to in his music – that will never in a million years translate to a mass global audience. That's the tragic paradox of Sajar Jopp.

So here I am. I *have* come all this way. I'm languishing in this plastic hotel room. I'm sitting endlessly by this fatuous swimming pool. And after all the effort I've made, effort I made only because I wanted to – for which I did not receive one penny of direct remuneration – Sajar it seems would not bother to piss on me if I was on fire.

And it would be typical of him that, if I was to confront him, if I was to say to him, 'What about everything I've done for you?' he'd turn with amazing impudent arrogance and say, 'You haven't done anything for me.' Oh, yes. Sajar and all his brothers and sisters, his apparatchiks and henchmen, they're forever getting in and out of gleaming Space Cruisers, in the latest designer sportswear. They've got the faxes, the computers, the mobile phones. But can they be bothered to return your call? You're just some stupid toubab they vaguely remember came here before. But it wasn't like that in the old days, when they were back in the dusty bustle of the Medina. In those days, if anybody wanted to write an article or make a film, they'd be all over them. They'd be made one of the family. And the first thing they had to do was visit Sajar's granny, the font of the family's griot wisdom, and she'd recite the genealogies. And all the kids of the quarter would descend on you in a screaming, hilarious rabble. Now if you go to them with a project like that, they look haughtily down their nose at you and say, 'Who exactly are you?' But they can't make a decision. Oh, no. Sajar's educated all these people up for these positions – at considerable expense – and you can only get to him through them, but everything still has to come back to him. So it doesn't work. He's made this nouveau-riche African parody of a Western major. And it does not work. That's the grotesque thing.

But why am I worrying about that? I've got a million and one far more interesting things I could be getting on with here. Only problem is it's Sunday, and nothing happens in N'Galam on a Sunday. Sunday is a day when you really need something concrete to do in N'Galam, or you could get very bored and very lonely.

That's why I decided to organise a bit of an excursion. Oh, yeah? Where to? The Isle des Esclaves? Too tricky with the ferries. Down to the plage for a swim? Er . . . I think you're joking. If I was to actually get down there without being hit over the head, my clothes, watch and money would be heisted the second I got in the water. No, I'm going to the museum. *The museum?* But Litch, I hear you say, you're into *living* culture – stuff that's *out there*, that's *in your face*. You're not into peering at what some fusty pompous bastard's seen fit to put in a glass case – which in a place like this is going to be what some fusty pompous French bastard in the 1950s put there. Right? Wrong. I am interested in things like that. Very interested. But not in your modern 'interesting' kind of museum with VDUs, push-button displays and politically correct neo-structuralist explanations. No, I like the

145

old, 'uninteresting' kind of museums, with long echoing halls, full of exhibits left unchanged for decades to steep in their doom-laden resonances, with painstakingly typed labels peeling from the displays. I like to visit them in the dead of winter, an hour before closing time, when there's absolutely nobody else there, and they're filled with an eerie spectral light. Spooky, eh? And there's something about the pathos of such places, particularly when left behind amid the sad irremediable scruffiness of a place like this, that I find profoundly moving.

It's like my collection, the voices and the sounds locked within the black vinyl grooves in the protective slithers of their inner sleeves, the defining covers with their images of the grandes vedettes, the most jondo del jondo, packed back to back, unseen, invisible in the darkness, the tomblike stillness of the many vaults, corridors and repositories of my collection, till the moment comes when I, the great custodian, the keeper, the defining intelligence, have the time to sort them according to chronological, alphabetical, geographical order or whatever other criterion I decide to use. That, when it happens, will be an immense satisfaction – when I create the world, as it were, in my own image, when all the resonances of this music that I have invested in, believed in, saved from the immense tonnage tumbling towards oblivion, will be paid back to me.

The Place de la République is frighteningly empty. Odd figures sitting listlessly in doorways, the occasional person standing totally motionless for no apparent reason in the dusty brilliance, and virtually no traffic. Once again, I'm tired. I'm shattered.

Under the overhang of that great tower block, where the touts, hustlers and cigarette-sellers hang out, it's virtually deserted. But I stay well out, heading calmly and steadily up towards the official district – not looking about, just walking purposefully onwards. It's not yet ten, and I imagine the bad people are mostly still in bed. But you've still got to faire attention. At the top of the great dusty expanse of the square heading into the Avenue Roume, I can see, from the corner of my eye, a loping, loose-limbed guy, crossing the street to speak to me. But all he wants is to know the time.

As I head on with the iron weight of the heat, the delirium-inducing brilliance upon me, into the deserted streets of the official quarter, the dust-blown ill-looking apartment blocks, the bunker-like official residences crouching behind their security walls and parched bougainvillea hedges, the peeling, flaking ministries, their endless rows of venetian blinds all hanging at different angles, I feel this sudden and overwhelming sense of loneliness and desolation. And it's not so much because of the rundownness, the dustworn, crumbling scruffiness of everything around me, not so much to do with time passing, with so many of the mid-century hopes and ideals of newly independent Africa having disintegrated into the brittle termite-ridden earth, with the fact of the moral epicentre of the city having departed from this quasi-European official quarter down into the teeming mayhem of the Medina, as with the deadening harshness and brilliance of the light itself – its relentless uniform monotony, day after endless day – and the grey, glittering monochrome it imposes. Oh, yes. You holiday in warmer climes because you think it's somehow inherently life-enhancing, that the sun of itself confers happiness. I mean, you're probably thinking, Litch – what's he complaining about? He's got the manor sorted. He knows everyone. He's got better contacts here than anyone. Why doesn't he just come and live here? 'I would!' you say. But you wouldn't. Not if you'd really seen it. Because, believe me, however much you may think you'd like to live in the tropics, if you did, you would one day find yourself walking down a street like this, through the empty, bleak brilliance that drives man and beast for cover, that seems to drain, to dissolve all hope and ambition, and you'd think, 'I shouldn't be here. I'm a man of the damp, green North, of the blushing, rose-laden temperate belt, its cool air fragrant with the moist fecund humus. I'm a mists-and-mellow-fruitfulness kind of guy. I should be up there saving the whale in an Arran sweater.' But by then it'd be too late. You'd have succumbed in some deep, irreversible way to the bleak tristesse, the all-pervading ossifying fatalism and corruption of the tropics. You'd already be half-withered into a brown-paper shadow of what you should have been. Oh, yes. It's all very well to stick a manicured toe in now and again. But to get yourself stuck here? Don't do it.

The museum lies on a corner of one of the huge, dusty traffic roundabouts from which the boulevards of the official quarter radiate. It stands amid parched and crumbling gardens, an imposing cream building, its heavy iron doors firmly closed. A handwritten notice informs visitors that entrance is forbidden – 'Prière de n'insister pas' – presumably aimed at American lady anthropologists who were thinking of trying tears. A guy sitting in the shade down the side of the building tells me the place has been closed for years – 'pour le refurbishment'. Yes, as I recall it, on my only other visit – what is it, eight years ago? – the masterpieces of African civilisation, the masks and magic objects of the ancestral cults of the savannahs, were all rotting away.

I head off down another deserted avenue and find myself at the side of the cathedral, a huge cream, neo-byzantine edifice rising out of a crumbling rubbish-strewn wasteland. Steps lead up onto the raised forecourt, beyond which stands the great gloomy portal decorated with carvings of angels with African features. The mass is in progress, people are entering, crossing themselves on the forecourt, and although I've always regarded this huge edifice in this ninety per cent Muslim country as a bit of a pompous, sad anachronism, I wander in after them. And to my astonishment, the place is packed. A stern young man points me through a side door up a staircase into one of the wide, bare galleries under the dome, the bare concrete tiers again crammed with people, a handful – less – of Europeans, a few Lebanese. Everyone else is Tekrurian. To my left, on the gallery facing the altar, are the choir, mostly young men and women, books in hand, faces uplifted in rapt attention towards their leader, a wiry man with his back to the great space below, who must be the arranger and composer. How can I tell? From the incredible delicacy and care with which he's conducting. Oh, yes. He's doing the bending backwards, the hands, the shoulders, the whole works. He's Tekrurian. The bishops in their scarlet and magenta are Tekrurian. And down there, in the great well of the cathedral, the drums are beating. It must have been in the mid-fifties that a Belgian missionary,

Father Guido Haazen, got his choir to extemporise in their indigenous styles, to create a 'Latin Mass in pure Congolese style' – the *Missa Luba*. They toured the world, the album was a best-seller – endlessly used in film, TV and radio. This music's come from that, conceptually, though it's come on a long way. It's more complex, melodic and sophisticated. The mass, from what I can understand, has bits of French and Latin, but seems to be largely in Wolof. Young men read from the Bible in Wolof. The Bishop of N'Galam, one of these cool, inscrutably half-smiling types, begins his sermon in French, but soon goes into Wolof. This young woman with braided hair in a blue ecclesiastical gown – what is she, a deaconness? I know nothing – does a kind of speech in Wolof. And as for the congregation: are they testifying and amen-ing? Are they jiving joyfully in their pews? No, man. This is Tekrur. The congregation are cool. They just stand and sit, intent, stone-faced.

And I'm surprised. I'm taken aback by the whole thing. I mean, to the extent I'd considered it, I was expecting just a straight Catholic mass in French, Latin, or whatever it is they use. And it makes me think I must have been pretty stupid not to realise it wouldn't be like that. It's as though the whole event is saying to me, Do you think we're stupid? The *Missa Luba* was half a century ago, and do you think that, when the whole world's heard that, we were just going to carry on doing what we were doing before? And do you think that just because you haven't given any thought to us, that in all that time we wouldn't have developed, that we wouldn't have moved on from that? This is our country, man. This is our religion, too. This is what we do here. You know, it makes me feel a little humbler.

For all the bombastic splendour of the exterior, the interior of the cathedral is remarkably bare – the massive monumental piers supporting the dome are bare undressed concrete. But round the interior of the dome frescoes have been painted, of figures in casual modern dress – in shirts and trousers and simple dresses, like people in the street outside, like the people in here, people of all races, but mostly black – starting to ascend, arms raised, up into the great, grey concrete expanse – an expanse that mirrors, whether deliberately or not, the implacable steely emptiness of the burning tropical heavens outside. It's quite well-painted, and I mean, I don't term myself a Christian, I don't *believe* . . . I haven't been to church since I got kicked out of the Cubs. But sitting here in this huge bare tropical cathedral, hearing that music, the serene uplifted faces of the choir across the gallery, the stern, earnest heads of the Tekrurian Christians, I can't say I feel any real fellow-feeling with these people, because I don't know what they're thinking, or what any of this really means to them. But there is something in all of this that I can relate to, something beyond the common feeling, or what I assume to be the common feeling, of alienation and separateness from the overwhelming tide of the Muslim majority, something beyond a sense of sympathy for what may be the precariousness of their position, something beyond the fact that amid the seedy, crumbling rundownness of N'Galam what they are doing may represent a more exalted way of thinking and feeling – or at least has a quality, a standard, something beyond the fact that these people are committed – something deep, something buried, something one would have to go to the unspeakable ends of the earth to realise was even there. And I look up at the tall figures in the frescoes overhead, floating, arms raised, up into the grey, unchanging blankness of the tropical sky – the brightness which, outside, brought on that sense of loneliness and desolation – and I think . . . I've gotta get outta here.

I hurry down the bare staircase, through the overarching portal, out into the dazzling brilliance where the line of abject, exhausted beggars sit and stand waiting for the largesse of the blessed. And beyond them under the trees on the other side of the street, more beggars, the improvised stalls of the sellers of cigarettes and cola nuts, the men sitting – not waiting, not watching, just there – and already I'm back in the tawdry everyday reality of N'Galam – the endless self-fulfilling, fatalistic spiral of begging, petit commerce and sitting around. But lacking on a Sunday its usual teeming energy, and seeming in comparison to the cathedral and what it represents – which although it's only a few yards behind me, already seems amazingly distant – incredibly squalid and depressing in its listless, tawdry fatalism, and I think, 'I don't want to be here.'

On the corner ahead, by the Lutetia – most archetypally French of N'Galam's patisseries, but long since given over to Lebanese ownership and anyway closed on a Sunday – is the lowering wolf mouth of the dim, tree-lined Avenue Wagane Diouf. No, I'm not going down there. So I head up the adjacent boulevard and turn left into a little old street of one- and two-storey terracotta-roofed houses, all visibly falling to bits, where a milder everyday reality of sitting about in doorways, women fetching water, washing clothes in the street prevails. There's a whole quarter like this, gradually getting filled up with high-rise buildings as the others collapse, and I always wonder who they were built for, these places: poor whites, blacks, Lebanese, Moroccans, discharged soldiers? This was the area where before they were expelled, you could always hear the hammers of the Mauretanian silversmiths, and there are a lot of shops selling 'African art' and 'designer' clothes and handbags in neo-traditional fabrics. And it's all very laid back, very tranquil on a Sunday, and if I don't draw attention to myself, nobody's going to bother me here. Down another side street to the left, squeezed between a photographic developers and an amazingly scruffy restaurant, is the entrance of the Hotel Ndar. *The Hotel Ndar.* That's right. And although the entrance is inconspicuous, the dim and spacious hallway beyond is immaculately clean, the dark silver of the black marble floor reflecting the reception desk which is constructed to represent the rippling flanged trunk of a silk cotton tree. Yes, the Ndar. I've heard of this place. *The* arty hotel of N'Galam. The place where the filmmakers, TV researchers and journalists hang out, where the attenders of symposia on negritude and neo-platonism put their feet up. Bang in the middle of town! Why didn't Sajar put me here, instead of that pompous plastic chain hotel stuck up among the banks at the dead end of the financial quarter? Typical! I wander in.

The girl at the desk is reading a magazine, but she looks up with an amiable, though rather shy and uncertain smile. The straightened hair, the tawny aquiline features. I've seen them before, though I'm aware I'm seeing them at a different angle, because this is the woman who was dancing so disturbingly and excitingly at Sajar's club the other night.

'Bonjour.'

'Bonjour, monsieur.'

'Do you speak English?'

'A little.'

'I know you.'

A look of doubt and slight confusion crosses her suave countenance. 'Yes?'

'Yeah. Last Sunday at Sajar's club. I was sitting next to you, on the balcony. You were dancing ... very well.'

'Oh ... You were there?' She seems astonished.

'Yes.'

'You like our music?' It seems incredible to her. But she's delighted.

'Loll!'

'*Loll?* And you speak Wolof, too?'

'No, no,' I chuckle.

'You seem to speak it very well!'

'I'd love to ... Do you have any rooms?'

'Rooms?' The abrupt change of subject and the question itself seem to throw her into a panic.

'To stay in.'

'Rooms. Yes er ... I don't know.' She pulls aside her women's mag and starts checking out the ledger. But the harder she peruses it, the more flustered she becomes. 'Er ...' She smiles sweetly, but hopelessly. 'I'll have to see ...'

She leans through a door at the back and speaks to someone. After a few seconds, a tall, very dark woman comes through and regards me disapprovingly through very large glasses. The glasses have thin frames, the kind where if you get very close you don't notice the person is wearing glasses. Her eyes are slanting, coolly appraising. She's got an enormous number of plaits pulled back from her broad, smooth forehead, and the severe, rather ascetic demeanour of an old-fashioned headmistress – not the kind who stopped you from going to see *Romeo and Juliet* for reasons of political correctness, but the kind who gave you

152

detention and the ruler the whole time and never got married. My heart's in my mouth. I can hardly swallow.

'Can I help you?'

'Are you married?' *What am I saying?*

Her brow clouds over. 'Comment?'

'I mean . . . Do you have a room?'

'For when?'

'Er . . . now.'

'We're completely full,' she says with a monumental finality, looking at me very full in the face through her big glasses.

'When er . . . would you have a room?'

She starts flicking through the ledger, instructing the girl in Wolof who murmurs embarrassed assent. 'Not before Thursday.'

'Ah . . . I'm at the Belotel.'

'If you're at the Belotel, why do you need a room here?'

'I . . . er . . . prefer it here.'

She pauses for a split second. 'You can stay at the Belotel till Thursday morning, then you can move here.'

Man, I'd love to move here, being serviced and pampered by this bevy of intellectual and not-so-intellectual amazons, with the opportunity to get next to BBC researchers and lecturers from SOAS in my spare time. But anything could happen by Thursday, and anyway, Sajar's got everything arranged at the other place. It could be complicated.

'Do you have any . . . deals or redu . . .'

'Non. Parce que nos prix sont déjà très économique.'

'Can I see the room?'

'Non. All the rooms are occupied. But I don't think that's a problem.'

'You mean I can see the room?'

'No, I mean the room will be fine for you.'

I realise I've been staring at her shining shoulders and her small but shapely breasts beneath her thin dress. I look up, and her cool slanting eyes are still full on me. And on her lips is a very, very faint smirk – a smirk of triumph. I'm shaking, though whether because I'm weak with desire or because I'm seriously ill, I can't tell. Probably a bit of both. 'We'll see you on Thursday, then.'

'Yes,' I gasp, and head for the door and the glare of the street outside. In the doorway I turn, and see the two women just standing looking at me.

Eleven

'The whole idea of Tekrur really does arouse an extraordinary degree of loyalty and . . . sentiment in France. There was a recent economic quorum here, and there were, I think, eight French cabinet ministers present. It really would be difficult to imagine any African country arousing that level of commitment from our own government, for example.'

I'm sitting on the terrace of the British Ambassador's residence, under a magnificently tall and white arcade, surrounded by unbelievable tropical plants – pendulous vermilion pods, dangling like great penises from spongelike purple flowers – sprawled back on a luxuriously padded cane sofa, as monsieur l'ambassadeur fills me in and madame, seated on the sofa beside him, regards me with a Giaconda-like mystical serenity through almond eyes – almond eyes, I love it, man! – as I shovel cashews into my gob.

Litch, at the British Embassy? you're thinking. Can this be right? Oh, yeah. When you get to my level, when you become a bit of an institution, you get called upon. And it's only right to show your face, if only because, let's face it, you never know when you might need to call upon these people's help. Though I must say, I had to crease when a Merc turned up at the Belotel, with a gold-edged card inviting me to a reception to celebrate the Queen's birthday. I mean, I would have to be fucking desperate to go to something like that.

155

'So what aspect of the economy in particular will you be writing about?'

I start, spurting a couple of mouthfuls of Coke down my shirt-front. I'm tired. I think I've told you that, haven't I? I'm so tired I can hardly function. Madame rolls her eyes slightly.

'How d'you mean?'

'In your article. For the *Guardian*.' He sits, expectant, calmly and tactfully oblivious to my sweaty, exhausted discomposure.

'The er . . . *informal* sector.' Well thought, I posit, cramming my cakehole. I hadn't noticed I was actually fucking starving.

'Ah, yes,' he purrs with a slight smirk. 'The informal sector! I daresay you'll find quite a few colourful stories there.'

Yeah, the informal sector! All those marchands ambulants, all those women sitting all day behind a pile of three oranges, all those boy hawkers of pirate cassettes, the traditional weavers packed into the area of waste ground between the back of Hakim Nder and the Texaco station, the sewers of sandals, the embroiderers of the robes of the faithful. The whole world, in fact, of traditional African commerce, everything from leprous beggars to . . . Sajar Jopp. Except that Sajar Jopp gets more formal as the days go by. You can hardly have a deal with the Motivate Corporation and claim to be in the informal sector.

'So how would you normally go about researching an article of this kind?'

'Well, I'm going to be interviewing Sajar Jopp.'

'Sajar Jopp! Well, he's hardly informal. He's become terribly grand, hasn't he?' He looks at his wife who looks back with her continual expression of inscrutable serenity. 'We were taken backstage after his concert at the National Theatre, and we couldn't get near, could we?'

'No,' breathes his wife.

'Terribly impressive, when you think he's come from absolutely nowhere. But you may not find it easy to get an interview.'

'Oh, that's all organised,' I say airily. 'I've known Sajar for years.'

'Have you really? How interesting?'

Informal sector, indeed! I mean, here we are in the British

156

Embassy. And while it hasn't exactly got marines on the gate, there's a sedateness and a solidity. You can at least enjoy the tropics as you'd like to. The fabulously coloured birds darting among the phallic flowers. But once you get out there, it's wide open. Out there in the streets everything is negotiable, and there's nobody, but nobody, who isn't open to suggestions. So, you ask yourself, how do all these French people who've been here for decades, the advisers and experts, the tie-in merchants, the multinational representatives – the people who probably do actually govern this country – how do they function? They're all up to their necks as well. They've got to be, or nothing would be done. Because nothing's fixed, nothing's solid here. You can't put something somewhere and say, Right, this is gonna be here. Because you can't trust anybody, you can't rely on anything. And the goal posts and the parameters keep moving. But what about the guys in the sleek suits and the starched robes, I hear you say. They seem pretty professional. Professional is right. But what are you gonna do, invade? Withdraw aid? Cancel the deal? You *can* do that. That's what the Big Boys do. But you and I can't do that, so we have to ride it. We have to adjust to the deceptive, vertiginous rhythms, the slippery surfaces. We have to succumb and yield a little when we enter the rubber labyrinth of Tekrurian commerce. *The Rubber Labyrinth of Tekrurian Commerce.* I like that! I may end up writing this article for the *Guardian* after all.

'The way I see it,' I say, stretching my legs and putting my hands behind my head, 'the entire Tekrurian economy is one big informal sector.'

'Well, that's a view, certainly. Though I don't know if I'd go *quite* that far.'

What the hell's an almond eye when it's at home, anyway? 'The almond eyes of Sajar Jopp.' How many hundreds of times have I read that in articles by people who've hardly even bothered to look at a photo of Sajar Jopp. It's like 'the long-lashed eyes of Michael Heaven'. It's completely meaningless. Does he have long lashes? I've never measured them. But some hapless hackette gushed it once and it became *true* – the thing that has to be said in

157

every consideration of Michael Heaven (of which there are way too many). But as for Sajar's almond eyes, who put *them* there? Me, of course. Most of these articles you've read on Sajar Jopp, I provided the journalists with so much information I practically wrote them. In some cases I actually did write them. There I was typing away one day – sort of, 'tap, tap er . . . tap' – and I thought, Shouldn't you go and look at a photograph to make sure he actually *has* got almond eyes? And I thought, Nah, fuck it. So for the rest of time Sajar Jopp has almond eyes. Which for all I know, he does have.

Bacon, She said. Get bacon. But don't go to Tesco's, go to Waitrose. It's nearer. Is it hell nearer, but I went. It gets like that, doesn't it? It gets so you can't be bothered to argue. So you can't be bothered to explain when you get back and they see the packet and say, 'Why didn't you go to Waitrose?' And I haven't done any arguing, or any explaining, for a long time. Also, I have to admit that in the back of my mind was the fact that Waitrose was in the old town, and over the zebra crossing is a narrow street that slips off parallel to the main road, between the old red-brick buildings, paved over now, and running off that is a sort of alley, and in that there's a record shop. And I've often thought, as I do when I see a funny little old record shop, that one day I'm gonna check that out, because it's in the most unlikely places that you find the good gear.

It was damp and black and drizzling. The old town was already long since deserted. Take your umbrella, She'd said. But I'd forgotten it.

The shop was half-timbered. Picturesque, valuable if it hadn't been dilapidated and half sunk into the pavement. But though the old town was deserted, and every other shop, except for the warm neon glow of Waitrose, was grilled and shuttered and bolted with a medieval finality against the marauding night, the low door of the record shop betrayed a light, and through the rain-besmeared panes I could see three figures snug in conversation at the counter.

A bell tinkled, and the three heads turned as I squeezed under the lintel, down the two uneven steps, then immediately turned away as I began to survey the neatly labelled racks of 'Indie, Thrash, Techno, Sixties, Classic Rock.' I flicked desultorily through the blues section. No, there was nothing here for me. Even if I'd been thinking of buying. Which I wasn't. Two quid is two quid, right? If he'd had anything for two quid. Which he didn't.

I was vaguely aware of the conversation behind me. Someone, presumably the owner, holding forth at some volume, to another who acted both as echo and prompter, and a third party who added nothing whatsoever, about some gig his band had just done or were about to do. I wasn't paying much attention, though in some small part of my consciousness I was wondering whether they'd be beefed-up folk, singalongaseventies or tasteful covers of 'classic rock'.

'Yes, mate?'

I turned. I was sweating, and I couldn't work out why. I looked at them, a small, pale wispy-bearded bloke in denims and his two dark, shaggy-haired cohorts, and all I could manage was, 'Errr?' That's what happens when you don't go out, when you hardly even speak to anyone for nearly a year.

'You looking for anything in particular?'

'You got any . . . African music?'

They looked at me. African music? The two shaggy-haired, no doubt Deep Purple-fancying yokels looked at the owner as though anticipating a signal to burst into derisive laughter. *African music? What's this fucker on?* But instead, he just looked at me, cool as you like, and said, 'Yeah. We get a fair bit of African music. But you won't find much now. I normally take it down the market at Great Snarden. Seem to get more of a call for it there. But see them boxes under there? Try the third one along. You may find something to interest you.' And they went back to their conversation.

I squatted happily down. What treasures would be revealed here? 78s from the very earliest days of anthropological recording? Ten-inchers from the fifties, preferably with plummy-voiced commentary? Stuff that had lain undisturbed for decades in the

159

attics of nearby houses? I love all that kind of stuff. It's got such atmosphere! But no such luck. Even if you've got no intention of buying, there's a sense of pleasurable anticipation and satisfaction to be had from working your way through several rackfuls of records. And there's an equal weight of disappointment when you realise after the flick of the third cover that there's not only nothing here that's within a million miles of what you're interested in, but it's all on the wrong side of the fine line between valuable archive material and a load of garbage to which no sane person would give house-room. That wasn't quite the case here. I mean, there was a double import of Tex-Mex music, a collector's item, it would have been nice to have. But it's a long time since I bought anything because it would be nice to have. Now I only bought things if I knew not buying them would lead to a lifetime of bitter self-recrimination. And this was mostly much-hyped and drearily predictable stuff from the World Music era that the purchaser had evidently soon got bored with. Ahmadou Toure in his kiss-of-death phase. Stuff from the New Age-Folk-World Music interface end of things. Mauretanians hit the Cotswolds – that type of thing. Soon, I found myself listening in to the conversation behind me, which concerned the night, some time in the mid-seventies, when the proprietor's band blew Orfaze Testament off stage. Orfaze Testament! That wasn't a name I'd had cause to consider for several cosmic light centuries. Weren't they some kind of faintly arty hard-rock band from somewhere like Sheffield, built around their guitarist's virtuosic skills and then-disconcerting habit of mentioning Jean Cocteau in interviews? Their name and the very term 'blew them off stage' took one back to a time, which in the light of everything that's happened since, appeared like some drably quaint adjunct of the nineteen-fifties. A simpler place and time ... Or it would have been, if I hadn't been putting everything conceivable up my nasal passage. I was, as I recall, managing a country rock band in those days. And it says something about the state of rock'n'roll at the time, that trawling a country rock band round the pubs, clubs and school halls of southern England seemed a radical thing to do. Fucking desperate, man! 1974. When Orfaze Testament were contenders, and our friend here 'blew them off stage'. And where did he achieve this feat? Bracknell! Yes, man! If you're gonna blow Orfaze Testament off stage, Bracknell is *definitely* the place to do it! And in the version I'm hearing now, of a tale that is I feel not infrequently aired in this establishment, the massed head-bangers of Berkshire, Oxfordshire and Hampshire are packed into the cavernous Sports Hall, and our hero and his bunch of screaming acid boogie merchants are going down a fucking storm. I see him now, hunched over his bass, gawping out at the head-shaking, air-guitaring hordes, awestruck at the power of rock'n'roll. When Orfaze Testament didn't appear, they were sent on to do a second set. And when the headliners finally did show up, they were booed off . . .

'You're not mixing them up, are you?'

I started, banging my head on the underside of the rack, nearly stunning myself in the process. I managed a sound between a grunt and a groan.

''Coz I'm taking them down the market tomorrow.'

By now I was through the modern jazz and into the Latin section. Yes, they actually had a Latin section – if you can call a two-inch space in a cardboard box a section. The Fania All-Stars. *Back to my Roots*. Something one really should have. Something that it is in fact extraordinary I don't have. Wait a minute . . . Eight ninety-nine? Here? He's gotta be joking! I mean, part of the point of putting in time, searching stuff out in places as unpromising and unlikely as this, is that they virtually give you the stuff.

'Not exactly giving it away, are you?'

'What's that?'

I stuck my head out, the shaggy cohorts peering down at me, bemused. 'I said you're not exactly giving this stuff away.'

'Not really, no.' He peered down, his eyes narrowing with a look that said, Who do you think you are? Don't you realise I blew Orfaze Testament off stage?

I threw him back an even harder look that said, Listen man, I don't care if you've been in Eric Clapton's backing band. I don't give a monkey's if you *are* Jack Bruce. I'm into something far deeper, richer and darker than that.

I could see him already starting to climb down as he took the album cover. 'See, an album like this is not easy to find. And there's a lot of people round here know their stuff and are prepared to pay proper prices.'

I love this! The idea that the satellite estates and twee villages surrounding this trans-M25 nowheresville are filled with people who can tell the difference between Monguito El Unico and Pete 'El Conde' Rodriguez . . . That is beautiful!

I got unsteadily to my feet as he went searching behind the counter. 'Tell you what, if you're into African music . . . How about this?'

I glance at it. Orchestra Super-Jive. 'Produced by Michael Heaven,' he said, proudly.

'No thanks.'

'Well,' he said, disgruntled by my ingratitude and at being shown up in front of his admiration society. 'If you don't like that, you don't like African music, do you?'

I hurl myself into the foyer, straight into the arms of the porter, the smooth, suave one with the hawk nose and the sparkling eyes. He waltzes me round the foyer, purring in my ear. 'I know you are a nice man. You have only come here to help us promote our culture.' He takes my forearm in a fierce grip. 'If you go to the counter, you will find a message from your friend Sajar Jopp.'

He loosens his clench and I go spinning to the desk, where the guy hands me a while-you-were-out slip. 'Phone Sajar Jopp immediately.'

I spot that guy in the blue suit, the undermanager, approaching. 'Ah, monsieur –'

'Yeah, later, man.'

A split second later I'm in my room, telephone receiver in right hand, expertly tapping in the number with my forefinger. This is more like it's supposed to be, things moving to a slicker, more adept rhythm – and I always was a bit of a principal soloist on the blower.

162

'Oui.'

'Sajar. Litch. What's happened?'

'I want to talk to you.'

'When?'

'Now.'

'Okay . . .'

'En personne!'

'What . . . Now?'

'Yes.'

'Can you send a car?'

'No.'

The driver has no trouble finding Sajar's house this time, and he's ready for the haggle on the price. He won't budge. Says it's a different rate after six o'clock. Bullshit.

Sajar's not there. His wife says he's at the new house which is too far to walk. Fortunately Abdou's chilling round the corner, and he runs me up there.

In the darkness it seems like the middle of nowhere, but all around are the houses of the richest people in Tekrur. I can't see anything of the outside, but we step through the front door into a vast lounge, like an airport concourse, with various robed figures lounging on Chesterfield sofas. Actually it's more like the lower deck of a great ocean liner, with the open staircases with their rounded handrails – just like the nightclub – sort of Californian Bauhaus Cunard, with a touch of Nashville in the guitar-shaped window on the circular central staircase.

'Music is the theme,' says Abdou.

'Right on,' I say.

We pass the bathroom on the first floor, where more robed figures are inspecting the gold taps, the marble sunken jacuzzi.

'Who are all these people?'

Abdou shrugs and goes into a gargling burble ending in 'relatives'.

'Sajar hasn't moved in yet?'

'We're doing it bit by bit.' He points to a doorway at the end of a darkened landing. 'Sajar's in there. You can just knock.'

'Oui,' comes a gruff voice.

The room is long, lined with shelves of box files, boxes of disks, video cassettes. Sajar is sprawled on a sofa, while a young guy in jeans taps into a computer.

'Ça va?' I proffer.

Sajar flashes me a dirty look and carries on talking to the young guy in Wolof. The guy, one of these people who through an accident of nature have their features fixed in a big sunny beam, flashes me a big sunny beam while looking slightly embarrassed, and carries on zapping and flashing. He certainly seems to know what he's doing – not, though, that I'd be any judge.

I slump down on the sofa beside Sajar, who keeps asking the guy agitated questions.

'I'm sorry,' says the guy, turning to me. 'What is your web site?'

'My what?'

'Your web site for the Internet.'

'I haven't got one.'

'You have no web site?'

'No.'

'You have no home page?'

'I haven't got a computer, man.'

'Then what is this?' asks Sajar, handing me a great pile of computer paper, an endless scroll filled with what seems to be just names of African bands and their records, an immense catalogue that reads like a surrealist poem that is better than most actual surrealist poems, a nocturnal leap into the unconscious – a list that might not mean much to you, but which glows and fizzes for me with its visionary nocturnal resonances. I chuckle to myself as I read through the names of Guinea's state-sponsored regional orchestras. The Vingt-Deux Band de Kankan. Yes, I can picture them grinning out of the orange and purple cover of their album, posing with their guitars in their preposterous flares, and I can hear their jangling, chiming music – like Bembeya jazz taken faster and harder. And what *was* that guy doing to that bass guitar? Or Le Nimba de Nzerekore. *Le Nimba de Nzerekore!* It's a long time since I even thought about them – a bunch of guys from

164

the forests of south-east Guinea who did this proto-Satchmo singing derived from their circumcision rituals, backed by deliriously wailing saxes and kamikaze kit drumming. Crazy stuff! I read on from the Guinean orchestras to the Malian orchestras through the Malian griots – and there are a lot of Malian griots – to the flamenco greats, all apparently in mint original editions – editions I have myself got. And I realise there's something in the shape and structure, the presiding will of this list that is frighteningly familiar. I flick on through the samba schools, the choirs of the candomble temples, the New York ... This is a list of my collection!

'What is this?'

'That's what we want to know,' says Sajar.

A slim guy in a grey suit comes in. 'This is Maître Sall,' says Sajar. 'Mon conseiller.'

'Your quoi?'

'Mon avocat ... My lawyer!'

'I thought Prosper Mbodj was your lawyer.'

Sajar darkens a shade. 'Non.' The lawyer, who looks very young, tries to appear stern and resolute. Sajar seizes the printout and points to the front page. 'You see this!' Every conceivable piece of Sajar material, from collaborations with Michael Heaven to cassettes for Tekrurian-only distribution, bootlegs, stuff taped off the radio, his earliest work with the Star Band, every single thing by the Lumière, every single thing by the Super Lumière, is carefully listed. Let's face it, even Sajar hasn't got anywhere near as complete a collection of Joppobilia as this. But what's it doing here? This is all my gear. No doubt about that. But I never made this list. I mean, I'd quite like to have done, but I never have. It's just too uncool, you know what I mean?

Sajar's eyes are blazing with reproach. 'We did not bring you here just so you could exploit us – so you could make *money* out of us!'

This is already getting on my nerves. Firstly, there's that thing you always get with creative people that no one, no matter how many thousands they've invested in their work, should be allowed to make one penny from it, that no matter what

165

suicidally generous terms you offer them, you're still out to *fuck* them, while commercial considerations never even cross their minds . . . Then there's that use of 'we' and 'us', which always comes out in Africa, which means that any African, no matter stupid or dishonest, is one of 'us', while you, the White Man, are always the exploitative neo-colonial outsider. I mean, it's not as though I haven't tried, as though I haven't done everything humanly possible – and for no payment.

'If you want to use our work, you have to license it formally,' says Sajar pompously.

'There are very strict international laws regarding music piracy,' says Maître Sall.

I can't believe it! If you go down to the Marché Hakim Nder any time of day or night, you'll find hundreds of people, shamelessly rerecording Sajar's entire catalogue. And has he lifted a finger against any of them? Je croix pas.

'Just a minute! *Just a minute!* Listen! I have no idea what this is! I've never seen it before! I don't know where it came from!'

'It came from your . . . ordinateur!' says Sajar.

'I haven't got an ordinateur.'

'What about this?' says Sajar, pointing to the two rows of digits, dots, dashes and backslashes at the top of the page, in the middle of which is: 'GILB\LITCH\COLL'. The truth starts to dawn.

'Where did you *get* this?'

They look at each other a trifle sheepishly.

'Off the Internet?'

'Well,' says the boffin. 'Not exactly.'

Sajar looks darkly into the middle distance. 'We had to do it. We had to find out.'

'About what?'

'The money.'

That's right, man. They hacked into my computer. I'm impressed. Africa is definitely on the move. And I don't mind in the least, because it's not my computer. Not any more anyway, not since, in a gesture of misguided magnanimity I gave it to that bastard Paul. I mean, I had no idea how to use it anyway. And this can

166

only mean that he is attempting to sell, market, reproduce or otherwise exploit my collection without my knowledge. But how could he? I did leave about a third of my collection at his place. But that was just the dross: mainstream freebies I'd never bothered to listen to, stuff even you could get hold of. And how did he manage to have such precise information about *exactly* what I've got? Because that's the sort of thing I'm very cagey about. Unless of course, he went through all my boxes, crates, cupboards, chests, sheds and lock-ups without me knowing. And I wouldn't put it past him. I wouldn't put it past him at all.

Twelve

'How about this? Produced by Michael Heaven...'

'What...?' I wasn't listening to him. Because I'd found something far more interesting: a sparsely designed blue and white record cover, a split-second glance at which yielded a flooding rush of memories and emotions. Suddenly I was in the world as it had been, what was it, four, five... six years before? I felt a warm chuckle deep inside as I scanned the meagre credits. 'Written and arranged by Mansouman. Spiritual Inspiration: the Almighty God. Produced by Litch for Monster Productions.' *Produced by Litch?* Absolutely correct, man. I'll never forget how I felt when I received the first copy. I just sat there staring at it, for about a week, with this little smile on my face. 'Mansouman Zarra and his Rockin' Hunters of Wassoulou: *Reflections on the Next World.*' Yeah! That was a *mad* record. Or it had been the last time I'd heard it, which must have been at least six years ago. I mean, you get so close to things you can't actually hear them. So you put them in this other zone till you need to go back to them. In the meantime, of course, the rest of the world can enjoy them at their leisure. I turned back to the front of the album and the little yellow price sticker. One ninety-nine. *One ninety-nine?* And this looked like a pristine unplayed copy.

'This is cheap!'

'What's that? Oh, yeah. *That.*'

'It's a brand-new copy.'

'Yeah, we got a load cheap off the distributor. They got lumbered with virtually the whole pressing, and they found they couldn't give 'em away. They were selling them in Sterns' in London for fifty pence each. You can have that for a quid if you want it.'

He takes the sleeve. 'How can you expect people to fork out for something like that?' There are knowing grunts from the other two at the cover which is simply a blunt, head-on view of Mansouman Zarra. 'See, people nowadays are used to a high standard of graphics. They want and expect class.'

Grunts of agreement.

The idea had been to protest against the fatuous yuppie exoticism of World Music graphics, to produce something that through its enigmatic simplicity would hint at the mystery and the power of the music inside. In fact, it just looked like a rather badly printed picture of an anonymous black man.

He peers at the credits. 'I don't know where this was produced. There's not even an address. But it's quite possible that an African record, actually from Africa, would look like this. But if people think "African record", they're more than likely to think the technical quality's gonna be iffy.'

'Yeah, well more fool them. 'Cause I've heard it, and it's a fucking brilliant record!'

The guy just stands there looking at me.

By the time I got out of there, Waitrose was shut.

Do I strike you as the kind of person who would bother to bring out an album if it wasn't a stone masterpiece? I mean, I think we've established that I do know my stuff. And there's been so much incredible African music that's never seen the light of day, why should I waste my own and everyone else's time and money bringing out something that wasn't at least a contender for the all-time top one hundred? That's right. I wouldn't do it.

I'm a Lebanese. In London a Lebanese is a shifty-eyed, rosary-flicking, hookah-sucking scion of the mad orient. Here, they're just jean-wearing Mediterranean shopkeepers. Italians, Greeks,

Israelis. Moroccans, Lebanese. What's the difference? Here they're all *whites*! Except that unlike the flushing, fragile children of the damp green North – the mists-and-mellow-fruitfulness crew – who walk into it the whole time, who walk around with a sign over their heads saying, 'I'm white – DO ME!', they know how to behave. They know how to behave because they've always been here. They were born here. Their parents were born here. Even back in the thirties, when their grandparents were refused the acceptance in white society they craved, the colonialists were up to their necks in hock to them.

And from the poor Lebanese with their corner shops in the Medina, to the rich Lebanese of the Plateau with their hair salons, supermarkets and patisseries, their kids going to the top schools, living an *American Graffiti* life in their open-topped cars among the teeming lepers, beggars and thieves along the Avenue Fouquet, sitting around till the early hours on their drop-handled motorcycles, in their leather jackets and aviator shades outside their dads' kebab joints, they still behave as though they own the place – because they do! And although they're hated – of course – the locals are saving all that up for the day the Lebanese *get it*. In the meantime, if you can pass yourself off as a Lebanese, you'll be all right. But I can't. I'm too greyly, greasily pallid, too lankly blue-eyed. I'll have to pretend to be a cold-eyed, hard-hearted French bastard instead. But that's not that easy, not when you can't speak French and you're feeling seriously queasy. Still, it gives you the downturned mouth and the measured tread, keeping an eye out for the open drains and the heaps of sand and rubble. And of course, you've got your shades on. The wiry, red-eyed marchands ambulants eye you ruminatively as you pass, a folded pagne perhaps draped over their head, a hand's span of cassettes held out, a pair of wire-framed shades dangling from each finger, and they think, 'Don't bother, he's just a cold-eyed, hard-hearted French bastard.'

The heat hasn't really got going yet. It's still got that tremulous liquid brightness that says, Come on out! It's not too bad out here. Then, when you're a hundred yards down the street – WHAM! I'm coming now to the area where the scruffy low-rise grid east of

170

the Avenue Wagane Diouf creeps into the interstices of the commercial and financial quarters. The guys in the suits – the cheaper suits – and the smart jeans and slacks, with the pullovers knotted around their necks Italian-style, with the fake Gucci briefcases, the attaché cases and the clutch bags, are on their way to work. Rolling along in gaggles, their arms draped round each other's shoulders, one guy holding forth to the spluttering red-eyed approbation of the others. Even that bearded, thoughtful-looking guy in the cream suit mooching along with his briefcase has a slight smirk on his face, as though there's a big secret, and he's definitely in on it. These guys are what, bank clerks, petits fonctionnaires – the ones who have to make their own way to work. There they go, grabbing each other's shoulders, slapping each other, deep in their lascivious elastic sniggering. These are the lucky ones, the exalted few with white-collar jobs, who've struggled, hustled and bribed their way into the neo-European formality of international commerce and their own government's structures, but they're all still in some way deeply and ineluctibly *dodgy*. Dodgy? you ask. Dodgy according to what standard of judgement? Dodgy according to the fact that I'm still feeling really fucking nervous.

Passing an alley between two anonymous modern buildings I catch a glimpse over heaped rubble and rubbish into a cramped world of corrugated-iron compounds, a guy, his features just a patch of shade beneath the rim of his baseball cap, strolling down over the rubble towards me. Oh, yes. The traditional African world starts here – with all its ashes, blackened wood, rusting corrugate, washing hanging out – crammed into the nightmar-ishly claustrophobic gaps between the tall buildings. You're walking along the suave façades of modern N'Galam, and just a couple of feet away *that* is all going on.

There's a white woman, tall, middle-aged, swanning along the street in a knee-length skirt and Hermès scarf. I mean, you've got to hand it to the French, they've got no problem with the idea of Africa as elegant, Africa as stylish, Africa as modern. The British, the second they set foot on African soil it's, 'We're on safari! Get the shorts on!' Even if they're driving round a major traffic intersection, they're on safari. No matter what you tell them, no matter how much you brainwash them, no matter how much you show them the traffic underpasses, the railway lines, the sky-scrapers, no matter how much you force-feed them African TV adverts and Sajar Jopp music, you cannot get them away from the wildlife travelogue scenario. Whereas the French, even if they're up-country, they've got the starched tablecloth, the silver, the major glassware. And if you find your residual Britishness coming out and you say, 'Yeah, but you're in the middle of the African bush, man!' they just shrug their shoulders and go, 'Donc?'

There she goes, striding nonchalantly along the streets of one of the 'least secure places on earth'. And like that older woman, choogling along minding her own business, like the big kids in their Tintin t-shirts strolling guffawing along the Avenue Fouquet on their way home from school, under the crumbling façades of the cinemas showing kung fu films, the big shoe shops, the remainder book stores, undisturbed by the thumps and slaps of the marchands des crap sculptures, the jabbing stumps of the leprous beggars, the grabbing at your ankles of the polio victims on all fours, she doesn't seem the least bit fazed by it. They've somehow accommodated to it, or been accommodated by it. It's only me, trapped in the prison of myself, who can't cope, who can't hack it.

I glance at my watch. The ferry's going in twenty minutes! I always do it. Every fucking time! You know, there's something in me, something fatal that says, 'No, man, don't stroll down there now, leisurely, while you've got plenty of time, leave it till it's touch and go, till you've got some adrenalin, some real *fear* going.' Yeah, every fucking time I do it. But you can't afford to do that here. You can't afford to be seen to panic, to get your knickers in a twist, to be *the white man running!* Quickening my step, but remaining calmly purposeful, I turn down into a sidestreet towards the port. Calmly purposeful. But this kid – one of those with the baseball cap and the wooden tray of cassettes, and I haven't looked at him, but I can sense him from the furthest corner of my eye – has clocked me, has sensed and smelled my

172

fear and panic. *I'm already prey.* On my left are open-fronted shops full of brassware and Moroccan leatherwork, and there, standing contentedly ahead of me, with his mirrored fez and his big gazelle eyes, is this Moroccan trader I remember from the Belotel. His eyes widen further on seeing me, and he breaks into a smile. No grudges held for the fact that I didn't buy any of his crappy souvenirs. I'm his friend. We don't so much shake hands as link them in moist-eyed tenderness. How *am* I? I'm cool, but I'm in a fucking hurry, man. How do you say that in French? He gets the message, and the lustrous and enormous pools of his eyes betray astonishment. If I'm about to miss the ferry, why am I bothering to hurry? That, I suppose, is the great theme of Mediterranean philosophy, but I'm still gonna try and go for it. I leave him standing as surprised as anyone as laid-back and fatalistic as him is capable of being and press on, the kid closing in on my heels. Far from being discouraged by my apparent familiarity with the marchands of the quarter, he sensed the dissonance of the encounter, its betrayal of my lack of composure. He can smell the dampness, the stinking fetid terror under my armpits. Like a lame wildebeest separated from the herd, I'm already marked down for death.

I turn into the Avenue Fouquet, picking my way among the impromptu half-formed stalls and booths, clambering over the lepers and women squatting behind their piles of oranges, and the kid's on me. 'Monsieur, cassettes. Cassettes, monsieur.'

Rule number one: never reply.

'Cassettes. Sajar Jopp. Cherry Jatta Samba.'

'Je l'ai,' I grunt weakly.

That's it! I'm lost. With one gasped phrase I've delivered myself up to them. The kid whistles, and there's a flurry of excited activity further ahead on the sidewalk. 'Get ready, there's one coming!'

Immediately ahead, the pavement is closed over by a dark arcade. But I'm not looking at it. I don't know what I'm looking at. I'm so frightened I can hardly *see*.

Don't go in the arcade!

On the other hand, one must maintain one's composure, one

must appear to know where one is going and not be diverted from one's chosen path, maintaining nonchalance at all costs.

Do not go in the arcade!

I step to the left, into the potholes between the parked cars and the pillars of the arcade.

Get on the outside of the cars, man!

Now I'm really walking fast, and I can hear the scuffling of feet running along the arcade beside me, the athletic bounding of the hustlers, their muscular spring booming in the rats' cage of the arcade. But they've already given up. I'm already virtually off their patch.

Cross the road, man. Get a cab like you should have done in the first place!

I find myself walking down a sidestreet on the other side of the road, with a taxi passing. I hail it, and ask to be taken to the port for the Isle des Esclaves.

When I first came here, the place had an amiably decrepit air of lost time. But each time I come it's more manicured, spruced and prettified. It's getting like Covent Garden or Fisherman's Wharf. It's getting like Clovelly! Oh, yes. They've turned the Auschwitz of the Black World into a twee little tourist attraction. And all people talk about is the feeling of peace and serenity in the silver-sanded streets, the rustle of desiccated palm leaves, the scents of jacaranda, hibiscus and bougainvillea, the pastel washes of the eighteenth-century houses, while the callously cynical inhabitants saunter arrogantly about in their designer sportswear, looking with resentful disdain on the odd tourist they haven't yet woven into at least one of their shekel-raising scenarios, daring him to try to take a photograph of anything. Every time I come here, I think, This is a nasty little place, I'm not coming here again. And every time I find myself coming back. Why? I've no idea. Maybe I'm just stupid.

Think I'll check out Henk Van Leer. A former ANC field commander, he runs some well-meaning leftie organisation based on the island because of its symbolic significance. Nobody seems to know precisely what he does, but he has no trouble raising

174

money to do it – and he may be a good source of info on Sahelfest 2000.

I leave the culture tourists to be descended on by the hustlers and guides and head for the Logis des Signares, the island's only hotel, where van Leer normally goes for a lunchtime drink, and settle myself on the terrace, under the wicker awning.

The signaras were the mulatto matriarchs who dominated the slave ports for several centuries, cheerfully profiting from the trade no doubt, and now managing to get themselves reinvented as proto-feminist role models. A bit like this hotel, trying to trade both on the pathos of its position and its laid-back historic charm. Below me, the Atlantic glitters brilliantly. I hate the Atlantic.

I order a Coke, and ask the waiter if he's seen van Leer. 'Il vient,' he says with a charming smile.

Visitors always head immediately for the Maison des Esclaves, the house with the extraordinary symmetrical staircases where the slaves were kept. A door leads out of the cellar onto the rocks where the slaves were led to the rowing-boats that took them to the slave ships anchored on the still grey sea beyond. It's one of the world's great evocative vistas. I challenge anyone to look through that door, and not actually *see* the slave ship anchored out there, and the manacled slaves clambering over the rocks.

I remember my first visit, reading the comments of Black American visitors, or pilgrims, as I suppose they thought of themselves, recording their feelings of gratitude to their ancestors for having endured so much on their behalf. One woman wrote, 'I came here in 1964, I came back in 1972, and I will return many times before the end of the world.' I wasn't sure what this meant, but I burst into tears. Because it seemed the place represented so much that was epic and awful, that the world had not even fully acknowledged let alone expiated itself of. Oh, yes. I cried. But you can't keep doing that. Anyway, I later learned that the cellars were in fact used to store grain, and the slaves were kept in a completely different building up the other end of the island. But they kept the Maison des Esclaves going because the other place didn't have the staircases and the view.

Where the hell is van Leer? When he's here, he does virtually all his socialising in this hotel. I've always liked the guy, though I'm beginning to think that anyone who would choose to live in this place must be fatally flawed in some way. I sit there under the thin awning with my Coke, loathing everything around me. The jovial banter of the waiters, the carefree gait of the islanders strolling past, the rustle and clatter of the palm fronds against the ancient walls, the chatter and squealing laughter of the largely black holidaymakers on the beach below, the glittering ocean, the sunshine. I'm feeling really sick. I think I've somehow managed to contract major food poisoning.

The tiled courtyard of the Institut Democratique Africain is full of mindboggling potted plants. A door leads up onto a red-washed arcaded gallery smothered in bougainvillea, frangipani, jacaranda and every other kind of herbal aphrodisiac. This place is more than most people would dare fantasise about living in. Even I've got to admit it's got charm. The red-tiled upper loggia is lined with huge succulents that look like they've been designed by some mad auto-erotic surrealist. A row of arched louvred doorways lead into what were once the apartments of the signaras. One of them is open. The tables inside are full of faxes, modems, telexes, terminals and the rest. At the end a stocky, brick-red figure in a yellow vest is sitting with his back to me, intent on a computer terminal. 'Litchfield,' it says in a dry monotone. 'What the fuck are you doing here?'

'How did you know it was me?'

'You were seen getting off the chaloupe at ten fifteen this morning . . . Give me two seconds.'

I peer at the vast frieze of laser-printed A4 sheets covering the walls. Phrases like 'effectiveness diagnostic curves' and 'power management inventories' leap out at me. That's right. Filling Africa with people coming out with stuff like that is really what we need.

'People come here and stay for a short time,' says van Leer as we stroll through the silver-sanded streets towards the restaurant, 'and they think they've come to paradise! They don't realise that living in a place like this can have its drawbacks the same as anywhere else.' He smiles in a slightly smug way, that suggests that he can nonetheless more than accommodate these drawbacks, and that I must share the wide-eyed wonder of his criminally naive visitors.

We pass the logis, where the waiters are all sprawled against the wall smoking.

'Hey! Van Leer!' they shout.

'Yeah!' shouts van Leer. 'Nangendef?'

I lean up to van Leer. 'I hate this place. I wouldn't live here if it was the last place on fucking earth, man.'

He snorts. 'That's another way of looking at it.'

'So, what's happened?' he asks, as we settle ourselves under the awning of a scruffily informal restaurant further along the beach. 'You used to like it here in Tekrur so much.'

'I'm ill, man.'

His brow knits as he sips his beer. 'Have you seen a doctor?'

'Yeah. But it's more ... spiritual.'

He grimaces. 'You're ill, spiritually? Can you be more specific?'

'I can't stand this ... rich and poor thing. It's doing my head in. You know, I'm from New Malden.'

He's never heard of New Malden. But he gets my drift. He's not stupid, van Leer. I would never say that.

'I'm a South African,' he says. 'The position I find myself in here is not that different to what I've grown up with. And it doesn't bother me day to day, because I've never known anything else. But it's no longer about black and white. It's not about continents or even countries. As you say, it's about rich and poor. If you have access to the international credit system, the Internet and all these other things, it doesn't matter which country, which continent you're in. The real distinction is going to be between the people who have access to these things and the people who don't. You know, people come here with no clear purpose in view, and they think that just by being here they're going to ... find something. But it doesn't always work. So if all you want to do is look at poor people, why don't you just go to Hackney?'

'I live in Hackney, man.'

As a matter of fact, I don't live in Hackney, but from this distance, the distinction is minimal, and it shuts the patronising bastard up.

'So there you are,' he says, tucking into his grilled chicken, covered with a delicious crust of charred pepper marinade. 'Anyway, I wasn't referring to you. You know that.'

My rational mind tells me the chicken is fantastic, but my stomach won't let me eat more than about two mouthfuls. The chef, who's grilling the food in the open air a few feet behind me, looks disconsolately at my plate. He seems genuinely hurt.

'He thinks you don't like it,' says van Leer.

'It's beautiful,' I say to the chef, who seems a genuinely nice guy. 'But I just, just can't . . .'

'If you're having such a bad time,' says van Leer at length, 'why don't you just go home?'

I don't reply. I'm too busy thinking that before I go anywhere, I've got to get myself off this island. I've got to confront the patinated lawless reality of N'Galam, negotiate myself into a cab and back to the hotel. Maybe that's why I don't feel like eating anything.

The city comes in and out of view as the boat heaves, its tower blocks glittering hazily in the late afternoon light, deceptively bland, giving no indication of the scurrying rat-like life below. On the far side of the boat, I can see this incredibly good-looking, but slightly sour Frenchwoman in shades. She must be what, ten, even fifteen years younger than me, but she's already got that slightly middle-aged look of icy bourgeois complacency that all Frenchwomen over the age of twenty-one go out of their way to achieve. The thick well-cut hair, neither long nor short, the simple blouse of indeterminate though no doubt extremely expensive cut, the serious cheekbones, the slightly pouting mouth. She could only be French. And put in this context she's like someone from one of those ludicrous French colonial nostalgia movies, where Catherine Deneuve swans improbably deodorised through Saigon, or a French family leads an implausibly well-laundered existence in the Camerounian highlands. All just an excuse for pouting in pith helmets. I'd probably fancy her if I wasn't so frightened. In fact, since she looks the type who's going to know where she's going, I'm going to mill along with her as we get off the boat. You know, I'm not actually going to follow her or speak to her, I'm just going to give the casual observer the impression I'm with her under the assumption there's safety in numbers, and what I'm gonna do after that I'm going to worry about when the time comes, because we're already pulling in to dock – the swelling and heaving against the quay, the overloud chugging of the engine, the throwing over of ropes. Yes, the venal, but Watteauesque interlude of the chaloupe and the island is over. You're back in the capitale de la douleur, the Big Bad City, and it's now not in the water where you're going to sink or swim. She's already standing, and I realise I've been sitting in totally the wrong place. She's going to be virtually the first off the boat, and I'm going to be last. I try to elbow my way through the tightly packed passengers, but it's not easy: they *are* tightly packed and they're Tekrurian. It's only the middle-aged culture tourists who're prepared to be elbowed out of the way. I can feel myself descending into a nervous, shambolic panic. For Christ's sake, keep calm!

I get off about three from last. The salle de disembarkation, or whatever the fuck it is, is virtually pitch dark through my Ray-Bans. I take them off, but quickly put them back on as I emerge all too soon into the crowded yard. A guy has recognised me. He's recognised me as the person he's going to rob today. 'Hello, my friend. How are you?' I push straight past. Oh, yes. I'm not a complete fucking idiot. The necklace or the piece of gold goes into your hand, they expect you to pay, and if you argue, out comes the knife. And the guy's immediately at my shoulder. 'You don't want present from black man?' I don't answer. Why should I? I speed up my pace, barging the middle-aged culture tourists out of my way. Why doesn't anybody bother them? There's two of these guys. I can hear one in each ear, and I can feel them in the back of my neck, as though they're going to sink their fangs in at any moment. And I'm still blinkered, half-blinded by my shades, but I haven't got time to think about taking them off. And about

179

twenty yards ahead, I can see the head of the Frenchwoman, walking quickly and intently. I break into a half-run. They don't like this, but they keep up. 'Hey, you fucking bastard. What are you doing in our country? Why don't you stop?'

Now I'm really running, crashing into everyone in my submarine murk. There goes a woman's basket of tomatoes. Serves her right for carrying them on her head. There are angry yells after us. What am I saying 'us'? I'm about to be stabbed! Now I'm clear of the crowd. Shit! Don't let them get me on my own. The Frenchwoman is hurrying past the taxi rank and crossing the road. Mindlessly I'm running after her, not even looking out for traffic. She can hear the commotion of running footsteps behind her, and she's speeded up her step, but she's not turning round. Now she's cutting through this narrow encrustation of market stalls from where she emerges onto another road. I crash, blundering, after her, trampling on the marchands' bowls, oranges and other rubbish. Where is she? Over there, getting into a taxi. As I reach the door I turn to my assailants, whose feet I can hear clattering over the crumbling asphalt behind me.

'Did Sajar Jopp try to mug me? Did the Minister of Culture try to mug me? So don't ask me what I'm doing in your country, right!'

I pull off my shades in a gesture of theatrical defiance, and look straight at the knife – the dull iron blade, the arm, the mad eyes and trembling lip of the guy holding it. I turn to the woman, who's right behind me, her eyes wide with terror.

'Get in!' I scream.

Thirteen

The last vestiges of the day's light are slowly dissolving, slipping away off the wall, through the window, out over the Atlantic, the ocean I'm lying high, high, high above. And they're welcome to do that. I can't stop them. So let them go.

I can hear the faint rushing of the gentle waves on the rocks, and the laughter, the throaty visceral chuckling of the taxi-drivers outside the restaurant, far, far below, carried on the faint evening breeze. The Laughter of Tekrurian Taxi-Drivers. Sounds like the title of a stylish, but superficial first novel by a former Peace Corps volunteer now working as an investment analyst on Wall Street. Come to that, it would make a great title for a compilation of the latest and most *in there* Tekrurian sounds. I must write that down. When I get up.

How long I've been lying here, whether it's hours, days or just minutes, I've no idea. I'm quite contented. But if I leave it too long, I'll miss the restaurant, and I'll have to make do with a sandwich fromage. And I don't want that to happen.

I find myself in the lift, descending.

And then I'm standing at the entrance to the bar, which I have to pass anyway, a dark, permanently nocturnal space. It's lively and full as it usually is, because for some reason, there's a certain kind of inhabitant of N'Galam who likes hanging out here. So I glance in, and I stop, because in the middle of all the smoking,

181

bonhomie and chatter, sitting at a table on her own, is the woman. She's sitting there, looking straight at me and smiling.

It's one of those low tables with low stools, where you either sit upright, which is a big effort, or you lean forward, and if the other person is leaning forward too, which they are, you're right in their face.

'I thought you handled that very well.'

'What?'

'Those guys.'

'Right.'

'You were very cool.'

'Yeah?'

'I thought so.'

'You're not French.'

'My mother's Swiss. But I consider myself English. You're English, aren't you? You're very English!'

'Yeah?'

'I'd say so.'

'Is that good or bad?'

'It's good.' She smiles. Normally, when I get in situations like this, I get nervous. 'Cause I'm thinking, this is too easy. I'm *bound* to blow it. But this time I don't feel that. Because although we're in a crowded noisy room, it's like we're enclosed by our own bubble of intimate togetherness. Because we're loin de notre pays, notre endroit, notre culture – loin de chez nous. We're loin, period. I mean, I can quite see that in another context this woman and I would have absolutely nothing to say to each other. But we've been thrown together, and it's like we're already sharing a deep and intimate secret. I can already feel this golden glow in my stomach radiating from my solar plexus.

And that sense of clinging together against the dangerous but intoxicating otherness of the surrounding culture, the milling shadows closing around us like a thick blanket, let me tell you that is a big, big aphrodisiac.

'It's so French here. I knew the influence was very strong. But it's so . . . It's like being in France and Africa at the same time.'

'So you've never been here before.'

182

'No. I only arrived yesterday.'

'Okay.' That's useful to know. Very useful. 'So what brings you to this thieving, rapacious city?'

She laughs. 'You don't like it here?'

'I love it.'

She laughs more. 'I'm here in connection with a festival I'm organising.'

I can feel the tingling in my chest, the fluttering in my throat, the rushing of blood towards my face. I resist the temptation to hit the table and let out a major wolf howl. Instead I say, incredibly calmly, 'Sahelfest 2000.'

Her mouth opens. Her pupils, which are virtually all I can see of her face, get even wider. 'How could you possibly have known that?'

'I keep my ear close to the ground.'

'You must keep it amazingly close to the ground. Are you hungry?'

Gabriella's in full flight. She keeps using phrases like 'social and critical spaces', 'framing devices' and 'issues surrounding'. But instead of thinking 'lemme outta here' as I normally would, I let her run on. Because whatever she's said about me – and comments about middle-aged fat white men elicit nothing more from me than a faint, ironic smirk – whatever she's heard about me, fate has slid our diverse destinies into another groove, another reality, where her post-structuralist babbling is just another abstract music. And the rhythm I'm clicking into, the resonance I'm vibing on, is the swelling undercurrent of passion. Oh, yes. The woman's on a crusade. And like all true visionaries, she assumes I'm on it with her. It's great. It's like having dinner with Joan of Arc. And I always have had a thing about gamine women in chain mail. Not that Gabriella's gamine exactly. She's more womanly. And that's cool too. Because as we get older, we tend to prefer a meal to a snack, don't we? And as she goes on, with me half, or maybe a quarter, listening, I realise that while there's nothing so outrageous about what she's proposing, which is basically that African artists should have some say in the way

183

their work is seen in the West – which is basically what I'm saying myself, isn't it – you can't help thinking that she's evolved her ideas in a critical space (as she would no doubt put it) far from the cruel and intractable realities of what's going on here. And that makes her seem touchingly vulnerable.

I realise that in some deep and elemental way, Gabriella is alone – that she always has been alone. With her Anglo-Swiss parentage, she never felt quite part of either environment, of either culture. So she shut herself up with her books and her 'texts', writing the theses that have got her in the position she's in today – to pull together a major world festival – so she missed out on some of those aspects of youth that some of us exaggerated, blew up and distended into an entire life's project. Gabriella is, in a word, definitely *not* rock'n'roll. And this endearing quality of aloneness is something which, for all the ligging, schmoozing and hanging out, I feel I share. Yes, here we are, two souls who are, in very different ways not only separate from, but also somehow *above* the rest of humanity, finally meeting, at last, far from our own culture, in this hotel at the westernmost point of the African continent.

'And,' says Gabriella, reaching a suitable break in her recitative, 'he'll be leading a workshop here for poets from all round the world.'

'Who will?'

'Serin Ahmadou Cham.'

'Serin Ahma . . .' I can't get the guy's name out. '. . . *He's* involved?'

'I just said so,' she says, as though to an imbecile child.

Serin Ahmadou Cham . . . Poet, platonic pantheist – or is it pantheistic platonist? You can't get away from him, can you? Those huge and immemorially expressive eyes, that smirk of imperturbable knowing, follow you from his book jackets, his promo posters in Waterstones, his myriad TV appearances. Even you've seen Serin Ahmadou Cham – you just don't remember it, 'cause you can't remember African names. The man who equated the civilisation of the savannahs – its ancestral cults, its age-graded initiation societies, its inscrutable cosmologies – with the mythology of pagan Greece, from the comfort of a writer-in-residenceship at Yale. Oh, yes. Unlike all the other Professional Africans who fill the conferences with their endless debates on whether we should be referring to post – or neo-colonial Africa, who get up after the screening at the NFT and say, 'As an African...', he's taken it to a whole other level. He's legit. He's incredibly legit. And the thing you always forget about him is that while through the accident of an elder brother who did well for himself in the States, he got shunted into an anglophone groove – I think he went to Oxford or somewhere – he is actually from *here*. You forget it, because he doesn't have that arrogant francophone gloss, that rangy street-hustling bonhomie which – not wishing to be racist or anything – you do tend to expect from people from here. Though that doesn't mean of course that if you dig deeply enough, that they're not there.

Gabriella's mouth is puckered in a faint and very slightly foxy smirk. She's looking straight at me, but she's not seeing me – her big velvet pupils have gone completely matt. Her mind is flooded with Serin Ahmadou.

'Mate of yours, is he?' I say, trying not to sound too bitter. Let's face it, man, I'm almost in tears.

'Who?'

'Ser . . . Cham.'

'That's one way of putting it,' she says, very quietly but with a playfulness that speaks volumes about the luminous, all-consuming, groin-straining athleticism of what they've been getting up to. And if I'm not careful, she's going to start telling me about it, in detail. I can't believe I didn't see this coming. I mean it was absolutely obvious. Wasn't it?

'So,' I say, 'What about the music?'

'Music . . . ?'

A sudden hunted look comes into Gabriella's eyes. As I said, she's not rock'n'roll. I've caught her well off her manor. 'Well,' she says uncertainly, 'I'm having a meeting with Sajar Jopp.'

'You're having a meeting with Sajar Jopp!' I say, as though this is the most banal thing anyone could think of doing. 'How about

Papa Gorgi Ngom? How about Elhadji Mamadou Seck? How about Sidi Taal, Nyanya Guisse and Coumba Gewel Mbaye?'

'I don't know them.'

'Well, I think you should.'

She's got out the notepad such people never have far from their fingertips, and she's scribbling the names down as fast as she can. Asking me all the correct spellings. I tell her I've got the phone numbers upstairs and I'll give them to her later.

'This is wonderful,' she says, looking at me with some of the warmth and confiding intimacy she had back in the bar. 'You're quite a goldmine.'

But I'm wary now. My guard's well back up. 'You didn't tell me what *you're* doing here,' she says with a pleasant smile.

'Me? Oh, I've got various ... business interests here.'

'I see,' she says, obviously imagining I'm talking about ... jute or something. 'So music's a sort of hobby?'

'A passion.'

'Do you know Simon Henchard?'

'Who?'

'Simon Henchard. He writes for the *Guardian*. He's a real authority on Tekrurian music ...'

'Oh, yeah. Simon. Yeah, Simon's cool.'

'He's going to be writing a very important article about us.'

I think I'm going to kill Simon off before he gets me into deep shit.

Mansouman Zarra was a kind of loose cannon percussionist-animateur-guitarist in the Super N'Tomo Band, who were then Mali's top group. They played wild, swinging Bambara rhythms with the crazy psychedelic guitar of their leader Seyni Kouyate growing all over it like dangerous madly coloured flowers. Anyway, I met this Zarra in Paris when they were playing there, and he was mad to come to England. I said, No problem. We'd love to have you. Meaning, We, the British people would love to hear your music. One night three months later, there's a knock on the door at three in the morning. I had that bad feeling you do have under such circumstances, but I was half asleep and I didn't

186

bother to look through the spy-hole thing. I just threw open the door and there's this massive black guy in a hooded track suit standing there. I froze. You do, don't you? But he just looked back at me with soulful imperturbability and said, 'How are you?'

He moved in. I thought, great. This is where we make an album under the controlled conditions of my choosing. This is where we show the world what African music is really all about. She was more ambivalent, but at first She didn't mind that much. This guy, this Mansouman Zarra, was a real African. Sajar Jopp is not an African. Cherry Jatta Samba is not an African. I mean, they're Africans, but they're first and foremost show-business people. You could even say they're artists. But this Zarra, though he was an incredible musician, didn't even think about what he did as music. In fact, he didn't think about it at all. He was from Wassoulou, the rocky, inaccessible area in the far south of the Mande region, where his family had been hunters since time immemorial, playing their hard gut harps and singing for the hunters' associations that ruled the villages of the bush. Iron scrapers created this bumping, swaying rhythm, the harps throbbing and whirring like the scratching and buzzing of the insects in the delirious brightness of the bush at noonday. This was the music it was in him to play, and that he did play, at times hardly even aware that he was doing it. Women singers have become really important in that music. Quite a number of their albums have been brought out in England, mostly licensed from Ahmadou Toure, so that he and his sidekick Mamadou Sylla have had their fingers all over them, with their fatuous synthesisers and drum machines, replacing the rasping one-string fiddle with violins. But the original stuff, by this Zarra, and particularly by his mentor Toumani Kone, had this frightening invocatory rawness that has been completely lost in the later stuff.

Zarra was big and very black, and it was great going into shops with him, 'cause the staff would all jump out of their skins. But violence wasn't something that even entered his world-view – except maybe under very particular circumstances. He was an African. Everything was negotiable. If he had any kind of problem, his attitude was, Okay, let's have a discussion. The fact that he spoke virtually no English didn't seem to matter. If he got caught travelling on the tube without a ticket, they'd end up giving him a free weekly pass. And they'd say, 'What a nice man!' as though he'd done them a favour. He had this incredible, not exactly charm, but this immense personal dignity and sense of sincerity that disarmed you totally. And the fact that he was six foot six and built like a brick shithouse didn't do any harm either.

He was an African, and like a lot of African musicians, he wasn't that interested in music. It was an ancestral craft they were using as a stepping-stone to some more lucrative business activity. Anyway, he'd been with us over a month before I sussed he'd actually come here with the sole intention of setting up an import-export business in electrical goods. Why he thought it would be a good idea to do this from a country where he couldn't speak the language, and with which his own country had virtually no diplomatic or trade links, I never found out. Maybe he thought there'd be less competition from his compatriots. Yes, he was an African. He only took people from his own cultural milieu seriously. Everyone else was just a cardboard cutout. That's why he had no trouble dealing with them.

But he loved England. He spent all his time combing the skips and rubbish tips of the Home Counties looking for exportable materials. Soon our house was full of defunct tellies and fridges he was going to have rigged up back in Bamako and sell for a huge profit. He had Her driving unlicensed, uninsured vehicles down to the ports. And at first She didn't mind, because like everyone else She was totally disarmed by him. But then it became apparent that distracting his attention from all of this towards the album we were supposed to be making was not going to be easy. And while all this was going on, I couldn't do anything else. So I wasn't making any money.

And after a time, She got fed up with it. She kept saying, 'When's he going?'

I'd say, 'Don't you like him?'

'Of course I like him. When's he going?'

'As soon as we've finished the album.'

'When are you starting the album?'

'Look, I'm doing it, right?'

By now it had become obvious that he had no interest whatsoever in making an album, and he treated each of my increasingly desperate enquiries as to when we were going to start it as a greater effrontery than the last – despite the fact that he was living off the fat of the land in my house, and doing untold harm to my marriage. But one night, I had it out with him – Big Time.

'It is not a problem. We can make the album whenever you like.'

'Like when?'

'Now.'

'What now, now?'

'Why not?'

'Er . . . solo?'

'Non. Avec mon groupe.'

'Où est ton groupe?'

'Holland.'

'What are they doing there?'

'Chercher l'argent.'

Turns out his group – there were three of them – were over there illegally, busking, playing restaurants and small clubs, sleeping on their compatriots' floors. It took me a couple more months to get their visas organised, which delighted Zarra, as he had more time for skip clearance. By now the tellies and fridges also filled most of the garden. We were getting complaints from neighbours and the council. I still hadn't been able to work, and my finances were ebbing terrifyingly downwards.

She said, 'I thought he was supposed to be exporting it.'

I said, 'He hasn't got any money.'

'Why don't you give him an advance, then he can get shot of it?'

'I'm not giving him a penny till we've done the album,' I said, not convinced events would take the direct linear course She imagined, and not wanting to inform her that Monster Productions' capital resources had dwindled to a frightening extent.

Then, one night, the group turned up at about three in the

189

morning, filling the place with their morose mysticism, the aromas of many days' travel and the dark hunted glances of the illegal immigrant. The fact that I'd got their paperwork sorted, and they had a right to be here, still hadn't sunk in.

And as soon as they started playing, all the warmth and meaning and the point flooded back into the thing. As always, as soon as the music started, I thought, Yes, *this* is what it's all about! And that was beautiful and deeply spiritual music. The vibrating buzzing pulse of Zarra's harp, the counterbalancing scraping on this iron cylinder, made you rock your head backwards and forwards whether you liked it or not. It went straight to your spine. That's the way it is in Mali. There's that continual pulsing and swaying to the gentle bobbing of the music that's a constant accompaniment to life. And there was this Fula guy who played this rasping, harshly breathy flute and a balafong that went spiralling off into deep space. The balafong player also played a bit of guitar, and it was obvious that he was the real musician. I could see there was going to be friction between him and Zarra. But Zarra was really into it. Discussing music alone with me, out of context, was a completely purposeless activity. But now he had his mates here it was all just happening on a kind of biological level. Only problem was they only seemed to be able to do it at night. And that meant that even if one had been able to get any sleep and wanted to get up, one wouldn't have been able to get into the living-room because they were all asleep or sitting chatting, watching telly, playing cards, bivouacked among the tellies and fridges. After about four days She said, 'Get that album recorded!' I was amazed it had taken her that long.

I also had the idea that I should get them into the studio before Zarra and the balafong player killed each other. I could now see why they'd decided to put the English Channel between them. I booked two days – or rather two nights – in a tiny four-track studio in Tottenham. I'd had the idea we were going to try all kinds of experiments. But I knew there was no way they were gonna be interested in that. They were going to do it the way they'd always done it, and that was going to be it. Now my sole

190

aim was to get it all down before some irrevocable altercation occurred.

There's this voice like subvolcanic activity. *'Laura's Lunchtime Experience!'*

'That's right, the Lunchtime Experience with Laura Liddington, taking it through till two with some news, chat and some killa choons on the Big One. And my guest today is Andrew "Litch" Litchfield. Welcome Andrew. Do I call you Litch, or what do you want me to call you?'

'Call me what you like.'

'I see! Taking a strong and difficult approach?'

'Yeah.'

'Good on yer. Now Litch, there's been an incredible amount of African music in the charts over the last few months. We had Sajar Jopp at number one. And anyone who knows anything about it knows you're the person who's largely responsible. Isn't that right, Litch?'

'Not really.'

'Okay, but Cherry Jatta Samba, Sajar Jopp. You're the one who went out to Africa and discovered all these people.'

'That makes me sound like Doctor Livingstone!' Gurgling chuckle from Laura. 'Like some Great White Hunter who went out there to get the darkies sorted out.'

'Steady on!'

'That's what I'm saying! I just happened to go out there. I met Sajar, heard the music, loved it, chilled with him. That was it really. Basically, Sajar's just a mate.'

'Too cool! Which brings me to my next point. 'Cause anyone examining your life would be forced to the conclusion that all you do is travel round the world listening to music. Would that be correct?'

'Er . . . more or less.'

'More or less! Sorted, or what! Laura Liddington talking to Andrew Litchfield on the Lunchtime Experience. We'll be hearing more about Litch's lucky life . . . after the break!'

Laura Liddington is Radio One's principal female deejay. There

191

are other ones who come on at night who're like more hip. But Laura's daytime, mainstream. She's flagship! She's horribly cheerful and jokey, though she's got this little chuckle in her voice that's meant to sound drug-induced, so the kids're supposed to know that while their mums like her, she's been there too. And she's always going on about all the raves and festivals she's going to, and trying to make out she's shattered from partying – when actually you can't get this irrepressible brightness out of her voice – and she says everything as though it's a question, yeah? Like the youth of today all do, right? But the place to encounter her is the telly, where she appears all too frequently. Because she's got this twinkle in her eye which lets you know that she's only going through all this crap till she can hop over into mainstream TV entertainment from where nothing will stop her in her rise to a position of media dominance second only to that of Noel Edmunds. Oh, yes. Because although, looking at the all-too-beautiful Laura – and yes, she is beautiful, seriously – trying to work out what race she is, you may think that this supra-racial, multi-cultural, hyper-effective, mega-confident woman who is young enough to be your daughter is a harbinger of some super-species of the future, it is reassuring to realise that basically this woman represents no threat to Judith Chalmers whatsoever.

Faced with her indefatigable joviality on the mainstream bastion of daytime Radio One, one has no option but to adopt that mainstay of permanent undergroundness: surly incoherence. One doesn't want to overdo it, however. Because, as I said, she *is* beautiful.

Two o'clock, she has a breezily flirtatious changeover with afternoon guy Davey Harbottle, off come the cans and the phoney smile, and she's asking me with a husky, intent earnestness if I want to go to the club where she normally chills in the afternoons. I say, why not, and next thing I know we're in a darkened booth with a bucket of champagne. I tell her I don't do that stuff. She says that's all right, she'll have mine. She's already got her arms round my neck. 'Why are you so cool?' she asks with a tone of reproach.

'Who?'

'You! *You!* Why are you?'

'Am I cool?'

'Yes you are – incredibly cool! You know you are!'

I'm floating, man. Every cell, every atom of my being is golden, glowing, distended. The room is full of light, the world is full of light and I am the light.

Suddenly I'm awake. It's dark. And Laura, covering me with the cloak of her raven tresses, kneading my chest in hoarse-voiced desperation, is utterly gone. Where's my dick, man? It's disappeared.

I click the light on, shaking. It's still there, the greasy colourless gristle, marked with burst veins and unnamable staining. Christ, no wonder they don't like showing them on telly. But it never used to look this bad. And it's shrunk. It's definitely shrunk. I sit up, peering down at it, examining it, as though it's not mine – *as though it's someone else's penis!* Because it doesn't feel like mine: it doesn't seem to be interested in anything I want it to do.

I head into the bathroom. And I hardly recognise the hunted, exhausted visage that returns my gaze – the jaw slack as though half-dislocated, the eyes exhausted from squinting in the brilliance, developing hoods and folds they never should have had. The contours of my body, thrown into hideously stark relief by the yellow over-mirror light, have all shifted in ways that bear no relation to the reality beneath, that don't even follow the patterns fat should form. I feel a thin shriek rising within me, 'That's not me!'

I alter my position, trying to shed light on the slug-like appendage between my overpacked thighs. One of the advantages of losing weight, which I must be with all the sweating and loss of appetite, is that it should make my dick look bigger. But it doesn't seem to be having any effect yet. I pull and tweak at it, stretching it, trying to summon Laura, the heavy witch of the airwaves, but she's not interested.

I sit on the edge of the bath as I try to imagine Gabriella with Serin Ahmadou Cham. Gabriella gasping out, like the enraged growling of a great steam press – a sound we men have to hear, if not every night, at least a *couple* of times in our lives – as he slams his body, frighteningly compact and muscular beneath his trademark caftan shirt, into her ripe velvet womanliness. For a time I think I'm getting somewhere. Then I get bored, and I go back to bed.

Fourteen

'Where are these people?' asks Sajar, looking at his watch.

'They're coming, man.'

We're in a room at the Universitaire Alhaji Malick Ndoye, waiting for the Sahelfest 2000 posse. Now that it's about to happen, the prospect of Gabriella's realisation that she has in fact been wining and dining on intimate terms with the Unspeakable Bogey Man of World Music doesn't seem so amusing. Or rather it's so amusing it's making me feel ever so slightly sick. What's the matter with me? So I've been ever so slightly duplicitous! How can you be the bogey man of anything without being ever so slightly duplicitous?

'They're ten minutes late,' says Sajar, in a state of some agitation. 'I've got a lot of things to do.'

This is Africa, where you simply assume everything's going to take place at least three hours late, where everyone just shrugs, smiles and says, 'African time,' where un rendezvous tekrurien is one that doesn't take place. But I'm with the guy who wants to change all that, and just about the only person who might be in a position to actually do so. That's why, in spite of everything, I give him deep, deep respect.

The room is a small seminar room, just like such a room anywhere, but a bit more mottled and marked, with red termite trails spreading up one corner of the wall; though I've stopped noticing things like that. Down below, across the campus, is the

195

corniche, with well-tended municipal gardens and the hazy, sparkling sea, and since it's midday only the odd jogger down on the foreshore. To the left, back up on its promontory, the tower blocks of the city rise, a grey flat blur, above the smoking, steaming rubbish heaps, the charcoal haze coming from the infernal yards of the metal-workers' quarter.

'What are you thinking, man?'

'Er?' says Sajar, blinking out of his fractious reverie. 'Oh,' he smiles for the first time. 'Rien.'

I can hear voices in the corridor outside. They're here. The door swings open, and there's Gabriella with Serin Ahmadou Cham, shorter than I expected and looking more like the photos on his books even than he does on the photos on his books. It's those big soulful eyes, man. They really are big and soulful, and they don't look particularly pleased to see me. Gabriella looks worried. She looks worried because I'm here. And she can't think of any reason why I would be here. No good reason anyway.

Sajar and Serin Ahmadou exchange warm, chuckling greetings. I didn't realise they knew each other. It never occurred to me to even consider the rangy, irreverent street energy of the one and the other's ponderous quasi-academic legitness as part of the same reality. But Cham's dressed considerably more trendily than I'd expected and, let's face it, Sajar gets more legit by the day.

Sajar does his whole Franco-African charm bit with Gabriella, while Serin Ahmadou gives me a limp handshake, his eyes, big and soulful though they are, not quite meeting mine.

Sajar gestures to me with a note of pride. 'Do you know Andrew Litchfield?'

Serin Ahmadou's face doesn't move a muscle, just a faint tremor in the deep, dark waters of his eyes, but Gabriella's visage is horrible to behold: it's like one side of it's sliding off the other. She looks like she needs helping to a chair.

We take our places at the table, Sajar thankfully oblivious to what's happening, Gabriella rapidly composing herself as she gets her notes out, while Serin Ahmadou fixes me with an intent and reproachful stare. What's *his* problem? He doesn't know me from Adam. *Does he?*

Gabriella, trying to respond to Sajar's oblivious enthusiasm and eagerness to get on, runs through developments, reading hurriedly from her notes – in French.

I find myself coughing noisily.

'Yes?' hisses Gabriella. '*What?*'

'I'm just wondering if we shouldn't be having this meeting in English?'

'For what reason?'

'In a lot, probably the majority of, the countries we're dealing with they don't speak any French at all. If we set a precedent now, we're just gonna alienate them.'

'You mean *you* don't speak French!'

'Well, I do but . . .'

She looks at Sajar.

'I don't mind,' he says, the soul of obligingness.

Serin Ahmadou is still fixing me with that unblinking gaze. What a ham!

'The Super-Session . . .' says Gabriella.

'Oui, the Super-Session,' says Sajar.

That's right. The Super-Session. The centrepiece of Sahelfest 2000. That's what we're interested in. The idea is to get some of the most heavy-duty musicians from Africa and the Black Diaspora – Brazil, the Caribbean, the U.S., Europe – together here on the earth of the Mother Continent to explore their common heritage, to find out what's been lost and what retained in all the musical comings and goings over the great ocean. There'll be an album, natch, to be premiered at the gig. Neat idea, and it's definitely tweaked Sajar's imagination. He'll be playing the role of honorary host. But he wants to know exactly who else is going to be involved.

'We've opened discussions with Stokeley Jackson,' says Gabriella. 'And he's apparently very, very interested.'

'Yeah?' says Sajar. 'C'est fantastique!' Stokeley Jackson started in church as a teenager. He went through Black Power, mystical introspection and back via multi-multi-multi-million selling ballads. Let's face it, Stokeley Jackson *is* Black Music. Only trouble is, he's mad as a hatter.

197

'Il est mon héros,' breathes Sajar.

'Je le sais,' breathes Gabriella.

'What if he doesn't turn up?' I wonder.

'Why shouldn't he turn up?' snaps Gabriella.

'He never does turn up. He didn't turn up for Paul McCartney, Elton John or Michael Jackson. He didn't turn up for Ronald Reagan, Bill Clinton, Jesse Jackson or Medgar Evers's widow. He didn't turn up for Haile Selassie, Kwame Nkrumah, Léopold Senghor or Nelson Mandela. I mean, he meant to. He wanted to. He just . . . didn't.'

'Est-ce que nous avons besoin d'un remplacement?' says Sajar.

'Je crois.'

'Mais qui?'

'How about . . .' and this *is* a stroke of genius, '. . . Isaac Hayes?' Gabriella exhales sharply.

'What's wrong with Isaac Hayes?'

'Is he . . . *relevant*?'

Is he relevant? 'What d'you mean is he relevant?'

'Well . . . who is he?'

I can't believe it. I mean, we all know Gabriella isn't rock'n'roll, but this is ridiculous. 'You must know "The Theme from Shaft".'

'No, I don't. Sajar, what . . .'

'You don't know "The Theme from Shaft"?'

'No, I don't know the theme from . . . whatever it is! Can we have the names of some *African* musicians?'

Sajar looks doubtful. 'Maybe Fela.'

'Non.'

'Non?'

'He wouldn't come,' I posit.

'How can we organise an event if you're just going to say that nobody'll come?'

'I know Fela Kuti, man. He's out of his box.'

'Well,' says Gabriella, looking down at her sheet of paper. 'How about Papa Gorgi Ngom?'

I can't believe it! She's got nothing to suggest other than the names I gave her in the restaurant last night. And that's not good. Knowing Sajar, he won't want any other Tekrurian artists

198

involved, unless they're his personal protégés and yes-men. And most of these people hate his guts. Papa Gorgi Ngom, Sajar's co-singer and rival from Lumière d'Afrique, a man whose pathetic demise is universally blamed on Sajar . . . I put my hand over my eyes.

'C'est possible,' says Sajar with a cold frown, clearly wondering where Gabriella got the idea of using *him* from.

Gabriella carries on down her list. 'Elhadji Ma –'

'How about Mbolo Mbango?' The veteran Zairean guitarist won't offend anyone.

'Yeah!' says Sajar with an enthusiastic grin. 'Bonne idée!'

'Abdou . . .' reads Gabriella from her book. The woman is *determined* to put her foot in it.

The door opens and a grey bearded man enters and tries to slip quietly into a corner. He's tall, gravely distinguished, a lot like Folarin Ayinla, the Nigerian playwright, doyen of African theatre, embodiment of its moral conscience. And Gabriella's already on her feet shaking hands, giving big respect, because *it is him*! Everyone rises, offering obeisance, which he, apparently here on some kind of sabbatical, residency or enforced exile, returns with a chuckling self-deprecation.

'This is . . . ,' says Gabriella, waving a hand in my direction, but is unable to finish.

'Pleased to meet you,' says Ayinla.

He seats himself on the edge of the group, radiating this cool modesty that is infinitely more imposing than any bombast, the sort of thing that only works if you've already made an incontrovertible impact on history.

Gabriella briefly recaps before going back to her list.

'Sebastaio Almador!' I throw in.

Sajar raises his thumb. 'C'est sûr!' Brazil's master of surrealist, political bossa nova. An inspired choice! Yes, Sajar can rely on Litch.

The others just stare into space, except the great man, who's racking his brain. 'How about Ray Charles?'

Sajar laughs. 'Why not?'

199

Gabriella is looking well pissed-off. Once again, the meeting is slipping away from her.

'And I think you need some Nigerian musicians,' says Ayinla.

'Ah oui,' says Sajar. 'J'adore la musique Nigérienne.'

'I spent quite a lot of time with Fela Kuti when I was in my twenties. But I'm told he's completely lost now.'

'How about Gentleman Femi Adewale?' I throw in.

Ayinla chuckles. 'Gentleman Femi Adewale! You obviously know Nigeria!'

I smirk modestly. 'A little.'

'Who would *you* suggest?' asks Gabriella.

Ayinla laughs. 'Ask our friend here,' he says, gesturing to me. 'He's the expert. These days I listen mainly to Schubert.'

'How about . . . , 'and this is an inspired idea, 'Raoul Garcia?'

'Oui, oui,' Sajar nods. 'C'est cool.' It certainly is. You need someone to represent the Afro-Cuban tradition that's had such a profound impact and says so much about the transatlantic interactions of the Black Soul. And Garcia is probably the hottest conga player around.

Gabriella turns to Serin Ahmadou. 'Isn't he that man we saw at Ronnie Scott's?'

Serin Ahmadou looks uncertain. 'I think you could be right.'

'Is he a Cuban drummer?'

'Conga player, yeah.'

'Well,' she gives an embarrassed and slightly patronising smile. 'I don't think he's suitable.'

'Why not?'

'Well . . . He's not black, is he?'

I feel a pall of incomprehension, confusion and anger descending on me.

'How do you mean?' I ask, my voice thick and slurred. 'How do you mean he's not black?'

'Well.' She gives a sharp and embarrassed laugh. 'He's white!'

I put my hand to my head. Okay, Raoul Garcia is of mixed race. He happens to have lightish skin and a not particularly African cast of features. But so what? He's from the Oriente province of Cuba, where the African influence is strongest. He's been steeped

200

in it since birth. He's an adept of Santeria, the Afro-Cuban religion, an initiate of Shango, the thunder god, of Ogun the god of iron, who protects and inspires musicians. To say he's *white* is like saying Tito Puente is white. I mean, what race *is* Tito Puente? I've never thought about it. I'm not in the fucking brain police.

'Raoul Garcia,' I say, 'is as black as I am!'

After a time, and particularly when you've heard as much stuff as I have, you get to the point where you expect to be very slightly bored, where you expect everything to fall in line with an expected mean of what you've already heard, and not go much beyond that. But that's reckoning without African musicians' capacity to play without what we in the West would consider the basic components of rhythmic regularity. Two drummers will get together and start jamming around a pulse they know is there but you can't hear. They don't bother to establish the beat, they just play the tunes in their heads, sliding and jangling against each other, the dancers swinging and swaying, their limbs twisted and pulled deliriously in the shapes between. It's jazz, man. Jazz at its most ecstatic and experimental. I mean, I've got tapes of lone herdsmen improvising on their flutes in the loneliness of the bush, that show that jazz has achieved *nothing*. I've got records of cow-horn trumpet orchestras playing on the mountainsides in the early dawn that show the Art Ensemble of Chicago where to get off totally. That's why I've always said that African music's going to progress by looking ever deeper into its own traditions, not by making albums with Brian Eno. Sorry Brian, but that's the way it is.

So while I wasn't expecting that much when we were unloading the gear into this studio in Tottenham, as soon as they started playing, it was like being in a house that was continually in the process of collapsing, but was somehow just staying up – thrilling, but definitely frightening. The bumping, rusting vibrato of the harp, the spinning tumbling syncopations of the balafong, diving off on apparently random trajectories. God knows where the scraper was, and Zarra's vocals came in with such sheer invocatory *attack* it made you jump out of your seat every time. I sat there terrified, not only by the sheer raw spirituality, the dadaist rhythmic daring, but by the thought that something might happen, they might do something to fuck it up, or that the tape recorder wouldn't be working. I thought, if we can get this out of here and onto disc as it is now, it's going to be fucking incredible, because there is nothing in the way. It *is* it! I did think it might be good to include an alternate take of one of the tracks with a back beat. So Zarra gets this snare drum, and just goes whack ... whack ... I thought, Where is he putting that beat, man?

As we were leaving, the engineer said, 'So when d'you want to do the mixing?'

I said, 'How d'you mean?'

He said, 'When are you going to mix it?'

I said, 'We have mixed it.'

He said, 'What, you're just going to leave it like that?'

I said, 'Yeah, we are.'

Now the musicians could see there was a record and they were going to be big shots, they were really excited. The group went back to Holland with the idea that they'd come back and do a tour at the time of the record's release. I made it my aim in life to make sure as many people in the world heard that record as possible. It seemed that it encapsulated the genesis of so much that was most exciting, dangerous and innovative in twentieth-century culture – jazz, blues, surrealism, the Uncertainty Principle, the works. I toyed with the idea of writing a sleeve note to that effect, but I thought, No, that's the sort of thing Michael Heaven would do. Just let it *be* it.

I don't get discouraged easily, but I found it virtually impossible to get any media interest. A lot of people, magazine editors and the like, said World Music was last year's thing. I said, 'It's not World Music, man. Just think of it as a dangerous record. If it was by a bunch of acned junkies from Detroit or a gaggle of black-clad anally retentive Germans, you'd be all over it.' They said, 'Yeah, well.' Other people, critics, journalists and the like, wouldn't play it because it wasn't on CD. I said, 'CDs are for yuppies and wankers.'

202

They said, 'No, they're not.'

It got rave reviews in *Tradewinds* and *Folk Roots*, and Dirk Samuels played it on his radio programme – once. After two weeks I phoned him up. 'What's the matter, man?'

'Oh, right, the er . . . Malian thing? I couldn't quite get my head round it.'

If you can't get your head round that, you shouldn't be a fucking World Music deejay, should you? I didn't say that, I said, 'Listen to it again, man.'

He said, 'Yeah, I will.'

He never played it again.

As for the tour, no promoter was remotely interested. They'd already overstretched themselves on tours by African, Asian and Latin-American artists that were going to lose massive amounts of money. The bottom had dropped out of the World Music boom even quicker than I'd expected. So I decided to do it myself. After a week continually on the blower, all I'd achieved was an Arts Centre in Lincolnshire, a wine bar in Winchester and Her school. ('This is Mansouman and he's from . . . MALI! Can you find it on the map?')

Zarra had become ill. He reckoned it was his liver. He went to the local hospital. They weren't sure what it was, but they booked him in for tests. He decided to go back to Mali, to seek help by traditional means. He was gone two months which was a fucking relief I can tell you, even though things in some ways did become more difficult during that time. But I was expecting him to turn up at any minute, all ready to start the tour. Then one day we got a letter saying he'd died. She was really upset. I was devastated. I felt more bad about it than I can possibly say, because in my heart I'd blamed him for the fact that we'd had our house repossessed.

I'm still laughing as the taxi pulls up at the Belotel. Gabriella and Serin Ahmadou had walked out in disgust. Sajar was furious – not with what I'd said, but for showing him up. Folarin Ayinla seemed to find the whole thing vastly amusing, in his cool serene way, and my remarks genuinely thought-provoking. Not that I'm relying on any support from him. He's on a plane far, far above my grimy, dishevelled reality. Not that I need help. Sajar'll have forgotten the whole thing by tomorrow, 'cause none of these Western things touch him that deeply.

As I approach the glass doors, a dark figure steps out of the darkness: the eagle-faced porter, his features earnest and intent, the suave smile gone. 'What is your room number?'

This is it. I knew this would happen. '253,' I say off the top of my head.

He nods and holds the door open for me. When he finds out there is no Room 253, things are going to get very nasty.

In the foyer, the blue-suited assistant manager is standing straight in front of me, a broad smile on his round cheeks. 'Ah, monsieur.'

'Yeah, I'm just going to . . .'

'This won't take a moment, sir.'

He leads me to the counter, where the thin guy, the one who doesn't like me, hands him an envelope, which he hands to me. 'Thank you, sir. This is the first part.'

The first part? Of what?

'Your bill, sir.'

Bill? What's he talking about? Why's he giving me this? Didn't Sajar . . . ?

'Didn't Sajar . . . ?'

I can't tell if he's playing a game with me or not. Surely he knows. 'Who is Sajar?' he asks, his cute bonhomie suddenly gone.

'Sajar . . . Jopp. Did he arrange it?'

'*Sajar Jopp?* I don't understand.'

Come on, man, get things straight. You were in fact booked in here by Sajar Jopp's people! 'I was booked in here by Sajar Jopp's people!'

'Sajar Jopp's people . . .' By now he's behind the reception desk, going through the ledger, while the thin guy flashes me looks of evil triumph.

'Ah, oui. C'est vrai. Yes, monsieur. Your reservation was made by a Monsieur Abdou Jopp.'

'Yeah.' So come on!

'If you have any further enquiries or we can help in any other way, please let me know.'

'Yeah. Wait a minute. This Abdou Jopp, did he make any other arrangements?'

'No.'

I tear the envelope open as the lift hurls itself skyward with indecent haste. Everything is going far too fast. Why don't things just slow down? Call this a bill? It's more like an extra volume of Proust. Endless thin blue sheets with carbon annotations of phonecalls, laundry details, dockets for drinks, sandwiches, meals and room service. I've eaten all this? Christ, man. I've been ill. I've had no appetite. And it just goes on. Page after page. How long have I been here? It must be over two weeks . . . I feel weak. My head's pounding. Gimme some water, man.

After the roaring, the booming of events, so loud you're not even hearing it, that you get when so much is happening you're oblivious of everything else, I find myself sitting on my bed reflecting that the worst thing is that not only did Sajar not make any provision for my stay, it never even occurred to him to think about it. And I came here for *him*!

Then I'm thinking, Fucking Abdou. He thinks, 'He's a toubab. Stick him in a big hotel.' Doesn't occur to him to wonder how I'm going to pay for it.

I grab the phone.

'Reception.'

'How much is the exchange rate?'

There's a pause, as the receptionist adjusts to the different language and the unbelievable peremptoriness of some foreigners. But I don't give a fuck about that. I need information, fast. 'Between which currencies?'

'CFA and pounds.'

'English pounds . . . One moment.' There's a pause that seems to go on for about a year, then, 'One pound is seven hundred and eighty-four CFA.'

I slam the phone down. Calculator! I haven't got a calculator. Pen and paper! I can't do maths, but after some manic scrawling I've managed to establish that it's *too much money*!

I grab my money-belt, pulling it furiously from my waist, and tear the zip open. A couple of dog-eared notes come away in my hand. I've been robbed! I'm shaking all my different pairs of trousers wildly onto the floor. A few coins jangle out and roll away over the carpet. What's happened to all those wads of notes I've changed? What's gone on?

What's gone on is that you haven't got any money. Those wads didn't add up to much. You hardly brought any money, and you've spent it.

It's too easy. I'm on the top floor. Two doors away, a door leads into a concrete stairwell to the bottom of the building. The fire escape. Across the terrace, past the restaurant, the entrance back into the foyer, where one doesn't want to be seen, and won't be – not at three in the morning. Down the far end of the terrace there's another entrance I've seen some of the staff, the grumpy sod from the swimming pool and the neo-rasta tennis professional, using. But can you get into the rubbish-strewn lane down onto the corniche? Or do you get led automatically back round onto the main driveway? The latter, obviously. Even if there's a gate, it's not going to be open. Gate? There is no gate. The fences are there for your protection. That's what's given you the tainted, absurd, pointless security you couldn't afford to pay for that you've been enjoying over however many days, weeks... Enjoyed? I enjoyed *that*?

I sit there. Time's gone into another frequency. This place isn't a hotel, a human organic institution. It's a shell of walls I have no right to be in, a set of barriers whose legitimacy I don't recognise, can't afford to recognise. And I'm certainly not going to stay here to be terrorised, imprisoned, preyed on by that evil bastard of a hall porter.

I cram everything into the holdall, swing it over my shoulder, turn out the lights and shut the door. I'm bringing my mineral water. The big bottles are heavy in the flimsy plastic bag, but this is Africa, and I'm not going anywhere sans hydration.

The humming corridor is deserted, indifferent. The bare concrete fire escape is flooded with moonlight. Good one. I can see where I'm going . . . Bad one. They can see where I'm going. I make my way quietly down, trying to muffle my scuffling on the raw concrete. But I don't make too much of a meal of it. Because there is no one whatsoever around, and a staircase is a staircase. It was meant to be gone down.

Yes. I'm told the moonlight in Africa is no stronger than in Britain. But as I never go wandering on the South Downs in the blue nocturnal brilliance, I never find out. Out here on the terrace, it's enchanted. There's no other word for it. Maybe I shouldn't have brought the water. It's fucking heavy, and the bag handles are becoming more elastic by the moment.

I approach the doorway between the poolside and the foyer, that entrance of which I've made so much use. The moonlight's gone as I peer into the yellow French-bulbed interior. There's a surprising amount of activity. One guy, maybe a cleaner, is standing in the middle of the foyer with his back to me, talking to someone out of sight, maybe the desk-clerk guy. I slide straight past. The moonlight's back on. If you've never tried it, you really should: the limpid, milky otherness. If I meet someone now, I simply sit down with him at one of the thatched umbrella things and have a good natter. I'm creeping through their pools of enchanted shade now. Did I see signs saying the grounds are patrolled by guard dogs? I really hope I didn't. And I don't think I did. Because the idea of someone wandering round with an alsatian in this mild and mellow moonlight is not on. They just wouldn't do it, you know what I mean? And anyway, the dogs in this country are mostly of the loping, skulking, feral variety. They don't look good on a lead.

I come to the corner of the blue-grey shrubbery. There are the tennis courts to the right, with the moonlit rubbish glimmering in the lane beyond. Could I just climb over? No. 'Cause all that parched and withered bougainvillea on top's going to be a bugger to get over even if I manage to get to the top, and it's probably got barbed wire underneath. Plunging away to the left is the great dark canyon down the side of the hotel building. There's what looks like a wall, and above that, the faint glow of electric light. I head towards it. There's a faint electric burbling: a radio or telly.

I'm feeling my way in the darkness, over the rough ground. The telly's loud now, and I'm approaching the wall. It's just a kind of stockade of old boards and brush. I pull at it, and can already see more of the electric-lit yard. What is this? The back of one of those restaurants on the corniche? A charmingly ramshackle beach bar? The stockade moves. The door was just one panel leaning against the others. I put a foot through straight into somebody's washing up – a load of metal bowls that crash down on top of each other. Right. Straight through that door and out. I grab the water-bottles under my arm, and head into a sitting-room. The pool attendant, the burly, grumpy bastard and his two mates, sitting there in their armchairs with the telly full on, look back open-mouthed. They are shitless.

'Bonsoir,' I say with a friendly grin and I'm through there.

Blinking in the darkness of the lane, the moonlight displaced by the lights flashing on and off inside my head. Okay. *Run!*

The bottles are shaking all over the place, the water sloshing around in the hard plastic like the liquid of my vital organs being shaken every which way. I go headlong. The rocks, mango stones, fishbones and other crap cutting into my hands and knees. I'm bleeding. I can feel it. Up! Grab hold of those fucking bottles. I emerge, my breath raw and dragging against my lungs, just beyond the taxi rank at the bottom of the hotel drive. No, man. Not here. 'Cause the hotel people'll simply ask them where they took you. Gotta be intelligent.

Only one guy is awake. He looks pretty surprised to see me, but manages to get an offer out. I thank him politely and head on, praying the guy at the hotel gatehouse didn't spot me. Little chance. Bound to have been asleep. I'm trembling all over. I can hardly breathe. The bottle-bag is going to give way at any moment. I head on, bracing it against my leg. The holdall, also heavy, bouncing against my arse, along the sandy ill-lit side street, leading towards Sajar's studio. Haha. Yes, Sajar's studio. Thank you, Sajar.

Cutting down towards the main street. No doubt also deserted. I arrive at a corner, and there's a taxi, cruising slowly towards me. I collapse inside with my bag and bottles. 'Hotel Ndar,' I gasp.

That's right. The Auberge des Amazons Intellectuelles – and Not
So Intellectuelles. It's Thursday. I hadn't forgotten. Or rather it's
Friday morning. Pray they've still got the room.

The guy nods smoothly and pulls away.

'The price will be mille.'

'The price will be cinq cents.'

'The price will be mille.'

'Okay.'

Within what seems like seconds, we're pulling up at the Hotel
Ndar. I pay the guy and stagger out, doubled up with my bottles.
I push the door with my shoulder and squeeze inside at the
precise moment the bag breaks sending the bottles thudding and
rolling away over the black marble floor.

The tall dark woman – the Headmistress – and the fair aquiline
Fulani woman – the sweet but slightly dim Student Teacher –
stand watching at the counter. 'I thought you weren't coming,'
says the Headmistress.

Fifteen

She hates it. You know, *there*. She can't stand it. But I mean, I've never minded it. I don't love it. I really don't care one way or the other. But She'd go on about how it was my kind of place, my level. That I'd lost the other houses on purpose, because deep down, subconsciously, I actually wanted to live in a place like that. Well, I can't be bothered with things like that. When She gets like that, I just walk out. I go in another room, and put something on. And She'll say, 'That's right, go and listen to your fucking crap! That's what got us in this situation in the first place!'

But as I say, I never minded it there. It just didn't really affect me. Until this guy came to mend the wall over the road.

Some piss-artist had come down the hill from the railway bridge too fast and gone straight into it. I hadn't heard the crash, hadn't even noticed the wall was smashed. Then suddenly, I could hear this noise out there, and when I go up into the spare room and look down, I can see this bloke out there, fag poised delicately between his lips, with a measuring string pegged out, and his radio on. I mean, I like music. I'm professionally involved in music. I practically live for music. And I've caused my share of mayhem and disturbance in my time. But that doesn't mean I want to hear *any* music blaring out of crap miniature ghetto-blasters so loud people can hear every word at the back of their houses with the blinds down. When She gets in, She says, have I had a word with him? I say, a word with who about what, which

210

seems slightly ridiculous, since we're having to shout to have the conversation. I say there's no point going over there, 'cause it's the end of the afternoon, and he'll be going home in a minute. She doesn't say anything.

Next day, about eleven, I go over there. Normally, I'd probably still be asleep now, but the bastard woke me at about nine, and my sleeping patterns are so fucked I didn't get off till four. So I'm feeling a bit frazzled, a bit fraught and a bit fucked. And I don't want to be going over there, because I've got a bad feeling about it. But I've got no choice. As I cross the road, I can see that a woman, presumably the houseowner, a shapeless personage in a navy track suit, is deep in conversation with the brickie. So much the better I think with a grim and rather unhappy sense of relief, I can address my remarks to her and cut out the brickie who I've already fingered as a difficult bastard. As I approach, they pay no attention whatsoever, and I stand there feeling flaccid, unwanted and pale in the unaccustomed brightness. 'I'll make you a cuppa tea,' she's saying, 'and I've got biscuits. You'd like some of them, wouldn't you?'

'Yeah, ta,' he says in a tone that suggests he's already had enough of her fussing over him.

Finally, she turns to me with a witless half-smile, clouded over with incomprehension, as though I've just been beamed in from Mars or something.

'Would you mind er ... turning the music down a bit?' I fumble, as she looks blankly back, with the look, I reflect later, of someone on major tranquillisers.

'*Shouldnyoubetalkinname?*' intercedes the brickie. Quite right. Yeah. I should be talking to him.

'Sorry, yeah. I didn't know who was er ... But it's a bit loud. We can hear it right round the other side of the house.'

He looks at me with cold, pale eyes for a long moment. 'Yeah, okay,' he says.

The volume is reduced, slightly. But by the time She gets home, it's resumed its former level. She gives me a contemptuous look. 'I thought you were going to speak to him.'

'I have done.'

211

I'm not going to discuss it any more than that. From the spare room, I can see his tight-jeaned arse sticking up at me as he bends over his work. He's shorter than me. Wirier. Fitter – needless to say. And a lot faster and nastier. And he's got this kid with him, this tubby fair kid who's strutting up and down keeping an eye out. And I've got to keep well down. Got to keep the top of my head well out of the picture. I don't want to give these people the wrong message. I mean, let's face it, if they're the kind of people who're so insensitive as to be blasting it out at that volume in the first place, they're hardly going to respond to the kind of polite, 'civilised' comments She'd have me make. I should have marched calmly over there with a major hammer, smashed his little ghetto-blaster to a thousand fragments, said, 'Okay?' with a friendly smile, and gone back into the house. He'd have understood that. He'd probably have firebombed my house, but at least we'd have been speaking the same language.

Next morning I wake up, and She's standing by the bed. What am I going to do about it? She wants to know. Christ, it's louder than ever. It sounds like Mick Hucknall's actually in here.

Blinking and stretching, I tell Her I'm not going to do anything. There's no point. I've already been over there. But I can tell She doesn't believe it. And that's the kind of thing that makes you realise there is no point, no hope.

Mid-afternoon, I get up and despite my embargo on the day, I allow myself to be sent out with a list. I ask the daughter to come, but she's busy with her homework.

I'm rattled enough anyway by the daylight, without having to pass *them*. The brickie's intent over his work. But I can feel the fair kid watching me with a contemptuous grin. What is he, twelve, thirteen? And the very air's shaking with the tinny volume. I'm surprised the entire neighbourhood hasn't been round to complain. Where's the fucking residents' association now?

I slip down to Tesco's as quickly as possible, and slip back, head down with two heavy bags. I studiously avoid even glancing at them, but as I turn into our drive I hear the kid shout, 'Why don't you come and complain about the music now, you fat bastard?'

Later, when they've gone, about seven, She gets out there and finds some cement on the back of the car and is immediately on the phone to the cops. I'm against it. I'm telling her to leave it. I can already feel his boot sinking into my ribcage as he growls, 'Who asked you to get the Old Bill involved, you fat cunt?' But She doesn't listen.

The copper's like a pig in shit. Sprawled back on the sofa in the warm glow of my living-room sipping tea with a *beautiful woman*. He can't believe it. A bit of class, in a place like this! And it's typical of the sort of person he is, that he thinks that because he can appreciate a woman like Her – not what the headbangers down the station would call a 'stunna', but a bit of cool class – he thinks he's a bit superior. And he wants her to know that. He wants to show her that the police can be friendly, helpful, *civilised*. He's loving it, stretched out, long legs wide apart. And anyone would think I wasn't there. He doesn't address one word to me, just gives a very occasional dismissive glance towards this pale, flabby presence in the corner, as though far from being her husband, I'm some mentally retarded half-brother. He's a picture of vigorous good health, as he warms to his theme.

'Honestly, I would *love* to take these people in for criminal damage. I would *love* to lock 'em up for a few days, scare the living daylights out of them. But to be quite honest, as you didn't actually see them doing it, we would find it very difficult to make it stick, and you might then have them coming round here giving you grief. You know, "Who asked you to get the Old Bill involved?" This type of thing. So if you think they've nearly finished the work, and they'll be gone in a couple of days, you might find it easier to just leave it. I mean as I say, I would *love* to take 'em in – *love* to. But to be perfectly honest . . .'

He looks round the room. 'You obviously like music!' He peers at a row of CDs. 'Oh, what! Michael Heaven! You a fan? I've got all of his.'

She stares at the ground. 'He's a friend of my husband's.'

'That you is it?' He looks at me with new eyes. It's *his* night. But I don't say anything. Suddenly he feels awkward. 'Okay, then. I'll just have another look at the damage on my way out.'

213

He finds he can brush the cement off with his hand, but tells her to get in touch the second anything else happens. He gives her his name, direct lines, the works. Good thing I'm in all the time, or he'd be round there showing her his gun, riding her to the sound of the latest Michael Heaven CD – or he thinks he would. Not that I'd particularly care. But I would still give her more credit. Oh, yeah. I'd still give her a *lot* more credit than that.

That night, I slept even worse than usual, as I tossed and turned trying to think what I should *do*. But I could think of no solution that didn't involve sneaking up on the fair kid in the most furtive and cowardly way and stoving his head in with a blunt instrument. Unsatisfactory in many ways, except that I would have the opportunity to tell this worthless, no doubt illiterate product of incestuous coupling, before braining him fatally, that it was in fact *him* not me who was a fat bastard. And unless I could totally conceal my identity, I could not allow him to live. Because if he was once able to identify me to the brickie – his brother/uncle/father, or whatever he is, probably all three – I'd be dead meat. I can already hear him screaming, as he disables me for life, 'You touched my brother/nephew/son!' And he wouldn't go down for it. Oh, no. He'd be fined – at most. But because he'd be on Social Security, he wouldn't be able to pay it, and he never would. Oh, yeah. I've read all about it in Tesco's. That's the beauty of papers in supermarkets. You can read the tabloids cover to cover. That's how I know there's nothing you can do about it.

I've just changed some money. That's right. I found a wad of travellers' cheques in a hidden pocket of my holdall. God knows what they were doing there, but it was just as well.

I love this hotel. You can stand on the front step, as I often do, with the street before you, its heaps of sand, its piles of white-hot rubble, its ragged sore-laden beggars, its endless ambling bana-bana men with their cassettes, their pagnes, their dark glasses. One guy with a couple of Bullworkers. Another offering a shovel to everyone he passes. That guy's got a hand's span of cassettes, a balloon whisk dangling from each knuckle, and in the other, a small rack with stainless-steel kitchen implements swinging from it as he makes his way up the street. A guy offered me a pair of shoes of different styles and sizes that looked like they'd just been run over. Yes, it's all there. The Algerian alimentation over the way with the shop next to it which is just one telephone you can pay to use, on the corner of the alley full of neo-rasta dealers in crap sculptures all with their ghetto-blasters blaring. Two steps back, and you're in the still, polished, ruthlessly modulated temperateness of the foyer – yes, man, another foyer! – and you think, Thank God. Because no matter how much you're up for the teeming heat and energy out there, you do need your bolt-hole. This place is pretty basic – a plant-laden stairwell, a landing with a parapet overlooking the street, and small bare rooms leading off it – but it suits me fine. And it's all down to the manageress (the owners, a Franco-Lebanese couple, you never see), the Headmistress elle-même, who presides over the foyer with her dark Egyptian-profiled composure, demanding the life-and-death submission of the underling porters, clipping the heels of the giggling provincial chambermaids with her cool-edged ruler, threatening the tall, glamorous waiters and waitresses with detention, eliciting the bobbing homages of the hapless guests as they make their way in and out of her domain.

I shoot the breeze with her as I put my carefully sorted cash into my wallet.

'I understand you're in the music business, Monsieur Litchwell.'

'Field . . . Litch*field*!'

'I understand.'

'Yeah. I work in music.'

'And what sort of music do you specialise in?'

'Ndagga!' Ndagga is blaring, rattling street music – Sajar Jopp-type music.

Her eyebrows knit with bemusement. 'You like that kind of thing?'

'Yeah. Don't you?'

'I prefer mellower sounds. Classical music, jazz and rock.'

'Yeah? Which bands?'

215

She shrugs. 'I don't know the names. To be honest, I'm not that interested in music.'

'That's a great pity.'

She shrugs.

'What's your er . . . name?'

'My name? My name is Njai. Aissa Njai.' Yeah! Njai is the most heavy-duty Wolof surname: the lion totem, the descendants of the kings of Djolof, the cradle of Tekrurian culture. And this being Tekrur, it's also the most common, including all their slaves and dependants and griots, and a load of other people who just happen to be called Njai. But I don't need a griot to tell me which branch I'm dealing with here.

'Njai!' I breathe. 'Dom ou gainde Njai. Njai Jatta Njai – *sahare wale!*'

Her eyes narrow. 'I didn't realise you were an expert in our culture.'

'I'm not.'

'You seem to be.' She studies me through her big-framed glasses. 'Do you have any books?'

'What sort of books?'

'Any books you have finished with.'

'No. No, I haven't. To be honest, I'm not doing much reading at the moment.'

'That's a great pity.'

That's right, man. Yeah. I know what you're thinking. We're back on that question you've been itching to have answered the whole time. Has Litch *been there*? Has he been . . . *involved* with a Tekrurian woman?

Good question. And the answer is . . . No. No, I haven't. African women, yes. Malians, Ivorians, Ghanaians. Even Nigerians. But Tekrurian? No. Some of the most beautiful, the most elegant and graceful, and proverbially the best-educated women in Africa, they're just too scary, too tough. They've got too many angles covered. Swanning through the streets of N'Galam in their incredible robes and turbans, their knifepoint stilettos, their shoulders magnificently polished over the necklines of their billowing boubous, absorbed in their supercilious smirking and pouting, their endless schemings, feudings and rivalries, their heads full of Mercedes limos, Cartier watches, diamonds, gold bath-taps. Oh, yes, they may look you up and down, assessing your value in hard currency, but don't even think about it. You're like me. You're a big, soppy, old English sheepdog in love. You're a man of the damp green north. You couldn't hack it.

Because however progressive they may appear, they're still into their immemorial groove of backbiting, politicking, poisoning and litigating. However sweet and demure – particularly the more sweet and demure they appear – when they've feasted enough on the fruits of the earth at your expense, when they've got as much cloth-of-gold, glacé silk, as many jewels, Cartier watches, BMWs, planes and marble baths with gold taps as they can out of you, they'll get their lawyers, marabouts, hood-boyfriends and relatives in high places to fleece, curse, abduct and deport you, before they toss your worthless fucked-out husk into the harmattan. And I'm not the only one who feels like this. Why do you think the men here look to Oxford anthropologists and BBC film directrices for a bit of light relief? And when these women come here, they're treated as honorary men, and if they know what's good for them, they stay well out of the coteries and cabals of the women of N'Galam.

'Papa Gorgi Ngom,' the taxi driver is saying. 'I haven't heard of him for years.'
  'No?'
  'No. I think he may be dead.'
  'Yeah?'
  'Well, no. Because his name still means something from Lumière d'Afrique. So I think if he'd died, we'd have heard something about it.'
  This is the reaction you get from everyone. They talk about Papa Gorgi as though he's a figure from the shadowy and irretrievably distant past. Half these people, you know they could locate him in a maximum of three phone calls. They just don't want it to get back to Sajar that they led you there. But this guy's not like that. He's got no axe to grind.

217

'These people were old-fashioned musicians. They were not organised. And Papa Gorgi was a big drinker,' he's saying, as we round a corner into a posse of troops in full riot gear.

Fuck.

The guy brakes, and they peer into the car, big Mickey-Mouse muzzles pushing forward, the eyes of their gas masks big and opaque beneath their anorak hoods. They see me and wave us off up a sidestreet, away from the centre of town.

What were they carrying? Tear gas? Rocket launchers? Bazookas? I'm not up on hardware.

'C'est dure,' says the driver raising his eyebrows. 'But they're not there for you.'

'What were they er ... there for?'

He shrugs. 'C'est les étudiants, je crois. Un sort de riot.'

Sajar's deep in some phone call as I arrive at the studio. He's alone – just him and the thin, lemur-eyed caretaker. The phone call goes on and on, gets deeper and deeper. I listen, not understanding a word. And there's a strained, almost tortured note in his voice I've never heard before. He puts the phone down and looks up, his eyes wide.

'What's happening?'

'Where?'

'Outside!'

'Looked like some kind of demo.'

He nods. 'That was my lawyer. The government want me to play at a concert for them, but I have said no.'

He's said no? Is that er ... *sage*?

'Sage? Ce n'est pas un question de sagesse! C'est un question de principe! Tu comprends?'

Yeah, yeah. That's absolutely right.

'Have you phoned Gabriella?'

Gabriella? I'd virtually forgotten that woman even existed.

'That was the purpose of this meeting.'

'Yeah, yeah.'

I try the Belotel, where I assume she's still holed up. Artfully disguising my voice, I learn they haven't seen her for three days. I could try Serin Ahmadou Cham's place.

'Non, non la femme est là!'

Which femme?

'La femme de Serin Ahmadou!'

Yeah, yeah. Bien sûr.

It's late by the time I get back to the hotel. I don't know what time, but the foyer's already taken on the dark and womb-like stillness of the deep, deep night. Aissa Njai – the Headmistress – is sitting behind the counter absorbed in a book. She's always reading, this woman, and always in English. One day it's Danielle Steel, the next it's *Hidden Vectors of Underdevelopment: the Example of the Sahel*. The other night she came in the restaurant when I was eating, and asked me if Robin Hood was still alive.

She looks up as I approach. She's sitting back in her seat, her braids hanging loose over her shoulders, and she's not wearing her glasses. She doesn't say anything, she just sits there looking straight at me, with a heavy, languid look as though she's just got out of a major steam bath. I want to turn and run, but I'm caught, hypnotised, though if I stay here much longer, I'm not going to be able to breathe.

She holds the book up – *The Mayor of Casterbridge*.

'You know this book?'

'Er . . . yeah.'

'You've read it?'

'Not all of it.'

'You must finish it, it's a fantastic book. Very passionate.'

'You're er . . . into passion.'

'Very much so. It caused a lot of problems in my marriages.'

Marriages? 'How many have you had?'

'Two.'

'That's er . . . beaucoup.'

'Not really.' She sits there, looking straight at me, her expression utterly unchanging, with the ruthless immemorial self-sufficiency of an Egyptian statue. 'My hubands were both highly educated men. But very conservative.'

219

'Yeah?'

'Yes. They believed that a woman should stay at home, do the housework and say nothing. But I can't live like that.'

'No.'

A faint, almost imperceptible smile plays over her lips. 'I'm sure you agree with me.'

'About what?'

'That a woman can be educated, live her own life and still be faithful in marriage.'

'Yeah . . . Definitely.'

'You look tired.'

'Yeah, I am.'

'You should go to bed.'

'Yeah.'

'Now.'

I don't like having breakfast here. Firstly, I don't feel remotely hungry, and the idea of eating their excellent all-butter croissants makes me feel really ill. Secondly, while the evening staff are all incredibly tall, charming and good-looking, the morning staff are all squat and sullen and behave as though having to fill your cup is a form of humiliation for which they will eventually pay you back tenfold. Employing them is probably Aissa Njai's way of getting everyone out of here so they can get on with the cleaning. Whatever, I shouldn't be here. I'm in the music business, and this is far too early for people in the music business. But I keep waking incredibly early.

I'm supposed to sign a chit so the breakfast gets added to my bill, but the squat, sullen staff aren't interested, and neither am I.

Unwashed, and more than slightly dazed, I wander out onto the front step and press flesh with the doorman, the couple of taxi-drivers who are habitually slumped out there, the odd beggar of my acquaintance and the Runover Shoe Geezer who's in attendance today – No, man, I'm not interested. It's dull and overcast. Hot. And oddly quiet, with fewer people, fewer marchands ambulants, fewer commuters, fewer amblers and loiterers. I wander over to the corner of the Avenue Wagane

Diouf and . . . What the fuck has happened here? Shopkeepers – mostly Lebanese, natch – are sweeping away the acres of broken glass. One of several burnt-out cars is being hauled away. One of those immemorial shade trees is hanging loose by its roots. What the hell happened to that? And there are cops and soldiers everywhere. A woman is trying to set herself up on the kerbside with her proverbial three oranges. Didn't take long for the insistent and enduring rhythms of the informal sector to try and reassert themselves – 'cause even the cops need oranges. But they soon move her on.

I wander on past the open-fronted shops of the cloth-vendors, their steel shutters half down, their owners standing around wondering whether to open or not. For these guys to pass up even the slightest possibility of doing business, things have got to be *really* bad. As I approach the crossroads at the Marché Hakim Nder, there are more and more people hanging about, civilians talking in low voices or just standing, watching, waiting. I squeeze up to the twisted, rusting crash rail, crowded with guys sitting, striding and sprawled across it, all peering across at the tank beside the market entrance. Or what passes for a tank in this country. A big armoured car. And it looks impressive, sitting there, its gun turret commanding this strategic crossroads. Most of the stalls are heavily shuttered, but a few are open as usual, their boom-boxes blaring. And what's that I hear from directly over the way? The swaggering, impudent bassline and resound-ing brass of Sidi Taal's 'Chômeur' – the Unemployed Man: 'My wife just asked me why we've got nothing to eat.' Only Sidi could invest a line like that with such husky, big-girthed plaintiveness against a background of such arrogant funkiness, Sidi, the man who speaks to the chômeurs, the students, the Gaddhafists and neo-rastamen. Playing his music here seems dangerous, seems nervous-chuckle-makingly provocative, guaranteed to get a fuck-ing riot started – or get that ghetto-blaster smashed by the pigs at the very least. But then again, this is Tekrur. So while Sidi's radical, if you look at it another way round, he's also conserva-tive. If the government organise some big jamboree, he'll probably find himself turning up in his role of national poet. It's

221

like the party that have been in power here since independence are called the Socialist Party, while they're the most capitalist organisation you can possibly imagine. The opposition party are obviously anti-socialist. But when I asked a leading political journalist if they were to the right or left of the government, he just said, 'We don't have that here.' It's like Sajar: where does Sajar Jopp stand politically? You can't possibly know. Because there is no ideology in this country. There is only deal-making. Until now.

'Hey!'

I turn, there's a familiar face smiling at me through the crowd.

'You never know me.'

'Of course I know you ...'

'Daouda Mboob.'

'C'est ça.'

We shake hands vigorously.

'Did you listen to my cassette?'

Lie, man, lie! 'Most of it.'

'Yeah?'

'I loved it. I can't wait to hear the rest of it.'

'Oh ... I'm so happy.'

We're standing, holding hands in the rapidly thickening crowd. I'm vaguely aware of something going on behind me. Did someone just jab me? Was that a hissing I heard. I turn and look straight into this pair of wild, bloodshot eyes.

'What do you want here?'

He's thin, with a prominent forehead and bulging fanatical eyes. The crowd are massing, squaring up behind him. They look indignant and mean.

'How d'you mean?'

'Why are you here? This is not for you!' That's right, man! Lessons in Anti-Colonialism, Number One: Get the White Man!

My musician mate's responding in indignant Wolof. Everyone's looking, turning, pressing in. We're on a cusp between support for my guy – Yeah, so what's it to you anyway? Let him walk where he wants! – and the very understandable desire to string up a white man. And my oppressor's got his mates with

222

him. More of them are crowding in behind him all the time. He's not badly dresed. A student zealot from Central Casting if ever there was one. And I'm old enough to be his father.

'I'm not with you, man.'

'I'm asking you what you are doing in my country?'

Oh, that! Yes, I could be a spy, an 'expert', a militaire or just a small-time exploiter, sucking the lifeblood of their country.

'Listening to music.'

That threw him. He wasn't expecting that.

The crowd are pressing in closer. They're agog. This is street theatre.

His response is limp and desperate. 'Why do you want to do that?'

'Because I love it.'

The crowd are really heating up. Come on, their panting breath is screaming, Stick it in! Mboob's leaning over my shoulder, bellowing in Wolof in my defence. But no one's paying any attention to him. The zealot raises his finger in my face. 'Why don't you go back to your *own* country and listen to your *own* music?'

I raise my finger. 'Because I prefer *your* music!'

'Why?'

'Because it's got something that our music in the West has lost totally – humanity! I love the rhythm, the feeling, the ambience. That's why I've been coming here for ten years. And I'm gonna keep coming back!'

He tries to speak, but I'm already into another volley.

'You see, I've got to be free, man. I've got to feel free! That's why I can't live in America. Because I can't feel free in a country where apartheid effectively exists! I can't feel free in a country where a quarter of the black population between the ages of sixteen and twenty-five are in prison. I can't live in Britain, because I can't feel free in a society where old people are being raped, tortured and murdered by children!'

'So you've come here . . .' The guy's relented totally. He looks like he's going to offer to put me up at his place. But once again I cut across him.

'Non! Parce que je ne peux pas tolérer l'inégalité de ce société! Here I'm a toubab! I'm separated from the people. But I can't be free like that. I can't do it. I cannot *be* a toubab! I'm from New Malden! I'm just *a man*, if you know what I mean. I can't sit in a fantastic restaurant if people outside aren't eating. I can't base my happiness on someone else's misery!' He tries to cut in, but I raise my finger for rhetorical emphasis. 'Hamga, gor, gor la! Jigenne, jigenne la! Toubab ak nit kou nyoul *yepp* benna la!'

A great roar of approval. Everyone's back-slapping and air-punching in sheer delight. I'm outta here.

'Stay and chat with us!' begs my former oppressor.

'I can't, man. I've got a meeting with Sajar Jopp. In fact I'm already late. Ciao.'

The Sahelfest Super-Session has been called off because they couldn't get a firm commitment from Stokeley Jackson. It was only because of his presence that not only the Africans, but the Cubans, the Brazilians and the Antilleans were prepared to put aside their rivalries, hatreds and demands for preposterous and vainglorious amounts of money, that the TV companies were going to mobilise the film crews who were going to tell the world about the event, the major in question would do the deal for the album, the video and the t-shirt that were going to pay for the whole thing. With Jackson there, it was front page, it was News at Ten, CBS, CNN, whatever they have in Japan and the whole works: the most extraordinary gathering of black musicians ever assembled, finally getting it together on the sacred earth of the Mother Continent. Momentous. Without him, it was a bunch of guys with unpronounceable names congregating somewhere you'd never heard of, that would merit an item in the arts pages of the *Guardian*, if that. Jackson had said he was up for it, that Sajar was his spiritual brother, that he would do it 'cause it was for Africa, and it was something of great importance for all Black People. But he wouldn't actually sign anything. Or at least, the people who stand between him and the rest of the world wouldn't allow him to sign anything. He kept saying, through the people with whom he communicates with the rest of the world, that it was no problem, that he was definitely gonna come. But without his signature, none of the South Africans, the Nigerians, Camerounians, Zaireans, Algerians or Malians would sign. Nor would the Brazilians, Cubans, Franco-Antilleans, Trinidadians, other Americans or Black British. And as time was passing, they were all getting sewn up into tours, recording schedules and holidays with implacable paranoid wives. So the Big Boys, the head honchos of the legendary Black American label for whom Jackson had recorded since 1962, the rival communications corporation who for some reason had been scheduled to do the album, brought in by the smaller British communications corporation who were making the film and had been contracted to oversee the whole thing, and all the mega-mega-mega-lawyers who could buy certain African countries outright if they wanted to, the managers whose word is law, the bullet-proof cashmere brigade who sit in gold-plated offices behind desks the size of small towns, all the hustlers, bastards and nasty pieces of work who've spent decades working themselves into positions whereby nothing can be done without them taking a cut, have to be got involved, and they pick up this letter from N'Galam with this list of unpronounceable names on it and say, 'What the fuck is this?' So Stokeley Jackson doesn't come.

Meanwhile at this end, the relatively paltry, but for this country, extremely significant amount of seed money put up for the Super-Session, has disappeared in circumstances that may or may not have something to do with Serin Ahmadou's wife's fury at his public carrying on with Gabriella. Oh, yes. While I'd always assumed he lived somewhere like Cambridge or Tufnell Park, it turns out he lives *here* and he's got a real-life Tekrurian wife and she's not amused. She's related to the Minister of Culture and various members of Sajar's band and she's trying to get them to withdraw their support, which, considering the Tekrurian government, in line with their policy of maintaining their position as the coolest country in Africa, are the honorary patrons of the festival, and Sajar and his band are supposed to be playing a massive gig to announce the launch of Sahelfest 2000, could make

225

things difficult. Back in Blighty, the BBC who, since the Americans have shown no interest whatsoever, represent the main mass-media vehicle of Sahelfest 2000, have said that all programmes in the proposed Sahelfest 2000 Season on BBC 2 will have to be fronted by faces familiar to the British viewing public, which means those great Africans Lenny Henry, Trevor Macdonald and Michael Buerk. In other words, compared to the way these things normally go, it's all going fairly smoothly – though Gabriella, not being attuned to the Ways of the World, has taken it all rather hard, particularly, I'm told, when Serin Ahmadou's wife turned up at the Belotel with a gang of kids ready to stone her. In fact, the last thing I heard, though I can't believe it, she'd totally disappeared.

Up two flights of stairs, through a door and I'm in Sajar's office. And it's packed! Soldiers and police sitting around drinking tea while they wait to discuss security arrangements for the launch gig, apparatchiks in designer sportswear holding languid, but intent conversations against the filing cabinets, while others elbow their way importantly through the throng with their files and bits of paper, peer at the bleeping video screens, tear massive lengths of paper from the chattering fax machines. Oh, yes. Sajar's operation's well into the Third Wave, and who was it told him to get tooled up? Who do you think? And crammed onto every spare chair and bit of bench, perched on the edges of the desks, crowded along the walls are scores of guys, Sajar's distant relatives, friends and relatives of childhood friends and anyone else who's had the front to come here in the hope that they can do something for Sajar, or that he can do something for them, just sitting and standing silently, with that defiant, defensive Tekrurian cool, that says, 'I may be unemployed, I may know nothing, but I am a man – so back off!' There's Salimata in her Armani-framed glasses, her normally unimpingeable-upon cool ever so slightly ruffled by the even greater than usual crowds of people. There's Soumano, who manages this end of the operation, cool, suave, but radiating this sense of 'Why when I've taken the trouble to get all these major degrees in law, accountancy and business studies, do we still have all these white people hanging

226

around?' Oh yes, as a White Man involved in Black Culture, you do come across that kind of attitude, but you can't afford to let it get to you, and you generally find that a very modest amount of schmoozing brings them round.

And there in the middle of it all, blithely and coolly affable as always, getting on with things, apparently unperturbed by the mayhem around him, is the man himself. He sees me and points, 'Yeah!'

I point back, 'Yeah!'

I don't so much see as feel the looks of resentment, but as I say, if you're sensible you don't pay attention. And let's face it, most of these kids haven't been around long enough to know *who I am*.

I make my way across the room, shaking hands, throwing out Salaam Aleikums, Nangendefs and Ça vas as custom demands, to a desk on which Nyanya Guisse is holding court.

'Yeah,' he says, taking my hand. 'Nice?'

'Nice, man.'

'Tous va nekh?'

'Wow, wow.'

'All right, man.'

And he's back into his lubricious narrative, the only word of which I can understand is 'jigenne' – woman – a word whose unguent plasticity, particularly in its French spelling 'djiguène', has always evoked for me a pair of *major* hips swaying slowly and complacently along a street. And Nyanya, with his great mouthfuls of words, is stroking, touching and poking this jigenne every which way, working her into a labial frenzy. I love this language, man. It's the only one I know where you can have sex verbally without even talking about sex. Then I notice another word sliding into the conversation – again and again – *toubab*, a white. Then the two words in ever closer proximity: the white woman. Everyone's chuckling and guffawing as Nyanya mimes someone having their bottom smacked. That's right, man. Not fair is it? Still, you've got to laugh.

There's a sudden crash from outside. Amazingly loud. And everyone's on their feet rushing towards the window. Sajar's already out on the tiny balcony. I squeeze out after him. If there's going to be some major mayhem, I want a grandstand view.

It's a jolt coming out into the light and noise. People shouting. Whistles blowing. Cars honking near and far. And feel the adrenalin, man! There's no substitute for the spine-tingling booming of a crowd in full heat, and it's like the entire youth of a country's down there, from the designer sportswear'd children of the élite to the ragged urchins via the numberless others who are simply getting through – hell, there's even a few *girls* down there. Some are carrying placards in French saying things like, 'Fuck off Fascist Government!' But mostly they're empty-handed, smiling as they march quickly towards the National Assembly. And there's a megaphone, its message utterly incomprehensible, already broken into this blaring, reverberating abstract music, powering the crowd, bringing a tear to an old man's eye – 'cause I love to see the young people enjoying themselves!

Then I hear other voices, other tones. Looking down, I spot the kids from this morning – Central Casting Revolutionary and his mates – all shouting and waving up at me. 'Come on!' I shout, raising my fist in solidarity. Nyanya Guisse, beside me, adds his stirring bellow, urging them to greater feats of courage and defiance in heavy-duty Wolof. They respond with whoops and roars of enthusiasm. Then someone spots Sajar, and the whole crowd's cheering and waving, giving him revolutionary salutes as they move past, the pace slowing as more and more people come flooding into the street. Sajar waves back, smiling nervously.

'Merde,' he says, under his breath.

'What's that, man?'

'My car is down there.'

I can just make out the silver roof through the trees immediately below. But I haven't got time to think about that, because suddenly, as if from nowhere, there's this deep and immemorially droll voice:

'*Sajar – Président!*'

There are whoops and shouts of laughter. The voice comes again, dragging the vowels out with a deep and immemorial languor.

228

'Sa-jah – Prési-dawnt!'

Other people echo the cry. Quickly it turns into a chant, 'Sa-jar, pré-si-dent!' Booming and resounding with the passionate energy of many voices, filling the canyon of the street, powering the crowd's movement along it. I look at Sajar, his features set in a strange expression of excitement and uncertainty.

There's a sudden crack, not that loud, like a firecracker going off a couple of streets away, and the sudden mad drumming of feet as everybody's running in every direction at once. People falling, screaming, getting trampled on, then dragging themselves to their feet and running clear – scattering among the trees and cars below us or running back the way they came. Within seconds the street is deserted.

There are a couple more shots, slightly nearer. We can see the people crowding behind the cars, including Sajar's car, below. Then there's a megaphone, very different to the students' megaphone, presumably telling people to disperse. We can see some of the people below slipping away along the side of the building. We hear vehicles grinding along the street, and then the troops come into view, rifles levelled, unhurried, anonymous beneath their helmets. Then a figure runs out from among the cars. At first I think he's going to throw something. But he's got nothing. It's my guy: Central Casting Revolutionary. *What's he doing?* He stands defiantly in the middle of the street. He's saying something. I can't hear it. Probably something like, lay down your weapons and join us. One of the soldiers raises his rifle. I can see Central Casting Dude bridling, he's going to raise his hands, but the guy's already shot him. He staggers for a couple of seconds then teeters over sideways. The soldiers move on without pausing, step over his body and on up the street.

I feel really ill, man. I've got to get out of here. I push back off the balcony, through the crush of people all trying to force their way forward. I've got to sit down. I get myself out onto the dark stairwell and sit on the top step. Everything sounds very distant. The shouting, whatever it's about, starts to seem further and further away, and it seems echoey and shiny, like it's moving round the inside of this big steel bowl that's encompassing my head, swivelling in the air around it. I'm going down. The stairwell is getting bigger and darker, closing in around me.

I wake up, and I'm cold. I'm in my room at the hotel, covered in just a sheet. It's pitch dark and the air-conditioning is full on. I can see the red pinpoint of the air-conditioning controls. I get up, stumble towards the light, and flick the switch. It's suddenly quiet. Then I'm aware of the roaring of all the air-conditioners in all the other rooms. I lie down, covering myself in the sheet in the darkness. In a few moments, the edge'll have gone off the cold. In an hour, I'll have to turn the air-conditioning back on.

I'm here.

The kid got shot. They just shot him! Just like that! Without even pausing to think about it.

Sixteen

'Do you speak English?'

'Oui. Mais je préfère parler en français.'

'That's funny, because I speak French, but I prefer speaking in English.'

'C'est rigolo,' he says, stone-faced.

I'm in the Air France office on the Avenue Guillaume Savary, where the Avenue Fouquet extends beyond the Place de la République – and it's a bit more tranquil here, a bit less hassle, a bit less fucking dangerous. Even so, there are still plenty of people hanging around, guys in robes just standing there looking mildly pissed off, guys in ragged trousers peering blankly in through the big glass window, eyeing the various bulges in my pockets with a detached, abstract interest. And of course, there are the beggars, people with no legs, polio victims crawling round on all fours staring reproachfully into the pristine, air-conditioned airline office, which with its big gold lettering, huge globes and tan leather seating, is an immaculately preserved relic of the nineteen-fifties. Yes, even down to the plastic plane on the counter it's exactly like the place where Jean Seberg books her ticket in *Breathless*. And like Jean, I want to escape. I don't know what decade I'm in here, let alone what continent. That's why I'm going somewhere where I'll know where I am, where I'll really know I'm in Africa. I'm going to the source, man.

'You wish to fly to Mali?'

231

'Oui.'

'When do you wish to fly?'

'Er . . . en peut-être une semaine.'

'En peut-être une semaine,' he repeats as he taps at his keyboard. The incredibly good-looking woman seated further along the counter looks at the burly dishevelled white man with the abysmal French with a mixture of pity and disgust. No, let's qualify that. There's no pity there. I'm trembling inside. Ever since the kid got shot, I've been trembling inside. Maybe I should see a doctor.

'Your name is Litchfield?'

'Yeah.'

'Monsieur Andrew Litchfield?'

'Yeah.'

'You have already made a reservation to Bamako?'

'Non.'

'I have it here. Monsieur A. Litchfield, Air France flight 1035, Bamako via Bissau and Ouagadougou. Tomorrow afternoon at 1600 hours.'

Via Bissau and Ouagadougou. That's a hell of a way round. And it's not the first time I've heard of that. It rings very faint bells, and I can hear them resounding, as though from distant parts of a house. A house I wasn't even aware I was in. A house . . .

Shit!

The guy is talking to me?

'What?'

'You wish to reserve the flight?' he asks with a look of slightly suspicious puzzlement.

'Er . . . non, non. C'est trop tôt. Est-ce que . . . Have you got anything in about a er . . . week.'

He goes back to his screen and his tapping. 'Oui. In eight days time. Bamako direct. 21.00 hours. Est-ce que c'est trop tard?'

'Non. C'est bien.'

'Il faut payer en deux jours.'

'Oui, oui. C'est er . . . combien?'

'Cent milles.'

232

'*Cent milles?*' Internal flights in Africa used to be amazingly cheap. They used to be virtually nothing. 'C'est beaucoup.'

He shrugs. 'C'est le prix.'

His incredibly good-looking colleague narrows her eyes, obviously wondering why this disgusting slob is able to jet round the world at will – and expecting to do it at less than market prices – while incredibly cool, immaculately sculpted people like her never go anywhere. That's another reason why I want to get out of here. There are too many good-looking people. If people are going to look at me with undisguised contempt, I'd far rather they were ugly.

Bamako via Bissau and Ouagadougou. That is a *hell* of a way round. That's like going to Berlin via Madrid and Istanbul. Must be a round trip.

And why, you ask, don't I just get that flight? By three tomorrow, I could be past the hustlers, through the customs, police and soldiery, sitting in the cool, pristine white room on the edge of the blank, sun-baked runway – out of here and onward, saying goodbye forever to this fucking place – where even when they shoot people in cold blood they manage to invest it with a degree of complacent cynicism and the response, even of people on the same side, shows unbelievable callousness. Response? *There was no response!*

So, you say, do it. Just go.

No, I don't want to do that. I can't . . .

Why not? There's nothing here for you. Nobody gives a damn about you here.

No, I . . .

And what are you going to Mali for? To hang around in more hotel rooms, making phone calls to people who aren't interested? They'll all be wandering around in their robes even more locked into their inscrutable purposes than they are here. And it'll be ten times hotter, and the hotels don't have air-conditioning and the phones don't work. Why don't you just go back where you belong, man, and face the music?

. . . I er, I can't go till after Sajar's gig. The Sahelfest 2000 gig. I've got to be here for that.

Why?

I've just got to be. Okay?

I'm sitting in the hotel bar, which seems to be a popular watering hole for left-field professionals and the more glitzy end of the artistic milieu, with Amadou . . . Okay, you're fed up with all these names you can't remember, right, so we'll just say they're a filmmaker and a journalist. The filmmaker specialises in low-budget music videos (the only sort they have here) and the journalist's into cultural gossip. My kind of people! Mind, they've slightly lost me, because although the conversation started in English, talking about major government corruption on the cultural front (what else?), we somehow drifted into French, and then after about twenty minutes of trying to follow that, I realised they were actually speaking Wolof.

You're not *still* here? I hear you ask. Course I am. Turned out that kid – Mr Central Casting Geezer – was only hit in the arm. As soon as the soldiers passed, Sajar and the others got down there, put him in the back of the BMW and drove him to hospital. A couple of other people *were* killed, but he's going to be fine. I visited him in hospital, told him not to pull a stunt like that again – if he's that determined to get his picture on the cover of *Newsweek* there are safer ways. He was dead chuffed. So was his mum.

I feel a sudden jab in the ribs. I turn and look straight into the haggard, make-up besmeared face of Gabriella Malinowski.

'Mr Henchard, I presume!'

I look at her, then turn back to my conversation, as a third of a pint of prime Tekrurian lager hits the side of my head.

'That wasn't very cool,' I say with icy calm. 'This is N'Galam. You've got to be cool here. You know what I mean?'

'Ya kna'aa myne?' she mimics, in a grotesque parody of a Black South London accent. 'Here he is, the great *expert*, the great *authority* on *African* culture. You make me absolutely sick!'

The filmmaker and the journalist are looking on open-mouthed.

I can feel everyone else in the room turning, gobsmacked. I've got to get her out of here. When you're professionally involved in Black Culture, it's not good to be seen to be associating with mad white people.

'Un instant.' I flash my companions a long-suffering smirk and take Gabriella's arm.

'Geddoff me!'

I turn and give the bemused intellectuals, embarrassed aid workers and mind-boggled bar staff a rueful what-can-you-do kind of smile, and get Gabriella out into the foyer.

'What's happening?'

'Oh . . . *Fuck off!*'

Aissa Njai's not at the desk – thank God. The inscrutable guy is standing up, looking very concerned. I give him a reassuring wave.

What am I going to do with her? I can't just push her out into the night. And I'm certainly not taking her anywhere. I'd better get her up to my room.

'That's right,' she moans as we ascend the stairs. 'Get Gabriella out of the way! Can't have her ruining our street credibility.' I put my arm round her in case she falls. A black couple coming the other way give us a dirty look.

The room is small. Gabriella only has a few feet to fall onto the bed. 'That's better. So this is . . .' She's about to fade away, then she comes back into focus. 'Any chance of a cuppa?'

Tea! Good idea. I'm out on the landing, then I go back. 'Milk and sugar?'

'I don't give a fuck.'

They don't do room service in this hotel. But the guy agrees to send some up. He wants to keep things as quiet as possible.

When I get back up there, Gabriella's dead to the world.

What am I going to do? I could fuck her in her sleep. But apart from the fact that it always seems kind of ungallant, she doesn't represent such a tempting prospect in this state. So I undress, shift her incredibly heavy body a couple of inches across the bed and crawl under the sheet.

235

'Have you got any drugs?'

Er ... I'm asleep, man. But the voice is insistent in my ear.

'Have you got any drugs?'

I frame my words with effort. 'Waddya wan' drugs for?'

The voice is cold and controlled. 'So I can kill myself.'

I'm awake now. 'You don't want to do that.'

'Don't tell me what I want to do. I must have a mania for self-destruction to be attracted to someone like you.'

'You're not attracted to me ... are you?'

'Of course I am. Couldn't you tell the first time we met?'

'Well, yeah. But I thought I was imagining it.'

'No.'

'So er ... if you're attracted to me, does that mean ...?'

'Don't be so stupid.'

'What about Serin Ahmadou?'

'He's absolutely pathetic. As soon as he found out we didn't have the money, he wasn't interested.'

This is going too fast for me. 'Didn't have what money?'

'The money for the festival, for Sahelfest 2000.'

'You haven't got the money for Sahelfest 2000?'

'No.'

'What about the money from BP?'

'There is no money from BP. BP are taking legal action against Sahelfest 2000 for using their name in our publicity. But they don't realise they can't take legal action against Sahelfest 2000, because Sahelfest 2000 doesn't exist.'

'Sahelfest 2000 doesn't exist?'

'No.'

Shit. 'What about the brochures?'

'I made it all up.'

'It sounded really good.'

'It would have been fantastic if that stupid little man at BP hadn't withdrawn the development money.'

'Why did he do that?'

'Oh ... I don't know. Some stupid reason.'

Yeah, like he realised he was dealing with a mad fantasist.

'So you just sent out a load of press releases, printed up some glossy brochures, and you thought that if enough people thought it was happening, it would happen?'

'No ... Yes.'

That's great. That's the sort of thing I would do. That's the sort of thing I *have done* – though not on quite such a major scale.

'Why did you do it?'

'For Serin Ahmadou. I thought if I organised this for him, he would leave his wife.'

'But what about your academic career?'

'What?'

'You know, your credentials in academe. Couldn't you have used them to do it legit?'

'What are you talking about?'

'Your thesis ... Surely you've got the contacts to do the whole thing properly.'

'I don't know where you get this stuff from! I haven't written a thesis. I haven't been to university.'

'You haven't been to university?' I'm feeling indignant now. I mean, I haven't been to university, but who does she think she is just wandering around, not having been to university?

'No.'

'I thought you were kind of a ... professor.'

'No.'

'But it said that in your brochure?'

'No, it didn't.'

'I could have sworn it said you were at the Musée de l'Homme.'

'No. It's another of your fantasies.'

What about her father? Surely he can help.

'My father? What could he do?'

'He's loaded.'

'Loaded? My father's a builder in Hornchurch. He's just about keeping up payments on his retirement bungalow ...'

I'm positive she said he was a millionaire industrialist.

'No. It's you. You're living in a fantasy world of your own.'

That's great coming from her. But what's she going to do?

'There's nothing I can do. I can't face all these people.'

'Who?'

'The BBC ... the Tekrurian government ... Sajar ...'

'Don't worry about Sajar,' I say, putting my arm round her. 'I'll sort it out with him. And don't do anything rash. We'll work something out.' That's right, now that she's here, in bed with me, a warm, live woman, I feel I could be very, very helpful to her. We could do all sorts of things. We could run away together. We could go to Mali ...

'I'd rather you didn't touch me.'

'I thought you found me attractive.'

'I don't know what I feel.'

And that's probably just as well. Because there's no way I could be seen to be involved with her. If I was once to get tainted by the fiasco of Sahelfest 2000, I'd never be able to do anything in this country again.

When I next wake up, Gabriella's gone.

Mor Jeng lives up in the dusty, windswept Beverly Hills of N'Galam, not far from Sajar's new house. Why the millionaires all want to live up here, I can't imagine. Jeng's the garage owner, importer/exporter and property developer who backed Papa Gorgi Ngom's Orchestre Fin de Siècle. He's now proverbially the richest man in Tekrur.

We come to a big windswept wall with smooth grey security gates.

'You want me to wait?' asks the cab driver.

'Er ...' If he doesn't, there'll be no way I can get back. On the other hand, if I'm unsuccessful, I won't be able to pay him. 'Yeah.'

I press the entryphone three times, then there's a voice buzzing through interference. After I've shouted into it and it's been buzzing for some time, it goes quiet. Then I'm aware of someone watching me. I turn and see a slight but severe-looking bloke standing at the corner of the wall.

'Qu'est-ce que vous cherchez?'

'I've come to see Mor, man.'

'Do you have an appointment?'

'I'm an old friend.'

'He doesn't see anyone without an appointment.'

'I've just come from England. I'm only here very briefly.'

He presses a code into a zapper, and the gates open a couple of feet.

'Vous savez que c'est dimanche?'

'Oui.'

'On doit préserver la paix sur le dimanche.'

'Oui, oui ... Vous êtes Chrétien?'

'Non.'

He leaves me on the terrace beside the grey bunkerlike house which gives little hint of what I assume to be the scale and opulence within. Because let's face it, if you've got as much money as Mor Jeng and you don't have scale and opulence, why are you bothering?

The guy reappears looking more disapproving than ever. He beckons me with a nod. 'You have a short time. C'est dimanche.'

'Yeah, yeah.'

Mor's by the pool, around which there will eventually be major tropical vegetation, though it hasn't quite got going yet. He's sitting on one of those rocking sofa-on-a-frame things you get by swimming pools, watching a young fair coloured woman I take to be his wife, who's in the pool with a young child. He's stocky, handsome, with a close-cropped grey beard and a pot belly. He turns only as I'm actually approaching. I take his hand, offering full formal greetings in Wolof. He gives clear, concise replies, but doesn't ask me to sit down – and apart from squeezing onto the sofa thing beside him or getting on the ground, there isn't anywhere.

'How's Papa Gorgi Ngom?'

'Can you tell me what it is you want, because I normally try to keep Sunday for my family.'

I give a hollow laugh of incredulity. 'I've just come to see you, man. Don't you remember me?'

'Of course I remember you. What exactly do you want?'

I tell him.

'So you've come here begging for money?'

'No. I'll send the money as soon as I get back to England.'

239

He looks at his wife and child cavorting in the water, utterly oblivious to the unseemly exchange taking place a few yards away.

'You know, I have a bad feeling about you. And I can't remember precisely why ... I used to carry the details of every transaction I'd ever conducted, down to the last quarter-franc, round in my head. That's the way we've always done it. And our memories for every kind of debt, for what must be paid back, whether good or evil, are very, very long. But as soon as you start keeping written accounts, which I now do, you lose that capacity.'

'Look, man ...'

'When I was a child, and I saw the whites in their official cars, with their pith helmets, I thought of them as close to gods. Even the petits blancs with their small shops had a status far above that of the highest black man. Then, when I first travelled to Europe, I saw a white man sweeping the street, and I was deeply shocked. Since then, I have travelled widely. I have seen so many white people allowing themselves to be subjected to the most unbelievable humiliation I don't even notice it any more. But when I am *here* in my own country, it's different. I don't like to see a white man falling from what the greater part of the population of this country still regard as his natural position. Sometimes when I am driving through N'Galam I look out of the window, and occasionally I see white people, whether they are hippies or what, I don't know, but they have allowed themselves to sink so low that even the beggars are kicking them. And it makes me feel very uncomfortable. I don't know why. I should take pleasure in the degradation of these people who have caused my country so much suffering through slavery and colonialism. But it just makes me feel ... *embarrassed*. This is why I am going to give ... not lend, *give* you some money. But after that, I don't want to see you here again, ever.'

André Chadid lives about half a mile away. I don't know how he scores in the league table, but he's hardly poor. A Maronite Christian, he put money into Sajar's operation when he first went solo – though I've no idea how things stand between them now.

There's a car and people outside the gates, which is good. Means I don't have to fuck about with entryphones and butlers.

Chadid, a wiry, stubbled bloke in shades, is loading his family into the Merc for what looks like an afternoon at the beach.

'Yeah, man! How's it going?'

Chadid, who's just filled the boot with buckets, spades, towels and the like, slams it shut.

'I was just passing . . .'

Chadid goes back in through the gates.

The driver is looking at the ground. Chadid's wife and the nanny are inside the car. A couple of the kids are peering out at me.

I catch the driver's eye. 'I knew André when he was involved with Sajar Jopp. I'm in the music business in England. I'm over for a few days. I thought I'd drop by.'

The driver looks back at the ground. Chadid comes back out of the house with his fags. He nods to the driver.

'I er . . .'

They get in the car and drive off.

'Those people were not so very, very friendly towards you,' my driver is saying as we ascend the lower reaches of the Avenue Wagane Diouf. 'This is why I don't like Christians. You're not a Christian?'

'No.'

'It doesn't matter if you are. I'm not a fanatic. I just don't like them.'

The soldiers are slumped on their tank by the Marché Hakim Nder. There are very few people around. The French naval base along the coast is on red alert. There's said to be a fleet of destroyers anchored just out of sight in the grey gluey haze off the coast. The paratroopers are ready in Marseilles. The Foreign Legion are sitting in Chad all tooled up. The Americans are on standby. This is Tekrur, *the* stable country in West Africa. There's no way anything's going to be allowed to happen here. Meanwhile in N'Galam, it's Sunday afternoon and nobody's bothered.

241

Aissa Njai's behind the counter. She doesn't look up as I approach.

'Ça va?'

'I hear you've been disgracing yourself.'

'How d'you mean?'

'I think you know the answer to that.'

She looks different. She's done something to herself. 'You've had your hair straightened?'

'You don't like it?'

'I love it.'

'I don't think so.'

'No, I mean it.'

Come on, you're thinking, shouldn't you be worrying about Gabriella? She's probably wandering empty-eyed along the Corniche through the wastes of noonday, a prey to every mugger, rapist and throat-slitter, or ODing agonisingly on paracetamol in a darkened room.

Who?

Aissa's not wearing her glasses. Nothing against glasses: glasses can be incredibly sexy. But without them she looks softer, more human. And while I've never been that into straightened hair, largely for political reasons, she's got a *big* wave in it that makes her look incredibly glamorous, like Martha from Martha and the Vandellas. Go for it!

'It makes you look incredibly glamorous.'

She snorts. 'That woman who was here, she works for the fête?'

'What, my ... colleague. Yeah, she's wasn't er ... well.'

'I can't believe that a woman in that position would behave like that.'

'She's been getting very over-tired. I'm having her repatriated.'

'I would love to go to England.' She's looking me full in the face now. Her tone has changed, and her slanting eyes once again have that hazy, satiated, sultry look. My skin is starting to tingle. 'I really love that place.'

'Yeah. You don't like er ... France?'

'France is also good. But I prefer England, for further studies.'

'Further ... What would you study?'

242

'Business Administration.'

Business Administration? That's a bit kind of *stark*, isn't it?

'I really love that subject.'

Mm. Maybe it's not such a bad idea. Maybe a course in Business Administration is exactly what I need. We could do it together. We could hold hands under the desks in lectures.

Aissa's face is now about six inches from mine. My throat's so tight I can hardly breathe.

Only trouble is, I'd have to pay for both of us, and the way things are at the moment, I don't think I'd be able to do that.

I'm lying on my bed. I'm shattered, but I can't rest. Every time I close my eyes, all I can see is Aissa Njai's satiated, implacable features, so big they totally fill my field of vision. But where the eyes should be are just holes – like one of these masks, burnished to an immemorial smoothness, that are suffused with an ancient and inscrutable knowledge and have always, in the full and complacent cast of their mouths, a barely perceptible smirk. Oh, yes, Aissa's just like one of those women you knew when you were about thirteen, who were the same age as you, but behaved as though they were a good ten years older, who went out with boys in the fifth form and took a distant, patronising interest in you while all the time you knew they were *subtly taking the piss* – the kind of women who on reflection had a seriously damaging effect on your ability to relate to women, and who still do occasionally flit across your mind during protracted bouts of onanism – and don't say you didn't know any women like that, because this is all archetypal. I could try and jerk off now while thinking of Aissa, but that would be too sad even for me, when the woman herself is just sitting at the bottom of the stairs. I mean, why don't I just go down there and . . . What? What would I say? What would I do? Do? I wouldn't have to do anything. She knows exactly what's going on. The woman's a total operator. And this is her domain. Whatever she wants to happen is going to happen, and whatever she doesn't want to happen isn't.

But let's face it, if she was to take me in the back room, get up on the table and say, 'Okay,' I wouldn't be able to do it. I just wouldn't. I'm not like that. I'm the sentimental type. I've got to feel there's more to it than that. And I just can't relate to Aissa Njai like that. Because I just know that if I were once to get ... involved with her, her entire extended family would be on my case to solve their financial problems, she'd get me involved in some scam of her brother's whereby I'd end up in jail while he went scot free and she betrayed me in endless humilating ways with half of N'Galam. She'd sell my record collection to fund her children's education, or even worse, she'd lend the rarest and most valuable items to her rangy, priapic boyfriends and they'd bring them back ruined, or they wouldn't bring them back at all. Don't get me wrong, I'm not saying she's a bad person. I'm just saying she's a woman of N'Galam, and *that is what it is like*. And let's face it, the moment she realises that far from being able to bankroll her degree in Business Administration at the LSE, Simon de Montfort Technical College or wherever it is, I'm practically destitute – that I have negative equity on life – she's not going to be the least bit interested. I mean, what possible reason *would* she have to be interested?

By the time I go back down, Aissa Njai's gone. Big relief. The inscrutable guy on the desk says someone called telling me about a gig in a certain nightclub. Probably that kid with the cassette – which I still haven't listened to. I should go. I may yet go. But the idea of staying up till four in the morning to see a band that I somehow feel I've already seen, is not really on. 'Cause they'll be good, but they won't be that good. And all the time I'll be thinking, How can I translate what's good in this into something that'll appeal in the Western context – which is what they, of course, want – without losing the funk, the feel and the taste that make it inimitably Tekrurian? And the answer is, you can't. The amount of bands you've come across in places like this who've got one song that is just so fucking brilliant. And you think, let's get them in a decent studio, re-record it – not poncing it up too much, but so you can actually *hear* everything ... And it never works. Somehow the magic is always lost, *and* it doesn't appeal in the Western context. Because it was in the first place only ever something for the Tekrurian or whoever-it-is people and the few fond and foolish souls like myself who bother to take an interest – that is the context in which it has real meaning, and it should really be left like that. But even assuming they've got that one killer song, how do you explain that to them, without them feeling you're trying to fob them off 'cause you're too mean to bother? Fact is you can't. That's why I'm not going to the gig. Meanwhile, I must see Sidi Taal and Papa Gorgi Ngom.

In the restaurant, I order capitaine with aubergine purée and pommes de terre vapeur, which I consider with a kind of abstract relish 'cause my appetite still isn't back in place, not fully, even though the food here is probably the best in N'Galam: modern French with a touch of African. The chef is a member of the Jola ethnic group, in case you're interested. The waiting staff, in contrast with the grumpy breakfast crew, are all incredibly tall and good-looking – like out-of-work actors – and they speak French with a suave and obliging graciousness that makes you feel that you speak it incredibly well too. The walls are a pale and soothing blue, though the golden light at ground level soon fades into the sombre, ominous darkness round the unused overhead galleries – a reminder of the heavy, dolorous darkness of the rainy season which will soon be upon us, preceded by a period of intense, maddening heat and its advance armies of mosquitoes, blister-beetles and plague-carrying parasites, and that I've got to get everything wrapped up and be out of here before that gets underway.

Meanwhile, I'd far rather sit quietly here than go haring off to some night club. Could it be, I occasionally wonder, that I'm actually losing interest in music? I still haven't bought so much as one cassette on this trip. Incredible, except that when you're actually here, the urge to possess and consume and to *have* is never as great as when you're scheming and brooding amid the dark canyon-like shelving of your collection. Because here, it's not problematic, it's not recherché, hard-to-get and therefore gruesomely overpriced. It's just there, just what's happening. It's not mysterious, distant and *other*. It's just a load of cassettes.

But of course, I will buy. I will have. Because I know that if I

245

don't leave this place laden to bulging, hardly able to walk for all the carrier bags, panniers, mud-cloth sacks packed to bursting with cassettes and any old records, CDs and printed archival material, I'll no sooner be on the plane than I'm kicking myself and by the time I get back into the vaults of my collection, I'll be actively grieving, marking out the spaces it would have filled, like a barren woman mooning over clothes bought for a child she never had.

I look up, and Serin Ahmadou Cham is sitting opposite me.

'Where is Gabriella?'

Shit.

'Why are you asking me?'

'I'm told she spent last night here.'

Christ man, that seems like years ago.

'She was too . . . tired to get back. So I let her crash in my room.'

He sits there. He's only got one expression, this guy: intent and immemorial knowing. And you can't change it, you can only turn the volume up or down. At the moment it's *up*. And it's making me feel bloody uncomfortable – particularly as I'm trying to eat a meal.

'Do you want some of this food?'

'No.'

He almost got annoyed there. I almost broke through the immemorial knowing. And that may not be such a good thing. He could be armed.

'I'll be frank with you. I don't like you.'

'No?'

'Not at all.' He looks at me, a faint smile on his lips. 'It is a matter of great regret to me that I cannot give Gabriella the commitment she desires. But I still feel very deeply for her, and I feel a profound need to protect her from people like you.'

'Yeah?'

'Yes. Because people like you are in a sense destroying the world.'

Fucking hell, man.

'I mean it. There is a cynicism, a deadness that you spread to everything you touch. And the tragic part is that you don't realise that the person you are hurting most is yourself. Whenever I see you I am reminded of the words of Babou Ngor.'

'Who?'

'You don't know Babou Ngor? He was a poet. He trained in classics at the Sorbonne and became Minister of Culture in the post-independence government – a man I admire enormously. He writes that the African, when he does something, becomes completely absorbed in that action – becomes in a sense one with it. Whereas the white man, because of his reliance on analytical reason, always stands apart from his actions – is in a sense destroying his actions.

'And you, though you probably don't define your operations in terms of analytical reason, but in relation to transient notions of something like "hipness" or style, are nonetheless a case in point. Because while you think you like African music, and of course in a sense you do, you cannot simply enjoy the music, you cannot simply let the music be what it is. You are prevented from fully participating in the music, not by your colour, but by your own deep-seated inhibitions, so you have to fret and fuss over it, you have to try to shape and mould it according to your own strategies and agendas.'

'And what are they?'

Floored him. Floored him, for an instant. 'I'm sure if you examine yourself, if you look deeply into yourself, you will know the answer to that.'

'So it was you who told Gabriella I shouldn't be involved in Sahelfest 2000 because I'm a fat, white bastard?'

'I didn't put it quite like that, but I felt it was necessary to avoid some of the mistakes of previous events of this kind.'

'Then when you realised the money wasn't in place you weren't interested?'

'If you think that you have a very false picture of the situation.'

'How did you know I even existed?'

'Oh, I've been watching you.'

'How d'you mean?'

'I've made a kind of study of people like you. I see you at the conferences and symposia, sitting there, always alone, and I wonder to myself, Who is this man? What does he want? Why is he here? And it's not that I resent your interest in Black Culture. Far from it. In fact . . .'

'You got this wrong, man. I don't go to conferences.'

He hesitates. 'I'm sure I've seen you at at least one.'

'I maybe went to one, once.'

'And you made a statement from the floor that was highly offensive to many people there.'

'I don't remember that.'

'I've made a collection of people like you. I've even thought of writing a novel on the subject. It would be called *The Africanists.*'

'Go for it!'

'I cannot afford to waste my time. Do you think anyone would want to read a novel about someone like you?'

'Yeah.'

'I doubt it. The average Western bookbuyer is not the slightest bit interested in Africa, unless the subject is approached from certain highly specific and very banal perspectives.'

'That is absolutely true.'

'Even with my own work, I have found that Africa and African culture have to be approached very carefully if one is to retain the attention of the Western reader – particularly the English.'

'The French are worse, because they're so fucking twee about it.'

'You think so?'

'Definitely. Do you want a beer?'

'Let me get them.'

Seventeen

'So what does Sajar think of it?' asks Michael Heaven.

'Oh, he's up for it.' Matter of fact I haven't even broached the idea – a compilation of all the other Tekrurian artists who've recorded at his studio, selected by me, natch – and I'm not going to, not till I've sorted out the matter of the twenty-five large – not that that's been mentioned recently. 'Yeah, I mean, it would be a great opportunity to get a lot of these people heard.'

'Yes, I can see that.'

The way this guy talks, with this slightly patronising sense of interest . . . It's like, because all his projects, all his shite music, have to be accorded the greatest respect, he gives whatever you're talking about a kind of respect, a kind of weight too. It's like if he gets in a taxi in London, and the driver wants to tell him about this fucking appalling novel he's writing in his adult education class, he'll listen and discuss it with him as though it's something incredibly important that's going to be published by Faber and Faber or somebody. This is the kind of thing that gets him his reputation as 'a nice man'. But all the time, people like me and the taxi driver, and no doubt you too, we're just dust to this guy – human dust!

'There's a guy called Mike Leedham at Sensor. If you discuss it with him, we could maybe work something out. I think it sounds like a really interesting project.'

Typical. Thinks he'll just casually absorb and subsume another of my ideas. No way. I wouldn't put this out on Sensor with Mike Leedham at the controls if it was the last label on earth. 'Yeah,' I say. 'I'll give him a bell when I get back.'

We've reached the beachside market area. Heaven forks to the right, up towards the Plateau. His driving is slow and careful. Methodical.

'It gets more built-up every time I come here,' he observes.

He's out here to do some filming for the video of his forthcoming album, which he's going to do in the south where they've got the forest, the major baobabs, silk-cotton trees and all of that. The crew are due in a couple of days, but he came early to get his house aired. That's right! Turns out he's got a house three doors along from Sajar on that grotty estate. He's had it for years, and I never knew.

'I may try and do some writing when the crew go back. Get a few new songs done. I've always found it very easy to relax here. To concentrate on whatever it is I want to do. Away from the pressures. I've done a lot of my best songwriting here.'

He glances off to the right at the Atlantic – this great sheet of faintly sparkling haze. 'Look at that!' he says. 'Isn't it fantastic?'

Yes, I suppose it is. When you're outside, when you're skating over the surface of things in a Mitsubishi jeep, it's easy to notice things like that. But when you've become absorbed into the fabric of the city, when you've started moving to its raffish rhythms, its ancestral codes, its dark and ambiguous undersway, you experience these things in a different way. That's why I don't feel annoyed with Heaven any more. Because I'm no longer fully part of his reality. But he doesn't know that. He thinks that because he's come here and he's seen the water sparkling, that he's really *in it*. But he's wide, wide, wide of the mark.

'Have you heard much about this Sahelfest 2000 thing?' he asks.

'Ah, yeah.'

'It sounds very interesting. I suppose you're involved,' he laughs.

'I'm ... helping out.'

'I bet.'

I knew it. He didn't just come out here to do his video and his songwriting. He heard about Sahelfest 2000 and he couldn't resist coming out to sniff around, to see if it could be of any use to him. But he doesn't realise that Sahelfest 2000 doesn't exist. Sajar's expressly forbidden anyone to speak about the problems till after the gig – which, incredible though it may seem, is going ahead. And obviously word hasn't got out in Britain yet. Poor Gabriella, she didn't realise that if people like Michael Heaven want to be involved, you can't stop them. And you shouldn't try. Because they're bankable. They bring the good things with them. If she'd had Heaven involved from the outset, she probably would have got her development money and she wouldn't have had to have topped herself or whatever it is she's done.

'Are you all right?'

'How d'you mean?'

'You seem very quiet. Less ... animated than usual.'

'I'm fine.'

'How's Sarah?'

'*What?*'

'Wasn't it Sarah, your ... partner?'

'Yeah.'

He feels the need to quickly change the subject. 'So how long have you been out, this time?'

'I dunno. Weeks.'

'That's great. I've always admired the way you just seem to be able to throw yourself into it. Unfortunately I've never had the time to do that.'

Did you hear what he said? Did you? *How's Sarah?* Bastard tries to tuck me up with Sajar over twenty-five grand. Twenty-five grand he has, for all I know, himself had and long since spent. And then he has the fucking nerve to say, *How's Sarah?*

We arrive at the studio, and Heaven parks his car. He reverses it into a space immediately behind Sajar's BMW. The way he just *parks* it, anyone would think we were in England.

We step onto the pavement, and Sajar appears in the doorway. A broad smile spreads over his face – a smile of tenderness and gratitude, a smile that acknowledges everything they've been through together, and the sadness of how much time they have to spend apart. They embrace, cleaving themselves tightly together, inhaling deeply, closing their eyes. Then they stand, holding hands, looking into each other's eyes for a long moment. Sajar looks as though he's going to cry. As an uptight, emotionally repressed Englishman, Heaven shouldn't be able to stand it. But he's been to men's groups, Navajo sweat lodges and tantric workshops, so he's cool.

'My elder brother!' says Sajar.

'It's been a long time,' says Heaven.

Sajar's functionaries and technicians standing around us on the pavement all smile with pleasure. After all, that's what they're paid to do.

'Gabriella,' says Sajar, when Heaven's gone. 'Il n'y a pas de nouvelles?'

'Non.'

He considers the matter gravely.

'We're going ahead with the concert?' I ask.

'Oui. Pour le moment.'

'Is Michael going to be performing?'

'Who?'

'Michael . . . Michael Heaven.'

'Non. It's nothing to do with Michael.' He considers. 'Anyway, he won't be here.'

You know when they take an Amazonian Indian to Manhattan, and instead of staring up in awe at the skyscrapers, he just goes into a kind of cultural suspended animation, staring mutely at the ground, 'cause he just *cannot* take it all in? Paul Gilbart's like that. He's like that in his own country. He's like that in his own city. For all I know he's like that in his own house – or should I say his mother's house.

And like a lot of mild-mannered, apparently inoffensive little men who don't say much but observe everything in a dank and ruminative silence, he makes women uneasy. She, for example, couldn't stand him. Typical that women generally find your

252

average charismatic megalomaniac rapist utterly charming, but get edgy round a guy like Gilbart who would never in a million years have the bottle to carry out any of the heinous sex crimes he is no doubt contemplating behind that blank façade.

And for someone who has managed to assemble what must be one of the largest World Music collections on the planet – and that's over and above what he's stolen from me – he is surprisingly poorly travelled. Not only has he never been out of the British Isles, his few visits out of London have been largely to gigs for which I arranged him free transport. To say he speaks no languages other than English would be an understatement. Let's face it, the guy can hardly fucking speak English!

How he managed to inveigle his way into my world-view was because he's the kind of person who's prepared to do virtually anything to get records, CDs and cassettes other than actually pay for them. Since he was in those days too lazy and cowardly to involve himself in outright crime, and too repugnant to all known forms of life to be offered vinyl for sexual favours, this came to consist largely of hanging round my office, answering the phone, putting things in envelopes and doing things on the cheap Amstrad computer I never managed to work out how to use, in return for which he took away all the gear of which I was mistakenly sent two or more copies (quite a lot given the myriadness of my addresses), all the reggae reissues ('cause I've got all the originals on mint vinyl), all the jazz, rock, MOR and all the tickets to gigs I didn't have time to go to, all the receptions, buffets and parties where he lurked lank and furtive and ignored by all. Plus he got to meet the great and the good. Oh, yes, Paul Gilbart has met Sajar Jopp. An event remarkable for the way he managed to piss the mainman off by mispronouncing his name – not easy to do, you'll concede, but Gilbart somehow managed it. He was showing a degree of unusual animation, 'cause he probably has got the world's largest collection of Joppobilia – other than mine – and I was thinking, Why's he suddenly started talking in a Geordie accent? And Sajar's standing there thinking, Who's this fucking idiot?

But Gilbart's like that. People take against him instantly, even blithely good-natured people like Sajar who normally don't give a toss either way. If you're with Gilbart, people instinctively avoid you. But I always liked him. I helped him. I gave him chances. Why? *Because I'm a nice man.*

Then one day, Gilbart was left some money by his grand-mother and he turned up at the office waving a cheque for three large. Within two hours he'd been made a director of Monster Productions. Yes, I know. I know. Don't say it. But I thought he'd be easy enough to control. But Gilbart, like a lot of dirty, feckless, lazy, apparently backward people, turned out to have surprising resources of low and feral cunning. That's how he became The Man Who Ripped Me Off.

'How are you, man? Everything working out?'

'Not bad, man.'

I'm lying on a bed at Nyanya Guisse's place with Doudou Ndow, Sajar's bass player, arranger and musical director. Most of the music you've heard on Sajar's records over say the last seven years, was actually written by Doudou Ndow, the burly boy wonder who was drafted into the band while still at school. 'Cause as Sajar's expanded his activities and found more and more of his energies sucked off into the business, the statesman-ship, the PR and the endless interviews, he's had less and less time for the music. And if you didn't actually like a lot of the music that was produced – thought it was a bit too smoothed out, a bit too blandly international – that's because while everyone brings something different to the group – Fafa and Nyanya those irrepressible street rhythms, Mamadou Faye his unashamedly rockist guitar, Tapha Jain the plaintive cadences of the khalam, transmuted through his trademark Fender Strat – Doudou's a jazzman. His elder brothers were musicians, so he grew up steeped in Charlie Parker, Weather Report and Roy Ayers. Highly, highly intelligent, he speaks a funky jazzman's English, 'cause while on one level he's just another Tekrurian dude, part of his mind sings in the supra-national, supra-ethnic language of jazz. That's why he says 'man' at the end of every sentence, that's

254

why we all do, to give respect to and show our identification with the jazzmen – the aristocrats of the Black Race.

'You have not heard any more from the Festival woman?'

'Nothing.'

'C'est bizarre, man.'

'Trop.'

He's raised on one elbow. I'm prostrate, pouring with sweat. That rainy season's definitely on its way. Rhythm guitarist Tapha Jain comes and slumps down beside us with a groan. 'It doesn't bother you?' he asks. 'The heat?'

'Yeah, it does. It's too much, man.'

'D'accord. So how do you see the concert, Litch?'

'How d'you mean?'

'Things are desperate in this country. There are tanks everywhere. People are being shot in the street like dogs. The people in the villages are starving. The head of the opposition is under house arrest. People are totally confused. Yet we are having a concert to celebrate a festival that is not for the people of this country, that most people in this country will not even know is happening. Can that be right? If it was up to me, we would not be involved in this festival or this concert!'

Tapha's about my age, but wiry. Nice bloke. Very sincere. A bit too sincere. A bit too inclined to go off the deep end about neo-colonialism and exploitation. He's the one who's always stirring it about how Sajar doesn't pay them enough. There's always one like that in every band. They're like the shop-steward. You've got to neutralise them without them realising you've done it. That's where your skill as a manager comes in. And what Tapha doesn't realise is that the government can't afford for this concert not to take place. They've staked too much prestige and credibility on their honorary sponsorship of Sahelfest 2000. If the truth were to come out now, that they'd been taken in by the delusional fantasies of a mad Englishwoman, that the president is patron of a festival that doesn't exist, there'd be mayhem. They just can't afford to have one more fuck-up on their hands. Even more importantly, the entire country's waiting for the concert with bated breath. It's Sajar's first big concert in over a year, the red-

255

letter day on everyone's calendar. They're opening up parts of the stadium they don't normally use, making it the biggest concert in Tekrurian history. It's been sold out for weeks, and the entire youth of the country is in a state of excited expectation. If it were to be cancelled, there really would be riots. Can you imagine it? A government brought down over a rock'n'roll concert? Could happen!

And the last thing Sajar wants is to give his many rivals, ill-wishers and detractors an opportunity for a field day. That's why he's given strict instructions that no one, not even his band – particularly his band – are to know more than is absolutely necessary about the problems with Sahelfest 2000. There's only a handful of people in the President's office, the Ministry of Culture, Serin Ahmadou Cham, Sajar and me who know what's happened. And we're keeping quiet – till after the concert. Because let's face it, after the concert Sahelfest 2000'll soon be forgotten about of its own accord.

'See, the thing is,' I say, 'It's all part of the system. The World System, which is completely mad.'

Tapha chuckles. 'Il est radical!'

'Tu es communiste, Litch?' asks Doudou.

'Non . . . Anarchiste!'

Nyanya Guisse comes swaying slowly into the room. 'Ai-yo!' he sings in a crooning parody of a griot voice. 'Litch is among us! Litch, the anarchist with the big wanger!'

Everyone laughs. Then Nyanya too collapses lifeless in a chair.

In the West, you've got your passes, your stickers, your massive laminated name-tags with elaborate graphics to deter fraud, holograms, mugshot, potted biography and credentials for Access All Areas. Oh, yes. You need that, so you can be waved through, so you can be stood aside for by all the jobsworths, minders and armour-plated gorillas, and gawped at enviously by the great unwashed. And it's all quasi-military: leggy broads, well past their sell-by date, but still frightening in their leather, leggings and shades, brandishing clip-boards and telling everyone where to go, and the grizzled old pros marshalling the roadies, drivers and equipment. And of course, the punters eye you, The White Man on the Sajar Jopp Tour, as you stroll importantly past, your pass, laminated talisman of your potency, swinging at your chest, and they can see you're not lugging gear and they can tell that for you, at your age, to be there, with your characteristic air of wry world-weariness, that you've been there, that you've seen things they could never hope to, that you're *business*, that you *are* rock'n'roll.

And when you get on these massive mega-tours, with maybe four or five *big* names touring the great stadiums of the world, with say Avedon taking the photos and Antonioni filming it all, it gets totally unreal. It's like a great army on the move, and you've got maybe ten or twelve categories of passes, signified by different colours – from the stars themselves, who move through it all with a god-like obliviousness, down to people who've maybe had to *pay* to get into the press enclosure, who're like the lowest rung of the rockocracy. It's medieval, man. To get backstage, you've got to go through maybe five levels of security. And woe betide you if you find yourself in the wrong area with the wrong pass.

'Let's see yer pass!'

'I'm just going to see Sajar Jopp, man.'

'Let's see yer pass!'

You proffer it, a foot-square sticker half-covering your Levi jacket. Category J.

'Right, Colin! Can we get this guy out of here!'

'I've gotta see Sajar Jopp!' you squeak plaintively.

'No, you haven't!'

Within seconds you're deposited unceremoniously into the bare and beleaguered tunnel leading back to where you should have been in the first place.

So, if you're not Category A, there's really no point in going. And if you've been in the business for a quarter of a century, your sense of self-respect shouldn't allow you to accept anything else.

But in Africa, it's different. And I'm not talking about the old days when it was all so loose and relaxed everyone knew who you were, and it didn't matter if they didn't. I'm talking about when they got their own stadium gigs together, when they got the army involved, got their own gangs of heavy-duty bouncers, minders and gorillas organised. Because the fact is, and you're going to hate me for saying this, and in a way I'm going to hate myself for saying it, if you're white and you comport yourself in the right way, you don't need a pass. They'll not only let you pass, the police'll be blasting on whistles, the troops'll have the sticks out and the arms raised, and the call'll go along the line from the bouncers to the minders to the gorillas: 'Get the guy through!' Oh, yes. It always used to be that if you were white in Africa, you were automatically a VIP. It's not so much like that now, but you can still play it to your advantage if you so choose. Isn't that neo-colonial, I hear you ask. Well, it is and it isn't, because not anyone can do it. You couldn't do it. No chance. You'd be at the back of the queue and the back of the crowd with all the kids and the yobs kicking you and pelting you with orange peel. In fact, you probably wouldn't get in at all. But that's what Africa's all about: politicking, making connections and creating zones of influence for yourself. You can't just turn up in Africa on your own and expect to have a good time. You've got to have your teams of fixers, minders and jobsworths working away, getting things organised for you. Basically if you're white in Africa, you're either a VIP or you're fucked.

So, here we are, another year, another stadium. Somehow, no matter when I go to N'Galam, things always conspire to climax with a massive stadium gig by Sajar Jopp. And when Sajar plays one of these things, everyone knows about it. It's like Cup Final day in London. There's a holiday air, and it's as though everyone's on their way there. This is the launch gig of Sahelfest 2000, but ninety-nine point nine per cent of the people there won't even be aware of that. They've just come to see Sajar.

So, you wonder, what is a stadium in Africa like? Well, it's much like a stadium anywhere else, but a bit more battered, a bit more worn down and stained by the wind. And of course, the ground in the middle is a bullet-hard desert of red termite-infested earth. But the most extraordinary aspect of the whole thing is the location. We're miles out in the suburbs here, the low hills desultorily covered in a shanty-like sprawl of mud and corrugate compounds, with patches of brittle rubbish-strewn scrub left exposed, giving the impression that the hills themselves are immense rubbish tips partially colonised by humanity, above which looms suddenly the vast, and I mean *vast*, outline of the stadium, like some immense extra-terrestrial craft unaccountably marooned among the ebbing tide of the city's suburbs. And by six o'clock, the roads leading out towards the stadium and the blue paths up over the rubbish hills are dark with figures, all swarming ant-like and intent towards the concert. It's like a great pilgrimage, and among the thronging crowds veer and sway the buses, taxis and pick-ups all packed to the gills. And all over the city great crowds stand waiting for more vehicles. The young girls, out of their school uniforms and into brilliant cotton prints, mini-dresses, boob-tubes, high heels, newly plaited, straightened, wildly sculpted hair, lip gloss. The guys are all in freshly pressed shirts and slacks, and a few shell suits, leather berets and heavy shades, but mainly shirts and slacks, 'cause this is Africa. Yes, it's all so clean, so wholesome. This is Sajar's New Africa on the move. And where's it going? To his gig, of course. Later, the older people, the VIPs, the suit-wearers, the starched robed merchants and their spectacularly boubou'd wives will be arriving in their cars and official limos.

Up on stage the band complete their soundcheck. Sajar's not here yet. He'll be off in some dark place, phoning a few thousand miles, conferring, sorting, meeting the shadowy titans of law and money, leviathans of the financial, legal and political nether-worlds through whose ties of honour, prestige, respect and sheer graft, formed over decades, he's been able to pursue his increasing domination of Tekrurian society. But it all takes time. That's why his cousin and backing singer Leyti Mbaye is at the microphone. A great morose bear of a bloke, he never smiles. But now he's unaccountably showing me some teeth and raising his eyebrows. Mamadou Faye, the lanky lead guitarist, earnestly cradling his Strat with its black and yellow Fender strap he's managed to keep in pristine nick all these years, looks at me uncertainly, as though waiting for something. A look of intent

259

and unspoken recognition passes between me and Doudou Ndow. Talking drummer Fafa Mbaye shakes his head, rolling his eyes as the curved stick flails limp-wristed onto snakeskin and this spiralling gurgling phrase bulges and booms out over the lonely hardness of the pitch and the acres of empty seating darkening in the dusty gloaming. And the rest of the band are already in there. When it gets this close, this tight, this telepathic, there's no need for counting in. The bass goading the wheezing synthesiser, the traps booting in, playing off the dry snap of the sabar, answered by the growling breath of the horns.

Outside on the teeming hillsides, among the crowds massing at the stadium gates, and on the swaying heaving minibuses, there's a sudden gust of excitement and panic. It's started! They're playing! And we're missing it! There's a second of rushing, clambering and shoving, which if it continued would almost certainly incur massive fatalities. Then the music peters out into random plonking and crashing, the musicians unplug their instruments, the stadium doors are opened, and soon there's only me left on stage watching the dark tide swarming across the steep sodium-lit banks of seating.

In the bowels of the stadium, the band sprawl around the white-tiled dressing room and showers, chatting, smoking, cracking the odd joke. How many are going to be here tonight? Seventy-odd thousand? But these guys have done it all before, many, many times. At least they'll be going home to their own homes tonight. There's going to be some limit to the endless, endless hanging around of rock'n'roll.

I wander out onto the pitch, along the route they're going to have to take to get to the stage. Yes, man! I can feel it as I step out under the great silver arc lights, the heat, the energy and the sound of the crowd – dark beyond the great brightness of the lights, the dull, ocean-like roar of a few tens of thousands of people talking and joking and laughing, and every single one of them can see me: that lone and mysterious white man wandering on that enchanted silver interim, the area of bullet-hard pitch directly in front of the stage, that glows spectrally and invitingly in the electric glare – the area that tauntingly distances them from

260

the stage, and which none of them are gonna get near, because the state is out in force tonight. Immediately beyond the touch-line begin the ranks of the combat-fatigued troops – no guns, that I can see – their faces, with the lights behind and above, dark and anonymous. The smell of soldiery, of boots, gun oil and ruthless hard-booted action hangs heavy in the air, the thought of the tear-gas brigades and the helmeted riflemen sitting outside in their armour-plated vans and troop carriers – just enough to subtly dampen the euphoria, deter the odd over-enthusiastic fan and anyone who thought they might try to use tonight to make some kind of statement. And they can see me, the troops. They're only in fact a few yards away. I can feel them watching me, half of them thinking, Who's that fucking guy? Let's arrest him just to see the look on his face, while the other half are thinking, No, leave him, man. That's Litch.

Reggae music suddenly begins to pump, at surprisingly low volume, out over the crowd. There's an appreciative ripple, and the buzzing murmur of the crowd goes into a slightly higher key.

Sajar still hasn't arrived. That's unusual. Because although there's an army of promoters, functionaries, middle-men and technicians wandering around backstage among the friends, relatives, well-wishers and high-league liggers, and everything seems to be running smoothly enough, he's normally put his face in by now, because basically, he doesn't trust anybody to do things right. The promoter, a huge bearded bloke, patent-leather shoes gleaming from beneath a cream damask boubou, takes my hand with a fruity chuckle.

'Long time since we saw you.'

'It's been hectic, man.'

'Welcome, anyway.'

'Cheers.'

Yes, man. Everything's buzzing nicely. You wouldn't think the country was on the brink of cataclysmic social upheaval.

There's some throbbing and crashing behind me: the support act, a comedian and his troupe of drummers and dancers, making sure their gear's working. The comedian, a roguish grey-bearded party, keeps coming over, smiling, winking and repeating his name in conspiratorial tones. It gets like that. You know what I mean?

There's a sudden roar of feedback from outside, then an unbelievable roar of excitement, as the disco suddenly cuts out leaving us hanging raw on the black abyss of expectation. Yes! We're getting there. I rush back out onto the pitch.

'We're in for a good time tonight!' booms the promoter, or some such all-purpose rock'n'roll banality, in his throatily guttural Wolof. Yes. The guy can talk, and when he gets to ... Sajar Jopp, he's already drowned by the roar. I mean, you'd think the novelty would have worn off. When Sajar's in town, he usually plays at least twice a week in smaller venues. Most of these people can't afford to go to his club or the National Theatre, but even if they could it wouldn't make any difference. These people have an unlimited appetite for Sajar Jopp.

The support act file on and the audience goes back to its chatting, joking and yelling to people several rows away. Oh, yes, I've been out there among the punters on many, many occasions, and you're forever being clambered over, stood on, shouted over the head of. The comedian's act consists mostly of furious thrashing on the mbungbung – a barrel-shaped drum, the comedian bellowing hoarsely into a microphone, as his two female cohorts perform wild stamping dances. Good honest entertainment! But the audience scarcely look up from their gossiping, networking, intriguing and eating, and the only laugh comes when the comedian falls over by mistake.

The promoter comes back on. Not long now before ... Again the roar, and somehow, one waggishly authoritative voice can be heard above it all, ringing out from God knows where: 'Sajar – Président!' There are hoots and howls of mirth, and a great gasp of admiring disbelief, and again the belligerently droll voice: 'Sa-jar, Prrrésidawhnt!' It's that voice, the voice I heard at the demo, the sardonic conscience of the Tekrurian people. It's like the soul, the spirit, the animating demon of the crowd. As the governor of the Bastille is being dragged through the streets by the baying uncertain mob, one man steps from the crowd, says, 'Kill him!', and immediately disappears. And who is he, the man with the casting vote of history? You can't know. You can never know. 'Cause he doesn't know himself. The officers are all running up and down, shouting into walkie-talkies, peering up into the great dark stands, thinking, If we can just isolate that guy, drag him squirming through the kicking, jostling crowd and dispatch him somewhere quiet, we can solve all our problems. But even they know it's impossible, that they could never, ever find him, and everyone else is just laughing, even the soldiers are laughing as he keeps prodding and goading with his ever more absurdly drawn-out vowels: *'Saj-awwh – Prrési-daahnt!'* And other voices take up the cry. Voices angry, passionate. And there's this kind of tumultuous whistling, which you realise is the astonishment and delight of the rest of the vast crowd, invisible behind the glare of the great arc lights. The soldiers below are becoming more and more uneasy, and this seems to provoke the crowd further, and there's this sudden booming swell, as what seems like the entire audience takes up the refrain: 'SA-JAR PRE-SI-DENT! SA-JAR PRE-SI-DENT!'

I move a few yards, crane my neck, and suddenly from being just an anonymous, amorphous mass behind the glaring curtain of light, I can see with profound clarity up into the heaving stands, the crowds of guys up on their seats fisting the air in time, that guy in the very clean white shirt waving his arms in indignant fury, while other sections of the crowd continue their gossipping and orange-peeling oblivious. The tide of the chant rises to break suddenly on a great shriek of delight. Yes! He's been seen. Everyone's turning – I'm turning, the troops are turning – getting to their feet, dropping their oranges, as *they* can be seen: walking across the darkened pitch on the far side of the stage – tall figures with the weary charisma of jet-lagged generals, the Super Lumière d'Afrique. Up there on the stands, the crowd are in ecstasy as the promoter goes into overdrive: 'Yes, the moment has arrived! Are you ready?' He's reeling off the names of the band members. All this, and I can see one army officer waving his arms at another saying, Get the guy off, he's stirring it up too much, while another says, Be cool, man, it's only rock'n'roll. Or words to that effect. The band are on stage, the audience reach a plateau of pleasurable anticipation. Then, suddenly, the lights go off. For a second, we're in total darkness, then there's another light, the light of a voice, golden, surging out of the darkness. The light of the golden voice of Africa, crooning, caressing the audience, spinning out those yearning griot phrases, the litany of the praise-names of one particular family, specific but somehow embodying the desires, the aspirations, the very soul of the Tekrurian people. The audience gasp, arms uplifted as a single spot hits the stage. I look up, and there is Sajar, just a few feet above me, tall, majestic in a magnificent shimmering robe, one arm outstretched, eyes half-closed, head swaying as he reaches a height of screeching, golden exaltation. I'm almost in tears, the audience are almost in tears, 'cause that voice – no matter how much he's fucked about with it, gone into bogus scat, Springsteen-style grunting to appease the expectations of Western record buyers – that voice that means so much to all of us, *the* voice of our time, now he's singing for us, his own people, in his own country, still has that golden, liquid purity, that molten griot otherness.

'Thank you, God. Thank you, N'Galam,' says Sajar, as the lights go up and the band hit a rocking dance groove, Sajar hoiking up his robe, as he and the guitarists jive Shadows-like back and forth across the stage. Yeah, as I said, it *is* only rock'n'roll. The audience up on the stands are rocking as one, the first-aid men are grooving, the police are grooving, the soldiers are grooving – 'cause, hell man, they're all Sajar fans too. I can't even think which song this is – though I know Sajar's catalogue back to front – I'm not even analysing which elements are traditional, which imported, which African, which Western – 'cause when you're here, when you're actually *in* the heat of it, you don't think like that, you can't think like that, 'cause you just know that this is what you *should* be hearing.

Into the darkness behind me are crowding all the apparatchiks, fonctionaires, relatives and liggers, all the first-aid men, roadies and equipment-luggers, all wanting a better view, and we're all swaying, grooving, pointing at each other, chuckling and making arch and dudish eye-contact – 'cause this music has got to be

264

shared. And up on stage, Sajar is swaying urbanely in his unbelievable cerise robe, smiling with pure pleasure. Because here he doesn't have to put on some big act, doesn't have to explain or justify himself. Here it's enough for him to just stand up there and sing.

Another number comes to a crashing conclusion. The first-aid man and I who've been ghosting each other's movements, however ludicrous, for what seems like hours, give each other five, and I look up at Sajar. We've been on a rhythmic journey into the deepest interstices of their culture, nodding at the Latin past, taking in the scratchily plaintive cadences of the khalam, even done one of those numbers he normally does as a duet with Michael Heaven. We've told in fact the whole story of the music, but we haven't yet hit the final overarching climax of the show. Sajar turns to wipe his brow, and I catch a look of exhaustion, of utter, utter weariness – the look only of a second, which only I at my vantage-point down at the very front of the side of the stage actually see – before he turns back to the audience with his usual smile.

'Thank you for coming,' he says. 'Because of all the people we play for as we travel round the world, we get more satisfaction and happiness from playing for you than any of them.' Enthusiastic applause. 'Wherever we go, we're always thinking of you and praying to come back to you as soon as possible.' Even more applause and cheering, which I join in, 'cause while on one level this is just transparent mass schmoozing, on another, he means it. Oh, yes. Sajar really does care. He breaks off 'cause there's some shouting coming from the front of the main stand. I move back where I can see round the glare of the lights, and there right down in the shadows at the front of the middle stand, I can see the crowd trying to break through the security barriers and the cordon of troops to the area of bullet-hard, spotlit earth at the front of the stage. The walkie-talkie men are going into a frenzy. More and more troops are moving over there. The nightsticks are coming out, beating back the long-shanked, baseball-capped exhibitionists who all want to be the guy who got down there and really strutted his stuff. You can see them down there in the hazy darkness, remonstrating with the trops to let them through, and the troops equally indignant shouting and waving their sticks, cracking them over the thighs and shins as they try to get a leg over. Shit, man. He just hit that guy over the head. He's cowering back, holding his head. Meanwhile, more and more people are climbing over the seats towards the front. I see Sajar watching, horrified. Yes, man, that *is* blood!

'Sa-jah – Prrézidawnt!'

It's that guy again. And it's frightening, because you can't tell where it's coming from. You can't actually hear as much as feel it. More angry shouts and the beginning of a chant: 'SA-JAR PRE-SI-DENT!' Sajar listens. Sajar, the prophet. Sajar, the Modern Messiah of Tekrur. L'homme de destin. Then his eyes flicker. He's back in the here and now. Let's do one more number, he thinks, finish the show and get the fuck out of here before the whole place goes up. He shouts to rhythm guitarist Tapha Jain, and they slide into a sinuous liltingly melodic groove, embellished by Mamadou Faye's flamencoesque guitar elaborations, Sajar holding up one hand, smiling broadly and shaking his head as he narrates his tale of lost love, found love or whatever it is. Most of the audience have totally forgotten what's going on down the front, carried by the sheer beauty of the melody – a good half of them singing along misty-eyed. And that includes me, 'cause this always was one of my favourite Sajar songs. But the trouble with this kind of music, or rather the great thing about it, is that it tends not to stop in one groove for long. If you want to keep things on a bland, predictable even keel, it's not for you. Fafa Mbaye's no sooner executed a bulbous paradiddle on his talking drum, than we're booting off in a completely different direction, the slithering synth progression and scratchy insistent guitar lines keeping up this deliciously slippery rhythm like the endless clenching and unclenching of some exquisitely lubricious organism – and I think you know exactly which organism I'm talking about. The hornmen jiving at the side of the stage blow out occasional rasping rejoinders, while the talking drum and the bone-hard sabars throw out thudding rattling salvoes apparently at random. Yes, man, 'Njouga', another of my favourite Sajar numbers, maybe my favourite Sajar number of all time – or it's gotta be when it's taken this fast and with this degree of crazy provocative *looseness*.

Sajar, totally forgetting the mayhem below, lets out this sudden screeching exhortation, immediately ghosted by the gurgling, insistent tama, the sabar cracking in hard behind. Then the whole band adhere in this hammering coda:

bah – bah . . . ba-bah!

The loins of the audience, who've all been swinging and swaying and thrusting all night, are right on time, with the snapping of taut bare thighs, the jutting of prehensile buttocks, the shaking of big traditional arses. Everyone who's not fighting the pigs down the front is practically falling over with laughter. Slapping his thigh, Sajar holds the mike up to the talking drum and Fafa Mbaye plays the whole melodic progression:

Ngghi-dungudu-dugu – dugidung . . .

And the rest of the band and the thrusting, knee-trembling audience react as one:

Ah – Ah . . . A-Ah!

Nyanya Guisse takes the mike – the stentorian streetbarker lui-même. Time to unleash *the voice!* There are certain things that can only be said in one language, and Nyanya's jagged alliteration is every bit as goading, as deliciously insinuating as Fafa Mbaye's tama. And which came first? Did they develop the talking drum to precisely echo the tones of their language, or do they talk like that because they happen to like sounding like a talking drum? Who gives a fuck? 'Cause here, rhythm and melody, language and dance are all one. Why play your drum solo when you can sing it? *Dance* your guitar solo – as Mamadou Faye has done before now! But first Nyanya's taking it down a bit, addressing

267

the crowd in tones at once masterful and insinuatingly conspiratorial, the organ riff elegantly grooving back and forth over the rhythm, the talking drum poking its way in and out of the rhythmic interstices apparently at random. Yeah, they could keep this up for hours. They could just coast on this kind of easy groove for years on end. And the audience, those who aren't, as I say, having their heads cracked down the front of the stand, have forgotten politics totally – cruising on the intimacy and the louche humour. 'Ye-e-ah!' Nyanya's saying. 'This is what it's all about – us grooving and chilling with the people of Tekrur! The beautiful people of Tekrur! Our people! *Wow-wow!* And that's important. It's something very precious between us, that we have to guard. Because you know me. I'm just a Tekrurian man – *a man, erh?* That's why I want to remind you of what our elders advised us, that we should never forget our own culture. Because the world is very hard, and finally our culture is the only thing we have, erh?' All the time, the rhythm's been building, and meaning, if there was any I wasn't imagining, is lost in a spiralling ithyphallic onomatopoeia of names, fragments of phrases used by the griots to praise the virginal blood, the hymenal flow of consummation, then tumbling shards of pure rhythm, bumping headlong over each other in careering patterns that have the squealing women leaping in pure delight. Then Nyanya gets behind one of his drums, the blunt-toned, barrel-hard lamba, and beats the whole thing out in one ferocious flailing volley, shards of shattering stick flying everywhere – the audience, particularly the women, up on their seats, thighs, buttocks and arms thrusting in all directions. All around me, the guys are giggling and nudging and winking as they demonstrate their dude-stepping, their high-crotched thrusting, their gluteal muscular twitching to each other and to me. Up on stage Nyanya does a strutting, leaping solo dance, executing an impossibly athletic twist in the air before landing in a pose of cocky nonchalance. And how do you follow that? Because the rhythm's still hanging in there, going back and forth through its progression as I said it endlessly could. But it still hasn't reached its height, its climactic epiphany of rhythmic intensity – though it's building, it's definitely building. We've reached that point where we're waiting, just waiting for it come spilling and flooding forth. But some final crucial element is missing.

Sajar, helping out on the sabar, lets out these golden peals at appropriate rhythmic intervals, while over at the front of the stand, the mad chaos and confusion goes on unabated.

A policeman points at me, stone-faced. Then he kicks one leg up and swings it out sideways, decribing a great arc in the air, as the booming crack of Nyanya's sabar comes thrusting in behind, propelling his massive lunging stride towards me, ending with a final defiant nod about two inches from my face. Everyone round about is roaring with delight. I nod back. Nice one, man! But, still stone-faced, he shakes his head and points at the bare hard earth. It's my turn! No, man. I can't do that. But he's resolute, his eyes narrowing, looking hard, straight into me. Everyone's slapping and prodding me. Go on, man! Get in there! In there? What do you mean, *in there*? But they're all pointing at the area of hard, blessed brightness in front of the stage, hit by the silver moon's edge of the great spot – just five or so yards away – where I would be clearly visible from all parts of the stadium. I'm laughing. I'm cackling hysterically. *Tu me taquines, wai!* To break the first law of the white man's involvement in Black Culture: that he must on no account make a prat of himself? To abnegate one's implicit and unspoken understanding with Sajar that one waits eminence-grise-like in the shadows till called upon to act? C'est pas possible!

But the rhythm's in my head, pumping, loud, gathering, volleying – one with the prodding, shoving, laughing hands – loud enough to blot out the even more cogent consideration of the fact that *I cannot dance!* Not like that, in that way you're either born to or you forget, with that ruthless athleticism that is either *right* or utterly, utterly wrong. But I'm already out in the silver brightness, hit by this great gasp of disbelief – 'cause the white man, the bloody toubab, is going to dance! There's much derisive laughing. But the rhythms from the stage are already cohering, already tightening for that final moment of unleashment. I'm bright – I *am* the shuddering brilliance of the great spotlight – and

269

there's a great shriek from the audience as I swing myself into a defiant, an arrogant posture of readiness: *He's going to do it!* I swing my limbs in time with the bumping and whirring of the tama, then *there it is* the hard, overmastering syncopation, cracking down from on high. I swing my right leg up and out, and it's as though all hell's breaking loose. Hundreds of people are running towards me. Shit – they're through the barrier! They're all around me, and they've no sooner started their long-shanked cavorting, than the cops are on them, thrashing out with their sticks in all directions. A cop's on me, baton raised. I shield my head as they grab my shoulders, and as I'm dragged away I catch a glimpse of Sajar looking down from the stage – open-mouthed in utter, utter horror.

Eighteen

'He was doing it like this!' says Nyanya Guisse, doubled-up and lunging gorilla-like, in imitation of my dancing. 'Then the cop comes in like this!' He thrusts his lower lip out, wagging his finger in mock-parental admonition, before collapsing onto the bed beside me, jolting my head onto Tapha Jain's helpless, heaving stomach. The muggy turquoise room is full of band members, apparatchiks and hangers-on, sprawled and heaped over the chairs and divans. We've been through the story of my performance, attendant mêlée and flight from the field about fifteen times, and we're still busting a gut.

Oh, yes. Far from cracking my head, the cops simply kicked my arse as I scuttled backstage, straight into the band's bus.

'Ki sayi-sayi bou maag la!' says Nyanya, lying back exhausted with laughter.

'It's true!' says someone else.

'The mad white man,' says a third.

I lie back contentedly. This is what Africa always was all about. Mirth and male bonding. The endless coming and going in the mugginess of turquoise-painted rooms, stretching oneself out on a bed or a wooden armchair, and always a ready greeting from and for everyone.

Someone else comes in the room, walking near the feeble overhead light so it seems dimmer than ever. Blokey grunts and greetings through laughter for Sajar's driver, who responds with his usual nasal gargle.

They're all taunting and teasing him, telling him to sit down, trying to draw him into their throaty open-ended banter. Then suddenly, no one's laughing any more.

'Litch,' says Nyanya. 'You have to go with this man.'

'Er . . . ?' I raise my head from the bed. Now what's going on?

'Sajar wants to see you,' says Nyanya.

I look round. Nyanya's looking at the ceiling. No one else will meet my eye.

Now what's going on? Have I already said that? I have? Probably something to do with Sahelfest 2000. But at this time of the morning? We're hurtling up the winding scrub road towards the area of beleaguered housing developments where Sajar's old and new houses are.

The driver suddenly turns to me. 'Hey!'

'Quoi?'

He flicks his right forefinger over his left wrist. 'Méchant! Erh?' He looks back intently at the road.

'Quoi?'

'Toi!'

'Moi?'

'Ouargh!'

What's he talking about? He turns off, bumping and careering down a dirt track. And he suddenly turns off the engine. All around, the powerhouse screeching of insects. We're by a huge unlit building. Sajar's new house. We get out. Someone's pointing a torch at us. The torch is pointed down. There's the outline of someone in the doorway. Guttural greetings. Sajar's butler, the thick-set, taciturn bloke.

'Ça va?' I venture as we enter the building.

He flashes the torch round the huge concourse with its suites of Chesterfield sofas, then leads me to the bottom of the stairs. 'Allez en haut!' he grunts. 'C'est en face.'

The glare of the torch follows me up the stairs, throwing the pattern of the banisters onto me and the wall. At the top of the stairs is total darkness. But ahead, along the hall, is the outline of a door lit by a light beyond. I feel my way forward and knock. There's a bark of assent from the other side.

I'm back in the narrow office where they hacked into my computer. Sajar's sitting down the far end in a pale yellow damask robe that I have to say looks fairly magnificent. Maybe I should get one. He's on the phone. I wave, but he doesn't look up. I settle myself on the sofa. Kind of a cosy little office, and the electric light's working in here. Sajar puts down the phone and stares into space for a few moments. Then he suddenly turns to me.

'How could you do that?'

'What?'

'Make a fool of me like that!'

'How d'you mean?'

'You ruined the whole concert.'

I gasp with astonishment. Come on, man! He can not be serious. 'A ... a policeman made me do it!'

He laughs mirthlessly. 'Non, non ... People in this country are not as stupid as you think they are.'

'I never ...'

'I encouraged you to come here, because we were trying to develop our music, and I thought people like you could help us. But I was ignorant then. I didn't know anything. I trusted you. I showed you things. I gave you opportunities I gave to no other white person. Things I didn't even do for ...' He pauses.

'Michael Heaven!'

'Yes, not even for Michael. I know you don't like Michael. At first I couldn't understand why you were always trying to ... push him downwards. But now I see it is simply that you are jealous because the whole world is looking to him, while you have failed in everything.'

'Look ...'

'I believed in you. I thought, This man really loves our music, and he really loves us. But now I see you as you really are.'

'How's that?'

'*Un criminal!*'

273

I'm almost laughing. They always use the word in that way. It's almost admiring. Like a rogue.

He pulls out a packet of Marlboro and lights one. I can't believe it!

'What you doing, man?'

'Quoi?'

'You're *smoking!*'

He pauses. 'Oui.'

'You shouldn't be doing that.'

He shrugs.

'There are so many things that need doing in this country, so many things that are lacking. And it is only me who can see what needs to be done.' He's got a look at once of slightly glazed determination and exhaustion.

'Listen, man. I have actually done an incredible amount to help musicians in this country.'

'What have you done?'

'I've ... talked ...'

'C'est certain!' He picks up a phone and starts dialling. 'People in this country are actually trying to create something. We cannot afford to keep carrying people like you.'

'So what are you saying?'

'It's over between us.'

I look at him. He's got the receiver up to his ear, but whether he's actually listening to the dialling tone, I can't tell. Come on. This is Sajar. My man! He can't mean it. 'You can't mean it, man!'

He dials his number again. 'C'est comme ça.'

I realise I no longer know this person. He's changed totally. 'You've changed, man.'

'Pas du tout. I've become realistic. I've realised we have to be professional and organised. Just like everybody else. We can't keep making excuses.'

'I agree with you, man. That's what I've been saying the whole time. That's what I've been helping you to do.'

'Helping?'

'Yeah, I've really put myself out, man – for you!'

274

He smiles, shaking his head, sadly. 'No. You have your own projects, your own dreams . . .'

'What's wrong with that?'

He winces, shaking his head.

'Who's been talking to you? Is it that fucking . . . ?'

'Please, don't say anything else! I have to make a very important phone call. The driver will take you back to your hotel.'

'But, what about . . . ?' What about the money, man? 'What about the money, man?'

He looks up midway through dialling. 'What money?'

'The money . . . You said I owe you twenty-five grand!'

A dark, slightly sheepish look comes over him. 'No . . . That doesn't matter. Forget that.'

I stand there gobsmacked. Sajar's already into his phone conversation, as though nothing's happened. He's just destroyed someone's life, and he's already onto the next thing. In a no doubt subconscious reflex action, he turns his back on me.

My life is over. Everything I've worked for and striven towards is in ruins. Everything that's of real value to me has been tainted – irrevocably. I've put so much into it all. I've invested *everything* in it. That sound, that yearning, aching intensity, that reaching out into the void, that bringing down of the power of the ancestors, of God, of destiny, that dark epiphany of exaltation and passion one finds in the singing of the griots, that's all gone now. I've lost that completely. That whole river of music is poisoned for me. 'Cause I was in there with the man by whose voice all others must be measured, the voice of burning liquid gold, the inimitable, the blessed, who took the whole thing to another level, another dimension. You were in there totally. You were so close to that. And now it's gone. So what are you gonna do? Are you, after that, going to say, okay, I'll work with the second-best guy, woman or whatever it is? I mean, you cannot – once you've been to the very summit – do that with any real conviction. And really, it's the whole of African music. Because when you've always worked with the mainman, what really is the point of working with anyone else? And going outside of Africa, there are of course, a myriad other possibilities. There's Cuba. There's Brazil... Spain... Morocco ... I mean, if I wanted to get seriously into say, flamenco – which I love – I couldn't be in a better position to do it. But I have to tell you that the thing that got me into that in the first place was the similarity, the equivalence of its fierce passion with that other declamatory intensity from across the straits and the great Saharan emptiness, with which it may possibly share some common roots, the music of the griots. So if I was to do the necessary hanging out at the fiestas and juergas of the great gypsy families of Jerez, Cadiz and Triana – which I easily could do – I know I would experience that terrible sense of emptiness, reflecting on the fact that this, however wonderful, was merely a substitute for other experiences that I underwent with an intensity that I would never find again. So really, there is no point.

These are the thoughts that engulf me, as the car plunges on through the flickering nightscape. Oh, yes. I'm in a state of irredeemable, irreversible and inconsolable bleakness. And yet ... And yet, I always knew it would end like this. I mean, how long have I been in this business? And what did I tell you about musicians? That's right. So you have to be prepared to expect this kind of thing. Because it's likely that conflicts of interest always will arise between people in my position, and those we term 'the artists' – particularly when the artists get a grossly overinflated sense of their own importance.

By the time we get back to the hotel, I'm already reflecting with derisive mirth on some of Sajar's more pompous pronounce-ments. What was it? 'The responsibilities I have in this country?' And didn't he say something about nobody understanding except him? I mean, Come on! That's the sort of thing rock musicians used to say in the 1970s. That's the sort of thing I got into African music to get away from. The sort of thing Michael Heaven would say if he wasn't so eaten up by English modesty and bogus diffidence. And what is it I'm supposed to have actually *done*? I got up to dance at Sajar's gig. I showed my appreciation in the traditional African way. I mean. Big deal.

I slap the driver on the shoulder and go into the hotel. Oh, yes.

No matter how bad things look, there always is, at the end of the day, another angle.

I'm in the foyer. Back in neutral territory. The light from the desk glowing sepulchrally on the black marble floor. Stillness. And she's sitting behind the desk. Oh, yes. There always *is* another angle.

Once again, she's sitting back in her chair, a book open on her lap. Once again, she's not wearing her glasses, her braids, hanging loose, swept back over one shoulder. I stand leaning on the counter, looking at her. And she in her chair looking back at me, her full lips very slightly parted, her slanting eyes with that heavy, steamed-over look. Looks like she's been getting heavily stoned on whatever she's been reading.

She stretches her back slightly – as though her body aches with all the passion and agony retailed in the book, scenes replayed now in the smouldering stupor of her eyes. I hang there on the counter, inhaling the musky heaviness of her limbs, transfixed by the smooth contours of her face, the rounded forehead, the exquisite curve of the cheek, anointed with the oil of Africa, melting in the golden dimness into an oozing caramel glow. And it's as though my consciousness, my will, are melting, are being absorbed by this mask of immemorial knowing.

She leans forward and pulls an envelope from under the counter. 'This came for you.'

Suddenly, the foyer seems very small, Aissa is just the receptionist in a funny little hotel in a run-down African city, and the envelope, its thick manila glowing in the glare of the overhead spot, seems very, very big. 'Mr A. Litchfield, c/o Sajar Jopp, Tekrur.' I feel a quiver of uneasiness running through my bowels. You know those packets that arrive so hammered by the rigours of travel, so matted with the franking devices of everywhere from Vladivostok to Tierra del Fuego, you can't even read the address? This one isn't like that. Considering it's come all the way from London SW1, it's in frighteningly good condition. It looks like it's hardly been touched by human hand, and the feel of the densely textured manila and the heavy indentation of the old-fashioned typewriter positively scream of the offices of expensive lawyers. *Expensive lawyers?* Is there another kind? Oh, yes. After a time, you find you don't even need to open these things. I mean, I used to love mail. Even as a kid I was always first to the doormat. And then when the freebies started coming, all the jiffy bags, parcels and packages from the furthest corners of the earth, people used to say, Every day's like Christmas for Litch. But not any more. I haven't opened a letter for . . .

'How did this get here?'

'A boy brought it, this afternoon.'

'From Sajar's office?'

'It could be. I was not here.'

I wake with that feeling of mild surprise and sheer physical delight you feel in simply being alive and conscious, and in good enough health to appreciate it – a feeling so transitory and fugitive you only know you've had it when it's answered by the overwhelming counterweight of ominousness and dread.

What have I done?

I've fucked everything with Sajar. Destroyed it totally. How could I have done it? A relationship like that is something so rare, so precious, you have to guard it, to nurture it with immense care. Because of Sajar's unique position, any relationship with him has got to be a bargain – and I've blown my side of it in the stupidest way possible, by trying to upstage him at his own gig. I'm writhing, literally, in an agony of embarrassment. But there's something else. Something far worse than that. The darkness, the utter blackness vibrates with the possibilities of the unspeakable. *What have I done?* I click on the bedside light. The sense of relief of the obliteration of the blackness is only momentary. I'm on my feet rummaging around among my clothes, but I'm blocking my own light. I flick the overhead light. Yes, let in the harsh, bleak reality. Let's have all of it.

The envelope's under a chair. I tear it open. 'Dear Mr Litchf . . . Beg to inform you . . .' Blah, blah. Yes, get on with it. 'Writing on behalf of our client, Mrs S. Litchfield, to inform you that . . .

278

commencing divorce proceedings . . . We would advise you to instruct your own solicitor as soon as possible.'

What am I doing here? *What am I doing here?*

Acts. That's why I came here. To get acts.

I pick up the phone and dial a number written on a scrap of paper on the bedside table. It rings a long time. Then it's picked up and someone who sounds like they've been drugged mumbles unintelligibly.

'Est-ce que je peux parler avec Daouda Mboob?'

There's an indignant burst of Wolof at the other end. Something about bloody toubabs. I quickly replace the receiver. I look at my watch. Twenty to five.

I put my clothes back on and go down into the foyer. Aissa's not there. The other guy who's normally on nights, the inscrutable guy, is there. I just stand at the counter for some time without talking, glad of another living presence to ward off the over-whelming bleakness – the fact that nothing can be done.

'You know,' he says, after a time, 'it is the policy of this hotel that all bills are settled at the end of each week. But I am going to postpone the processing of your account.'

I don't say anything.

'When you leave, you can give me something, if you wish. Not much, maybe six or ten thousand. If I am not here, you can leave it behind the desk. Say it is for me, and they will understand.'

'Right,' I say, and head back upstairs.

Nineteen

I like the provinces. I'd never lived in the provinces before, but there, not an hour out of the centre of the metropolis, you're already well past some invisible barrier of the soul that separates the last houses of the suburbs from . . . the provinces. I mean, I'm from the suburbs. When I was a kid and I used to go into London, I used to love it, because everybody you saw on the tube and in the street looked somehow important. And I loved it, because very few people in New Malden looked important. I used to think this is where I want to be, because this is where it's at. But that was then. What I like about this place, is it's the sort of place where you come and think this is where it *isn't at*. It's the sort of place where absolutely nobody looks important. In the end you get fed up with London, because every second person you meet is famous. Half of them are busy writing books, articles, papers and briefs about what ought to be done about the other half. Even if they're not actually responsible, they behave as though they are. Here nobody looks as though they're responsible for anything. I'm amazed this place is represented in parliament, because they all look like the kind of people who don't vote. They all look like the kind of people who wouldn't think they were important enough to have an opinion about anything. And I don't suppose a 'famous person' has set foot here for decades. A bit like New Malden, in fact.

It's the sort of place that people who don't live there look slightly sorry for you when you tell them that you live there. The sort of place where if you weren't living there you might worry that if things went bad for you, you might end up living. So if you do live there, that's at least one worry you don't have. The sort of place whose name people who've never been there laugh at without quite knowing why. A place the sound of whose name has merely the bathos of signifying nothing. A place physically unprepossessing, with its fair share of social problems, but to which people in really hard-core places feel immensely superior. Not of course, that the people who live there are aware of any of this. They're the sort of people who are quite happy for the place they live to be nothing more than the place they live.

Not, however, that they are without their interests and passions. But they're the sort of obsessive one-dimensional interests that are outside the prevailing currents of history and the vicissitudes of taste and fashion. I mean, I'm not saying I've seen many trainspotters the few times I've stepped onto the bleak windswept platforms of the station, but I have noticed that the stock of the one bookshop is composed ninety-five per cent of hardcore fantasy. Guy with major broadsword versus gronormous monsters in Götterdämmerung dignified by gobbledegook title. And there're a lot of people who bury their sexual interests a lot less deeply in their pastimes than that. All these videos they're out there watching with the blinds drawn in the middle of the day on the outer estates – and in a place like this even the inner estates by their very nature feel outer – how many of them are legal? And of course, there are the hardcore hobbyists: the model-makers, the people who play one instrument in one amazingly narrowly defined musical style, the people who dress up as Red Indians, the pathological attenders of car boot sales. And like many English towns, it's an amazing repository of ossified youth cults. The outer estates, the surrounding villages, and even more so the nearby older market towns, are full of skinheads from Central Casting, rockabillies without a cause and bikers on the edge of time. When you drive through these places, you don't see them. You don't have to see them. You just *know they're there*.

I like it, because when you're in Tesco's, nobody looks at you, nobody checks you out, because it would never occur to them that there would be anyone in Tesco's who ought to be checked out. And they like it like that. No, the only time people look is if we're at the deli counter and She opens her mouth. I mean, She's the sort of person who will think, I've never had that kind of salami before, I'll try some of that. And if She can read the name off the label, She'll do it. Whereas they're the kind of people who can't read the name off the label because it's foreign, and wouldn't ask for it anyway because they only go in there for what they always have. Oh yes, there are still plenty of these kind of people out there. That's why the supermarkets in this place don't stock a lot of the things they do in other places. Because the people here wouldn't buy them. Unless of course they're featured in TV cookery programmes. Because it's in the nature of places like this that there is a certain percentage of the population who will make religiously whatever is on TV cookery programmes. Anyway, whenever She opens her mouth, you can feel them bristling and turning startled as if to say, 'Who does she think she is?'

Needless to say, She can't stand it here. She thinks they're all downtrodden, abject and pathetic. To me they're just ordinary people.

You see, New Malden isn't the provinces. It's manifestly part of London. Even when I was a kid, it was quite a way in from the boundaries of Greater London. But administratively it was still under Surrey, and people used to talk about London as though it was hundreds of miles away. A slower pace of life still prevailed there. A lot of people still accepted that things were a certain way and they were quite happy to accept it. I mean, I got away from the place as soon as I possibly could, but it doesn't come as a surprise to me that there are a lot of people like that, and I don't blame them for it. Whereas She, She can't understand why if you want to do something, you can't just do it. But I have tried to remind her that a lot of these people, they don't do it because they don't want to do it. But She can't see that. And that's where the problems start.

I'm on the street, and it's that time of day I'm not going to describe to you again, 'cause you know what it's like by now: the best time of day, when the world's on that beautiful cusp between everyone *hitting* the street and everyone *leaving* the street. When the buildings are disgorging their inner life, letting it hang out, literally, 'cause everything you might expect to be happening *inside* – all the stretching, the smiling with the sheer satisfaction of being alive, the lying down to put your feet up, the handslapping, the embracing, the protracted handholding, the putting the kettle on for an impromptu cuppa – is happening *outside*, in the middle of the pavement. You're making your way through and round it, grooving on it, inhaling it one great pungent wave of energy, and you're not even bothering to look at it, not in detail, 'cause you know it and it knows you. You're part of it. You've earnt the freedom of the streets. You wear the city like a garment, shabby but comfortable, so threadbare and so light you could be naked.

Okay, so I had a bit of a tiff with the mainman. So what? 'Cause this, teeming, immutable, fatalistic reality is just going to keep on going on, whatever I or Sajar or Michael Heaven or anyone else says or does. And these are the kind of people I can relate to: the *real people* – not the people who think it's their function to get everybody else organised, not the chauffeur-driven paper-shuf-flers, not the money-men, the power-trippers and their sharp-elbowed female protégées who've always got a lot to say – and not equally the thieves, the beggars, the pot-bellied, sunken-eyed and mad. I'm talking about the kind of people who are forever waiting at bus stops, who haven't got time to be either for or against you, who don't want any hassle, who just want to get by, who desire nothing more than to be able to nurture their tiny corner of personal progress – to make things just a *little* bit better for their kids than they were for them – yet who always get it in the neck. People like me, and I venture, people like you. I'm talking about *ordinary people*. And if you lose contact with that reality, because for reasons real or imaginary you feel you can no longer walk the streets, if you allow yourself to *totally lose your sense of humour*, to feel you have more in common with some international coterie of rich, powerful and influential people than you have with your own people – the people from whom you sprang, who *created you* – you can lose something integral to yourself and – more importantly – to your art. That's why although I've got all Sajar's cassettes, CDs and promo vinyl from the last five or so years, I've hardly even bothered to listen to them, because they are so fucking boring. I mean, you can hardly even describe them as Tekrurian music; they're, what, international jazz-soul with a mildly Tekrurian flavour. And the only reason the entire world thinks Sajar Jopp is the be-all and end-all of Tekrurian music, the only reason the Tekrurian people think that, the only reason Sajar himself thinks that to quite the extent that he does, is because people like me have, for what I can only describe as *political reasons*, encouraged them to do so.

But in fact, while Sajar's off collaborating with Brian Eno and Michael Heaven, an incredible amount of music that resonates with the immutable, fatalistic rhythms of the N'Galam streets, music that smells of N'Galam, continues to blare and crash and boom from a million-odd cheap boom-boxes, continues like all of this, to *just go on* – so the fact that I've fallen out with Sajar, however permanently, however temporarily, really makes no difference to anything. It could even do me a great deal of good.

I'm nearing the crossroads at the Marché Hakim Nder. Over on the other side of the road, the fronts of the Lebanese cloth emporia are starting to dissolve into the thick olive shade under the huge overgrown shade trees. But ahead, light's still falling onto the crowds converging on the crossroads, the vehicles trying to honk their way through the irrepressible mass of pedestrians spilling from the pavements, and then suddenly there's another tone, another buzz cutting across it all. People are turning to look, moving aside, being forced to swerve into the paths of oncoming vehicles by some other force, some other energy coming from among the crowds along the pavement directly ahead of me. And at first I'm seeing only the outward rippling, the people turning and stepping aside, the marchands ambulants – hopeful as always – holding up their cassettes and sunglasses and lengths of cloth in the direction of whoever it is. Then I see the outer protective shield of minders, fixers, translators and guides. What the hell is this? Some kind of party or group, moving not with the heaving tide of commuters, but at its own ambling, discursive pace. And while half the minders, fixers and bodyguards are shooing aside the marchands ambulants, beggars, loiterers and ordinary private citizens who just happen to be in the way, the other half are turning inwards, taking in the tenor, the vibration and the sheer importance of the company they're in.

As I approach – and no one's gonna bar my path, 'cause, let's face it, I'm white – I glimpse, in animated conversation with someone deep in the group, another white face . . . Gabriella. *Gabriella?* You cannot be serious! You'd have thought this was the last place she'd be showing her face. But it is, and she actually looks incredibly well. And if the twentieth century's taught us anything, it's that today's pipe-dream of a crackpot outsider is tomorrow's ideological cataclysm, and a second more's perusal of the scene ahead is enough to tell me she's done it – she's turned the whole thing around. Sahelfest 2000 is once again a reality. And I can tell that, because coming towards me are all the kind of high-grade social- and cultural-development liggers who *would* be involved. Whites, with that unnervingly white, fresh-out-of-the-box and stunned look, which means they're straight off the plane. Other whites, cooler, rangier, more stained of skin, who'll be workers for appropriate Western governments and NGOs – the French Cultural Centre, Oxfam's cultural division, assuming they have one. There's Henk van Leer, chuckling away with some guy from the Tekrurian Ministry of Culture, and there's quite a few of *them* here, keeping a suavely proprietorial eye on things. There are other Africans, looking about with a nonplussed detachment, who are the playwrights, poets, painters and academics from other African countries, who're all thinking fair enough, but it's not that different from where they come from. Oh, yes. I've walked slap into the middle of the Sahelfest 2000 posse. And right in the middle, with this continual eddying of interest around him, blocked from view by the great shoulders of the minders, by the animated gesticulations of Gabriella, who's deep in conversation with him, by the craning heads of the passers-by, by the deferential nods and glances of the other

285

members of the group, is the tired but still finely chiselled figure of Michael Heaven.

Oh, yes, no one bothers to check my advance, no one thinks to check me out, because it doesn't occur to them that a white man is going to pose any kind of threat to another white man on the main street of an African city at seven in the evening. It could happen. But it's not likely.

Gabriella is one of the first to see me.

'Oh, Christ!'

'Yeah? I thought you said it was going to be different from all other festivals of its kind. That *certain people* weren't going to be involved!'

'Look, why don't you just disappear in a puff of smoke!'

I turn to Heaven, who hasn't quite taken in what's happening.

'Couldn't resist it, could you? I liked the idea so much I bought the company! Did you realise the main premise of this thing, the whole point of it, was that you weren't going to be involved!'

Henk van Leer's got his hand on my shoulder. 'Andrew, this isn't the time for this!'

'Fuck off, man.' I'm right on Heaven's case. 'What about the twenty-five grand, man? Did you tell Gabriella about the twenty-five grand? Did you tell Sajar about the twenty-five grand?'

One of the minders has got his hand on my shoulder. 'Monsieur . . .'

'Just a minute, man. I'm trying to talk, yeah?' I'm back on Heaven. 'Haven't you got enough to do without trying to fuck up other people's operations?'

Heaven's just looking back at me.

'I'm talking about the money, man. What about the money?'

One of the minders has got me from behind. 'This way, monsieur.' But Heaven holds his hand up.

'Just a minute. Look,' he says, suddenly coming on all sincerity, now I'm safely in the grip of a twenty-stone bodyguard. 'I don't know what's been going on, and I'm very sorry if things haven't been working out for you. As I said the other day, I've always had a lot of admiration for the way you go about things. But in this instance, I honestly don't know what you're talking about.'

My arm is fucking hurting. 'Lemme go, man!'

The guy releases his grip. He looks embarrassed rather than annoyed. 'Monsieur! Remember yourself! Erh?'

A great crowd is standing looking. They can't believe it. A white minibus jammed in the traffic is honking wildly. Guys are leaning out of the window, waving at me.

'Litch!' That guy looks familar. 'You have forgotten me again?'

The cassette guy. I need to talk to him.

'We are playing tonight at the Salle Municipale de Djembereng – en vedette! Don't forget! I will leave your ticket on the door.'

A stylish jeep, bull-bars, the works, pulls over.

'Hiii! I might have known you'd be here!' Mike Leedham of Sensor Records leans out. 'We're just doing the video for Mike's new album. We're heading down south tomorrow, to do some filming in the rainforest.'

I just look back at him.

'So you're still mad for it all, eh?' He turns to his driver with a grin. 'This guy knows more about Tekrurian music than anyone!' The driver looks unimpressed. 'We're meeting up for a bite to eat later – Mike, Gabriella from Sahelfest 2000 and a few others. Gabriella's very keen to get us involved in the festival. Are you coming?'

'No, I've er . . . I'm having dinner with Sidi Taal.'

'Dinner with Sidi Taal! Well, you would be!' He turns to the driver. 'See what I mean? This guy is always right in there! Look, I've got to go. Maybe catch you when we get back.'

They pull away.

The crowd's more or less melted away. I find myself standing on the corner opposite the Marché Hakim Nder. Has time passed? I don't know. There's a lot fewer people about, and it's getting dark. Dinner with Sidi Taal, eh? I head off across the street and down the lane along the side of the market. Aliou Ndoye, Tekrur's main cassette distributor, is letting down the steel shutter over his booth.

'How is the evening?'

'I am here only.'

'God be praised.'

And he's quite happy with that answer. It's incredible how someone working day in day out in the middle of a place like this, and who must be regularly stabbing any number of people in the back, can maintain such serenity. Maybe that's how he does it.

'Where is Sidi Taal?'

'Sidi Taal is there.'

'Where?'

'He's at his place. In Grands Baobabs. You wish to go there?'

The car's grunting and spluttering, dim headlights full on. The conversation's good-natured but limited, 'cause he's naturally quiet and non-communicative, and we're speaking Wolof, and I can't speak Wolof – not really.

We turn off the main road up beside this massive rubbish tip, over which the last few scavengers are returning from their labours. I don't have any desire to see Sidi Taal whatsoever. Not this minute. I'm not in the mood. But that doesn't matter. He won't be there.

Ndoye drops me on the corner. 'It's the fourth one down.'

I knock. A miserable-looking woman answers it. We exchange grunted greetings.

'He's not here?' I venture.

'Who?'

'Sidi Taal.'

'He is here. Come in.'

Ah.

Large-eyed non-committal kids appear in the hallway, then disappear.

She shows me into the living-room, where Sidi and two friends are watching football on telly. The usual African musician's living room: three-piece suite, antimacassars, chrome-and-glass coffee table, glass cabinet full of hideous ornaments, big painting of the guy's marabout. There are murmured greetings, limp hand-shakes. Everyone's absorbed in the game. There are groans as Lyon, who have a Tekrurian player, hit the crossbar in the closing moments of the game, and the morose-looking woman comes in, and heaves a huge covered enamel basin onto the coffee table.

Mm. Another epic bowl of oil-laden rice, tough meat and melting vegetables. I'd forgotten I was hungry.

The volume is lowered and Sidi slides the lid off the bowl. A spoon is provided for me. Sidi invited me without saying anything and I accepted in the same way.

'Ça va?' says Sidi, registering my identity for the first time.

'Ça va. Rer bi dafa nekh loll.'

He and the others snigger through full mouths. 'Thanks be to God,' says Sidi. See what I mean about acceptance? No big deal. Just getting on with it. And that's what we're gonna do. We're gonna make music, real music. Music that's as real and as spicy and as earthy as this food. Music you can feel through your mouth. Know what I mean?

'How about you?' I ask. 'What are you up to?'

He sighs and stares off into space. 'I'm just about to sign to do another album in Paris with Ahmadou Toure.'

This is my moment.

'Don't do it, man! It'll be just another Ahmadou Toure record. You know what I mean? We'll do it together – *here*! It'll not only be more real, more African, it'll be much more commercially successful. People will say we're now hearing Sidi Taal for the first time as he really is!'

Sidi looks back at me for a long time, a mixture of emotions playing across his broad dark features. 'You know,' he says at length. 'It was how many years . . . ?' He squints as he tries to work it out. 'Six years ago, almost exactly. You came to me. I was about to do a cassette with Ahmadou Toure, and you said exactly the same thing to me. I was impressed by what you said. I was ready to do it. I waited a long time, maybe six months, and I never heard anything from you.'

Dark half-memories flood in around me, as they all look at me full of reproach and disappointment.

'In the end,' continues Sidi sadly, 'I recorded the cassette with Toure anyway. So I think that if I listen to you again, all that's going to happen is that I'm going to waste a lot of time.'

Fortunately I had enough coins to get me back to town. 'Cause there was no way, under the circumstances, I could have tried to ponce even four hundred off Sidi.

The usual gloomy and rather uneasy nocturnal quietude has fallen on the upper reaches of the Boulevard Wagane Diouf. The usual couple of cabbies slumped outside the hotel entrance.

I suddenly remember: that kid's gig. I run upstairs and rummage frantically in my holdall. Every time I've looked for anything over the last however many weeks, days, months or whatever it is, that frigging cassette's been in the way. Now when I desperately need it . . . Here it is! I snap it into the Walkman and lie down on the bed. I'm already shaking and it hasn't even started yet. Calm yourself, man!

Did I tell you that Tekrurian rap tended to be pretty feeble stuff? That the grooves didn't have the killer instinct and the homeboy choruses lacked conviction? I did? That's right. But this isn't rap. This is . . . I don't know what this is. It's like the singing the Laobe, the caste of woodworkers – who're like the lowest level of the griots – do, or used to do, as they processed the blood-stained nuptial sheet round the marital compound. Praising the virginal blood, the hymenal flow. And they didn't mince words about it – illustrating it with graphic explanatory dances! Hard, visceral stuff. It's like that, mixed with overheated religious ranting and the street-corner jivetalk of a hoarse-voiced geezer I take to be Daouda Mboob – backed by a chorus that sounds like it's comprised entirely of thieves, muggers and murderers. And there's a woman's voice that keeps cutting in – not a griot voice – but just your average throaty housewife yelling from the taps. All going on over a heavy-duty bass riff, murderously hard sabar drumming piling on the rhythm with ever-greater ferocity, till this squealing, sawing one-string fiddle comes sawing into the mix . . . That's it. I click it off. No one – and when I say no one, I mean no representative of the multinational Coca-Cola complex or, even worse, the chi-chi little World Music labels – must be allowed to get their hands on a copy of this till I've got that kid sewn up so tight he can hardly breathe.

The hotel bar is deserted except for one white guy. He turns as I enter, a bearded, swarthy guy in glasses, as though he might be glad of some company. 'All right?' I say, settling myself in the seat beside him.

'Ah! You're English.'

'Of course. And you?'

'Italian.'

'Nice one!'

'Thank you.'

'You here on holiday?'

'No, I came for a conference, on environmental science. I'm a . . .'

'Did you take in any culture, while you were here?'

'Culture . . . No. I . . .'

'You weren't interested?'

'Of course, but . . .'

Next thing he knows he's in a taxi, descending the muggy sodium-lit dimness of the Avenue Wagane Diouf towards the quartiers populaires.

'I hope it won't go on too late,' he's saying. 'My plane leaves very early in the morning.'

'No, no.'

He doesn't seem convinced.

Outside, the streets of the lower commercial quarter are dark, shuttered and almost ominously quiet.

'Everyone seems to have gone to bed,' observes the Italian.

'This is just like the commercial quarter, man. Nobody lives round here.'

He looks doubtful. 'Is it far? Because I have to be up very early in the morning . . .'

What's the matter with this guy? I thought these Latin types were really loose about time. I thought they *always* went to bed late. I thought they only went to bed in the afternoon, and then only for extra-marital nookie. He sits, already in a state of nervous tension, staring fixedly out of the window.

'Where you from in Italy?'

'Oh, er . . . Turin.'

'Right.' Did I do a gig with Sajar in Turin? No, it was Milan. 'You know it?'

'No. Milano, Roma, Napoli – si. Torino – no.'

He laughs. 'You speak Italian?'

'No.'

He chuckles uneasily, and looks back out of the window, obviously wondering where the fuck he is.

Good question. Where the fuck are we? The road's rolling on through the dusty corrugated-iron suburbs. Quite a lot of people are wandering about.

'C'est loin, maintenant?' I shout at the driver.

'Pas trop.'

'These are the quartiers populaires,' I say to the Italian. 'This is where the real things happen. Not back up there on the Plateau.'

'I hope so.'

'What's your name?'

'Giovanni.'

'Nice one. Litch!'

We turn off along a bumpy half-made-up road between corrugated-iron stockades, stretches of crumbling wall with crudely painted images of marabouts showing up in the car's beam. Odd kids scattering, groups of dudes sitting in doorways, a muffled figure here and there.

The taxi pulls up at a long shed-like building, with crowds of kids hanging round the entrance, all immediately swarming, moth-like, into the headlight beams, their hands thudding and drumming on the vehicle, touching us through the windows. 'Monsieur, monsieur . . .' , 'How are you?', 'Give me one pen!' The Italian, who's got only a few more hours here, should be drinking it all in in great gulps. But he's not.

'I really can't stay long here.'

'Je comprends, man.'

'Huit mille,' barks the driver.

'Eh?'

'Huit mille. Le tarif est huit mille.'

'You're joking, man!'

'Pas de tout. C'est tres loin.'

'We can't pay it.'

'If you can't pay, you don't take a taxi. C'est normal.'

The Italian pays him.

'Fucking criminals.'

From inside the building comes this exhilarating booming and tumbling, like the drumming of thousands of children's hands on rusting corrugate, all part of the dust-laden night. A huge guy in a robe bars our way.

'We're with Daouda Mboob, man. He left tickets on the door.'

'Qui?'

'Daouda Mboob. La groupe Laobe.'

'Ce n'est pas la groupe Laobe. C'est Jaliba Jabateh.'

'Oui. C'est Jaliba Jabateh *et* la groupe Laobe.'

The Italian's already paid and we're in, one of Jaliba Jabateh's long nasal refrains floating on the relentless, bumping, jangling wall of sound. A seated audience composed largely of middle-aged women in major robes and turbans watch as Jaliba, a burly, broad-faced bloke, like a huge and amiable skinhead, moves continually two paces back and forth, the great bowl of his kora, his twenty-one string harp-lute, before him, holding endlessly to the same tinkling, vibrating run. There's a manic, muppet-like percussionist in shades, an expressionless balafong player and a gauche middle-aged backing vocalist, like an off-duty geography teacher who's wandered on stage by mistake. The cooled-out bass and drums look like if they played any less they'd fall off the back of the stage, and all the time a mandrill-faced animateur in t-shirt and tracksuit bottoms wanders back and forth across the front of the stage, wagging his finger reprovingly at the women and occasionally slapping himself across the arse. Jaliba's soloing now, binding his silver notes ever deeper and tighter into the dense, rippling textures. Yeah. This is *real* African music – the sort of music one thought Africa had lost the abilty to create. If I had any bottle I'd sign these guys up. In fact, I probably will.

I raise my thumb to the Italian. He's trying to say something over the din. What's that?

'I have to go back.'

'Two minutes, man.'

'Two minutes.'

I head out through a door to the left of the stage, onto a piece of waste ground, where a bunch of geezers are standing and sitting around a tree stump.

'Mister Litch!'

'Yeah! Mister Man! Ça va?'

'Bien, bien. Thanks be to God.'

'Amin Allah. I heard your tape.'

'Yeah?'

'I loved it, man.'

'That's great. Thank you very much.'

'In fact, it's incredible.'

'Thank you. Thank you for everything you have done for us.'

'That's all right. We need to talk. 'Cause there's a number of ways we could do it.'

'Any time. Any time. But I just want to thank you for all the kind efforts you have made on our behalf.'

What's he actually talking about?

'Talking about us to Magnet Records. I know it was you who played them our tape.'

'How d'you mean?'

'It was you who recommended us to Amanda Jefferies.'

'Who?'

'Amanda Jefferies from Magnet Records. She was here two days ago. You know Amanda. She is so nice! Everything is now signed. But . . .' His brow clouds over. He can't understand my apparent ignorance of what he's talking about.

I can't understand my apparent ignorance of what he's talking about. If I'd known about it, Amanda Jefferies, whoever she is, would never have been allowed off the plane.

'Yeah, right,' I'm blathering. 'Amanda, yeah. Amanda's cool.' That's the trouble with being in the vanguard, with being out there and *in there*. While your back's turned, every jumped-up telephone-answerer's slept, wheedled and schmoozed her way into prime A + R positions, every bit-part youth journalist you gave information on Sajar Jopp for an unreadable Trotskyite magazine's running Channel 4 and won't return your calls.

'I can't believe it,' he's saying. 'We will go to London, New York. And it's all thanks to you.'

294

Fuck. Fuck. *Fuck*.

'Maybe even Quincy Jones will produce our album.'

'I doubt it.'

'No?'

'No. He's not right for you.'

'Who would you recommend?'

'I'll do it.'

'Yeah? You would do that? That would be wonderful.'

'I've gotta go, man.'

'But we haven't played yet . . .'

'Yeah, I know. Catch you later.'

I stumble back into the hall. I can't see the Italian. A thin guy is standing in his place along the back. 'Where's the toubab, the one who was standing here?'

'He has gone.'

I rush outside.

'Where's the toubab?'

'Who?'

'A toubab. He was here a minute ago. Fat, glasses.'

'What's he talking about?'

'A toubab in glasses.'

'He has gone. He went in a taxi.'

Next thing I know, I'm wandering along a road, or rather stumbling and tripping along it, and it's almost totally dark. I can hear a lot of dogs, near and far. And I definitely don't want to encounter any of them. And I can hear people too – throaty voices, indeterminately distant. I don't particularly want to encounter any of them either. This was a fucking stupid idea. It's all very well getting freaked-out because I lost an artist to another label. But I've got to get back to wherever my true destination on this earth is, in one piece. I should have just gone back and got a lift in Daouda's van. But I wasn't thinking. And that's the point. You've got to think. A couple of hundred yards ahead is a dull yellow street lamp. It's beyond a rise in the road, so all I can see is the pool of blackness in front of the ridge ahead, masking all the potholes, sand, crumbling asphalt, heaps of ashes and rubbish

295

over which I'm stumbling. God knows how long I've been walking. I hadn't realised the taxi had come so far. But this city is enormous. It's got vast outlying shanty suburbs, some of which are bigger than the city itself, and they aren't even marked on any map. I could be twenty miles out of N'Galam.

And this isn't the way to do it. When you're in Africa, you should do it the African way. Negotiate your way out of it. Stop at the first dim, turquoise-painted cubbyhole of a shop – of which there will inevitably be one, even at this hour. Get them to knock someone up on the understanding you'll pay him back over the odds when you get your hands on some loot tomorrow. Or ask them if you can share a bed. That's what you're supposed to be able to do. That's African civilisation. But would it work? Would it work here? Can you really expect to invoke the ancient hospitalities amid all this thieving shantytown desperation? I mean, isn't the opportunity of shafting passing ingénues one of the chief reasons that people come to live in cities in the first place?

There's a shop now, and it's exactly like you'd expect it to be – a doorway off the blackness, figures moving against a feeble light. It's even painted turquoise.

'Salaam aleikum.'

'Aleikum salaam.'

These guys are really surprised to see me walking in out of the night, though they're doing a bloody good impersonation of not being. They just stand there, expressionless, the guy behind the counter and two guys who are kind of *behind me*. I'm vaguely aware that while a lot of these shops haven't much to sell, this one doesn't appear to have anything.

'Nangendef?'

Murmured responses.

'Parlez vous français?'

What a fucking stupid thing to say! Why did I say that?

The guy behind the counter shrugs non-commitally. It's so dark in here I can hardly see his expression. There's just a hurricane lamp in a corner. I try to shift round so the guys behind me are less behind me.

'Mane, bugana taxi, wai.'

'Taxi? Il n'y a pas.'

Right. 'Qu'est-ce qu'on peut faire?'

A scarcely perceptible shrug. Can't tell whether he understood me or not.

'Amga telephone?'

Another stupid question. He shakes his head.

I think I'm in the wrong place here.

'Man gui dem.'

Murmured response.

I'm a hundred-odd yards down the road, when I hear footsteps behind me. I quicken my step, and twist my ankle. Oh, my God.

'Monsieur.' The voice is thick and throaty. 'Hey, Monsieur!'

Why I'm bothering to keep hurrying away, I don't know. But you do, don't you?

'Hsss . . . Mon ami.'

It's one of those guys from the shop. Why am I running? I haven't got any money. It's just fear. Pure fear.

I'm aware of a grinding sound. A car engine. Please come this way! In this darkness, you're aware of the lights from miles away: sweeping tiny fragments of detail massively over the walls and the huge trees I now find are all around. Then it's much louder.

'Monsieur . . .'

Suddenly details of the road half a mile ahead are coming into view. I turn, and there are the headlights. I run into their path, waving frantically. It's a big vehicle. It pulls to a stop beside me, and I hear Daouda Mboob's voice.

'Mister Litch! What are you doing here?'

Twenty

I'm sitting on the beach on the West side of the Medina, beneath the Muslim cemetery, staring aimlessly at the sea. How did I get here? I walked. In the expat-lore of the city, you are advised on no account, under any circumstances, to walk alone on the corniches. But nobody paid any attention to me. An old man with a stick is picking his way along the beach somewhere behind me. A bunch of kids are playing around on some rocks down by the water. Otherwise, there's no one around.

This morning, I phoned Prosper Mbodj to try to subtly wheedle out of him what this whole money thing was about, but there was no reply. I phoned Sajar's office to find out where he was. They were cagey. At first they didn't want to talk to me at all. Then they said Mbodj no longer worked for them. They said he was now working in Canada. And how long would he be there? They had no idea.

I can hear the old man getting nearer. I can hear the dry gasping of his prayers as he works his way through his rosary. Probably he's begging.

'Salaam aleikum,' comes a hard, dry and surprisingly vigorous voice.

'Aleikum salaam.'

'What are you doing here?'

I look up. From a distance, the figure's long gown, walking stick and dark glasses gave an appearance of gaunt and decrepit

298

ancientness. Close to, I can see he's not old at all. In fact, he's probably younger than me.

'What are *you* doing here?' I counter.

'I live here.'

'That's true.'

'I didn't know you were even alive,' I say as Papa Gorgi Ngom settles himself effortfully on the sand beside me.

'You don't know much.'

'What happened?'

'A car hit me.'

'Merde.'

'I was drunk.'

'Right.'

'But that's all over. No more alcohol. No more drugs. No more music.'

'So you don't want to do an album?'

'No.'

Damn.

I tell him everything, about Sajar, about the gig, about Michael Heaven and Sahelfest 2000. He listens in bemused disgust. 'These people are all idolaters and drinkers of alcohol.'

'Sajar drinks?'

He snorts. 'Sajar is nobody.'

Then I tell him about the money.

'It's obvious,' he says. 'It had nothing to do with the toubab Heaven. Prosper Mbodj and Mbaye Njai, the manager, have been eating Sajar's money for years. He realised what was happening, so they looked round for different people to blame. They saw you coming, and they thought, this toubab does not know what is happening, and it will not matter to him because he is rich. So they just put some of the money onto you.'

'So where are they now? Prosper and Mbaye Njai?'

'En Canada.'

'How do you know all this?'

'All N'Galam knows it. People have talked of nothing else for weeks. Now they have stopped talking about it, because the news is old.'

'How do I know you'll pay me back?'

I give a short laugh. 'I'm an Englishman!'

'That doesn't count for much these days.'

I'm in Ahmed Singh's office at the back of his shop on the Rue Mbokar Chong. He's big in cloth – big.

'Can you offer any kind of collateral?'

'I've got a record collection.'

'Here?'

'In England.'

'Let me have a look at your watch. Is it Cartier?'

'Timex.'

'This is five minutes slow.'

'It always is.'

'This is worthless. Have you got any jewels, diamonds with you?'

'No.'

'Passport?'

Now that is naughty. If I was to be hauled in by the authorities without papers, I could be in *deep* shit.

'Not at all. You simply instruct your embassy to issue you with an emergency one.'

My embassy! Of course. God, I'm slow on the uptake.

It's nearly dark as I approach the Residence. The guard's standing bolt upright in a dark blue uniform with white gloves. 'Hello, sir,' he beams. 'Happy Birthday.'

Birthday? Not me, man. I'm a Sagittarius.

'Not you. The Queen. You have come for the party. Do you have an invitation?'

Unreal, man. Unreal. And yes, deep in the pocket of my Striders, I find a mangled piece of card, thickly scrawled with telephone numbers, but still bearing the glint of its gold edge. I cursorily flatten it and hold it out, as he waves me on.

Ahead, the neo-classical portal of the Residence glows invitingly out of the darkness. Yes! I fancy a canapé. In the doorway is a guy the size of a house in a dinner suit. In the dim yellow glow, the dark suit and his blackness reduce him to this massive overpowering presence. He glances at the crumpled invite. I proceed.

The atrium's milling with people. Government ministers, leading figures from business and the arts and their glittering spouses – Oh, yes, the Queen's birthday gets a better turnout here than it probably does in England – and some of those old English people you get a sprinkling of everywhere in the world. Lady Somebody or other left over from something or other who carry on as if they're in Berkshire and everybody loves them for it until they're found beheaded in their bath – you know the type. And here's an exquisitely beautiful girl with a tray of those smoked-salmon cushion things.

'Yes, darling. You read my mind.'

She looks down demurely as I take one.

'No, no, don't go.'

I take another five.

'I love you,' I breathe through a mouth crammed with brown bread and salmon, and she slips quickly away.

I could really murder a drink. I mean I could murder a glass of British Embassy Sancerre. But the trouble with a glass of British Embassy Sancerre, is that it is going to make me feel totally omnipotent. But is there anything wrong with that? I mean, it's been ten years. But what's a decade either way.

The guy with the tray approaches, one of these handsomely-smiling types. 'Jerejef,' I breathe, scooping one of the pale amber goblets towards my lips.

'You speak Wolof?' he says, raising his eyebrows in feigned surprise, as the great wad of my soul's tissue rises to gratefully absorb the exquisite sting.

'Touti,' I breathe, as I go with the swell, and the delicious subsiding, and all around the gracious golden bonhomie. This is really very pleasant. Though they could have got some sounds in: maybe a string quartet. There are string quartets in Africa, you know. It's not all jungle drums.

And there's the Ambassador's wife. La gioconda elle-même. Yes, I definitely fancy the Ambassador's wife. She catches sight of me, and turns, colouring – I might almost say blushing. I'd like to

301

come here late morning, just wander in, go into one of the bedrooms, where the waitress who is also the maid is making the bed. I take possession of her from behind – without asking permission, if you know what I mean. And as I'm having her doggie-style on the half-made bed, the Ambassador's wife comes in . . .

And here's the Ambassador himself, exchanging fruity guffaws with some sleek-suited ministerial type. I need to talk to him, but I think I'll leave it till he's a little less pressed.

Suddenly, it's thinning out. I've schmoozed with the Minister of Culture – at least I think that's who he said he was – and various high-level business types who were very interested to hear about what I'm doing. Now I need to speak to the Ambassador.

'He has just left with Lady Michaelson,' says the waiter.

'Who?'

'That old woman who was here. He always gives her a lift home.'

I'm out in the portico. 'Where's the garage, man?' I ask the gorilla.

'A droite.'

It's now almost completely dark and I've practically collapsed on top of the Ambassador and Lady Michaelson before I spot them in the garage entrance.

'Who's that?' asks the Ambassador, sharply.

'Oh, hi. Yeah, it's er . . . Andrew. Andrew Litchfield. I came to see you . . .'

He turns to Lady M. 'Just a moment . . . Now look. You have absolutely no business to come here . . .'

'I had an invitation!'

'I did invite you into my house initially, under the impression that you were writing an article for the *Guardian*. But there was something in your whole . . . persona I didn't find quite credible. And when I telephoned the *Guardian*, I found they'd never heard of you.'

'I write under a pseudonym.'

He grunts scornfully, as though this is not even worth responding to.

'I then faxed London, and learnt that my predecessors at this embassy and colleagues at other embassies have wasted an enormous amount of time getting you out of the most idiotic scrapes – something, I can assure you, we're most anxious not to do again.'

'I –'

He raises a finger. 'You were invited here tonight because my wife has a policy of helping and encouraging young and artistic people. But you are by no means young and from what I gather, your artistic credentials are extremely dubious, so I would be most obliged if you would make your way out of here without causing a scene.'

I'm aware of the gorilla behind me.

'Who was that?' I hear Lady Michaelson asking.

'No one,' says the Ambassador.

Humiliating? To be ignominiously ejected from one's own embassy, in front of an old lady? Are you joking? The way these people can spend years, decades of their lives in these countries without having a fucking clue about what they're like, would be hilarious if it wasn't so frightening! 'Cause they're representing *you!* Chauffeured every inch of the way in air-conditioned limos, cossetted in embassies and residences of seldom less than architectural masterpiece status, pampered, fawned-on and no doubt sexually serviced by whole posses of servants, gardeners, nannies, drivers and security guards, they've got no idea of the indignities, the discomfort, the sheer fear undergone by their compatriots when they visit these countries, never mind the miseries of the millions of nameless indigenes. And *you* are paying for it all.

You think I'm drunk, right? That I actually took a drink back there? No, mate. I'm not utterly stupid. Turned out to be Tekrurian ginger cordial – supposedly a tremendous aphrodisiac – though I can't say I've ever noticed it myself. On the other hand, as I stroll into the hotel foyer, I'm just in the mood for a chinwag – at the very least – with Aissa Njai.

The inscrutable bloke hands me an envelope.

'The owner has asked me to process your account as soon as possible.'

'The owner or the manager?'

'The owner.'

'Gotcha.'

Parking my arse on the karsi, I open the envelope, which having only my name and no foreign stamps on it, escapes my normal embargo. It is handwritten on hotel notepaper:

'Dear Monsieur Litchfield,
There will be a fête at our home tonight.
You are invited.
Yours sincerely,
A. Njai (Mrs).
Directrice.'

Yes!

'Aissa Njai's place? It's er ... two blocks this way.' He waves a hand vaguely. 'But ...' I'm already out the door, along the street, crossing the Avenue Wagane Diouf, before I hear the warning note in his voice, and even then I don't pay much attention – it'll only be about some angle of his own. I plunge on down the unlit continuation of the Avenue Ass Malick Ndow, and I can already hear it, the urgent bump and clatter cutting into the muggy darkness. And I can feel the fervour before I hear the agitated clamouring voices – female voices, forever chattering, arguing and debating round the dancing circle.

All goes suddenly quiet. I see the silhouettes of a group of guys in the glow of a shop doorway.

'Salaam aleikum?'

'Aleikum salaam.'

'Ana fête bi?'

They grunt hoarsely, gesturing on up the street.

304

I come to a corner, and I can hear it loud and clear, the harsh declaiming of a big-voiced griot, answered by the great chorus of the crowd and the humping of the drums – sounds heard deep under the skin, sounds heard through the blood. And what is that they're singing? The praises of Njai. Blood returning to its source, the purest of pure blood. The blood of the lion. Njai, child of the lion. I'm cackling inside. Yes. What else would they be singing about?

Round a corner and I lose the volume. I can hear my footsteps, my breath, voices in the darkness around me. Hands grab my shoulders, push me onward. Then suddenly I've walked into it: the drums reduced to a solemn thudding clatter that nonetheless resonates with the imminence of unleashment, while a griot voice bellows hard and metallic out of the darkness directly ahead, with that spine-tingling edge you can only get if you're using a PA that's practically worn out. A female voice, higher and piercingly nasal, cuts in, obliterating the other with the long litany of the genealogy of Njai – becoming as I get nearer, louder, more exercised, the drums thumping and rattling, harder and drier than the hot asphalt under our feet – the bass notes booming deep in the solar plexus. And all around there's warm chuckling, excited chatter, voices agitated with that petty bickering and reprimanding and grumbling which in Africa is never quite extinguished, no matter how solemn the moment. I can't see a bloody thing, but I'm passed on from hand to hand through the crowd, more and more of whom the further I get are joining in the surging anthemic chorus. What is this? The baptism or wedding of some relative of Aissa's? 'Where is Aissa Njai?' I ask the world in general. 'She is there,' come the thick and throaty responses.

I find myself sitting, or being sat down, in a wooden armchair. Hands pat my back, arms and thighs approvingly, warm and earthy voices welcome me. I'm being sat among the mature women, the major matrons stitting back in their huge and voluminous robes and turbans. But that's normal. The drums are ahead of me and all around and in me. Are they loud? I feel like my head's thrust up against the skins – hot, hard, smelling rawly of goat. And the rhythm's changing again, building, the bass

305

notes keeping up this sawing insistent pulse, bending, sinuous, defining the deep, thick darkness. Yes, man. Bending. There's none of the metronomic stiffness you think of as rhythm here. This is rhythm as tunes and melodies colliding fiercely in the wild dust-laden darkness, this is the freedom of people who really know what they're doing. This is jazz, man.

Yes, I'm smiling to myself, 'cause I'm thinking about this kid who was trying to tell me that the success of 'house' and 'beats' was 'the return of rhythm', and how as a deejay, he was educating people about rhythm. I said to him, have you been to Bahia? He said, No. I said, Have you been to Rio? To Havana, Port-au-Prince, to Dakar, Cotonou or Ife? Have you been to one of these rooftop rumba sessions in the Bronx? Have you been to N'Galam? He said, No. I said, Go to all these places and then talk to me about rhythm. Totally flustered the guy. Mind, he wasn't a bad kid. Meant well. I'd like to give him a plane ticket to be here now, just to see the look on his face. Rhythm!

Louder, harder rhythms come bumping crashing out of the darkness, piling themselves on the taut booming that's holding everything together. Mad fragments of rhythm chewed sinuous, rhythms felt beneath the skin, rhythms heard in the centre of the brain, forming their juddering sentences hard, hard under the main rhythm. And I'm thinking about this woman, young enough to be my daughter, who didn't know who I was – nice enough, you understand, but not that bright – who asked me in the faintly patronising tone of one who assumes that no one over the age of twenty-one could have any conceivable knowledge or understanding of youth culture – if I ever went *clubbing*? I narrowed my eyes slightly and said, Eh?

She repeated the question, and I said, 'Listen, darling, I got into the Marquee carrying Cyril Davies's guitar case when I was thirteen. I was backstage at Monterey with Otis and Jimi. I was spreadeagled somewhere at those ludicrous, but epoch-making space-outs at the UFO and Alexandra Palace. I was a godfather to punk in a way that has never been fully acknowledged. I've been present at many of the most significant drug busts, overdoses and stabbings in the history of rock'n'roll. And if you want to talk about trance music, I've been with the sufis of Lahore for days on end. I've been with the gnawa men of Marrakesh, in the Candomble houses of Bahia, the juergas of Triana. I've been with the Cubans, the Haitians, the Santeros of Brooklyn. I've been to gigs in Africa that were just me and two thousand women in the bush in the middle of the night. So in answer to your question, I just don't *need* to "go clubbing!" '

The rhythm is really starting to bite now.

Suddenly a light – or rather several naked bulbs hanging over the street – flashes on. There's a great wheeze of delight from the audience, or there would be if you could hear them above the tumultuous clamour of the drumming. All around, wide eyes, delighted faces of children, the serene expressions on the heavily made-up faces of the fabulously attired women sitting and standing round the circle. The street is narrow, with hundreds of kids and onlookers trying to squeeze their way in behind the ranks of the women. Yes, everybody's waiting for the moment. The drummers, a motley crew of pirates, ragged neo-rastas and assorted baseball-cap wearers, cluster round their leader, this bearded guy, with the raw, red-eyed muscularity of a stevedore or furnace worker, who sits with the lead drum, the lamba, clenched between his knees, his temples and his bulging sinews already pouring with sweat. He looks wildly around, occasionally slapping randomly onto the rock-hard skin with the ball of his hand, making theatrical passes over it with the long thin stick he holds in the other. All around, the crowd surges with feverish expectation, the women at the front clapping with a big-eyed impassivity behind the eighteenth-century masks of their make-up. This skinny kid in a vest, his pin-head sprouting stubby locks, stares madly ahead as he holds the main rhythm, his cohorts blocking in random, capricious fragments of rhythm, stinging the heat-burnished skins, adding to the sense of fearsome agitation all round, as they wait for the moment.

The leader nods with a teeth-gnashing grimace, thrashing hard onto his drum, and suddenly the place is just a mêlée of twitching buttocks, rolling, thrusting loins – arms curving sinuously in the air, shaking the acres of cloth-of-gold and glacé silk, shimmying

307

silks up splayed thighs. Oh, yeah. It's all happening. And I'm actually not paying that much attention to the rolling eyes and tongues darting through tittering teeth. I mean, I'm enjoying it, but I'm not bothering with the details. 'Cause I've seen this type of thing so many times before, I'm happy just to let the whole thing wash over me. Unless of course, I'm watching the drummers, the lead guy leaning forward, his face a contorted mask of effort as he thrashes out ever more complex syncopations.

Then suddenly, he throws his arms wide. The rhythm stops. The women scurry and scamper laughing from the circle. Buckets of water are thrown onto the ground to settle the dust. Two of the drummers set up a loping, swaggering rhythm, the other drummers almost immediately piling in on top. The circle's milling with women, swinging their shoulders and hips to avoid colliding, tossing their heads with theatrical arrogance – then the rhythm starts to heat up and the circle clears. I sit forward as the deep thrusting from beneath is answered by pan-hard syncopations each crashing down harder and more furious than the one before. The lead drummer's swapping with one of his ragged pirate crew – furiously strapping the sharp-voiced gorong-yegel round his waist. Yes, man. The moment is coming. He stumbles forwards, looking wildly around, waving the milling kids back into the crowd. And then he's flailing out these jagged, hammering syncopations, shards of splintering rhythm flying in all directions. And this woman's already leapt from the circle, and all I can see from my angle is flailing, whirling robes, the stamping and swinging of shining legs and the swish of glistening underwear. Yes, man. I'm in a prime position. And one after another they throw themselves into the swirling madness of the dancing circle, two or three at a time, leaping and stamping before the drummers, I with my practised eye scoring them all off for elegance, grace and sheer athleticism. For maintaining a proud and serene smirk rather than an eye-clenching grimace of effort, for effortlessly combining vigour and purity of line, for the quality of their underwear. Stuff like that. People cast glances at me to see how I'm enjoying it. If this were some village out in the bush, or even in the suburbs, they'd have had me in there making a fool of myself hours ago. But this is the heart of N'Galam, the Plateau itself. There's no way they're going to admit anything I could do could be of the slightest interest, but they want to know I've clocked they can party. Then suddenly, another figure's prancing into the circle, tossing back armfuls of braids, preposterously tall, a Masai essay in lips and cheekbones in a coral-coloured business suit, looking straight at me – her face and legs and no doubt the rest of her too, plastered in what looks like red ochre mud. I feel myself colouring to the roots. Aissa Njai, the dom-ou-gainde, the mad powerdresser of N'Galam, kicking off a pair of red stilettos – and I'm praying in one small part of my being that whatever she's got on isn't skin lightener. You can see rather than hear the great roar of delight as a leg swings round in front of my face. Oh, no. Please . . . Leaning back, arms outstretched, she advances on me, thighs thrust forward, scissoring the air. Then, as the drums snap in behind, she's doing that dance – you know, the one I was trying to do, that I thought I *was* doing at Sajar's gig, where you swing your leg over, she actually *is* doing it, in a skirt that wasn't long or loose in the first place, that's going to split at any minute, right in my face. I can't look! The high-striding drum pattern cracks and booms to an abrupt climax, and with a nonchalant shrug she's picking up her shoes and slipping back into the crowd as though nothing's happened. The place is in uproar, everyone howling and slapping their thighs with delight – not at what Aissa's done, but at the look on my face. The music's broken down as the drummers collapse in shoulder-shaking mirth. I get to my feet, and the drummers start reaching frantically for their sticks, thinking I'm going to try and dance some pithy and hilariously appropriate response. But to their and everyone else's astonishment, I follow Aissa into the crowd.

'Where are you going?' everyone asks.

'I'm going to the house.'

'Where's he going?'

'He's going to the house.'

309

Hands push me forward. People shift to one side, gesturing me onward. Ahead is a black slit in the wall.

I'm dragged in to see the child, the week-old baby whose baptism this is all in aid of, in a dim room full of turbanned women. I have to sit holding him in his brilliantly patterned swaddling clothes, and make polite conversation. Time is passing. As I feel his hot urine seeping through onto my clothes, I hand him back, together with a handful of loose change, and head out, straight into this big bloke in a tracksuit.

'Yes, my friend. You play ludo?'

'Yeah ... Look, man, I want to see Aissa Njai.'

'You want to see Aissa Njai? Why didn't you say so?'

He leads me off into the darkness, round a corner into another courtyard that is full of the voices and laughter of young women and girls. 'Okay, my friend,' he says, and disappears. Ahead, by the light of a tiny lamp and by the blue glow of a moon that has suddenly ridden out from the pall of dust over the city, I can see women: women half-naked, wrapped only in their traditional cloths, sitting and sprawled and draped over each other, their supine, languorous limbs interweaving, all talking, grooming, breastfeeding, their laughing eyes glittering out of the darkness – a scene from some overheated Orientalist fantasy – and there at the centre of it all, I can just make out the recumbent form of Aissa Njai – Aissa, the super-jigenne, the dom-ou-gainde herself – a girl seated at her head, either plaiting her hair or picking it over for lice. Everyone's talking at once, and all apparently saying the same thing: 'Toubab ... Aissa Njai ... Toubab ... Aissa Njai ...' Aissa tells someone to fetch a seat. 'Come and sit here, Monsieur Litchfield,' she says, as one of those tiny, ludicrously small stools is placed at her feet. I squat down, feeling absurdly overlarge, unkempt and sticky, as though on some idiotically small potty, as the women discuss me in frighteningly personal detail. 'Did you dance, Monsieur Litchfield?' asks Aissa Njai. Everyone roars with laughter. I can't see her face, but I can hear her deep gurgling laughter, very close to me – I can feel it vibrating through her long body. I'm that close to her. I can practically feel her heat, and I can sense in that laughter, a warmth, a tension, an excitement.

I shouldn't be here. I should be outside with the guys, playing ludo, hand-slapping, chuckling and bantering on the corner, sniggering and joking and *talking about* women *with men* – not actually *in here* with them, sitting practically between the legs of these heavy-duty women I hardly know.

Hardly know, I hear you say. *Hardly know?* Here he is, the Soul Adventurer, the Culture Conjuror, protesting at being with people because he *hardly knows* them!

Yeah, but this is Africa, man. You can't just walk into these things. As a man, you can't spend too long in the society of women without compromising yourself on some deep, deep level.

A door opens somewhere, and a shaft of light falls on the scene. I see Aissa Njai, fixing me with a look of almost proprietorial tenderness, with a smile of what I can only describe as genuine affection. The door closes.

Because quite apart from all the cultural stuff, there's all the *other* stuff. Like the fact that she's a *woman*, with all her warmth and wants and biology, all her insecurities, emotional, spiritual and economic – particularly economic – all her children, her family, her culture and her own fantasies, kinks and desires. All the things that make her a human being separate from me.

I'm outta here.

The place is in uproar, everyone shouting at me to sit down, to stay, to chat longer. Aissa Njai is on her feet. 'What is the matter, Monsieur? Can't you stay longer?'

'No, I gotta go. I'll see you.'

I'm round the corner, stumbling across the darkness of the other yard. The drumming has finished. I can see the wall of the outer courtyard and the doorway. I fumble with the door, plunge through it, someone gets me in a headlock, forcing me downwards so I can hardly breathe, hissing in my ear.

'On aime les tam-tams?'

Shit, man. It's one of her husbands, and he's gonna kill me!

'Tam-tams et jigennes grandes! Erh?' There's that familiar

311

gargling laugh and he loosens his grip. The fucking driver! Thanks for scaring the shit out of me, man!

I see him wagging his finger at me by the dim streetlight. 'On est méchant, wai!' He makes the action with his fingers of a pair of legs sidling furtively in through an open doorway. 'Elle est belle, erh? Belle et très grande!' He seizes my hand as he creases up, cackling hoarsely through the side of his mouth like Muttley from *Wacky Races*. 'Est-ce que tu a besoin de mon aide?'

'I gotta go, man.'

'Hey, c'est tôt, erh?'

'I gotta go.'

I'm up early. Earlier than you'd have expected. Earlier than I'd have expected. But the day has already found its rhythm, the brightness is already imminent, there are already plenty of bana-bana men cruising the crumbling walkways. A few yards up the Avenue Wagane Diouf, I meet a guy with a length of rope. He holds it up with the habitual fatalistic motion. The chances of me wanting it are unbelievably remote, but needless to say he shows no surprise when I do. I haggle hard – I need to – and head back to the hotel. The smacked-in-shoe man is standing grinning near the entrance, raising his eyebrows in greeting as he holds up his ill-matched wares.

'I want these shoes,' I say. 'Comprends?'

He nods.

'But I don't want them *now-now*. Comprends?' I position him a few yards to the left of the entrance. 'Don't move. I'll be back in ... deux minutes. Something will come down. Down, yeah? Du ciel? Bon. Take hold of it. Don't give it to anyone else. Go round that corner and wait there. I'll be there in deux minutes ... Pour les chaussures!'

He nods.

I head back into the building, nod to the porter and the inscrutable desk dude and head smoothly upstairs. In my room, the holdall is tightly packed. I tie one end of the rope round the handles. Then I slip out, checking there's no one in the stairwell, and head along to the end of the landing, to the parapet that looks

312

down onto the street. I lean over. The porter, thank God, is inside talking to the receptionist. The taxi-man who habitually slumps himself there is off on a fare or he hasn't arrived yet. I hiss to the shoe-man, who looks up with a winning cross-eyed smile. I wind the loose end of the rope round my forearm, then lower the holdall slowly and gently over. I don't look over, 'cause I don't want to draw attention. As I feel the weight of the bag giving into the shoe-man's arms, I toss the other end of the rope over and run down into the foyer, straight into Aissa Njai.

'How are you?'

'Cool.'

'You left so suddenly.'

She looks somehow younger, her eyes wider. She's standing right up close to me, and it's like her whole being's dilated.

'Yeah, I was er . . .' I'm shaking and out of breath.

'Are you all right? You seem . . .'

'Yeah. I'm just popping out for a . . . paper.'

'A paper?'

'Un journal.'

'Ah, oui.'

'Yeah . . .' I give an imitation of a nonchalant wave, and practically fall out into the street. I try to walk in a straight line the few yards till I'm out of sight of the hotel windows, then I run straight round the corner and into the shoe-man.

I grab at the holdall. 'Brilliant, man!' But he's got a tight grip on it, pushing forward the shoes with his usual friendly smile. 'Yeah, right. I need to buy these. How much?'

He holds up his flattened hand. 'Cinq?' I hazard. He nods.

'Hundred?'

He shakes his head.

'Thousand?'

He nods.

Five thousand? For a pair of beaten-up shoes in different styles and different sizes, that look like the same ones he's been trying to hawk for however many weeks it is since I first saw him? He fixes me with a firm and unnervingly knowing grin. I haven't got

313

time to fuck about. I give him a fresh new five-thousand note, and I'm off.

Twenty-one

I'm on a train. No, I'm literally *on* a train – a t-shirt tied burnous-like round my face, with just enough room for my Wayfarers to peer out. But I'm not the only one. There must be a couple of thousand people crammed onto the roof of the immensely long goods train as it creaks and grinds its way ever onward into the immense light and the immense heat. It's easy now to say I shouldn't have gone on the roof, knowing it was going to be this bright and this hot – I mean in the interior of Tekrur in the middle of the day, what's it *going* to be like? – but there was no room in the packed cattle trucks below, I mean *no* room, and I didn't have time to blag myself a lift in a car, van or donkey cart, 'cause I didn't know till this morning I was coming. We're all sitting side by side, packed three rows deep on either side of the hot iron roof – all the young dudes of N'Galam, all the thugs, louts, geezers and hustlers, all the students, schoolboys, junior accountants and petty civil servants. We're all together. No one's better or worse than anyone else today. And further up the train, they're standing, holding on to each other's shoulders – but this being Tekrur, not that tightly, in fact frighteningly casually – swaying with the movement of the train as it picks up speed, trembling in the blasting heat from the diesel engine and the shuddering brilliance of the white-hot sky.

All around, as far as the eye can see, is just an endless scrub of low dust-laden trees, hanging ghostlike over the desiccated earth

– cleared over vast areas in readiness for the coming rains, and over others left, blocking out any real sense of space or distance. Nobody's saying much, the excited banter, laughing and joking with which we left N'Galam has petered out. Now we're mostly just waiting and enduring. I've long since finished the small amount of water I brought, and no one else has brought any. In fact, no one brought anything, because that's how you go as a young man. You just get up in the morning and go, as you are, impulsively, because everything you need will be provided when you get there.

Yes, we're on the Demal, the great pilgrimage to the tomb of Mam Sheikh Jarra – the guide, the spiritual grandfather of the Tekrurian people – the Prophet of Tekrur. In Islam, you can't say anyone after Mohammed is a prophet, so they say Nassir-al-Rhassoul – the Servant of the Prophet. But it's said by members of the other brotherhoods that the tariqa, the spiritual brotherhood of Mam Jarra, which is roughly half the Tekrurian population, venerate him above Mohammed or even God Himself. I can't say if that's true or not, but there's no doubt they're relying on the baraka – the spiritual power – of Mam Jarra, to get them to where it's the entire purpose of their actions in this world to get them: Paradise. And as I may have said before, while in this world the White Man has access to all the riches and knowledge of the earth, in the next world, it is the Black Man who will sit on the right hand of God. That, although I don't know if anybody has actually said it, is the implicit message of all of this. That's why every year, they make their way through the burning light and heat to Kagor, where they've built the biggest mosque in Black Africa.

So, I hear you say, you thought you'd just slip along? You who referred to all this as fatalistic, feudal bullshit!

I may have said that. But I was ill, I was raving, I didn't know what I was saying. 'Cause I always have, ever since I first became involved in Tekrurian music, had heavy respect for this kind of thing. Not just because practically all the musicians are members of the tariqa of Mam Jarra, and lyrical references are practically continual, but because the essence, the vibe of it, permeates the

316

music to an intoxicating extent. And if you're living in that society, as I now am, it's around you the whole time, it's hanging over you, enveloping you. You're imbibing other people's faith like passive smoking. So when the time comes for the Demal of Kagor, you've gotta go. Literally. This morning, Papa Gorgi Ngom, whose compound I'm now living in, told me that today was the day and I was going to go. And that was that.

Yes, I'm living with Papa Gorgi in one of the more pungent and *in there* of the quartiers populaires. And it's not as difficult as you probably think it is. In fact, if you understand the ethos and imperatives of the culture, it's really very easy. And in that world, the sort of money I've got goes a *long* way. The room I share with Papa Gorgi's younger brother is a glorified packing-case lined with mouldering lino through the holes in which you can see straight out into the street. But compared to the conditions most Tekrurians live in, compared to the conditions *most people in the world* live in, it's luxury. We've each got our own bed, for Christ's sake!

I came with two of Papa Gorgi's nephews. We got separated in the milling crowds at the station, but that doesn't matter, 'cause here we're all one. We've all got everything and nothing. There's a unity and a bonhomie, a sense of automatic friendship and common purpose, that I haven't come across since I went to Southend with several thousand other mods in 1964. Oh yes, that night in the cells was one of the happiest of my life.

Now the railway's running close beside the road, and you can see the great cavalcade of battered cars, painted Peugeot pickups and those blue and yellow minibuses with no glass in the windows, known with unintentional irony as 'cars rapides' – all crammed to the gills with the muffled and turbanned faithful; people on bicycles, donkeys, low-slung carts pulled by bony horses; people on foot, women carrying their great bales and baskets and basins on their heads through the endless brilliance; boys, bundles on their heads and backs; groups of the Gor Yallah, the Men of God, dreadlocked zealots of the brotherhood, walking the whole way barefoot, carrying nothing but their begging bowls and the great clubs with which they beat themselves during their

317

rituals. It's biblical, man. And every so often, one of the dark-windowed Mercs or BMWs of the Big People comes honking its way along, weaving among the battered cars and buses, throwing up great clouds of dust, scaring the horses, scattering the hapless pedestrians. Each time, someone says, 'That is Sajar Jopp's car.' And each time I say, 'No, no. Look for a silver BMW.' And everyone chuckles with affectionate approval, and a certain pride, because the man who knows Sajar Jopp is with them.

At Mboul, the country's biggest railway junction, we wait in a siding for what seems like years. People start to talk and complain. They stand up and stretch and walk about, to the disgruntlement of everyone seated. They go and piss over the side, to the annoyance of those wandering about below.

Then there are shouts from further up the line. Craning over the heads of those on my right, I can see some kind of commotion going on on the ground about a hundred yards away. There's a truck parked by the sidings, and among the people around it are some *white people*. White people? What are they doing loitering by the railway line in this unpropitious middle of nowhere? Whatever it is, the people on the train don't like it. And the anger's spreading this way. What's happening?

'They are photographing us,' says the guy next to me, in a tone of cold anger.

I take my Wayfarers off, then put them back on in an attempt to see what's going on. Yes, there in the middle of the group, on its tripod, is what looks like a film camera. A white camera crew with their Tekrurian minders, assistants, clapper-loaders and best boys, filming the pilgrim trains laden to breaking-point with the black and anonymous faithful, as they make their way on their immemorial journey across the brilliant immensities of the savannah. Time-Life, or what? *National Geographic* or bust! But the dark and anonymous faithful aren't interested. They don't want their pilgrimage roped into somebody else's documentary, CD-Rom or postcard without their permission, and certainly not without payment. There's some uncertainty down there. The minders, clapper-loaders and best boys are saying it's probably better to leave it. The grizzled white technicians, the bacon-

318

sandwich men, don't give a fuck either way as long as they get paid. The director, the lean guy in the safari suit, is thinking, If we can just get another thirty seconds we'll be covered, and we can get the fuck out of here. And the producer or whoever she is, that woman with the clipboard . . .

There's a sudden creak and the train lurches forward a few yards. Now I can really see what's happening. That woman with the clipboard. It's . . . *Gabriella*. Who else was it going to be? Deep in conversation with the head minder, who's telling them they should withdraw. She's telling him that if they can just get another thirty seconds, it'll be perfect for the title sequence to the Sahelfest 2000 season on BBC2 – just a few seconds, if that, of the pilgrim-laden train, with some appropriately moody music, looming out of the midday brilliance, shot from a dramatic low angle, will melange beautifully with the freedom-dancing crowds of Soweto, the swaying camels of the Sahara. I can't bear it, man. 'Cause on the one hand, I want these people to get whatever's coming to them because of the unbelievable arrogance with which they will blunder into any situation, no matter how profound, no matter how secret, no matter how *other*, and somehow reduce it just to the . . . *subject matter* of their activity – generally getting away with it because of their ability to pay. And on another level, I'm thinking these people are probably English, one of them is Gabriella, and you know . . . I'm a nice man.

Unbelievably they decide to go for another take. The guy's about to shout 'Roll it' when there's a sudden hard clattering on the ground below the train, and the film crew are scattering. The cameraman's down behind his tripod, folding it and climbing into the van all in one movement. He's been in Somalia, Bosnia and Rwanda, and he knows how to make a hasty exit. Everyone else is getting behind the van. Yes, they're being stoned from the train. And as soon as it's had the required effect, it stops. The stone-throwers – and God knows where they got the stones from; unless they brought them for precisely this purpose – drop to their haunches. A few bits of orange-peel and other refuse thud listlessly to the ground in front of the van. After a time, the crew, the assistants, the director and Gabriella peer gingerly out. And

319

from the hubbub of angry voices, one – male, hard, weary with a
dour experience to which all others cede authority – rings out:
'There are two things!' Suddenly, there's total silence. 'First, the
slaves. Second . . . les Tirailleurs!'

Yes, the Tirailleurs: Tekrurian soldiers, who fought on the
Allied side in World War Two. A bunch of them mutinied after
the war over back pay, and were pulverised by the French tanks
for their pains.

Those on the train stand and sit in grim silence, reflecting on
the truth and bitter justice of what's been said. Gabriella and her
crew stare shamefaced at the ground. There's a grinding of brakes
and the train lurches forward.

The edge has gone off the brilliance. The sun has kind of
dissolved into the dust. But it's still horribly bright, and it's hotter
than ever.

I feel terrible. Coming up on here was a bad idea. You hear of
people dying of sunstroke and dehydration, don't you? I should
have got off at Mboul, blagged a lift back to N'Galam with
Gabriella's posse – Tirailleurs or no Tirailleurs – and never mind
the Demal of Kagor, 'cause at this moment, all I want to do is live.
I want to drink and then lie down somewhere dark and quiet and
cool. No one else seems bothered by it. They're used to the light,
heat and the dehydration, and any hardship they undergo on the
way to Kagor will count as a blessing for them in God's great
account book.

Then suddenly there's a shout, and everyone's looking ahead. I
thought I saw something hanging, hovering up there in the dust-
laden sky. And then, there it is, trembling as it emerges out of the
shuddering whiteness: the minaret of the biggest mosque in Black
Africa. There's a great gasp – though everyone's seen it many
times before – and everyone's holding out their hands in prayer –
because it *is* big. And seeing it looming up over the mean and
total nothingness of the bush, hanging there in the immense and
empty sky: that is fucking awe-inspiring.

Next thing I know, the train is pulling into a station. It's
suddenly almost dark. Everyone else is standing. They have been

320

standing, possibly for some time. I'm helped down the narrow and precipitous iron ladder. I put my foot onto the platform and collapse.

There's a minor track on a less well-known album by one of Britain's most well-known rock stars (no, not Michael Heaven), that starts off with this wailing distorted blues harp, immediately challenged by a filthy, screaming feedback guitar, a demonically swaggering bass lunging into the mix, booting the thing further into a howling rusting mayhem. The lyrics are the usual garbage about copping dope in L.A., but they're largely inaudible anyway, and the guy deserves a Nobel Prize for the way he goes, 'Oo-YAY!' on the chorus. Only trouble is, it sounds like they've got the drummer from the Sunday lunchtime trio in the pub round the corner sitting in on a kit that cost about thirty quid. Nothing against cheap instruments! Most of my favourite music has been recorded on instruments that were hardly working, but in this instance, it has just *not got it*. And the whole thing's so close to being a masterpiece, an apogee of swaggering rock'n'roll preposterousness – an 'Air Guitar Greats: track one, side one' if ever there was one – it's a fucking tragedy. I mean the sense of bathetic let-down when those drums come in, just destroys it every time. But that's the early seventies for you. Only about three people knew how to mike the drums properly. I bumped into the guy once at an awards ceremony, and I told him one of my lifetime's ambitions was to remix that track and re-record the drums. Nice bloke – very sharp, very cool, not your typical casualty by any means – but he couldn't remember the track I was talking about. But that's artists for you.

Litch, I hear you saying. Litch! What are you on about? You don't even like white rock! Yeah, okay, in general that's true, but if they can manage to keep a sense of the ludicrousness of the whole enterprise, while still booting into it with real *appetite*, and without descending into self-parody, white rock can be a gas. I mean, punk was a laugh – for about five minutes. Only trouble is, there's only about three people who can actually make it work. (No, not you, Mick.)

Anyway, I have this nightmare, this recurring nightmare – occasional, but it's getting more and more frequent – where I'm on *Desert Island Discs* or one of those programmes like *My Top Twelve* with Brian Matthew, which doesn't exist any more, and I find myself asking for that track I've just been talking about. Which is slightly surprising, because although I do like it, it's not exactly central to my life's work. But then it gets worse. Instead of taking advantage of a once-in-a-lifetime opportunity to get Sajar Jopp and Papa Gorgi Ngom played on Radio 4, instead of demanding Mbolo Mbango's unbearably exquisite 'Kinsione', without which I wouldn't go anywhere, never mind a fucking desert island, I find myself unable to help asking for things like 'Your Song' and 'Nessun Dorma'. And it gets worse. I always wake up in a cold sweat just as I'm about to ask for 'Bohemian Rhapsody . . .

Well, you say, that's hardly surprising. That's exactly the sort of music someone from New Malden *would* want to take to a desert island. And you know, you're not wrong. Because in a funny way, I wouldn't, with the exception of 'Bohemian Rhapsody', have any objection to being represented by that music. I mean, music, culture, art – whatever you want to call it – if it's to have its full generative, healing, total, all-encompassing power, has to work on levels sometimes so deep that it's only when you're in danger of losing the things they represent that you're fully aware of them. That's what Sajar Jopp was doing, wasn't it? Taking the things the people had lost sight of through colonialism, through the rush to urbanise and westernise, things to which in their newly aquired habits of living they'd given no conscious thought, things they'd buried deep within themselves, that they regarded with embarrassment, even disgust, and he said, 'Come on! This is you!' And take 'Your Song'. It's not just that I think you probably do have to be British to fully appreciate how bad a line like 'If I was a sculptor, but then again . . . no' actually is. If I got bored sitting on the beach of my desert island speculating on how many millions Bernie Taupin has made from writing lines like that, I could wander off under the palms and think about the fact that my wife once said she thought that was quite romantic.

322

When I awake, I'm aware that I've already woken and I felt so unbelievably bad that I decided not to hang around, but immediately retreated back into unconsciousness. Now I feel bad, but I have that immediate and instinctive feeling of gratitude and relief that I don't feel as bad as I did before. I'm lying on a bed. It's not uncomfortable. I turn and see, silhouetted in the doorway, a tall robed figure, standing watching me. All around is the humming and roaring of the city, the sounds of two million-odd people milling excitedly through the dusty darkness, the buzzing and wailing of hundreds of P.A. systems, all reduced to one thick wad of sound, like the wall of the womb enclosing me.

When I awake again, there's a light on in the room and it's full of people who all nod and greet me smilingly as though there were nothing at all remarkable about having someone fast asleep in the corner of the room – 'cause this is Africa, and there isn't. A guy tells me I'm in the house of one of the high marabouts, one of the direct descendants of Mam Sheikh Jarra, one of those who are close to God – and when they say that they don't mean it in some vague, like-he's-really-close-to-God-man kind of way, they mean he's *actually* close to God.

'Come,' he says, taking my hand. I feel someone getting to their feet. It must be me, because next thing I know, I'm out in a courtyard, the vast hubbub of the starless night suddenly overwhelmed, overmastered by the call to prayer from the immense minaret that looms invisible above us.

We enter another room, brightly lit, where more people, even more spectacularly berobed than in the first room, are sprawled around on massive leather sofas, among brass'n'glass coffee tables, cabinets full of cut glass, neo-rococo light fittings and the like. They all greet me with this smiling, blissed-out courtesy. I hear someone reply. It must be me.

We head into another room, half-filled with this immense canopy, with two doors leading directly out into the night. Through one, I can see dozens of expectant pairs of eyes, waiting. Under the canopy, on a great chair like a throne, is a figure berobed, beswathed and bescarved in damasks that glisten and glimmer in the golden light. On his knees in front of him is a man holding the marabout's hand to his forehead. The marabout, sprawled back on his great throne, talks to him in a low voice. Another man takes the man by the shoulder, and leads him away. I notice the police outside the other door, holding back the crowd. But don't think this is the head guy, who they call the caliph, the last surviving son – or is it grandson? – of Mam Jarra. This is just one of the grandsons – or is it great-grandsons? – or great-nephews. But he's still got his hundreds, maybe thousands of followers and disciples who are looking to him for salvation. The vizier, or whatever he is, signals to my guy to lead me forward. I take the marabout's hand, and I'm about to fall on my knees, but my guy holds me back. Don't overdo it, man. Don't overdo it. I meet the marabout's eyes. He's in a groove so different from mine, I can't even tell how old he is. He could be very much older than me or very much younger. He murmurs prayers for my benefit to which I just say, 'Amen ... Amen ...'

'You are feeling better?'

'Yeah, much. Cheers.'

'This is your home. Stay here as long as you wish.'

And I'm being led away.

Everybody – everybody who's ever been anything in Tekrurian music – is here. Except Sajar Jopp. And they're all hanging out in the houses of their own personal marabouts, who they dedicate a song to on each cassette, maybe even naming a whole cassette after them. Particularly these griot women. Their cassettes are mostly just endless paeans of praise to the marabouts, the parents of the marabouts, the villages they come from. So come the Demal, they get privileged treatment, their own rooms in their marabouts' residences. And that's where you hang out, not overtly trying to network – not needing to, because just by being here, just by being seen to be here, you're already clocking up major brownie points.

You're sprawled on cushions in some marabout's courtyard with Elhadji Mamadou Seck, Omar Sarr and Mbaye 'Boy' Jallo, being fanned by some impassive, velvet-skinned odalisque, and all the time people are coming and going, the sabar player from this band, the guitarist from that. You're meeting people you haven't seen for years and you're making new friends all the time – because in Kagor everybody's in a good mood. Through a gateway, you can see the thronging multitudes moving through the streets. You can hear the continual buzz and roar of two-million-odd voices all talking at once – the distorted wailing of hundreds of sound systems near and far, all praising God, the Prophet, the Servant of the Prophet. More and more people are still arriving as we approach the high point, the Night of Demal itself.

I wander out into the street. It's late afternoon, but the air's still massive with heat and brilliance, and everyone and everything looks bigger, as though magnified by the sheer size of the brightness. And all these people, who just keep on coming, larger than life in their huge robes, the women, the great layers of their muffling scarves and veils pulled back in glistening piles over their foreheads, all bludgeoned by the heat and the heaviness of their faith into this expression of spaced-out serenity. And all these men: do they know that wearing dark glasses gives them a look of intense and inscrutable mysticality? Of course they do. It's like the sound systems continually booming out over the crowds: there's nothing like a nasal voice coming through a heavily distorting sound system, to give an edge of raw and slightly dangerous spirituality. Oh, yes, there's an edge out here, all right. Because there are just too many people, all trying to move in every direction at once. Someone just shoved me from behind, which I definitely did *not* appreciate. And as I move further, there are more hawkers holding up marabout scarves, keyrings, stickers and car-window talismans, as well as all the usual junk. There are hundreds of stalls and great shops temporarily taking up half the street we're trying to move down. It's getting tighter and tighter. There's a policeman blowing a whistle, trying to direct the crowd. Suddenly there's a space opening ahead and I'm shoved forward. There's a flash of red. I look down, and my shirt's spattered with blood. A guy's cutting a sheep's throat, sacrificing it, right here in the middle of the crowd. Fucking hell, man! It was clean on this morning.

'It will be a blessing for you,' says a voice at my elbow.

'Yeah, I hope so.'

There's another voice. 'Hello, my friend. How are you?' A beaming face: the philosophical métro-mender from the Medina. 'C'est philosophique, erh?' He waves his arm in an all-encompassing gesture. 'All of this is African philosophy!'

'Great.'

'What happened to your shirt?'

I tell him.

'Maybe it will be a blessing for you,' he says, doubtfully.

'Yeah.'

'Have you been into la mosquée?'

'Not yet.'

'Come on! Let's go together!'

There's a vast square around the mosque. But you're not aware of that. All you're aware of is the immense number of people desperate to get into the mosque, the vast looming minaret throwing its shade over the crowd, the whistle-blowing police pushing people into semblances of queues which immediately dissolve again, the muffled but howling sound systems: 'La Ilah illa Allah – *Lailah-illa-Allaaah!*' On and on and on, the intense nasal voices getting more and more exercised as the afternoon passes into evening and the Night of Demal. Suddenly there's a flat doom-laden drumbeat as if from nowhere, and this wild, red-eyed figure's suddenly materialised in front of me: dreadlocks flying, ragged patchwork motley, great gris-gris collars and a portrait of his marabout round his neck, like a huge access-all-areas pass. One of the Gor Yallah – the Men of God – the zealots of Mam Jarra. He's looking straight at me, not seeing me but some visitation of his own mind – either stoned out of his brain or bananas or both, and he's got a huge club. The crowd draws back as his cohorts keep up a deranged nasal singing and the deadpan drumbeat and he swings the club around his head, bringing it down on his back with a resounding thud. The crowd gasp. He seizes my hand and presses it to his forehead, muttering in some unidentifiable language. Then he turns and pulls me on through the crowd. Ahead, a posse of gendarmes reach out to touch the portrait round the guy's neck, and hold back the gaping onlookers. I'm dragged onward into the yawning portal of the sanctum itself. A gendarme gestures me to remove my shoes and by the time I've done it, the Gor Yallah have disappeared, so's the métro-man. I've lost him totally. And there's another kind of buzz in here, the hoarse murmuring of the thousands of people making their way towards the tomb of Mam Jarra. And you can feel, you can breathe, you can taste the sanctity in the heavy dimness. Yes, finally you're in it. For all the images and names of the marabouts you've seen on shop signs, carrier bags, taxi dashboards, all the lyrics in the thousands of songs you've heard in the ten years you've been listening to Tekrurian music, this at last, is it. You're as close to it as you possibly could be, pulled onwards by the crowd – feeling their breath, breathing the minty tang of the sinuous bodies crushing around you, up to the brass grille around the tomb. How can you not *believe?* There it is under the massive chandelier of French bronze – paid for by Keba Sall, once the richest man in Tekrur, who it was said had been killed by Sajar Jopp by spiritual means – the great sarcophagus, wrapped in what looks like bubble-wrap.

There are two enclosures round the tomb, two entrances and two exits from the mosque – one for the men and one for the women. As I make my way out, I'm carried within a few yards of the women, queuing to get in. I notice a tall figure silhouetted on the threshold. As I pass, she half-turns, the light hitting the side of her face, and I see above a white veil, the slanting eye of Aissa Njai.

Did she see me? I doubt it. And I'm not thinking about that, because I'm clutching desperately at my trouser pockets. My wallet. It's gone.

Night. Night, man. And I'm carried on the swelling movement of the crowd round the mosque, the lower portion of the minaret just visible, reflected in the dusty glow from below, the twinkling lights at the top seemingly miles up in the starless blackness.

327

We've prayed. And when you're with two million people who are praying, you *do* pray. We've eaten. Or most of us have. And the singing is well under way: the singing of the poems, the gnomic spiritual maxims of Mam Jarra, that we've all come here for. Voices, raw-edged, nasal, raised hard and plangent – higher – then the dying fall, and already more voices surging like waves on a great sea, and before they've hardly got going, more voices – this great chiming, surging round of voices led by ... Led by nobody. Everybody's just singing whatever they feel like, wherever they are, and it works, it coheres, moving like this great wheel of song turning infinitesimally ever further into the night. And as the singing moves, so the crowd is moving, heaving and eddying around the great mosque.

I seem to have fallen in with this bunch of guys, and at every heaving crescendo, I'm carried up with them, physically, on the surging swell of their exultancy. Am I singing? Of course I am – the choruses anyway, which are mostly variations on There is no God but God, which even I know. Mohammed is his Prophet. Jerejef, Follower of the Prophet. It goes on endlessly. Then you listen and you realise it's totally changed. The women are in their groups, the men in theirs. But its not organised – it just happens like that. I'm laughing, man. I'm laughing as I'm singing, because I love it. I'm laughing because I'm with two million people I don't know – at least, I don't know anyone I'm with at this moment – celebrating a religion that's not mine, and I feel totally part of it. Wallet? What about it? Why get worked up about a worthless piece of leather containing a tiny amount of cash and fifteen non-functioning credit cards? I'm pressed up against these guys physically, the dudes of the Medina in their tracksuits and hooded sweatshirts, and all their mums and aunties and sisters are singing in their groups, their fathers, uncles and grandfathers in theirs. And there's an acceptance, a generosity about it that's so automatic you don't even have to think about it. You just empty your mind as you go with the movement of the great wheel.

And deep beneath it all, there's this pumping vibration you can feel in your feet. It's like the resonance, the vibration of the crowd on the earth, the animus of the earth itself vibrating back into us.

And then I think, is that drumming? Because it's suddenly closer and in the air around us. Or is it some kind of thudding circular echo of the singing? Or am I imagining it? The singing's going on unabated. You can pick out the shining, exhilarated faces in the half-light. Then suddenly, the vibrating's much louder, much harder, more insistently regular and everywhere the singing's breaking off and everyone's looking up with a great gasp of wonder and terror because there, around the top of the minaret, is a great glow of silver radiance. Everyone's staring transfixed, women are whimpering and screaming as the light disappears behind the minaret and the chugging metallic vibration gets louder and louder. The light begins to travel slowly down the other side of the minaret, throwing a hazy silver glow around the black shaft, then seems to light up the whole of the other side of the sky, while we are thrown into darkness. You can feel this tremor of terror and wonder passing through the paralysed and petrified crowd. *What the hell is it?* And you know what they're thinking – that it's a spiritual visitation. What else would it be, on this night of all nights? And half of you's thinking they're probably right.

Then the great light starts to move round the minaret towards us, and the people start running, or trying to run, as this massive searchlight plays down over the crowd. Everyone's panicking. There's gonna be a stampede. People are gonna be killed. Then there's this great rush of wind, and everybody's crouching down, pulling their shawls and their scarves, their robes and their sweatshirt hoods up over their heads. I try to shield my face as the dust comes up over the great crowd of shrouded, cowering figures, whirling into the massive glare of light from the helicopter.

That's right, man. A chopper! But what's it doing here? Descending into Kagor in the middle of the Night of Demal? That's got to be a major, major sacrilege. Everyone covers their heads as the chopper lands in front of the mosque and the blades come slowly to a standstill. Then, some standing, some still crouching, peering gingerly out from underneath their cowls and shawls, others frozen in an attitude midway between the two,

329

they watch awestruck as the hold opens and a bunch of soldiers spring out. What are they, paratroopers? Do they have paratroopers here? Then everyone's talking. But not in the indignant frenzy you might expect at the hand of oppressive authority coming right into this most important religious event of the year. There's going to be no tearing limb from limb of the soldiers, no burning of their helicopter. And it's not just because the soldiers are heavily armed. There's only this soft murmuring, as they wait utterly passively to see what's going to happen. Then suddenly, everyone's turning to see where everyone else is turning. And I'm turning to see where they're turning. I'm trying to see where they're looking. Each time it's as though they're looking at something right behind me. Then when I turn, they're all looking back at me. It's like when you were a kid, and everyone's laughing at someone and running away from them, you're laughing and you're running away – then you realise the person they're laughing at and running away from is . . . You! The crowd parts, and the soldiers silhouetted in the light from the chopper are walking towards me, and no one in this great crowd with whom a few minutes ago I was sharing so much, is doing or saying anything. I open my mouth, but no sound comes out. The officer's already got a piece of tape across it. Now I do try to speak, but my head's thrust down, my arms pinned behind my back, a rifle muzzle in the back of my head. Hands unfasten my trousers. No, no. Not my trousers . . . Then I'm dragged towards the helicopter. The engine explodes into life as I'm bundled sack-like up through the hatch.

My eyes come into focus, and it's loud. It's like being *in* the engine, this thick, booming vibration, encompassing everything. I can see the eyes of the guy sitting on the other side of the hatch, huge and doe-like in the dimness, regarding me totally impassively. His broad face is young and smooth. And he's massive, his enormous weapon lolling between his thighs. He hoists it up so it's pointing directly at me. He's wearing a white silk scarf, his maroon beret tilted just so, his immaculately pressed combat fatigues only slightly rumpled by the effort of having to

330

apprehend me. Oh, yes, these aren't some drunken, disorganised rabble who go looting and raping to make up their back pay and then run away at the first sign of trouble. These are *crack troops*. They've seen action in Zaire, Chad and Rwanda. They were in the Gulf, and for all I know they're in Bosnia too. That's right. They're on *our side*!

I'm trying to keep this in mind while, screaming in my head, crawling in my bowels is the voice of the American anthropologist I met, who'd worked in Sierra Leone and said that Africans had a fundamentally different attitude towards death and killing – that in some parts of Africa killing is seen as a cleansing process – for the killer! – and in others, one takes on the *power* of the person one has killed. I remember saying to him, 'You've been listening to old wives' tales, man,' 'cause half these anthropologists are being paid by the CIA to come up with this Dark Continent stuff to justify the neo-colonial policies of the IMF. But now all I'm thinking is, *Sierra Leone!* That's not far from *Liberia* . . . Don't mention Liberia. Liberia itself is not nearly as far away from where we are now as I'd like it to be.

I'm feeling ill, man. 'Cause someone hit me as I got in. They just kind of slapped me round the head. And if you're the sort of person who gets in fist-fights as part of your average weekend's entertainment, if you and your best mate like to smack each other around just to show how much you like each other, you probably wouldn't even have noticed. But it's put my entire body into crisis. I'm trembling all over. And I'm trying to remember where it was that I read or heard, or even if I imagined it, and let's for Christ's sake hope I did, that the Tekrurian troops are notorious for their cruelty. That's right, man. Even in your Hampstead living-room or wherever it is you are, that phrase *notorious for their cruelty* sends a chill through your very blood. Half-formed images your squeamishness, your middle-class inhibition, your fundamental decency won't allow you to complete, rush helter-skelter through your mind before you quickly turn the page, forcing your mind into another track, but with one question flashing on and off in mad neon: *'How bad can it get?'*

Yeah, okay, these people are on *our side*, but can I still be considered to be on *our side*? I've always laughed at the expats, leading their charmed lives in their bougainvillea-smothered bungalows, with their tennis courts and official cars, treating their domestic staff like pets, buying them presents, paying for their children's education and fondly imagining they're thereby getting *close to the culture*. Oh yes, standing filthy and dishevelled at a bus stop with the vast crowds of the *real people*, I'd always smirk as the expats came cruising by in their air-conditioned land cruisers with their well-scrubbed kids. But now, now I realise that these people, who are by and large *nice people*, got it right. Because by staying well clear of the culture – even without having meant to – by not going within a million miles of the culture, they preserved their innocence. If they were here, these guys would be saluting them, asking them to please wait patiently while they make the radio message that'll sort out the confusion – not just because they can tell from the way these people are dressed that they're Grade A Whites, but because of their unimpeachable air of *uninvolvement*. But me, they're gonna look in my eyes, they're going to see that I've spent too long *in it* – that I've stood too close to the flame, that I've transgressed not only in the ways I transparently have transgressed, not only in the ways I haven't told you about, but in ways even I don't know. They're going to look in my eyes and see the guilt long before they see the causes of it. And that's when it's going to start getting nasty.

As the chopper descends, I can hardly breathe. Then it lands with a jolt. I'm bundled out and half-dragged, half-pushed across the hard earth. All around I can feel the crowds of soldiers standing watching from the darkness. I know all about places like this. I made the mistake of being an impressionable adolescent during the Congo Emergency, and I know that when you go into a place like this, you don't come out. I'm taken into a shed, and suddenly everything is grotesquely bright. A bunch of soldiers are playing cards. The leader, a big, belligerent, shambolic bloke, can't see why they've brought me in here. I'm a consignment, of no more interest than the sacks of grain piled round the room and potentially much more inconvenient. I'm dumped in a chair and they go back to their card game, which had been at a critical juncture, the big guy at loggerheads with this thin, Moorish-looking guy. This very young soldier's standing with an assault rifle levelled at my head, his eyes fierce and intent. He's loving it. This is the best thing that's happened to him since he joined up. With any luck I'll do something that'll justify him emptying the magazine into me. The air's vibrating with the soldiers' guttural ejaculations. Everything's big, vivid, loud and hard-edged in the hard light. These guys look considerably less crack, or maybe it's just 'cause I can now see their bloodshot eyes, their uneven cola-stained teeth, their bristly jowels, their sweat-stained uniforms. Now I can see what's going on, things are reverting to a level of banal humanity. It's usually at the moment of arrest that people get carried away and *things* happen. If I can get through this without the kid shooting me by accident or the big guy punching me in the face because he's lost his card game, things'll probably get onto the usual African level of negotiability. That's what they say, the real Africa hands, the people who've been hustling around the edges of African commerce for decades, real repro-bates most of them, and they've got to know how to work the system: if you get into trouble, make friends with them. And how do you do that? You give them something. Preferably money. That's the problem. I haven't got anything. I've got nothing left to negotiate with.

These people aren't the real guys. These are just the interim, the storemen, the semi-civilians. I'll be here just long enough to lull me into a false sense of security, then they'll hand me over to the hard men. The Elite Squad. And they always have them in these kind of places, don't they? Guys, usually from the President's tribe, who've been given carte blanche for every kind of burning, maiming, electrocution and small-time genocide that suits their purposes. Guys that make this kid with the rifle look like the naive boy amateur he is. On the other hand, the naive boy amateurs are usually the worst ones, because they've got no fear and no feelings. They'll do *absolutely anything*. Nowadays, heavily-armed twelve-year-olds have got the Elite Squads on the run all over Africa. And as the twelve-year-olds close in from the

333

bush, laden with their rocket-launchers and unspeakable talismans, the Elite Squads go apeshit, burning their uniforms, spraying the streets with random gunfire, setting fire to churches with whole ethnic groups inside, before they disappear into thin air.

But I'm thinking about the wrong parts of Africa, I mean the *wrong parts*! Or am I? Here they're so full of their bogus francophone cool you can't tell what they're capable of. And where are the French? There should be a steel-hard crewcut Frenchman here, keeping a cold-hearted cartesian eye on things. They dominate the country with their cable TV, their croissants and their Faustian economic aid, but when you need them, *they're not there*.

I'm busting for a slash, and the tape is making my face hurt.

A slim, efficient-looking officer with a clipboard comes in. He pulls the tape from my mouth with a moderate amount of care.

'Parlez français?'

I nod.

He says a load of stuff, which I don't get.

I shrug.

He sighs and tells the big bloke to untie me, which he does with an air that suggests it's being done purely as a favour. The officer gestures at me to do up my trousers. The kid goes into an overdrive of Ramboesque posturing – right elbow raised, breech up to his ear. The officer snaps at him and he relaxes.

'Allons,' says the officer, pointing at the door, and we troop out into the darkness.

Twenty-two

It's Sunday. I've worked it out. I should be out cleaning the car in the drive. It's a fantastic morning. May: the puffy clouds passing through the blue Surrey sky reflected in the gleaming bonnet, all ready to go and do the things that people in New Malden do on a Sunday. Like going to the retail park. Maybe lunch at Pizza Hut. That's what I should be doing. Then tonight maybe meeting the lads down the pub. You know, those people I thought were incredibly boring. I mean, they were boring. But they weren't. It was just because I was stupid and arrogant. They were *nice people*. You know, if you were to ask them to do something for you, like help you start the car, they wouldn't think, Yeah, nice one, what angle can I work on this? They'd either do it for you, or they wouldn't. And I'm almost sure they would do it. You know, they were real people.

Why, I hear you ask, do you keep going on about New Malden? You haven't lived there for the best part of thirty years. Your wife can't stand retail parks. You keep referring to cars but you can't even drive. And as for those blokes in the pub, how dare you patronise them like that. You haven't been in that pub for twenty-five years. What makes you think they're still going there. They're probably hundreds of miles away somewhere – getting a life!

I should never, I should *never* have been buying records while she

335

was delivering our daughter. Oh, yes. I know what you're thinking. You're thinking, You're sick, man! Even to be thinking about records at a time like that! You deserve everything! But I mean, you've got to look at things in context. This was ten years ago. (Ten years, man.) And ten years ago, it was less normal . . . okay it was *slightly* less obligatory for the man to be there. And let's face it, she'd shown no interest in me being there. There'd been no harassment, no coercion, no brainwashing with all the covert intravenous subtlety of a flying mallet to get me to attend ante-natal classes. Because even then, things were far from in their first blush. We'd managed to get sex down to once a year, or was it every two years, during one of which loveless perfunctory fumblings she'd managed to get pregnant. But it was from the moment that she, sitting back against a heap of pillows the size of a stately home, utterly wasted, but with that magnificent beaming contentment and our daughter in her arms, noticed the fact that amid all the Sainsbury's bags of scarves, umbrellas, paperbacks and other crap I was carting in there, there was the thin, brittle plastic of the square flat carrier bag of one of London's leading second-hand record shops – yes, it was from the look she gave me when she saw that that I date the transition from the merely passionless and unsatisfactory to the irremediably damaged, hopeless and bleak. And that was ten years ago. But, as I say, it wasn't like you think it was. I mean, I was early. Early? you say. There is no *early* in these situations. You just go there and get stuck into whatever's happening!

No, listen, man. Come on. I've got feelings too. I didn't want to be in the way. I didn't want to be going bananas in foyers, waiting-rooms and corridors, clogging up the entire NHS in the process. Oh, yes. Don't get the idea I didn't care. This was my way of caring.

There I was, on the packed tube, my head jammed against the steel handrail, with a faceful of steaming burberry and a folding umbrella in my ribs. And I was thinking there's a shop a few doors down from the next station, which is the one before the one where I'm due to get off, and I can easily, in the fifteen minutes I've got, get out of this crush, up the escalator, flick through the half a rack relevant to me, and be back down here on a less crowded train with time to spare. Oh, yes. I know all about filling in time. It's like some people, when you arrange to meet them, and there's like a gap between appointments, they panic 'cause they might have half an hour to kill. Not me. That's half an hour of gawping, browsing and dreaming that's to be looked forward to, that's probably going to be more productive than either meeting. Next thing I know I'm taking the stairs of the escalator five at a time, and I can already smell the slightly sour damp'n'dust tang of many thousands of old record covers mingling with the nicotine of the chain-smoking assistants, the dull neon bleakness, the bowed monastic intentness of the other browsers, nodding imperceptibly to seventies funk. A quick dash through blackness and wetness, and I'm in the shop exactly as I'd imagined it a few moments before. Exactly. That guy behind the counter on the right has got his fag hanging out of his mouth at the exact angle I'd imagined. There's a guy in my way thumbing through 'Irish Traditional' which is right behind 'African' and 'International Folk', but sensing the manic, and possibly homicidal urgency with which I'm hanging over his right shoulder, he moves over to 'Blues'. I steam straight in. What I want is for there to be nothing of remote interest, which I would have put money on being the case, so I can be careering back down the serrated escalator steps in a matter of seconds. But it's not like that. Things never are like you want them to be. The section is not only three times as large as I would have expected, it's brimming over with records I've been looking for for years, records I failed to buy at other opportunities and kept myself awake regretting for years, and new discoveries of mind-blowing import. First album by El Camaron de la Isla con la colaboracion especial de Paco de Lucia, in mint condition judging by the cover, comes into the first category. Second album of same, which features our hero in tight trousers in front of a massive crucifix, the same. Fanta Damba – le rossignol de la savane. Unbelievably rare. Now I don't have to blame myself for not buying it in Paris eight years ago. And what's this? *Thiapathiouli* by Etoile de Dakar in an original Senegalese vinyl version I didn't know existed. There it is, just

337

sitting there in the rack, looking cheerfully and impudently back at me. Admittedly it's got a sticker on it saying 'Property of Bromley Library Service', but it would, I hazard, be worth a tenner of anyone's money if it had been run over by a truck.

No problem, you say. Get the gear up to the counter, buy it, and get back down that escalator. But it's not as simple as that. I'm a surprisingly poor impulse buyer. Not that, considering their import, these could be considered impulse purchases. But it always takes me time. I like to stow them fractiously under my arm, shaking, mumbling and sighing as I flick mindlessly through racks of stuff I'm not remotely interested in, as I wonder whether to go through the agony of actually buying. Even with stuff I unarguably must have, I have to put myself through the ritualistic agony of a few moments' exquisite, self-lacerating doubt. Then I have to check the vinyl, peering, poking and fretting over every blemish, discussing the quality, the music and its significance with the utterly uninterested assistants, even when I'm not trying to actively haggle the price down. Oh, yes. I have to talk, 'cause when I'm buying, I go into a state of jabbering transcendental hyperactivity. There's no time now. But even so, I must check the vinyl. There are signs alongside the ones saying they won't buy stolen goods and 'Absolutely No Haggling' advising you to do that. The Camarons are, as I thought, mint. The Fanta Damba is, as we say, 'good'. And the Etoile de Dakar has a label hanging from the cover by a tiny fragment of glue from which I adduce that in all its eight years residency in Bromley it was never once taken out. A glance at the grooves suggests it's never even been played. 'This is out of a library,' I say to the guy accusingly. He takes it and holds it up to the light, twisting his face doubtfully. 'The thing about library records,' he says, 'is that while they may not look scratched, they've often been worn down through continuous play. How much are we asking for this?'

'A fiver.'

'Have it for two quid.'

I cackle inwardly.

Oh, yes. I didn't run down the escalator. I rode down in a trance of satisfaction and inner well-being. I'd scored. I'd bought.

And in doing so, I'd not only acquired items for the physical reality of my collection, I'd added another piece to some inner and invisible structure, a subconscious edifice the significance of which I was only gradually and dimly becoming aware.

It was only when I actually walked into the hospital that it occurred to me that I possibly should have bought flowers, rather than buying records for myself. That of course would have been an unnecessarily harsh way of looking at it, because for me being in record shops is work. It's what I do. But it did definitely occur to me. And as I went into the lift, I thought maybe I should have been there rubbing her back or whatever it is they do. I know she hadn't asked me to, hadn't shown any interest whether I was involved or not. But maybe I should have done it for, you know, *me*. Maybe, I thought, as I rushed along the corridor, maybe I've actually missed something, something important here.

You know, after a time, and it's usually not long, you stop seeing people for what they are, and you start seeing them for what they mean to you. And I'm sure you know that after you've lived with someone for any length of time, and I mean really *lived*, when you see them you don't think, Yeah, they're beautiful, 'cause you're too busy thinking about what you should and shouldn't say or do to get into a major argument. And the things you notice about them physically are usually to do with expressions and looks that precipitate annoyances deep within you. I mean, that's what living with another person's all about, right?

But occasionally, like about twice in your relationship after your first meeting, something kind of jolts you into another view. That was what it was like as I came hurrying rain-soaked into the warm stillness of the ward: occasional baby shrieks, conversation of other people's visitors, but this stillness and this dimness in the great body of the ward. And round my wife's bed there's like this golden light. It was just the bedside lamp, but it was like a blessed radiance, and she was sitting back on the pillows looking totally wrecked, but at the same time serene and open like a flower, fully dilated, exposing for a few moments the golden beatific beauty of

339

her soul. And I thought, she's fair. It seems ludicrous, but I realised I had totally forgotten she was fair. I could see, through this glistening translucence, into the beatific essence of her soul.

She saw me rushing along the ward towards her and she looked pleased. I realise now it was simply a look that said, Okay, I've delivered safely, so I'm even going to be nice to you. But at the time I thought for a brief moment that everything had now changed so utterly that things were going to be different.

'Where is . . . ?'

'She.'

'She.'

'They'll bring her in a minute. What have you got there?'

'Where?'

'In that bag.'

'What? Nothing, just my umbrella and stuff.'

'Not that one, the other one.'

'Nothing. How did it go?'

'What's in the bag?'

'I had to go to Island on the way here. They gave me some stuff. How did it go?'

She just sat there giving me a look of such naked and unequi-vocal contempt I didn't quite know what to do. I realised that her sister, who I've never liked, was already there, had been there the whole time.

She'd already gone dark again.

I've often thought about what I should have said. 'How did it go?' What a fucking thing to ask! I mean, she didn't care. She was already, within two minutes of seeing me, already beyond caring. But I've often wondered, simply from the point of view of intellectual curiosity, what I could have said. I mean, what did men used to say when there was no question than that they wouldn't be there? They'd just stroll into the ward, cigar between their teeth, hold their new-born child up to the light as though checking a ten-pound note, glance nonchalantly at their wife and say, 'Good one.' But you can't do that now. There's nothing you can say. Unless there are seriously extenuating circumstances, you've got to be there.

Sometimes, not very often, it occurs to me that my collection is just a load of records, cassettes and CDs. I buy. Occasionally, I buy importantly. I buy records that are actually very rare, that it's important someone has a copy of. But more than that, when I get something that's filling a gap in my collection, or that completes something that I want to say through my collection, and I have this sense of satisfaction of putting something into place in a way that goes beyond the actuality of my collection and its components. And then at other times, like when I've had quite a lot of this stuff lying around for ages, maybe heaped against the bottom of my record stacks, I'll think, Yeah, I'll just put them where they should go. And I'll take something, the purchase of which had been an event of momentous satisfaction, and as I slide it into its place in the categorical order – a categorical order only I can understand, a poetic order, an order that could only be achieved by actually doing it – and for a split second it'll occur to me that these are just records, and that since I don't get time to play any of them, I'm not getting anything from them. And because they're all stacked with their spines outward I don't even get any pleasure from looking at the covers. So what's the point of it? And although I've made a statement in choosing what I've bought, perhaps I've actually chosen the wrong stuff. This is not only just a load of old African records. Maybe they're actually the *wrong* African records.

Chris Knowles and Dave Aggs were a couple of teachers from Leigh-on-Sea – Economics and History respectively, I think – who decided, against all apparent reason, to go professional as an R'n'B band. This was a long time ago. This was nearly a quarter of a century ago, a time when in reaction to bombastic super-groupism, playing honest, good-time bar music in small venues was *the thing to do*. Knowles and Aggs would take it in a slightly swampy Meters-type direction, then at other times they'd go in a more classic Memphis soul direction. Were they any good? Of course they weren't any good. By absolute standards, they were fucking awful. If I were to put one of their records on now, you would, because of the flatness, the sheer banality of the recording techniques of those times, be shouting 'Geddidoff!' within moments. But at the time . . . At the time, it all seemed like fresh harmless fun. And they were, in all fairness, a hell of a lot funkier live than they ever were on record. But I realised, long before they realised it themselves, that their real strength lay not in their bluesmanship, but in the fact that they were actually very *clever little songwriters*. That's why I became their manager.

Jackie and Sarah were two former colleagues of theirs – primary school, so they didn't have subjects – who used to go to all their gigs. The joke was that they were the 'fans and groupies'. Not that Knowles and Aggs so much as snogged either of them, 'cause it was just a joke. Yeah, haha. But while Jackie was the jovial extrovert one, Sarah was more quiet and wryly observant, more of a specialist in flat put-down humour. The sort of thing you might expect from someone from somewhere like Cheshire. Not that she was some kind of hardbitten scouse harridan. The accent was hardly there, just enough to confer a faint tinge of exoticism, and she was actually very, very sweet. It was just me who brought out the tough sardonic side in her. I encouraged her to develop it as an erotic weapon. Jackie had a lot of curly blonde hair, and I remember mentioning Sarah to Aggs as the dark one. He said, 'What are you talking about? Neither of 'em are dark!' I looked back and I realised he was right. We established, during marathon sessions in pubs, while Knowles and Aggs did their interminable sound checks, this banter, this repartee, where I was this slightly stupid person who was lying to Sarah all the time, and she of course knew. Jackie stopped going after about the tenth gig, 'cause she felt left out. Sarah stopped going out of moral support for Jackie, and because she was bored with it. But by this time we were already seeing each other under other pretexts.

Knowles and Aggs played everywhere: pubs, clubs, schools, American air force bases, working men's clubs on top of mountains in Wales, Italian seaside resorts. They developed a small following, and critically, the response was surprisingly good. They got a recording contract and support gig on a couple of tours with bands who are now themselves utterly, utterly forgotten. Then punk happened, and suddenly everything was totally different. I got them to push the quirky, left-field aspects of their songwriting and play as jaggedly and atonally as possible. This was a time when a lot of oddball, square-peg people who'd been around for ages – the Ian Durys, Elvis Costellos, Talking Heads – were suddenly making it massively. Didn't quite happen for Knowles and Aggs, but they boomed around promisingly in the background. Then after punk there was this yawning energy gap, and suddenly Knowles and Aggs had a hit single. Not a sudden rushing-in-there-at-Number-Three type hit single, but the kind that hovers around between sixteen and twenty-four for about six months. And that is money. Then they had another one, even bigger. You can't remember it. You can't remember Knowles and Aggs. They didn't record under the name of Knowles and Aggs. You wouldn't remember the name they did use. But if I was to play you one of their hits, you'd go, 'Oh, yeah. That!' The album did pretty well here. It went triple platinum in Germany. Knowles and Aggs still are major cultural figures in Italy.

By this time, I was married to Sarah, and the banter, the repartee – you know, about me being slightly stupid and lying and her knowing – that had become the de facto actuality of our relationship, and it wasn't a joke. But I was leading such a fast-moving rock'n'roll lifestyle I hardly noticed. I was making so much money – twenty per cent of Knowles and Aggs, which believe me, I had well earnt – and she was having so much fun spending it, doing up our house in Ladbroke Grove, it didn't seem to matter.

Then things started to slip. I started to make mistakes. I started to miss opportunities. Because there's an Olympian satisfaction to be had from seeing a couple of guys bashing out their songs on an out-of-tune upright piano and thinking, this could be a massive hit, and working on it for a couple of years in a way that at the time seemed uphill, thankless and never-ending, but in retrospect was actually quite enjoyable, and then it is a massive hit – in a way so like you predicted, it is slightly frightening. You've looked Destiny in the face and said, 'Yeah, yeah. Don't worry about it.' At first you feel great. Then you realise the music is not exactly crap, but definitely not what you got into this for. You're taking on more acts: synth duos, Power-Pop, New Romanticism. Desperate stuff. And all you're listening to is old blues records. And you start doing stupid things. It's like . . . what were they called? You know them. Electro anthem band who bestrode the sales figures of the mid-eighties like a brass colossus. They came to me with their little demo. I could tell it had the potential to be enormous, and in its primitive bedroom-in-Basildon version, I even quite liked it. But I thought, Can I really be bothered? And why was that? Because of the drugs and the drink? No, because the drugs and the drink were never that important. I never took them to the extent people think I did. I never did them to the extent I encouraged people to think I did. It seemed like a good rock'n'roll reason to be fucking up, 'cause in that world a bit of serious abuse is always good for the CV. Then one day, I thought, I'm doing so much serious abuse to convince people I'm seriously abusing, I am actually seriously abusing. She was putting pressure on me to do something about it. Knowles and Aggs were making it clear that if things didn't improve they'd be finding new management – gratitude or no gratitude. So I did something about it. And it wasn't that difficult, because it never was the drink and the drugs that were the problem.

After that, I was depressed. I was really depressed. I went into a kind of emotional paralysis. Then one day, practically by chance, I went to Africa on that budget package tour, and I was sitting on a beach and I heard the music that seemed to me to be everything that music should be, that – unlike the blues – hadn't already been discovered and done to death by the generations before mine, that seemed to answer all the needs of my obsessional nature. The music that had always been there waiting for me – the music in my head. That was when things really started to go wrong.

So, you ask, whatever happened to Knowles and Aggs? Knowles and Aggs now beaver away in womb-like and hermetic anonymity, programming rhythm tracks for things like car adverts, for which they make an annual wedge roughly equivalent to the

344

GNP of Tekrur. So, you say, why don't you beseech the guards into letting you contact the British Embassy who could then fax Knowles and Aggs to send the money to bail you out?

Well, apart from the fact that the guards have so far ignored all threats, promises, pleadings, tearful implorings and conniving attempts at deal-making, I don't think . . . In fact, I *know* that Knowles and Aggs would not respond positively to such a request. And I'm not gonna go into it, but if you knew the full facts, you'd realise I was right.

At first, she was all for it. She thought, at last, he's found something, something wholesome – and in comparison with other branches of rock'n'roll African music is pretty wholesome – to sink his teeth into. She thought that was me sorted. And she liked meeting the musicians, because they were funny, charming and half of 'em didn't even drink. She liked telling her colleagues at school about Michael Heaven's parties. And she betrayed – though she vigorously denied it – a wistful regard for Heaven himself. She only played African music in her car, and she liked it when people said, *What's that?* Then it started getting on her nerves. She'd start saying things like, 'Sajar Jopp is not God' or 'Sajar Jopp's boring' – particularly about the later stuff, which actually *is* quite boring – and I'd say, 'Yeah, I know.' So she'd say, 'So why are you spending so much time on it without being paid?' I'd say, 'Because it's politically important.' But she couldn't understand that. Then she started saying things like, 'I hate Africa. Africa's just a corrupt mess, full of selfish callous people!' If she'd ever have gone to Africa, she'd have loved it. But at the time she would have liked to have gone, she always had something else on. And then she lost interest totally. I begged her to come with me. But she wouldn't. And every time I came back, we were slightly further apart. I'd be God knows where, having the most incredible adventures, seeing and hearing the most incredible things, and I'd be thinking I can't wait to get back and tell Sair – that's what I used to call her, *Sair* – and I'd get back and she wouldn't be remotely interested. So after a time I just kept all that stuff in a totally separate place. It's like I was in a house, and one day I found a door through into the house next door. But it wasn't the actual house next door, it was another house in another parallel reality, that had its own laws and norms. And if I'd gone to look for the door back into the old house it would have let me not back into there, but into another part of the new reality. But it's only now I've even thought of trying to find that door.

Twenty-three

Is this Africa? Can it be Africa? 'Cause no one's so much as spoken to me since they put me in here. The guards have resolutely ignored my threats, promises, pleadings and tearful implorings. They also haven't tried to extort money from me, torture me or even wind me up. What's going on? And why am I here? Do you get held in a remote military installation for not paying your hotel bill? No. You're taken to the police station, slapped about, dumped in the city jail where you have time to contract a major gastric ailment before your amabassador expedites your release with promises of financial support from home. So why am I here?

I could have done anything. Okay, maybe not an astronaut, mathematician or brain surgeon. That's not my area. But senior civil servant, cabinet minister, humanities professor – anything that's about blathering, schmoozing and manipulating reality – no problem. These people are just doing what I'm doing, but in a different context. When I got back from my first time here, I thought, 'Right, I'm gonna learn French.' I'd done some French at school, but I'd forgotten nearly all of it. So I bought this book, read it for a couple of weeks, then went on a month's intensive course, after which they said, 'Right, you're at O-level standard.' I thought, 'This is a piece of piss. If I keep this up, I'll be doing an Oxbridge degree in six months.' As a matter of fact, within six months I'd forgotten most of what I'd learnt. But I had confirmed what I'd always known: that it's all about *wanting to*.

My father was a signalman for British Railways, my mother a cleaner – quiet, modest, old-fashioned people who believed in working hard, being polite and not giving anyone any hassle. The sort of people who don't exist any more. The sort of people who *can't afford* to exist any more. But they'd been told by my primary-school teachers that I was exceptionally promising, not to say gifted, and they nurtured through me fragile but exalted dreams of betterment – that I might get a job behind a desk at BR or the drug company where my mother worked.

I'll never forget the day I received the letter of acceptance from the Royal Kingston Grammar School: the joy and pride of my parents, the massed clinking of Corona bottles, the playing of the 1812 Overture at full volume on Dansette record players all over New Malden, the deep and satanic laugh I let out across the playground: 'Now it's *my* turn!' I equally well remember the disappointment I experienced on arriving there and finding the place stuffed with exactly the same kind of nerds, time-servers and petty thugs as primary school. How it had occurred to anyone that I might not get in here I could not imagine. But for a while, I really steamed in there. Latin, chemistry, poetry – I was agog for it all. At first I even had the maths under control. My end-of-term report that Christmas: what a glittering document!

Then I just lost interest. By the summer, my marks had fallen off dramatically, and it was downhill all the way. A matter of considerable bitterness to my parents and the teachers. When I was pissing about in the third form or whatever it was, with all the meatheads who should never have been in a school like that in the first place, the teachers would always look at me with particular resentment. '*You* could be doing this!' Meaning, *they* couldn't but you easily could.

Was I a source of immense disappointment to my parents? Inevitably. But when *she* came on the scene their hopes revived. The fact that I'd managed to ensnare such a 'lovely girl' meant I must be doing something right. 'She's a doctor's daughter,' they never tired of telling people, 'from Cheshire.' I don't know why, but they loved that Cheshire part. Oh, yes. They worshipped Sarah to an almost idolatrous extent. Sadly, but probably fortunately, neither of them lived to see my first repossession and the irreversible decline in my material fortunes.

So, I hear you wondering, how *did* someone as sensible, as down-to-earth and as unimpeachably and ineluctably mainstream as the coolly personable Sarah get involved with a flaky, drug-addled slob such as yourself? Good question. But you have to realise that those were utterly different times, when the whole of the youth of the Western World genuinely believed, from the noblest and most honourable motives, that personal liberation could be achieved through the derangement of all the senses. And you have to realise how this filtered down through the entire consciousness of a generation. For years the doctor's daughter from Cheshire made it a matter of principle to smoke at least one joint a week just so she didn't get 'too straight'. Next thing you know, it's the mid-eighties, she can't remember when she last had a toke or why it was she didn't want to be 'too straight' in the first place, and our house is about to be repossessed. Everyone else is going up on Thatcher's credit boom, and we're on our way down. And you're going to hate me for saying this, and in a way I'm going to hate myself for saying it, but it's an interesting and undeniable fact about women – and this is true from Barbara Windsor to Virginia Woolf – that as long as there is a certain amount of loot about, they can put up with quite a lot. Oh, yes. Even then it was about putting up with things ... with the way things were: the 'situation'. Oh, yes. I can't remember when it wasn't about putting up with, about tolerating, when she didn't have that set look on her face. Yes, she put up with it because once things have gone so far in a certain direction it's bloody difficult to change them, and when there's a bit of money about there's less incentive to, and by the time you've clocked the fact the money's definitively gone, you've had sex for the first time in five years, or whatever it is, got pregnant and things are even more difficult to change. I put up with it because ... because I fancied her, because I maintained a belief, long, long after I had

349

any right to, that if it came down to it, I would still be able to win her round . . . and because, because I loved her.

Oh, yes, I know that now. I loved her. I still do love her. Yes, I know that now. Now it's too late.

It was when I started losing money on it – or rather the point, quite a lot later, when she *realised* I was losing money on it – that she really started to get pissed off. Oh, yes. By that time all this stuff I'd got into was World Music, and it was *happening*. And it's all very well being the person whose brain the entire world wants to pick, who every journalist in media-land is on the case of, tipster-in-chief to the TV companies and the multinational majors, but are you actually making that much money from any of that? And when we had to move out of our house in the Grove, which she really, really had loved, to that place by the North Circular, things got critical. Then they languished, then they festered. Then we moved to that place where we are now, or where we were last time I saw her. And by that time, we weren't even getting invited to Michael Heaven's parties any more.

I'm going to die. If they don't decide to dispatch me for reasons of expediency, the rains are coming. The great clouds are massing over the immensities of the savannahs – 'cause the heat, the presaging heat's already started – and with them come the swarms of mosquitoes. You don't see them. You don't hear them. Then suddenly, they're all around you. A few bites, some flu symptoms, and you'll be gone before you know it. That is if you haven't already been driven insane by their insistent drill-like whining, their hairy fluttering as they feast on your skin. Christ, man. It was hard enough when you had insect repellent. And in the meantime I've got the bed bugs, waking me with a shouting jolt, and whatever's in this blanket. I can feel them swarming, holding their field events and gymkhanas all over my body. I'm a mass of red bites, any of which could at any moment turn septic. I'm trying not to scratch myself. But can I help it? Of course I can't.

Yes, the guard chucked a blanket in here the first night. Just as well, 'cause it gets really cold in the dead, dead of night – you could catch your death – and it doesn't start to warm up till it gets light, which it does very suddenly. Then it's day. Oh, yes. I see it all, because I don't sleep. Not more than an hour at a time.

But the fact they gave me that blanket must mean they want to keep me alive. Or must it? 'Cause the iron and implacable silence of the guard, as he brings in my twice-daily dish of grey slime, refusing even to look at me, bodes badly. 'Cause it takes them a long time to give up on a toubab here. Your circumstances are gonna be really fucking dire before they deem there's not one more drop of value to be squeezed out of you. 'Cause they're gonna think a white man is gonna somehow always have access to money. That he can get his friends and relatives to send it. That his ambassador will kind of tip him on grounds of racial fellow-feeling. That the white man will one day be released and will maybe remember them. I can imagine being led to the scaffold and one of the guards asking if I'll sponsor his children's education. I say, 'Listen, man. I'm about to be executed.' 'Yes,' he says, 'but you have a last wish!'

So the fact that over however many days, no one's tried to tap me for any cash shows an ominous lack of ambition.

Yes, I hear you say, but whatever Sarah's doing now, whatever she thinks of you now, you have to face the fact that she has by any standards been remarkably patient, remarkably loyal to you: to have been ... faithful to you through all of this ...

Ah, yeah. Yeah. But has she been? What about that time you got back to find this guy, this lanky, balding congenital squash-player type, taking his ease on your sofa? Turned out he was there to discuss the decline in his son's educational progress. Yeah? What about parents' evenings? What about turning up, cap in hand, at ten to four like all the other anxious mums and dads? But I didn't say that, I said, 'Nice one, man. Have a drink!' But he was out of there before I'd had time to put my bag down, and I'd seen the *fear* in his eyes. I didn't ask any questions, and she certainly didn't offer any explanations. Then I found out they'd been out for dinner. She *had* met him at a parents' evening. He was a local businessman, recently divorced, and he *was* very anxious about the impact on his son's development. He was loaded, apparently, lived in this big house on this posh estate on the wooded fringes of the town – and even in places like that, they *do* have posh estates. He'd got really involved in the school, and was making moves to get himself made a governor. That's commitment, yeah? She said there was nothing in it, she'd just agreed to see him for a bit of company. And he wasn't interested in her, like that ... He was just lonely. I laughed.

'Daddy?'
  'Yeah.'
  'Why do you keep going to Africa?'
  'I don't keep going to Africa.'
  'Yes, you do.'
  'I just go for short trips. On business. For my work. But I always come back as soon as I can.'
  'Daddy?'
  'Yeah.'
  'Mummy says you like it more in Africa than you do here with us.'
  'That's not true. I like ... both.'
  'Daddy?'
  'What?'
  'Why did you leave without telling us?'
  'I didn't leave without telling you.'
  'Mummy says you did.'
  'Well it's not true.'
  'Why did Mummy say it if it's not true?'
  'I don't know. Sometimes people think things are true when they're not.'
  'Daddy?'
  'Yeah.'
  'When are you coming back?'
  'Soon.'
  'When?'
  'As soon as I can.'

'When will that be?'

'Very, very soon.'

'Daddy?'

'*Yes.*'

'When you come back, are you going to talk to Mummy?'

'Of course I am.'

'Daddy, I don't like it when you're not here.'

'Look, I'm coming back as soon as I can. I'll be there very, very
... very soon.'

'Daddy?'

'*What?*'

'I don't think you're going to come back.'

'*I am* ... I'm coming ...'

'Daddy?'

'Yeah?'

'*Daddy!*'

'Yeah ...'

'*Daddy* ... I can't hear you ... Daddy ... Where are you ... ?'

Records, man. How did I get into that? How did I get into the
permanent twilight, the death-in-life of collecting? 'Cause it's
Faustian, isn't it ... collecting? And I used to be the last person
who would collect anything. 'Cause I never had anything. Okay,
if you're in the business, you accumulate a lot of stuff, it's
inevitable. It's an aspect of your work. But I didn't think of it as
collecting. Far from it. I'd give half of it away as soon I got it. It
was just like water flooding through the system. 'Cause I was all
about the here and now, about *doing it*! I was pop. I mean, I had
some classic blues stuff, major rarities, which I could no way have
parted with. But the fewness of them was all part of the pleasure,
and if I'd got too serious about it, if I'd actually gone out pursuing
stuff, it would have spoilt it, because it would have been too
uncool.

And that was right. 'Cause that was when I was a doer and a
maker. Even if I never actually played any instruments – though I
am of course credited on several records: 'Andrew "Litch"
Litchfield – Chair Leg', stuff like that – I fundamentally saw

353

myself as a creator – as a shaper, a moulder, an enabler, a taste maker, a . . . not as a consumer. Good heavens! I mean, I had a record collection. Of course I had a record collection, but I didn't go out and pursue it, it was just there 'cause of the work I did. But I lost it, didn't I, that freedom – that sense of . . . action. God, how innocent it seems when I look back on it. 'Cause I changed so many of my perceptions when I went to Africa, when I went into that other house. I changed my relationship to the music. Because in Africa, no matter how involved I was, even if I'd actually *produced* the record, I was always an *outsider* to the music. I realise now that any five-year-old born into that language and that rhythm had more intuitive understanding, more *right* to the music than I'd ever have. The same as I had more *right* to bad seventies rock music than he'd ever have. That is the bleak reality. But I didn't see it like that. And that was good, or I thought it was good, 'cause it was like I could see everything very clearly, the African thing and the Western thing. 'Cause by that time, I was like an outsider to the Western thing too. It's like I'm floating between the two. And what I've collected becomes my comment on that. And at first, it's like a working collection – I don't even think of it as a collection – it was just like stuff accumulated in the process of working, which is gradually taking up more space. Then, without me realising it, acquiring this stuff becomes an end in itself. I find that I jet into places, and I'm not doing anything but browse the cassette stands of the markets, the old record shops . . . And all the other stuff that's there, I'm not only missing it, I'm not interested! I meet the most incredible musicians – the most jondo del jondo, the works – and all I'm interested in is the part where I blag a copy of their latest cassette. So what? I hear you say. Most people in the music business are like that. Yeah, but not me, man, *not me*! I'm supposed to be the one who's alive to it all!

So, getting the stuff starts to become *the point*. It starts to seem more creative than the actual creative stuff. 'Cause as you pile this stuff up – creating the world in your image – you can see a shape emerging, and you're wondering what it is.

Occasionally, you wonder where this is going to stop. Occasionally, as you come out of some seedy nicotined little second-hand record shop where you've spent far, far too much time browsing, clutching that roughly fourteen-inch square bag, you think, *Why did I do that?* Oh, yes. As you stood there at the racks with Curtis Mayfield blasting away, you looked at that item, which was nothing like Curtis Mayfield – peripheral to your life's task, but essential if however infinitesimally in defining it – which with its portrait of smiling tuxedo'd Dominicans, or whatever they were, seemed to become so big it filled the entire shop. And all the resonances of that cover as a cultural object, right down to the way it's printed, flood your mind, and you can feel the overmastering urge rising within you till there's nothing, nothing more important in the entire world than that you should have that record. Then as you slink limply away along the cracked pavement, you're filled with guilt and shame and self-disgust, and the creeping knowledge that you are unlikely to ever listen to more than three minutes of that record. Oh, yes. 'Cause while I've spent years of my life doing nothing but listen to music, half these records I bought I never listened to. 'Cause by that time, the *idea* of the music had become more important than the music itself.

Now I know what it was, that shape I was creating as I withdrew, spent less and less time anywhere but in the dim vaults of my collection. It was my own tomb. I was burying myself alive under this stuff. And even without consciously realising it, I'd known that for some time. And had that stopped me, had it discouraged me in any way? Hardly at all. No.

'M'sieur . . .' There's a voice coming from outside the door, thick and furtive. 'M'sieur.'
  'Oui.'
  'Any fifty francs?' He qualifies that. 'Francs français.'
  'Non.'
There's silence for a few moments.
  'Any ten francs?'
  'Non.'
  'Oh.'

I haven't spoken for so long, I don't know what to say.
'Where are we?'
'Prison.'
'Oui, mais, où? L'endroit?'
'Quoi?'
'Le pays?'
'Tekrur.'
'Oui. Quel part?'
'Er . . .' Long pause. 'Je ne peux dire.'
'Pourquoi?'
'C'est secret.'
Shit. I thought he was going to fall for that.
'C'est bien disciplinée, votre armée.'
'Merci.'
'Vous êtes qui?'
'Le chef.'
'Du camp?'
'Non, de cuisine. C'est délicieuse la cuisine ici?'
No, I feel like saying, it's fucking disgusting.
'Superbe.'
'Merci. Je dois partir.'
'Pourquoi?'
'Je ne dois pas être ici. Mais . . .'
'Oui?'
'Je vais te donner des os.'
'Merci.'

I don't want his bones. What am I going to do with them? Are
they going to be raw or cooked? How long are they going to have
been left lying around with vermin and insects crawling over
them? Not that I've seen any flies here. It seems too hot, like
they've been burned off – till the rains come. We must be far up in
the north-east corner of the country, close to the edge of the
desert. 'Cause you can smell the iron heat on the endless
immensity of sand and rock, you can feel the villagey gregarious-
ness of Black Africa starting to give way to the unspeakable
solitudes of the great ergs.

356

I should have said, No, I don't want your fucking bones. On the other hand, if there was anything edible about them, they'd make a welcome change to the dishes of grey slime they no doubt call porridge that are passed into this cell twice a day. I don't know how many times it is now. I've lost count. Same as I've lost count how many days I've been here. And apart from that guy with his bones – and that was pretty low-level stuff – no one's tried to work an angle, nobody's tried to tap me for more than fifty French francs. Because there's no point making deals with a condemned man.

Condemned? What am I talking about. All I've done is do a runner from a couple of hotels. Yeah, I know it was wrong! I know it was stupid. Particularly the last one. I could easily have done a deal with Aissa Njai. I could have just said, You make it all right with the owners and I'll send the money when I get back, plus something for you. That would've been fine. She would have trusted me totally. I should have done that. Why didn't I do that? Because I'm totally stupid. I am a sad deluded wanker carrying myself away on the tides of my own self-aggrandising bullshit. And I've blown it with everyone who's ever tried to be good to me. My wife. Sajar. Aissa Njai. Even . . . Michael Heaven. Yes, I can see it now. Michael Heaven is actually a very kind and honest man . . .

I mustn't cry. I can't afford to lose the precious bodily fluids and salts. 'Cause I'll never replace them, not with what I'm eating. If you can call it eating. Maybe I should have those bones.

But let's go back to what I've done. Yes, it was stupid enough. But does it justify this? I would have thought a couple of days in a city prison, a few deals, the usual routine, intervention by my ambassador, after which I'm deported. Yes, that's all bad enough. But it tallies, you know what I mean? Not like all this Frederick Forsyth stuff.

I can hear the rats. They're out there. That's why I stay on this bug-infested mattress rather than sleeping on the bare earth. 'Cause of them, and 'cause I want to stay further out of the roadways of the ants and scorpions. And the rats. Not big rats.

Not rats the size of cats, 'cause this is Africa and they won't get enough to eat to be really big and glossy. They'll be sinewy, hard-eyed, punching bantamweight. I can hear them at night, rattling against the door, like they're headbutting it. Lucky for me the door was such a tight fit. But it won't hold them for long. 'Cause I can hear them rushing around on the rafters, and it's only a matter of time before one of the bastards drops onto me.

It's dark. It's been dark for maybe an hour. And suddenly there are voices in the corridor, a thud against the door and a fumbling with the lock. The door swings open and a torch is pointed at me. I cover my eyes, edging back over the mattress. All I'm aware of is my defencelessness, my proneness, the light and the crunching boots of the guys behind it.

There's a hard grunt.

'Er?'

'Montre. Votre montre.'

They've come for my watch.

'Je n'ai pas de montre.' Shit. They'll probably torture me to make up for it.

There's a brief exchange between them. Then one of them bends down and tugs at the hem of my trousers. Oh, no. Please! Please!

He rubs the material connoisseurlike between his fingers. It's the big untidy guy I saw in the storeroom when I arrived. 'C'est un sort de nylon,' he grunts to the others.

'Vos pantalons!' comes the voice from the darkness.

I find myself taking them off. They are immediately snatched away. They trudge out, leaving me in darkness. It's going to be draughty tonight.

Some time later, I hear a voice.

'M'sieur!'

'Oui.'

'C'est moi. Le chef.'

'Ah, bon. Ça va?'

'Ça va. J'ai tes os.'

'Ah . . . er. Bien.'

'Ouvrez la porte!'

'I can't, man. I'm a prisoner.'

'Ah, oui.'

Some minutes later there's grumbling disputation between him and the guard and the door swings open. I catch sight of a gaunt, bright-eyed face of indeterminate age. I take the bowl.

'Bon appetit, wai!'

'Jerejef.'

'Je suis Sulaiman Sy. N'oubliez pas, erh?'

'Non, non.'

The guard swings the door shut. I sit down and feel the food in the darkness. Yes, it's food. I hadn't realised how hungry I was. I cram handfuls of the steamed rice sodden with a savoury broth finely laced with chilli into my mouth. I suck vigorously on the bones – yes, the bones! – fragments of gelatinous flesh still clinging to them, almost weeping with grateful ecstasy. Then I lie back, exhausted and replete on my bug-infested mattress.

I wake, and it's freezing. It's utterly black. I said it was dark before. Now it's dark. Now we're in the deepest and remotest watches of the night and I'm feeling weak and queasy. It started with a nagging bloated sensation and the suspicion it was going to get worse, which it then proceeded to do. I'd better get over to the bucket, because while this place isn't exactly Le Petit Trianon, you've got to maintain some standards. Though I'm not sure which end to start with. I don't actually mind throwing up or emptying my bowels in a sudden volcanic explosion per se. It's the waves of nausea that come with it that make you feel you want to die. You're telling yourself you'll feel better when you've got it out, but when it comes it's not in a smooth flow, but in this tortuous spasmodic jerking that racks your entire being. Like everything you've ever eaten is coming up, booting out at your innards and throat as it goes. And you're waiting for that sense of relief, however momentary, and it doesn't come. In fact you feel far, far worse. It's coming out of your nose, man, bruising your internal passages as it goes. There's this band of metal round your head that gets tighter and tighter, and this guitar playing. A fucking guitar. It's incredible. And its incredibleness is all part of

359

its horror, with this rich ornate glissandoing that's just going on, flooding the room, flooding my head, flooding my stomach... And it's too rich, too sickly, too ornate. It's got behind my eyes, man. Please turn it off! Please! I promise I will never listen to music again...

Go out and get bacon, She said. Bacon? you say. Again? Does the woman eat nothing else? Interesting that, because looking back I can't explicitly recall ever seeing her eating bacon. But that's what happened.

Breathless, I dashed upstairs, seized the holdall that lay already packed, just out of sight on the other side of the bed. Street light fell through the window – the curtains not yet closed. Without turning on the light, I slipped downstairs and out into the freezing mist, through which the lights of the New Town sparkled like uncertain stars, towards the Siberian bleakness of the railway station. I bunked down in a grotty little hotel in Bloomsbury, spent the early part of the morning getting jabs, medicines and essential gear, and I was on the 2 p.m. from Orly. And She, in the steaming kitchen, the metal-framed windows pouring with condensation, conscious without really hearing it of the front door clicking shut over the sound of 'Just a Minute'. Did she think then, That could be the last I ever see of my husband? Of course not. Why would she? But if she had known, could she have managed much more than a shrug?

So you say, Is that all it boils down to, that he simply walked out on his wife and daughter in the most cowardly, heartless manner possible – without so much as a word! And you're not surprised, are you? It's exactly what you've come to expect.

But you also know that, in doing that, I was simply making concrete what had been the de facto actuality for years. I dare say she even felt grateful. You noticed that letter didn't say, 'Dear Sajar, You haven't seen Andrew, have you?' 'Mr Andrew Litchfield, c/o Sajar Jopp, Tekrur.' The forthright confidence of that shows that once she'd established that I actually had gone, it took her about fifteen minutes to work out where I was.

So why the subterfuge? Why didn't I just say to her, 'Look, a

360

cheque's slipped through the net. I'm going out to N'Galam to see Sajar, to blow away the cobwebs, and hopefully do a bit of business that'll reverse the disastrous state of our fortunes'? And what would she have said if I had? Would it have been a cold, Okay, without even bothering to look at me? Would it have been, 'No, you don't. You can hand that money over, right now!' Or would it have been, 'You do that, and that *is it*!' Or would it have been, 'Go on! Go and play with your trainset with your little friend Sajar! Go and try and do some business with those people who're all laughing at you behind your back! They all think you're a bigger idiot than I do. And take your fucking record collection with you. I hate you, you fucking bastard! You've ruined my life!'

But whichever of these alternatives it would have been, there was no way I could have said anything to her. I just couldn't have. You understand?

Maybe . . . Maybe she wasn't so cool about it. Maybe she did phone Sajar's people in tones of utter desperation and say, 'Have you seen my husband?' And they said, yes, *then* she got the letter organised. Maybe she's been at her wits' end. Maybe she's been on major anti-depressants. Maybe she's gone grey. The fact that she may have done any or all of these things wouldn't necessarily mean that she liked me of course, but you have to face the fact, or *I* have to face the fact, that she has, by any reckoning been, probably without meaning to be, remarkably . . . unbelievably loyal to me. And I probably have ruined her life.

The most civilised country in Africa . . . On *our* side . . . If I get out of here, I'll destroy their tourist industry with a harrowing documentary . . . or maybe a feature film starring Bruce Willis. Or both. And a book . . . *Hell in the Savannah*. Too crassly populist? You can't be too crassly populist. That's one lesson I've been late in learning . . . It's broad daylight. It's afternoon, and I'm still throwing up water I drank three years ago, while someone's boring nails into my head. I'm not going to get out of here to tell anyone. I'm going to die here. Sarah . . . *Sarah!* What have I done?

The soldier grunts with the effort of lifting the bucket and the smell. 'C'est trop, erh?'

'Oui.'

'Tu étais malade.'

'Oui.'

He nods and leaves.

It's the next day. I'm weak. I'm shivering slightly. But I don't feel nauseous any more. My head's not aching. I haven't eaten anything, and I've got no intention of eating anything. But I've been drinking the water and God knows what that's going to do to me. I fall asleep, dimly aware that the guard just spoke to me.

I'm awakened by the door opening, and the sound of boots on the earth near my head.

'Get up!' says a tough voice.

I get effortfully to my feet.

'Vous voulez boire?'

'Oui,' I gasp.

A soldier passes me a plastic cup.

'Allons.'

It's night. But not too late. I'm dimly aware of the soldiers standing around in the quadrangle. We go into a building. Ahead is a room lit by electric light. An officer is working behind a desk. He looks up, mildly irritated at seeing me.

'Where are your trousers?'

'They were stolen.'

'In Kagor?'

'Here.'

His eyebrows knit. 'What are you saying?'

'Some people came into my cell and took them.'

The officer barks something at the guard. He leaves.

'Sit down.'

I sit on the chair opposite him. I feel fucking terrible.

He peruses some papers – like a hospital consultant reading through the notes sent on by your GP.

'Andrew Graham Litchfield. Otherwise known as "Litch" . . . You're a very lucky man, Monsieur Litchfield. In a lot of these countries you'd have been tortured, shot in the head and thrown in a swamp for the crocodiles to eat.'

I don't say anything.

'Isn't that right?'

'Yeah . . .'

'You've made a lot of people in this country very annoyed. Are you aware of that?'

'Yes,' I say in a squeaking gasp.

A soldier comes in and hands me a filthy bloodstained rag. What the fuck is this?

'Your trousers.'

'These aren't my trousers.'

'They don't fit?'

'I . . .'

'Put them on.'

I put them on.

'Your ambassador and his wife were very kind to you, and all you did was insult them. You deliberately tried to sabotage a very important cultural collaboration between your country and ours. You made a proposal of marriage to Madame Aissa Njai of the Hotel Ndar when you already have a wife, then you disappeared without paying.'

'I never . . .'

'You did not disappear without paying?'

'No, I never proposed to her.'

'You expect me to believe your word against hers?'

I shrug and shake my head.

He's got my passport out. 'You managed to lose this.'

'Er . . . yeah.'

'Fortunately, a concerned member of the public, a Monsieur Ahmed Singh, was kind enough to hand it in. The other thing I don't understand is how you managed to get into this country without a visa.'

No, I don't understand that. Normally Sajar or his people are there, and they just wave me through. But they weren't there this time. The guy must have just forgotten to look.

'I'm with Sajar Jopp,' I croak.

'You're with Sajar Jopp! I don't think your friend will be much help to you now. He's in prison.'

He's in prison. If I felt a bit weller, I'd find this a lot more surprising.

'Wha . . . er . . . ?'

'He was arrested as he got off the plane from London on eight charges of sedition and attempting to subvert the state.'

What? *London?* What was he doing in London? In spite of everything, the fact that he went to *my* town without me knowing about it is hard to take.

'What . . . What was he doing in London?'

'His record is very big there. Something like . . . Number One in the charts. He was doing a television appearance . . . You did not know this?'

'No . . .'

Sajar was on *Top of the Pops*. Now he's in prison. I'm definitely dreaming.

The guy shakes his head sadly. 'Sajar has the Western success we have all been praying for, then we have to lock him up. He's someone we all admire so much, but he should never have tried to meddle in politics. He will be released tomorrow. We cannot hold someone like that for long. Hopefully he will have learnt his lesson.'

He looks up at me.

'Naturally we had to investigate all his foreign connections, which is why you were held here. But you proved to be totally insignificant. You will be deported tomorrow.'

'What about . . . ?'

'What?'

'No, er . . .'

'The hotels?'

'Yes,' I gasp drily.

'Normally you would be sent to a civilian prison in N'Galam. Very different to here. Fortunately for you, a compatriot of yours agreed to settle your accounts.'

'Who?'

364

He looks at the papers. 'I cannot remember the name...
Something ... religious ...'

'Heaven? Michael Heaven?'

'That's it. I trust you will reimburse him when you have the
opportunity.'

The Andalusian plains hang in deep shadow, the river-beds and
hills glowing red like the rumples and furrows of a bloodstained
blanket. Or is that Morocco? I keep blanking in and out. And I
look down with a kind of absent satisfaction at the thought that
I'll probably never see any of these places again. Sites of the
imagination I have already consigned to the past.

I've got half the plane to myself here. Because there aren't that
many people on it, and they've put me away from the others
because I haven't had the opportunity to give that much attention
to my personal hygiene. But the staff, the cabin crew, have all
been very nice to me. Everyone's been very, very kind.

And I'm not really thinking about much. Because I've had the
chance to think about what I'm going to do when I get back. And
I already know what that is.

Twenty-four

I get off at the Siberian railway station. The sun's blazing. Well-polished cars slide through the gluey brilliance. Paint flakes from the balustrade of the pedestrian footbridge. The grass verges are scorched brown. It doesn't look like it's rained for weeks. Summer. I'd totally forgotten about that. I thought it was always gonna be dark and damp and twilit here. And of course, there's the ozone layer. I'd forgotten that too.

Screwing up my eyes against the limpid brilliance, I head off across the carriageway. A car hoots. I don't know why. It's nowhere near me.

I've never been to this part of town before. But I can sort of feel where I'm going. The roads have immensely broad verges with big hedges behind tall wire fences and small roads leading off into implausibly named estates. There are cycle routes and special paths and subways leading under the massive traffic roundabouts, but I don't bother with that, I just cut straight over everything. There's a fair amount of traffic, but no pedestrians, no cycles on the cycle routes. I turn off down one of the side roads, and ask this bloke clipping his hedge the way to the school. He jumps at the sight of me, then points me straight ahead. That's right. I told you I knew where I was going.

The playground and the sports field are deserted. But through the long frieze of windows I can see the classes in progress, hear the teachers' voices through the open windows. You can picture it all exactly, can't you? The children's artwork up on the walls, the history charts, the pine cones on the nature table. The second I've got my foot over the low fence, I can hear this bloke's voice: '*Oy! What d'you think you're doing?*' I pay no attention, but head on up over the lawn, towards the main entrance with its swing doors of reinforced glass and its small hallway. A small hallway for small people. I can hear the bloke's enraged voice getting nearer. '*Oy . . . !*' I look through the window of the first door, and there she is with her back to the class writing on the board. I open the door and go in, but she doesn't seem to hear me, too absorbed in what she's doing up at the board, which I in turn don't hear. The children all stare at me agog, but she carries on oblivious. Then she turns and stops in mid-sentence. Her jaw literally drops open. Otherwise she looks well. She looks extremely well. The care-taker, or whoever he is, grabs me from behind. 'Right . . .'

'It's all right, Jeff,' she says, already composed. 'I can deal with this.'

'You know him?'

'Yes . . .'

Sunday. And on the site of a demolished factory not far from where we live is held one of the biggest car boot sales in the Western World. And from dawn I'm busy carting barrowloads of stuff over there: records, cassettes, CDs, the works.

By nine, the sun's already high. It must be midsummer. And the place is thronged with families, groups of lads and the odd obsessive loner, all sifting through the most improbable garbage imaginable. It's Third World, man. Forget the three oranges. Here you'll see a poker-faced middle-aged woman sitting all day behind a table with one hideous Japanese ornament on it. Over there you can rummage through Laura Ashley children's dresses at fifty pee a throw. And if you go in one of those vans down the end, you could find the entire contents of your garden shed, or even your house. Know what I mean?

Most of the population of this part of the country are here. And if I knew anyone round here, I'd doubtless be bumping into them now.

I've got a little ghetto-blaster, and one of those signs saying 'Now Playing'. As the pumping tama and blaring trumpet of Sajar's 'Ngente' blast through the tinny speakers, this kid in a Stussy t-shirt examines the cover, his two mates in woolly hats peering over his shoulders.

'That's Sajar Jopp, man. It's a classic.'

'It's fucking shit,' says the kid, impassively.

This middle-aged guy, maybe a jazz buff, pores long over a Tito Puente CD, unplayed, still in its cellophane cover, but already unavailable, even as an import.

'Ten quid, mate.'

He puts it quickly back and scurries off without a word.

Always it's the same questions: 'Got any house? Got any techno? Got any thrash? Got any Chris Rea?'

But here is a familiar face. The slight, wispily bearded figure of the Old Town record dealer in his trademark faded denims. And he's got this faint condescending smirk. 'Decided to do it yourself, did you?'

I ignore his patronising and barely supressed glee.

'Everything in that box is a collector's item,' I warn as he heads instinctively for the best stuff.

He pulls out a cassette, holding it between his thumb and forefinger, the Arabic lettering barely visible beneath a case scuffed almost to opacity.

'I doubt if you'll get much for this.'

'That's Papa Gorgi Ngom, man. Unbelievably rare!'

'But it's a copy!'

'And where are you going to get an original? He gave me that himself. That's a piece of history.'

He shakes his head sadly.

'Didn't a German company buy up the rights to all that old Tekrurian stuff? They're bringing it out in a collector's edition on CD. Designer artwork, the lot.'

It's the first I've heard of it.

'I think you'll find a lot of this stuff isn't as valuable as you think it is. But tell you what, I'll give you . . . two hundred quid, the lot.'

I shrug and look away.

'Okay,' he says. 'Let me know, *when* you change your mind. But don't leave this stuff out in this sun much longer, or it won't be worth anything.'

It's hot. And it's bright. I'm sure Britain never used to be like this – this blazing unmediated white light. But I keep forgetting, don't I? It's the ozone layer. The ozone layer. The world's not what it was.

And all the dealers, all the browsers, all the strolling, laughing holidaymakers with only half a mind to consume, recede. And although new people are arriving all the time, it's as though the collective unconscious of this part of the world has already checked everything I've got to offer and made its decision. And the figures milling past start to blur, their colours fade, till there's just me sitting alone in the heat and the brilliance – the white light.

And my collection – I'm not talking about the freebies and all the other shit you've probably got, that, as I told you, that bastard Paul took – I'm talking about the real stuff, the tasty stuff. Stuff that you would never be able to get again. Stuff that carries with it whole histories. It's melting. The records are warping and blistering, their immortal grooves coagulating into a tarlike unplayable mass, their covers fading and curling in the wasting brilliance. The precious iron-oxide particles, the diaphonously thin brown magnetic tape of some of the few remaining copies of cassettes that contain music the like of which the world will never hear again. The music of the Moroccans, the Spaniards, the Cubans, the Brazilians, the Africans and so much more. Music I could never tell you enough about, unless I was to sit you down and play you each track, and talk to you about it, about how I came to get it, how much I paid for it – or more likely didn't pay for it. Yes, those thin brown tapes all softening inside the cases that are already cracking in the heat while the card inserts, like the covers of the records, many of which are, as you know, important works of art, fade and curl in the all-consuming brightness.

When I look up, the shadows are long over the rubbish-strewn immensity of the factory floor, the sun disappearing behind a huge warehouse and the long row of poplars beyond. I sit there in the middle of the great space, long since deserted of other stallholders, surrounded by the wreckage of my collection, reduced now to what some people said it always was – a load of rubbish. And I'm aware of someone walking over the darkening floor towards me. I look up from my disinterested perusal of how the face of a Dominican merengue singer has faded into this abstract pattern of blue and yellow and how quickly the thin layer of plastic that gave record covers of the mid-sixties their seductive classy sheen has puckered clean away, and see Her standing there regarding me with an intent and analytical frankness. My daughter runs towards me. I bend and pick her up, squeezing her to me as she bursts into tears. 'There, there. It's okay.' I look over her shoulder and meet my wife's gaze. Is she dark or fair? I've no idea. Because I can't see her as you would see her, I can't see her as anyone else would see her. I can only see her as the person I happen to love. She looks back. There's a reproachfulness, a resignation and a resilience there, a combativeness, a defiance in the set of her shoulders. I tilt my head towards the remains of the collection.

'I did it for you,' I say.

Twenty-five

Together again. And it's not easy. But nothing, nothing really worthwhile ever is. We're back in London. The city we should never have left. The city which whether we like it or not is our place – the place that was always destined to form the background to our small dramas. Our accommodation is kind of cramped, but that's just a matter of time – until I get some work and some proper money coming in. I haven't found anything yet, but I'm talking to people all the time, and I'm of the belief that something will . . . yes. What am I gonna do? you wonder. Anything. I'm totally prepared to do anything, as long as it doesn't involve music.

I spend a fair amount of time tramping the streets, just because . . . Just because I like tramping the streets. It was midsummer when I got back. There was an Indian summer. Then suddenly Christmas was upon us, the way it somehow always is.

I find myself at Marble Arch, descending the escalator into the tube, and there are these two buskers at the bottom, standing there in black overcoats, playing 'In the Bleak Midwinter' on electric guitars. The younger guy's strumming the chords, while the older one, in a black trilby, is picking out the lead on an amplified acoustic. It's about seven-thirty. It's freezing outside, but the residual rush-hour crowds are swelled by hordes of shoppers. And the relief of getting out of the cold is, like the glow of the festive windows outside, all part of the energy, the rhythm

371

of the year racing towards its conclusion and the new life that will follow – a feeling, a rhythm which, even if you think Christmas is a load of shit, you cannot, in our culture, escape.

I'm half-listening to these guys' music. And if you should never be afraid of the obvious, these guys are really going for it. The incredible banality of the way that guy renders the melodic line – only someone with real musical vision would have the bottle to keep repeating that with such chiming mantric insistence – going on, round and round, like the ceaseless circular movement of the escalator, like the movement of the crowds still thronging in from the freezing street. As I reach the bottom, I look at them, staring impassively ahead as they twang endlessly away at the oncoming crowds – wolfish, slightly dangerous characters, the kind of people who in a fairy-tale would lead you off to unspeakable adventures. No offence, but they've got to be Irish. Real professionals. The griots of the underground.

And while I swore to myself six months ago that I would never listen to music again, I find myself going straight back up the opposite escalator, because already it's forming in my mind: a film. A Christmas film. I can already see the credit sequence. Tracking shots among the shoppers along the darkened, snow-flurried streets. The crowds in the tube corridors. With these guys' music playing. Maybe we even see them playing it. Maybe we see them in a tracking shot as we come down the escalator. Setting the scene: the rawness, the incessant movement of the city. Yet there's a tenderness, a humanity there. It'll be my kind of film: quirkily humorous, yet powerful. You cry all the way through, but leave uplifted.

I've got to get home. I've got people to phone, people to speak to. Yes, film, television – that's what I should have been doing all along. Not music. 'Cause as the teacher told my parents when I was in the third form at school, I am actually totally unmusical. I step off the escalator a second time, give the griots fifty pence for the idea, and fuck off into the underground.